Books published by The Random House Publishing Group
are available at quantity discounts on bulk purchases for
premium, educational, fund-raising, and special sales use.
For details, please call 1-800-733-3000.

CAPITOL OFFENSE

A Novel

WILLIAM BERNHARDT

BALLANTINE BOOKS • NEW YORK

2010 Ballantine Books Mass Market Edition

Copyright © 2009 by William Bernhardt
Excerpt from *Capitol Betrayal* copyright © 2010 by William Bernhardt

All rights reserved.

Published in the United States by Ballantine Books, an imprint of The Random House Publishing Group, a division of Random House, Inc., New York.

BALLANTINE and colophon are registered trademarks of Random House, Inc.

Originally published in hardcover in the United States by Ballantine Books, an imprint of The Random House Publishing Group, a division of Random House, Inc., in 2009.

ISBN 978-0-345-50300-8

Cover design: Carl D. Galian
Cover photograph: © iStockphoto

Printed in the United States of America

www.ballantinebooks.com

9 8 7 6 5 4 3 2 1

The distance between insanity and genius
is measured only by success.

—BRUCE FIERSTEIN

Prologue

CHAPTER

1

I DIED THREE days ago.

I never saw it coming. It had been a difficult day at the hospital, shocking even—but when was it ever different? St. Benedict's is one complication after another, especially in my line of work. There are too many patients, too many bureaucrats, and too few happy endings. Midday, I took a long stroll through the children's ward just to hear the high-pitched voices raised in song or play. Even when there is great pain, the young always seem capable of mustering optimism and innocence, two qualities I see too infrequently.

"Dr. Thomas, you're pretty."

"Thank you, Jonathan."

"My dad thinks you're pretty, too."

"I'm flattered." And I was, genuinely. Compliments are sparse in my line of work.

"When I get better, do you think you could come over for dinner? Not for me. But I think my dad gets lonesome sometimes . . ."

"I'm married, Jonathan."

"Oh . . ."

"But I'd still love to have dinner with you sometime."

With innocence can also travel disappointment, but here at the hospital, time travels like quicksilver and long-term consequences are overwhelmed by the need for emotional satisfaction in the here and now. I was so accustomed to thinking of my patients' immediate happiness, I never realized how quickly my own happiness could be curtailed.

This was not a day like any other. What I saw in the hot lab disturbed me, perhaps more than I was willing to admit to myself. I didn't know how to respond. I did not perceive it as a tolling of the bell, as a sign that the End of Days was upon me. I climbed into my Land Rover and headed for home. The drive to Skiatook is almost forty minutes even if I don't get caught in a traffic snag, and the drive down Lombard Lane is always dark. Too many curvy country roads with little traffic and no witnesses. Deep ravines on either side. Not the place to be driving after a long hard day's work in the healing arts. A girl had to be careful.

All I saw was a flash of light and suddenly I lost control of the Rover. Heat, squealing tires, heart racing, eyes searching desperately for the road. The impact was sudden, shattering. The wheel wrenched out of my grasp, sending slivers of pain racing up my right arm. My Rover lurched off the road into a ravine, fell for what seemed an eternity, and crashed. Did I hit a tree? A house? I still don't know. I only know it hurt. I blacked out. Not from the impact, though that was fantastic, unlike anything I had experienced in my life. I blacked out from the pain. And then I died.

I awoke many hours later, unsure of anything. Where was I? What had happened? I had no answers. Answers are for the living, not the dead. I tried to make an inventory of everything I knew, everything about which I could be certain. I could not move. Not an inch. Not so much as to scratch my nose. I was in excruciating agony—I would describe it as unbearable, except that I did bear it, I had to, I had no choice. I still have no choice.

There's something sharp and metallic piercing my left

leg! Please, God, is there no mercy? I've helped so many others cope with their pain, can no one help me? It's bleeding and infected and I can't move and I can't even see and I just want this torture to be over. I don't care how. It hurts so badly. Oh, God, it hurts, it hurts!

I catch my breath, inhale deeply, murmur my mantra, and try to block the agony out of my mind. No help has come. I have no reasonable expectation of rescue. Dennis and I chose to build out in the far reaches of Skiatook for a reason. We were on a spiritual journey, trying to nourish our souls and find a better way of life. We sought seclusion, the peace that comes from knowing that you have removed yourself from the bustle and impurity of the city. What I never realized was that we had traded one form of danger for another. No one would come out here, no one but my husband. He will never see me, and no one else will have any cause to come this way. I am off the navigational charts of the rest of humanity, dead to the world.

The accident was three days ago. Since then, I have remained trapped here, mired in my own blood and waste, scared and angry and filled with a bitter pain that blackens my tongue and my thoughts and makes every breath an ordeal. As a physician, I am all too able to assess my hopeless situation—and all too unable to do anything about it. For days, I ran the standard ER checklist through my head. Check for concussion. Rather difficult to do when you're pinned down like a butterfly in a collector's tray. What's my white blood cell count? Who knows? Multiple lacerations, severe abrasions, internal bleeding—did this mean anything? They were just words, they had nothing to do with my body, with the life essence I could feel seeping away from me.

This much I know: My clavicle is broken in two places. At least two of my ribs, also. My shoulder is dislocated and something traumatic has happened to my left leg. I not only can't move it—I can't feel it any longer. That leg is gone; no science known to man could bring it back to me. I feel an aching in my gut that the scientist within recognizes as kidney failure, the sure product of dehydration. How long has it been since there was anything in my mouth other than the taste of my own blood? Too long. Far too long.

It was almost a year ago that I first expressed my unhappiness to Dennis, not with him, not even with our life, but with myself. I had once considered myself a spiritual person, but that spiritual side had been lost somewhere in the shuffle of quotidian duty, the drudgery of medical school, the internal ravaging that comes from watching so many people die, day after day. That was when I started attending the Shambhala retreat, where they taught me about meditation, hypnotherapy, Buddhism. Not a religion, they told me. A way of life. A way of incorporating harmony and balance and peace into your own soul. Initially, I wasn't very good at it. What was the point of all the breathing and humming? Did it matter how I held my hands?

And now it seems that's all I have left. I cannot block out the pain, but I can distract myself. I can't have a moment of tenderness, but I can breathe, and hum, and try to clear my mind. The Paramhansa Yogananda taught his followers to outwit the stars, that we may be guided by these heavenly sentinels but needn't be controlled by them. This is what I must do, at least until I become one of them. If nothing else, I can ease the passage.

The last drop of life may not have seeped away from me, but I am truly dead, just as surely as if my heart had stopped beating and blood had stopped circulating through my veins. Death, I remember hearing a yogi say, is not an ending. It is when the soul separates from the body. This ordeal is so intense, so intolerable, it pierces my spirit and leaves me unable to feel anything else. I miss my life, my work, my husband, the children I never knew. But I can no longer feel that aching, because the new one is so intense, so overpowering. When existence in the body becomes intolerable, the soul seeks other lodging, safe havens, snug harbors.

I can see the sky at night and it fills me with regret. So much I could have done, so much I never did. So much I needed to tell my husband. That is perhaps the greatest pain of all. Can I find another path, another way? Can I wring something positive out of this bitter ending? My teacher said it's all perfect, that things happen for a reason, that we are capable of turning poison into medicine. But what good can come from the suffering?

My meditation may save my sanity, but what will save my soul?

Physician, heal thyself. I must find a way to triumph. I will find a way to make this matter. I will remain on my path. I may not have planned this, may never have seen it coming. But I am stronger than the rippling tide of human happenstance. I can still make my life count for something. I can outwit the stars.

DENNIS THOMAS TOOK the proffered chair beside Detective Sentz's desk. Could it possibly be? Had he finally found someone who would listen?

"I understand you've filed a report."

"Yes. A missing person."

Sentz pressed his lips together. "Who is it?"

"My wife. Joslyn Thomas."

"Why do you think she's missing?"

Dennis looked at him, desperation etched in every line of his face. "She hasn't come home for three days."

"Anything else?"

"Isn't that enough?"

"Well, frankly, no."

Dennis gripped the armrests tightly, trying to contain himself. He'd been fighting this bureaucracy for days. Three days now he'd come to the Tulsa Uniform Division East station and the Skiatook police station. Three days he'd tried to motivate the police to take action. Without success. The only person doing anything was him. He had talked to all of Joslyn's friends, all her coworkers. No one knew anything. He'd searched the hospitals, called her relatives, driven back and forth over the roads she normally traveled, all without success. He had done everything he knew how to do and he still hadn't found her. Couldn't the police help? Wasn't that why the police existed? So far, he had not been successful at getting anyone to do anything. He'd filed a report the first day—a COS (Check Own Satisfaction) call issued—and he was told it was forwarded to a police detective who would decide what action, if any, would be taken. He'd come to the downtown Detective Division to see why nothing was happening.

"My wife wouldn't disappear for no reason. Certainly not without telling me."

"How do you know?"

"I've been married to her for seven years!"

Sentz made a grunting noise. "Seven-year itch."

"You don't know her."

"No, friend, I don't know her, but I have been at this desk for eighteen years. Two years and I can take early retirement. I've seen many guys like you walk through the door complaining that their wives have disappeared. It's always the same. Girl decides she's had enough, has to get out, doesn't have the guts to tell you face-to-face."

"That's not what happened."

"You'll probably get a call in a couple weeks, once she's safely settled into what she's running to. Parents, boyfriend, whatever."

"That's a lie!"

"Hey, don't kill the messenger, pal. I'm just telling you what I've seen. Over and over again."

"That man at the front desk—Sergeant Torres—he said you'd help me."

"I am helping you. You just can't see it yet."

Dennis felt his jaw tightening, felt the sinking feeling that told him this was just another false hope dashed, that there would be no more action now than there had been before. "I demand that you do something! I've reported a crime."

"But that's just it, buddy—you haven't. All you've reported is that your wife hasn't come home. And not coming home is not a crime."

"What about kidnapping? Is kidnapping a crime?"

"Do you have any evidence that she was kidnapped?"

"She's disappeared."

"I'll take that as a no."

Dennis reached across the desk. "Please. There must be something you can do. They told me in Skiatook you could initiate an investigation once she's been gone twenty-four hours."

"Only if special circumstances are present." Sentz cleared his throat. "There aren't any here."

"How many days must she be gone before you take action?"

"It's not a matter of days. It's the absence of a crime. She could be gone a year and there still wouldn't be any evidence of a crime."

"She's disappeared!"

"Do you have any evidence of foul play?"

"She wouldn't not come home without a reason."

"But you don't know what that reason is."

"Something must've happened to her."

"Does she have any special vulnerability?"

"Like what?"

"Well, I gather she's not a minor."

"She's thirty-two."

"Or elderly. Does she have a mental condition? Dementia?"

"Of course not. She's a doctor!"

"Like that proves anything. Is she off her meds?"

"The only thing she takes is omega-three."

"Suicidal?"

"No."

"History of drug abuse? Alcohol?"

"No."

"Depression?"

"No! I mean—she works in a cancer ward treating women with inoperable diseases. It's not exactly a good time. But she isn't mentally ill!"

"Then I can't—"

Dennis rose to his feet. "Are you telling me that since she's a normal healthy adult you're not going to do anything?"

Sentz shrugged. "If you want to put it that way."

"Listen. I know my wife. I know what she would do and would not do. Something has happened to her. Something bad."

"I know you're worried. But if we went running after everyone who doesn't come home on time, that's all we'd ever do. It's a manpower issue. We have to prioritize serious crimes. We can't look for everyone."

"I'm not asking you to look for everyone. I'm asking you to look for my wife."

"Look, go home, try to get some rest. Chances are she'll turn up or at least call in a few days—"

Dennis lurched forward and grabbed his arm. "My wife has not run off with another man. She's in trouble! And if you don't—"

"Whoa, whoa, let's all calm down now." The man Dennis recognized from the front desk, Sergeant Torres, stepped between them, breaking Dennis's grip. "No need to let things get out of control."

Sentz scowled. "Why did you send this man to me? You know there's nothing I can do."

"Oh, there's always something we can do," Torres said, smiling. "Maybe just give him some good advice."

"I did. I told him to go home and wait."

Dennis's face was flushed and covered with perspiration. "My wife is . . . is . . . maybe hurt, trapped, kidnapped."

Torres cleared his throat. "Well . . . actually, I don't think that's true."

"How would you know?"

"She's disappeared before, hasn't she?"

Dennis fell silent.

"Pulled it up on the computer. She was reported missing. Police searched. But it turned out she had just gotten in her car and started driving. Called in a week later."

"That was a long time ago," Dennis insisted. "Before we were married. She was just a kid. She got depressed after some jerk broke up with her and didn't know how to deal with it. Her mother got worried so she called the police."

"Uh-huh."

"This is totally different. She's matured. She's married. She's a doctor! She has patients, responsibilities."

Torres shuffled a sheet of paper in his hands. "I'm really not supposed to do this, but after we talked, I had someone in the computer room run a search on your wife's credit cards." He handed Dennis a piece of paper. "As you can see, a day after you say she disappeared, she bought gasoline at a place outside Skiatook."

Dennis scanned the paper. "That's impossible."

"No, that's a fact."

Sentz made a grumbling noise. "Guess her boyfriend lives near home."

Dennis launched himself toward the officer, but Torres held him back. "Please! Stay calm! This will not help your wife."

"Why won't you do something?" Dennis shouted at Sentz. "Do you want her to die?"

Torres continued to restrain him. "Come on now. We don't need any new trouble."

Sentz pushed himself to his feet. "Show this jerk the door."

"And you're not helping, either, Detective." The sergeant spoke quietly, obviously intimidated by the superior officer. But he still spoke. "I don't know what happened with this man's wife, but I can see he's very worried about her, so be a little sympathetic, okay? What would you do if Bernice didn't come home?"

"I'd go bowling."

Torres grinned a little. "Yeah, well, this boy hasn't been married as long as you."

"That much is certain."

"Isn't there something you could do, Sentz? Maybe off the record? Authorize some more computer time? Send out a quiet APB?"

Dennis felt his heart quicken. That would make a huge difference. If everyone on the Tulsa PD were looking for Joslyn, surely someone would turn up something.

Sentz considered for a moment. "I don't know. Perhaps . . ." As Dennis watched, Sentz's eyes traveled across the room.

Dennis turned and saw a tall man in the corner on the opposite side of the room standing in shadows, staring at them. How long had he been there? His head was bowed and Dennis couldn't make out his face, but it was obvious he was listening.

The man's head moved, only slightly, barely perceptibly, but it moved. From left to right. *No.*

Dennis turned back toward Torres. The sergeant didn't appear to have even noticed the man. But Sentz had.

"I'm sorry," Sentz continued, barely missing a beat, "but that would be against regulations. I can't authorize it."

Dennis's eyes ballooned. "What happened? Why can't you do anything? Who is that man?"

"Just a friend reminding me that I need to go by the book if I want to make it to retirement with my pension intact."

"Who's pulling your strings?" Dennis turned around again, ready to charge the tall man and throw him to the ground—but he had disappeared. "I don't care about your pension!"

"I do. Look, go home, and if she still isn't—"

"Why don't you want me to find my wife?"

Torres laid his hand on Dennis's shoulder. "Sir, the police department has rules, and for the most part they're good ones."

"What he's saying," Sentz interjected, "in a nice way, is, get lost."

Dennis flew forward. He grabbed Sentz by the collar and shook him, his face contorted by rage. "You've got to do something! Find my wife!"

Sentz shoved him back hard, knocking him to the floor. He breathed heavily, in and out. He looked furious. "You lousy—"

"Sentz!" Torres shouted. "Don't say anything you'll regret later."

Sentz's lips were pressed together so tightly they turned white. "Get him away from me. Now. If he's still here in thirty seconds, I'm filing charges."

Torres helped Dennis back to his feet. "I'm sorry, sir. I think you should go."

"But Joslyn is in trouble and—"

"And you can't help her if you're behind bars. Go!"

Barely suppressing his rage, Dennis grabbed his coat and headed out the door. He had never felt so helpless. They had worked so hard to put their lives together. Slaving away at the university, saving every penny, getting Joslyn through medical school, building their dream house. They had a good life, damn it. What right did these people have to act so cavalierly? What right did anyone have? How could they stand idly by while he lost everything he loved?

He threw himself behind the wheel and slammed his car door shut. He would drive all night. He would search every road, then search it again. He would hire a detective. He would never rest.

Until this moment, he had not fully realized how much he cared for his wife. She was everything to him. Everything that mattered.

Hang on, Joslyn! Please hang on! I will find you. *I will!*

CHAPTER
2

I'VE BEEN TRAPPED here for seven days now.

How can I still be in my body? How can I still be trapped in this metal cauldron of eternal torment?

I know so much about the human body's ability to handle pain. I knew there would come a time when the sensory neurons could no longer process so much negative stimulation, when they would shut down and I would feel some alleviation, however artificial. Somehow I would find some measure of release.

That release has not come. The agonizing aching has changed, mutated from the sharp splitting pulse to a hollowness, a sense that something has been lost. It still hurts, but it is a different hurt, perhaps more tolerable physically, perhaps more unbearable spiritually. It is as if I were swimming in the ocean, struggling against a sudden overpowering wave that carries my body away and slowly crushes the life out of it. I have swum too far from the shore. My hands are numb, aching, bloody. I can no longer swim, not even tread water, and I know I will never see land again . . .

I no longer deceive myself into thinking it will all work out. I don't seek miracles. It would be good to see Dennis again, to tell him what he needs to know, but I realize that is unlikely. Death has consumed my body, my brain, my very blood. It is what I have become. It is omnipotent. It is Krishna. It is God.

I don't seek the miracle of rescue. I seek the relief of oblivion.

FOUR HOURS AGO I realized I still had my cell phone in my jeans pocket. How much charge could it have after so much time? And what difference did it make when I was so powerless to get it out? Aren't I?

I thought about it for hours before I even attempted movement. The mere act of concentration made my head hurt, my brow sweat. It was too hard, too impossible . . .

I moved a finger.

Only the index finger of my left hand. But it moved. Twitched, perhaps more accurately. Could I possibly do more?

Two fingers this time. My hand was pinned down, pressed against my side. My fingertips lay perhaps six inches from my pocket. Surely this is a distance they can traverse. Surely I can make this so.

I moved my whole arm, but oh God how it hurt. Something had happened to that arm. The shoulder above was dislocated and the clavicle was broken and all movement sent lightning bolts of pain radiating through my arm and the rest of my body. This is so hard. Why is this happening to me?

Is this perfect? My spiritual teacher in Malibu tried to convince me that everything was perfect. The Universe does not make mistakes. That's why the Universe has lasted so long and will continue to do so. Everything happens for a reason. Don't greet misfortune with despair; try to discern what you will learn, how you will grow from the experience.

Like most all-encompassing worldviews, it is too easy to poke holes through. The Universe continues to exist because there's a natural scientific progression from creation to extinction, perfect or imperfect. How can this cheesy philosophy encompass huge tragedies such as starvation in Africa or the Holocaust? Did millions die so the world could learn a lesson? Can we seriously believe that's perfect? But my teacher was not moved by my protestations. When I stop objecting and accept, he said, I will see the truth. Because bad things will happen to all people. Do you let them destroy you? Or do you choose to let them make you better?

This is not perfect! It hurts! Dear God, how it hurts!

I think my wrist may be broken, too, but somehow I managed to ease it sideways, pivoting it around until the fingertips touched the mouth of the pocket. Baby steps, that's all I needed. An inch at a time, a micron even. Slowly my fingers oozed into the portal. Gently, tenderly they slipped inside until they touched the cold, hard shell. Naturally I opted for the sleek Razr, so damn hard to get a grip on . . .

My whole arm trembled, throbbing, and my forehead bled as I closed my fingers around the phone and tried to ease it out of the pocket. My leg was pierced, possibly severed, just a few inches below the phone. Every movement was torture. The slightest twitch was excruciating, unbearable, but somehow, I tensed enough hand and wrist muscles to close those fingers around the phone and slowly draw it out. My hand was slick with sweat and my arm shook violently, but still I continued to pull the phone out of that damnable pocket.

Until it was free. Inserting my index finger under the phone, I flipped the lid upward and turned it on. I heard the beeping sound that told me it still had power, however slight. Even though I could not turn my head enough to see it, I sensed the flickering illumination provided by the screen. Hand trembling, I groped for the button that would alert the police . . .

Noooooo! Dear God, no!

The cell phone glittered on the floor mat, shining, twinkling, beckoning, impossibly far out of my reach.

"SHE DIDN'T MAKE this charge. I did."

Sergeant Torres looked up from his paperwork, blinking. "Huh?"

Dennis slid the credit card receipt across the desk. "It was me buying gas. We share the credit card. If I hadn't been so upset, I would've realized that immediately. See? Here's the receipt. With my signature on it."

Torres took the translucent slip of paper and held it up to the light. "You bought gas after your wife disappeared?"

"Repeatedly. Because I was driving around looking for her all night long. Have been all week."

"She still hasn't come home?"

"No. Not all week. Seven days. No one has seen her at work. Her family hasn't heard from her. Nothing. Vanished."

"No history of drug use, or—"

"None. I've already answered those questions. Can you please do something? I've been in here every day, begging. I know I look terrible. I've barely slept. I must seem crazy, but I'm not. I'm worried about my wife."

"I'll take you to see Detective Sentz."

"No!" Dennis held out his hands, pleading. "I already know what he will say. He's said it every day this week. And no one will let me talk to anyone else."

Torres peered down at him. Dennis thought he seemed sympathetic. But he had no way to help. "I'm just the front desk clerk here. I don't make policy decisions. Detective Sentz—"

"Wouldn't budge if I had a ransom note from the Taliban."

"That's not true. We have to follow procedures—"

"Do you know who my wife is?" Dennis asked, his head tilted at an angle, his throat pulsing. "Do you?"

"I believe her first name was Joslyn . . ."

"Dr. Joslyn Thomas. She's an oncologist. Works in the cancer ward at St. Benedict's."

"She must be a very strong woman."

"She's a saint. That's what she is. A saint." Tears appeared in his eyes. "You think a policeman's job is tough? Try spending every day watching the people you care for slowly slip away. Watching them die. She works with women primarily. Trying to ease their suffering. Sometimes the cancer goes into remission, usually not. Even when it's gone, it all too often returns, like a bottled imp that keeps pushing the cork out. But she never gives up. Never. No matter how hopeless the case."

Dennis leaned across the desk, water streaming down his face. "And that's why it's so important that you look for her, Officer. Because I know that no matter what has happened to her, no matter how bad it is, she will never give up. She is not a quitter, not my Joslyn. She's still out there, somewhere, waiting for me to come get her." His voice cracked. He laid his head down on the desk. "Please help me, Officer. Please help me find my Joslyn."

Torres stared down at the crumpled man crying on his desk. He laid his hand against his chest.

"I suppose . . . we could put out an APB on her and her car. But honestly, if she were out there, stranded or something, she would likely have been spotted by now. I don't think—"

"What about her cell phone?"

"I assume you've tried to call her."

"Yes, and there was no answer. But when I called today I didn't get the quick cutoff voice mail message you get when the phone is turned off."

Torres's eyes flashed. "If her cell phone is active . . ."

"I know." Dennis slid forward a folder filled with pages printed from his computer. "You can track her down from the signal her cell phone emits."

"It's not that simple. Even if her phone is active, if she's too far from the signal tower—"

"Will you please just try? *Please!*"

Torres breathed heavily. His eyes darted around the station, as if his heart was in conflict with his head.

"Detective Sentz is out on a call. I know his assistant. I think I might be able to persuade him to do . . . something. At least see if we can get a trace on that phone."

Dennis's eyes closed. "Thank you. Thank you so much."

"Save the thanks until we accomplish something. It's still a long shot. Especially when she's been gone so many days. Statistically, it's still most likely that she's somewhere of her own accord."

"But you will look?"

Torres began the paperwork. "Yes. Of course we will."

I DROPPED THE phone. I should have seen that coming. How could I not, given my current state, my arms, trembling, unable to steady even for a second, my hand and fingers barely operational? It was hopeless. Now that little pink hunk of metal lies at my feet and there is simply no chance I will ever be able to retrieve it. My last hope is gone. My final dream is shattered. I am well and truly dead.

Perhaps it's better this way. Did I ever believe I would be rescued? What have I told my patients so many times? Sometimes acceptance is best. It is not perfect. But perhaps it is my finest choice. The dead can only expect so much.

The pain has subsided somewhat, but I'm not foolish

enough to imagine that means I'm getting better, or that my efforts at meditation have saved me. The serotonin sedation must be kicking in. Still, it does help to have that training, to know how to reach a better place and stay there, as long as may be necessary. My teachers taught me to find my inner strength, not physical strength but something better, something more important, more than the recognition of constant pain, the realization that this is my body's final resting place.

I had a dream just a moment ago. A hallucination, perhaps. There was a clamor outside, the thudding of boots, the flashing of lights. A rescue fantasy, no doubt. I even thought I heard Dennis calling for me. Ridiculous. But I think I will not resist. Perhaps this is the final gift the Universe has for me. Perhaps I will feel his arms around me one last time, if only as an illusion. I loved you, Dennis, and I know you loved me with a greater need and passion than I could ever match. Can you feel my arms around you, just as I feel yours? The little light I have left is fading, but with my final breath I send this wish to you. Accept what has happened. Don't give in to despair. Don't let it change you, ruin your life. Move on. Find the lesson. Tell yourself it's perfect, even if you don't know why.

I worry about you, Dennis. I worry so much.

Do not let this destroy you!

There is pain in dying, as I know now, as I have always known. But the pain of living can be greater.

Please, Dennis! Outwit . . . outwit . . .

"JOSLYN! DO YOU hear me? Honey! Can you hear me?"

It's starting over again, the whole dream fantasy sequence. I wonder if I have the power to alter it. Make it more immediate . . .

"We're coming, honey. I'm sorry it took so long. Your car ran off the road and plummeted down a very deep ravine. There was thick brush all around the car, black-berry hedges. I couldn't see you! I drove by here a hundred times, but it looked as if nothing was there. I didn't know!"

"Sir," Officer Torres said, "I need you to move away from the car."

"Can't you get her out of there?"

"We're trying, sir, but she's wedged in but good. Strapped down by her seat belt, pinned by the air bag, something stabbing her leg. We're going to have to cut the roof off to get her out."

"Then do it!"

"The equipment is on its way. We just have to—"

"What in God's name is going on here?"

Dennis and Torres whirled around and saw Detective Sentz marching toward them.

Torres stepped forward. "We've found Dr. Thomas, Detective. We're trying to extract her—"

"I didn't authorize this operation!"

This is new, Joslyn thought, smiling a little. Interesting. A nice bit of plot thickening. Heightens the drama. My Dennis is so sweet . . .

"No, sir, but—"

"In fact, I expressly refused to open a file. Didn't meet the criteria."

"Doesn't matter, sir. We found—"

"Doesn't matter? I'll decide what matters!"

"But—"

"Have you received a sudden promotion I don't know about, Sergeant? Or am I still your superior?"

Torres's eyes narrowed. "You're still my superior."

"I'm glad to hear it. Consider yourself on probation. Suspension without pay until—"

Dennis jumped in between them. "Would you stop this? My wife is trapped in that car. That's all that matters!"

Sentz pursed his lips, obviously angry. "You can't initiate an emergency rescue operation without the authorization of a senior officer or—"

"She's dying!"

That's my Dennis. Always a fighter. To the bitter end. Give him what for, Dennis!

Sentz took a deep breath. "Mr. Thomas, it might be best if you waited beyond the perimeter."

"I will not!"

"You will do as instructed, or I will regretfully—"

"I'm not moving an inch until my wife is out of that car."

"You are interfering with a police operation, leaving me no choice but—"

"*Why are you doing this?*" Dennis screamed, blocking his path. "Do you know how long she's been trapped in there? She's dying, and you're bellowing about regulations and—"

The detective moved so quickly Dennis did not know what had happened until it was over. Detective Sentz lifted him off his feet and threw him sideways. He fell face-first onto the ground.

Dennis screamed, clutching his face, bloodied on the right side. "Why are you doing this?"

Sentz ignored him. "I want to talk to the operations officer. These things have to be handled carefully. One false move could kill the person you're trying to rescue."

Are you still there? Is it over already? This isn't a very satisfying ending, Dennis. But it's too late. I know that. I can feel it inside. I can feel the transformation coming, the passage. And I'm ready. But I would like to talk to you, Dennis. One last time. I have a message . . .

"WE GOT HER!"

Dennis rushed forward, still holding the right side of his face. "How is she?"

"Not good," Torres replied, "but she's alive. Barely."
He led Dennis past the barricade back toward the car,
where attendants were lifting Joslyn's broken body onto
a stretcher. "Medics say she has broken bones, a
severely lacerated and infected leg. She's dehydrated,
malnourished. Judging from her skin color, she's got
liver damage, with the resultant buildup of toxins."

"Will she be okay?"

"They just don't know. We've got to get her to a hospital . . ."

Dennis rushed forward, grabbing the gurney. "Joslyn!
Can you hear me? Can you hear me?"

Her eyelashes fluttered briefly, barely signaling a trace
of life still residing inside.

"Joslyn, I'm sorry I took so long. I'm sorry! But we're
going to get you well. You're going to be fine, honey. I
promise. You'll be just like new. Back to your patients
in no time."

One of the medics stepped forward. "I'm sorry, sir,
but we have to get her to the hospital."

"Of course. I understand. Just—"

Joslyn's right hand suddenly wrapped itself around
Dennis's arm.

"I'm here, honey," Dennis said, eyes bulging. "I'm
here. I'll stay with you."

Slowly her lips pressed together. He could see she was
trying to say something, but she barely had the strength
to make it happen.

"What is it, Fizz? What?"

He leaned forward until his head was barely an inch
from her lips. Her voice was more breath than sound.

"Out . . . wit . . ."

"Outwit? Is that what you're saying?"

". . . stars . . ."

He felt the grip on his wrist loosen, then felt her hand
fall away altogether.

"What's happening? What's happening to her?"

The chief EMT rushed forward. "Get me an oxygen mask, now. And the defibrillator."

"They're in the ambulance. Up on the road."

"Then hurry!"

The paramedic in charge gave her an injection. "Something's wrong."

"What is it?" Dennis asked desperately. "What's happening?"

"How can I know? I haven't had a chance to examine her properly. She's been trapped in her car for seven days. Most people wouldn't have lasted this long."

"There must be something you can do!"

The attendant pounded on her chest. "I assure you . . . I'm doing . . . everything I know . . . how to do . . ."

"Please!"

Across the gurney, Dennis saw the paramedic in charge step away, shaking his head. "She's gone."

"What?" Dennis's eyes went wild. "She can't be gone. She's alive. I'm telling you, she's alive!"

Dennis felt a hand on his shoulder. "I'm sorry, sir, you need to move away and—"

"She can't be dead. She can't be!" He turned and saw Detective Sentz peering across at him.

"It's a tragedy." Sentz cleared his throat. "We did everything we could."

"Everything? You didn't do anything!"

"I know this is hard, but—"

"You killed her, you son of a bitch! *You killed my wife!*"

A second later, Dennis's fist clipped Sentz across the jaw. Sentz took a step backward, then recovered himself, rubbing the sore spot on his face. "Officers, restrain him."

Officer Torres and another grabbed Dennis by the arms,

holding him in place. Dennis strained against his captors, trying to get free, trying to get to Sentz. "This is your fault! You killed her!"

"It's an unfortunate incident, but there's only so much you can do when someone goes off a country road like this. I wonder if she'd been drinking . . ."

"You killed her, you son of a bitch! You killed Joslyn! You'll pay for this!"

Sentz sighed. "Mr. Thomas, I'm afraid I'm going to have to press charges. You threatened and committed battery against a police officer. Those are felony charges."

"You're going to lock me up? Someone should lock *you* up!"

Sentz turned away. "Take him downtown and book him, officers. I'll finish up here."

The two officers dragged Dennis away, but he fought them, struggling, screaming back at the departing detective. "This isn't over. You're not done with me. There will be a reckoning, do you hear me? Your time will come. *There will be a reckoning!*"

ONE

All Kinds of Crazy

CHAPTER

1

BEN KINCAID THUMBED through the case file, wondering what he had gotten himself into this time. As if he were not busy enough already. Just back from Washington, a much-delayed honeymoon waiting in the wings, a senatorial campaign to plan. And yet here he was, tackling a small-time criminal case. Was this really how he wanted to spend the two months the Senate was in recess? But when Marty from Legal Services called, he found himself unable to say no. As usual. He knew there were people who couldn't afford attorneys who seriously needed them, and he had often spoken of the importance of lawyers finding time in their busy schedules to help others. Time to put your money where your mouth is, right, Senator?

He stared through the acrylic separator at his new client, one Anson Thorpe III. He was a lean man, mid-twenties, scruffy beard and moustache. He did not look great, but the orange coveralls of the Tulsa County Jail rarely improved anyone's appearance.

"So, um, if I understand this correctly," Ben said, "the only things you stole were dolls?"

"Not dolls. Action figures."

"Okay . . ."

"Do you have any idea how much these action figures are worth?"

"I understand some are collector's items."

"And some are beyond collector's items. This was the classic run of Mego Super-Friends figures. Still the standard-bearer for the entire field."

"So . . . they're particularly attractive action figures?"

"Actually, they make the entire Justice League look like trolls. But they were the first."

"And they're valuable?"

"If they're in good condition."

Ben tapped his pencil against his lips. "So I'm going to assume the ones you, um, borrowed—"

"Rescued."

"Rescued from the store . . ." He checked his file. "Starbase 21, right? They must've been in very good condition."

Anson's eyes widened. "They were still in their original packaging. That makes them most desirable. So few understand."

Ben's brow creased. "What's the point of having a doll if you don't take it out of the packaging?"

"It is not a doll!"

"It's not anything if you can't take it out of the box."

"These are not mere toys. These are popular-culture icons. Artifacts of our time."

"Uh-huh."

"I have over two hundred action figures."

"All still wrapped in plastic?"

"Of course."

Ben's eyes rolled skyward. "And they call me a nerd."

"If you take them out and play with them, their value diminishes dramatically. Practically worthless."

Ben glanced at his watch. Marty so owed him one. Possibly three. "You decided to take the action figures for yourself?"

"Those barbarians were going to open the packaging!"

"They deserved to die."

Anson leapt to his feet. "Yes!"

"I was being sarcastic."

"I—" Anson deflated like a leaky balloon. "Oh."

Ben rifled through his papers. "You used a paint can to break the window."

"Had to get in somehow."

"Red paint splattered everywhere."

"But I got in."

"And you took the—action figures."

"Allegedly."

"And you went home."

"I definitely went home."

"Then the police showed up at your door . . ."

Anson folded his arms across his chest. "Outrageous. Total invasion of privacy."

". . . asking for the action figures . . ."

"I had to go to the door in my pajamas!"

". . . because they followed a trail of red footprints to your front door."

Anson looked down at his hands. "Yeah . . . that wasn't so good."

Ben stared at him. "Did you fall asleep during crime school or what?"

"I had a lot on my mind."

"You've got a lot more now. Burglary, theft, and criminal mischief, to be specific."

"My cellmate says you're a really good lawyer."

"You don't need a good lawyer. You need a change of profession. And some kind of twelve-step program for people addicted to action figures."

"He said you could get me off."

Ben closed the file. "I couldn't get you off if your mother was the judge. The state is offering you six months if you return the figures. Take the offer."

Anson looked at the wall, sulking. "Any more brilliant advice?"

Ben grabbed his coat and headed toward the door. "Yeah. You're really too old to be playing with dolls."

JONES PACED A circular path around Christina and Loving. "So, are we all together on this?"

"*Comme ci, comme ça,*" Christina said. "We're together in the sense that I'm perfectly willing to listen to you try to convince Ben." It was not a court day, as evidenced by her attire: a sporty white sailor suit, complete with blue kerchief, short skirt, and blue-brimmed sailor cap.

"Me too," Loving said, with his usual easygoing grin.

"But will you support me, Christina? You're Ben's wife. He listens to you."

"Yes," Christina said wearily. "He listens. And then he goes right on doing whatever it is he wants to do. As far as influence goes—well, I can't allow myself to believe that even for a moment. *La grande illusion.*"

"Oh, come on now," Jones said. "We all know wives have ways of persuading their spouses. Ways of . . . withholding favors."

"Do you know how long it took that man to propose?" Christina brushed her long strawberry-blond curls behind her shoulders. "I'm not withholding anything."

"Maybe you should!"

"I dunno about that, Jones," Loving said, "but I think this gives me a lotta insight into your relationship with Paula."

"Oh, ha ha."

"I wondered how she managed to score that big rock on her ring finger. Now I think I know."

"I gave that to her because I love her!"

"Or hoped to."

Jones leaned right into Loving's face. The office investigator was twice as wide and almost a foot taller than the office manager, but that didn't intimidate him. "Now you listen to me, you big . . . galoot!"

"Who's a galoot?"

"You're a galoot!"

"Do you even know what a galoot is?"

"Well . . . not exactly. But I know you are one!"

Christina eased herself between them. "Would you two stop acting like third graders? You work for an important attorney and U.S. senator, for Pete's sake. Show a little *je ne sais quoi*." She paused. "Besides, the client might hear."

"I don't care if—" Jones stopped short when he heard the jangling bell that told him someone had opened the front door to the seventh-floor offices of Kincaid & McCall. Jones waited a good three seconds until their titular boss reached them.

"No more pro bono cases!" Ben said, flinging his briefcase on Jones's reception desk.

"Ben!" Christina replied. "You've always said it was a lawyer's duty to help those in need."

"I've had a change of heart," Ben groused. "I draw the line at morons who leave the police a map to follow." He did a double take. "What are you wearing?"

She did a little pirouette. "Just a little something I picked up. Do you think I look sexy?"

"I think you look like Donald Duck."

Loving cut in, presumably to prevent an incident requiring medical attention. "So, Skipper, are you sayin' you're too important for cases like that one?"

"I think everyone's too important for cases like that one. I'm going to call Marty and tell him to take me off the referral list."

Christina gently laid a finger on his cheek. "Now, Ben. Isn't that a bit drastic?"

"Do you have any idea how much stuff I have to do right now?"

"Probably better than you, since I look at your calendar occasionally. But you have an obligation to others, don't you?"

"Well, of course, but—"

"Haven't you talked about the importance of reaching out a helping hand?"

"Well, yes, but—"

She ran her fingers through his hair and talked in baby talk. "You don't want to become an old sourpuss, do you?"

He frowned. "All right. I won't call Marty."

"Thank you, snookums."

"And thank you," Jones muttered, "for demonstrating how he never listens and you have no influence over him."

Ben's brow creased. "Why are you three standing around? Don't you have work to do?"

Jones stood at attention. "I have something I want to discuss with you, Ben. We all do, that is."

"I don't like the sound of this already."

"I'll cut straight to the chase. We want you to go back on the billable hour."

"No."

"Ben, everyone does it."

"My mother used to say, if everyone jumped off a cliff—"

"Oh, spare me the homilies and look at it from the standpoint of your office manager. You're a U.S. senator. You've defended cases that received national attention. And we still barely make ends meet!"

"The billable hour is the worst thing that ever happened to the legal profession. All it does is stir up a lot of dissatisfaction and suspicion. And it destroys lawyers' lives. Leaves them no time for pro bono work or mentoring. Drives women out of the profession. Justice Breyer wrote, and I quote, 'The profession's obsession with billable hours is like drinking water from a fire hose. The result is that many lawyers are starting to drown.' "

"Excuse me, did I ask for a Ben rant? I'm just trying to put a little change in the Christmas fund."

"Lawyers got along fine without the billable hour until the nineteen-fifties. They will again. Many corporations are refusing to pay them, demanding flat fees. Consequently, the smart up-and-coming firms are giving them what they want and stealing business from the old guard. Pretty soon—"

"We'll all live in Cloud-Cuckoo-Land and eat bon-bons all day! Honestly, Ben, when are you going to get a clue?"

Ben assaulted Jones with his deadliest weapon, the raised eyebrow. "I think the firm is doing just fine. We charge a fair fee without milking clients with billable hour charts. We make ourselves affordable to those who need help."

"Oh, I give up!" Jones said, throwing his arms into the air. He marched back to his desk, the usual exasperated expression on his face.

Ben stared at his wake. "He seems upset."

"Yeah," Loving agreed, "but he's happier that way."

"Think I've heard the last of this?"

"Sure. Till tomorrow."

"Ben," Christina said, tapping him on the shoulder, "Harvey wants to talk to you about the campaign."

"Ugh. Can't I just be a lawyer for a little while?"

"For a very little while, yes. But he has to start making plans."

"Have him do that. And send me a memo."

"Also, there's a client waiting for you in your office."

"More Legal Services referrals?"

"No. This guy has a little money."

"How refreshing. Know what he wants?"

"Nary a clue."

"Well, life is either a great adventure or it is nothing at all. Want to sit in?"

"No, I think the distinguished senator from Oklahoma should meet clients on his own. Besides, I have an appointment to see my personal shopper."

Ben blinked. "You have a personal shopper?"

Christina took his arm and rubbed her nose against his cheek. "Just since I married you, my little sugar daddy."

Loving bristled. "I'm so outta here . . ."

"Why do you need a personal shopper?" Ben asked.

"Because I'm a busy important lawyer woman. Besides . . ." She grinned. "You think I could pick out clothes like these on my own?"

BEN PEERED THROUGH the window in his office door, stealing a look at the client before the client saw him. His first impression was favorable; the man was not wearing orange coveralls. In fact, he was well dressed and groomed neatly and seemed like a perfectly normal urban professional, the sort you saw hustling about downtown all around Bartlett Square, even now that they had removed the fountain and allowed traffic to drive through it. Ben got the impression that he was smart and educated, which would be a refreshing change of pace.

Too bad Christina hadn't come in—she was always so good at sizing people up. Then again, he had been practicing law for—how many years now? He was not without intuition. Perhaps he had become too dependent on her. Perhaps it was time he flexed his own muscles . . .

The man sitting in his office had an air of confidence about him, which suggested that he was not here on a criminal matter. Some sort of business affair. Judging from his dress, his briefcase, and especially his shoes, Ben surmised that he owned his own business. He was wearing glasses and had two pens in his shirt pocket. No pocket protector, but still, he screamed computer industry. A software company, probably. That was the avenue many young go-getters had traveled to recent success. So what was his problem?

If he wasn't in trouble, it must be an employee. Contract dispute? Sexual harassment? No, Ben had it— immigration law. Not long ago, Oklahoma's extremely conservative legislature had passed the strictest immigration laws in the country, much to the dismay of most local businesses. Thanks to 1804, as the law was called familiarly, it was a felony to transport or shelter illegal immigrants. Employers could have their business licenses revoked for hiring illegal immigrants, even if they subsequently became legal to work. They were forced to fire employees, even when they weren't sure if they were legal. Since the law passed, more than twenty-five thousand immigrants had left Tulsa County alone, many of them legal citizens with illegal family members. With a smaller pool of workers, higher prices and wages soon resulted. Some predicted this would spur the greatest economic disaster for the state since the Dust Bowl.

Yes, that had to be it. And that was fine. Ben would be happy to deal with anything as calm and rational as an immigration problem. It would be a welcome change of pace, in fact.

"Good afternoon," Ben said as he entered the office, extending his hand. "I'm Benjamin Kincaid." They exchanged introductions. "How can I help you?" He grinned a little. "An immigration difficulty, perhaps?"

The client leaned forward. "I was wondering if you could arrange a pardon for me."

Ben stared at the man. "You say you want—a pardon?"

"Yes. Someone killed my wife. And no one is doing anything about it. So I wondered if you could arrange a pardon in the event that . . . someone does."

Ben fell into his chair. Maybe it would be better to leave the character assessments to Christina, after all.

"I'M SORRY, Mr. Thomas, but I don't have the power to grant pardons."

"I thought maybe you could put in a good word with the governor who appointed you. Or the president. You worked with him on that constitutional amendment, didn't you?"

"Well, yes, but I don't think he liked the way it came out."

"The governor would be sufficient."

Ben stared at the man, wondering where to begin. He had been right on one point—Dennis Thomas was smart and was well educated. He taught Victorian literature at the University of Tulsa, which had one of the finest English faculties in the nation. But on this subject, he was clearly not objective. Possibly not even rational. "I hope you're not contemplating doing something . . . extreme."

"How do you mean?"

"I'm not here to help people get away with crimes of revenge."

"Aren't you a lawyer?"

"Yes . . ."

"And you handle murder cases?"

Ben felt his heart speed up a beat. "Well, yes . . ."

"You got that senator off."

"He was innocent."

"Yeah. Look, all I want is a pardon. I don't think I should have to spend the rest of my life in jail because some bastard cop killed my wife."

"Cop?" Ben took a deep breath. "In the first place, Dennis, you won't get life. You kill a cop, you'll almost certainly be executed. In the second place, what are you talking about? I haven't heard about any cops out on murder sprees."

"He refused to investigate. Wouldn't even open a file. I asked him repeatedly. Every day from the moment she disappeared. He wouldn't do it."

"He must've had a reason."

"He had lots of reasons. But he didn't do it because he didn't want to. He's just occupying oxygen, waiting to put his twenty on. My wife wasn't enough to get him off his butt."

"So you blame your wife's death—"

"She didn't just die, Senator. She suffered. She was seriously wounded, trapped in a car for seven days, slowly dying. In excruciating pain. Can you imagine what that felt like, to experience that kind of agony, and dehydration, and starvation? For seven days? Eventually, I got someone else to authorize an investigation. Do you know how long it took them to find her? Three hours! She suffered for seven days because that dirty cop couldn't spare three hours!"

"I can tell you're upset, and I don't blame you. But believe me, revenge is not the right course of action. File a civil suit if you must."

"Civil suits against the police never succeed."

Sadly, Ben knew he was largely correct. "I can't condone crime. And I certainly can't in any way support you in a crime that hasn't even happened yet."

Dennis drew himself up slowly, folded his hands, and took a deep breath. "I'm sorry. You must've misunderstood me. What did you think I was proposing—murder? Gosh, I guess I didn't explain myself clearly. The truth is, I'm writing a book."

Ben looked at him levelly. "Go on."

"That's life in academia. Publish or perish. And I'm sure you know how important research is for a scholarly book. You've written books yourself, haven't you?"

"Yes. Nonfiction."

"Well, I'm planning a literary novel, something different from my usual critical analyses, and in my totally fictional story, a man commits murder, but then tries to get a pardon to get himself off. Or failing that, takes steps to establish a claim of temporary insanity."

"Do tell."

"So my point in coming here is to find out what would be the best steps to take to support a subsequent claim of temporary insanity. You can help me with that, can't you? Since you are an author as well as a lawyer?"

"But I'm not a total idiot."

"I understand that you—I mean, the lawyer in my book—would need to be able to show that I was unable to distinguish right from wrong at the time the murder was committed."

"Yeeeeeesss . . ."

"What if I were on some kind of drug? Would that help? Or maybe if I forgot to put my clothes on? That would certainly show diminished capacity, wouldn't it? If I were standing there starkers wearing nothing but a gun?"

Ben rose to his feet. "Look, I don't know who you think you're dealing with, but this has gone far enough. Despite what you've said, this sounds a whole lot like you're planning a murder and trying to get advice on the best way to do it!"

"What about irresistible impulse? I'm thinking that might be the best way to go."

Ben's brows knitted together. "Exactly what kind of research have you been doing?"

"I think the jury would believe that I was unable to

control myself, after all that's happened to me. And that's all you need, right? Just an excuse for jury nullification. Getting the jury to ignore the law and reach a verdict based on sympathy for the defendant."

"Why temporary insanity? Why not just claim you're absolutely totally stark raving insane?"

"Ah, but then I—I mean, my character—would be committed, right? If he succeeds on a claim of temporary insanity, however, he goes free. No jail because he wasn't responsible for his actions, and no commitment because the insanity was only temporary."

"You wouldn't go free. Not after killing a cop, not even on a temporary insanity defense. You'd be committed for observation."

"Yes, but for how long? Until the doctors think I'm well and won't be a threat to society? That shouldn't take long."

"Look. I'm not going to have anything to do with what sounds to me like a very twisted little scheme."

"I'm just doing research!"

"Yeah, and I'm just waiting for my Yankees tryout. I'm a member of the bar, Mr. Thomas—"

"Dr. Thomas, if you don't mind. I'm a Ph.D."

Ben drew in his breath. "—not to mention a U.S. senator. I'm an elected—well, appointed official. I can't assist you in the commission of a crime. In fact, I have a duty to report any plans to commit a criminal act."

"I said nothing about any plan to commit a crime. I told you, I'm just researching a book. Although . . ."

"Although you might just lose your head and take drugs and go commit a murder with your clothes off? I want you out of my office."

Dennis picked up his briefcase. "Fine. If you say so." He stood, then hesitated a moment. "You know, Mr. Kincaid, I have to say—I'm disappointed. I heard you were different. I heard you didn't just take care of your-self. I heard you cared about other people."

"Way too many people are talking about me these days. Look, I care about other people, but—"

"No, you're covering your own butt, like everyone else. Playing by the rules. The same attitude that got my Joslyn killed in the first place."

"That's not fair."

"It's disappointing. I heard you weren't afraid to bend the rules here and there in the name of justice."

"Bend the rules? You're talking about murder!"

"No. I'm talking about the man who killed my wife. Deliberately." He hunched forward, leaning against Ben's desk. "Did I tell you that my wife's liver failed? Totally shut down. The buildup of toxins in her body was horrifying. Physicians have told me that's the worst kind of pain it's possible to experience. Constant. Inescapable. Imagine enduring that for seven days, help-less to do anything about it."

"My heart goes out to you for your loss, but—"

"Her left leg was gangrenous. Even if she had lived it would've had to be amputated. She was so hungry she tried to eat the vinyl upholstery on the seat she was pinned down against."

Ben felt a dryness in his throat. "You have my sym-pathy, but—"

"You're a married man, senator. Do you love your wife?"

"Of course I do. More than—"

"Would you want to see her tortured for seven days?"

"Of course not."

"I know you wouldn't. I can see it in your eyes. If you were in my shoes, you would feel exactly the same way I do."

"But I would never contemplate murder," Ben replied, realizing how weak and unconvincing he sounded.

"Did I tell you I didn't get to say goodbye?" He collapsed on the desk, his head falling onto his arms. "I saw her for only a moment, when they pulled her out of the car. Then the . . . the bastard cop had me arrested for hitting him. What self-respecting husband wouldn't?"

Without even thinking about it, Ben placed his hand on Dennis's shoulder. "I'm so sorry."

"I was locked up late on a Friday. I couldn't get an attorney, couldn't get released before my arraignment. By the time I was out—" His voice cracked. "They had already cremated Joslyn. That was her wish—but it was implemented before I was released. She was gone. I never got to see her, Mr. Kincaid. I never even said goodbye!"

Ben pressed against his shoulder, hoping to somehow feed the man the comfort that eluded him. "I know how hard dealing with grief can be. But murder is not the answer. It won't help anything. And you won't get away with it. You'll be convicted. Would your wife have wanted that? The best thing you can do is move forward, get on with your life. If you want to bring some action against the police department, I will help you. Sure, the odds are long, but I have personally experienced police misconduct like you wouldn't believe. I know it happens—much more frequently than anyone wants to acknowledge. I will fight to the last to see that your wrong is righted. I promise you."

Ben knelt down beside him. "Will you let me? Will you let me do that for you?"

Dennis slowly rose to his feet. He brushed his wet face, then tugged at the lay of his shirt. "I'm sorry you weren't able to help me, Mr. Kincaid."

"Dennis . . ."

"Even though you won't be representing me, I assume

this conversation is protected by attorney-client privilege. Since I came in as a prospective client."

"Yes, but that doesn't extend to planning criminal—"

"I didn't say anything about any plan. I'm researching a book. So the privilege applies. And we have nothing more to talk about."

CHAPTER
2

CHRISTINA PEERED ACROSS the fifteen-by-fifteen grid, obviously not pleased.

"There is no way I am accepting this, Ben. *Za* is not a word."

"It is."

"What does it mean?"

"It's slang for a slice of pizza."

"If it's slang, it shouldn't be in the dictionary."

"But it is. And that makes it a valid Scrabble word."

"Use it in a sentence."

Ben contemplated a moment. "Whenever I look at you, I think, Wow-*Za*."

She gave him the look that he had come to recognize as the sort of serious irritation that only total acquiescence or pizza from Mario's could fix. "I am not going to let you make sixty-two points for playing one lousy tile!"

"There just happened to be an opening on the triple-letter space. I got lucky."

"It might be the last time."

"You mean I can't play *qi*?"

She closed her eyelids. "No, you innocent waif. That is not what I mean."

Ben normally looked forward to these evenings when no one was in trial and they were both home at a decent hour and they could unwind with a round of the greatest of all board games. But Christina seemed uncommonly stressed tonight.

"Something on your mind?"

She flopped around and lay down in his lap. "As a matter of fact, yes. I'm concerned about that client you saw today. Dennis Whatever. The professor."

Ben stroked his two young cats, Mellisandro and Dellisandro, and they curled themselves against his foot. Their mother, Giselle, watched from her cushy bed in the corner. The cats loved Ben, followed him everywhere, mostly to the exclusion of all others. Christina patiently tolerated their unmitigated partisanship. "He was a little creepy."

"He was more than just creepy, Ben. He's planning to kill someone!"

"He never actually said that."

"He didn't have to. It was obvious. That's why he was there."

"He said he was there because he wondered hypothetically if I would be able to arrange a pardon. Because he was researching a book. A work of fiction."

She took his hand. "Ben, I don't want to see you get in trouble over this. Especially not when you're planning a reelection campaign. Maybe you should report it to the bar association."

"If he had said he was planning to commit a crime, I would agree. But unless and until he does that, prospective client interviews are protected by privilege. Even though I didn't help him, I'm still bound not to reveal anything I was told."

"Unless he says he's going to commit a crime."

"Which he did not. The test is whether I believe he's planning to hurt someone. And I don't."

"And that's based on what? Your profound understanding of human nature? Give me a break, Ben.

You're clueless when it comes to people. You couldn't psychoanalyze a Barbie doll."

She had a point. He wanted to argue and defend himself, but unfortunately, he could never win an argument with her, especially when she was right.

"I know what you're saying. I've been agonizing over this, too. I just don't know what to do."

"You have to protect yourself."

"I have to protect the victim. If there is one."

"That's another problem. You don't even know who it is." She raised her hand to the side of his cheek. "Well, sleep on it. Perhaps in the morning it will all be clear."

"Good idea."

"Sleepy yet?"

"Not really."

She sat upright and smiled. "Good. Let's go to bed."

And then he heard the Blue Danube waltz. His cell phone. This sort of untimely interruption seemed to happen more frequently these days. Or perhaps it just seemed that way because, being newlyweds, something else was happening more frequently . . .

He flipped open his phone. "Yes?"

"Boss? Jones. Having a good evening?"

"Trying."

"Still wringing your hands over whether to report that guy who might be planning to kill a cop?"

"Pretty much."

"Well, you can stop."

"Can I now? Why is that?"

There was a brief static-filled pause before Jones continued. "Because he just did it."

CHAPTER
3

AFTER BEN showed his ID, the uniform at the door allowed him to pass beyond the crime scene tape. The room at the Marriott Southern Hills was a spacious suite, but it didn't take him any time at all to determine where the action was. Crime scene techs scrambled all over the site where the body was found. Videographers recorded everything. Two outlines had been drawn on the carpeted floor.

Major Mike Morelli stared at the scene, standing just above one of the outlined figures and a huge patch of bloodstained carpet, his hands deeply thrust into his coat pockets. Ben had seen this expression before. Mike was not pleased.

"That looks . . . awful," Ben said, staring down at the carpet.

Mike nodded. "April really is the cruelest month, huh? 'The blood-dimmed tide is loosed, and everywhere / The ceremony of innocence is drowned . . . '" He exhaled heavily. "Miles to go before I sleep."

"So if I'm not mistaken," Ben replied, "that was Eliot, Yeats, and Frost, all in one breath. That may be a new record for pretentious allusion, even for you."

Mike shot him a wry smile. "Good to see you, Ben."

"Thanks for letting me in."

"I gather from your presence here that you will be representing the alleged perpetrator?"

"He's called for me," Ben said, not filling in all the details. "I haven't taken the case."

"Don't." Mike replied. "This probably appeals to your insane predilection for representing underdogs and lost causes, but this is going to be ugly. It's premeditated. And a cop is dead."

"Even assuming Dennis Thomas committed the crime—"

"He did."

"You must admit, there were some keenly sympathetic circumstances."

"When it comes to cop killers, sympathy does not exist."

"Thomas blamed this guy for the death of his wife."

"So he killed Detective Sentz, who also had a wife, not to mention two daughters. I'm telling you, Ben, stay away. This is a loser."

Ben frowned. There was no point arguing with Mike about this. Better to change the subject. Try to slip in through the back door. "You're, um, looking good. Walking without a cane, I notice."

"Didn't like it. Made me look prematurely old. And you know what they say. 'This is no country for old men. The young / In one another's arms . . .'"

"That more poetry?"

"Yeats."

"Right. Sergeant Baxter been making you go to physical therapy?"

"You know it." Mike glanced his way. "To tell the truth, you look pretty good, too. Can barely see the scar."

A few months before, Ben and Mike'd had the misfortune to be at the epicenter of an assassination attempt. Trying to escape, they ended up in a car a few seconds before it exploded. Mike threw Ben clear, taking most of the damage in the process. Ben had a small crease from a stray bullet on his right cheek. Mike had been in the hospital for months and was only now getting back to work. Ben and Mike's partner, Kate Baxter, had been nursemaiding him most of the time. He was a difficult patient. He didn't like people fussing over him. Or so he said, anyway.

Ben and Mike's friendship was a resilient one. They had known each other since college and at one time had even made music together, Ben on the keyboards, Mike on the guitar. Mike had married Ben's sister, a union that did not turn out well or last long. But that was years in the past. They had managed to hold on to their friendship, at least as well as could be expected, given what each did for a living.

"I guess you knew the, uh, victim?" Ben asked.

"Of course I did." Mike was the senior homicide detective on the Tulsa PD. "I know his wife, too. Both daughters. Real cuties." Mike gave Ben a pointed look. "They don't have a daddy now. You have any idea what that's going to do to them?"

"I can only imagine."

"It won't be good. Sentz was a fine officer. A little grumpy, perhaps too rigid, somewhat unimaginative. But you don't make detective by being a dummy. He had the right stuff and he kept it together. I didn't see him ever making the transition to homicide, but I knew there were other jobs he could perform perfectly well. There was no need for him to come to an end like this. No need at all." He shook his head bitterly. "Such a waste."

"I'm sorry, Mike."

"He was hoping for my job one day. Wanted to be my second, to get Prentiss's old position. 'Oh, the vanity of earthly greatness . . . '"

"Why was he in this hotel room?"

"I don't know all the details. I think some of his co-workers were here, too, judging from what the clerk at the front desk told me. I'm trying to track that down. Apparently they were on some kind of stakeout. Drugs, I assume."

"But you're certain Dennis Thomas was here?"

"The first responder found him in a lump on the carpet." Mike pointed to one of the outlines on the floor. "That's him."

"Why was he here?"

"To commit murder, obviously. Why Sentz agreed to meet him, or let him into the room, I don't know. He probably felt bad about what happened to the guy's wife and wanted to help him. And you see what he got for his kindness."

"There must be more to it than that."

"Why? Because that's how you get people off? By complicating things that don't need complicating?"

"That's a little cynical, even for you."

"An officer died here, Ben. If you were expecting me to be jolly, you were sadly mistaken." He jammed his fists into his coat pockets. "Times like this, I really miss smoking." He stared out the hotel window. "I just wish I'd seen this coming, you know? Had some hint."

Like maybe having the killer come to your office to ask if you could get him off the murder he hadn't committed yet?

Ben couldn't help but wonder if he was responsible, at least in part. He prided himself on his determination to do the right thing. Had he just allowed a man to be killed? A good man, a public servant?

"I don't suppose your forensics people have turned anything up?"

"Not yet. Too soon. But honestly, what would they find? It's not as if there's much question about what happened here."

"Any traces of people other than the victim and the alleged assailant?"

"Yes. But remember, this is a hotel room. People come in and out every day, leaving behind their hairs and dead skin cells."

"Blood?"

"A lot from the victim. No one else."

"DNA traces."

"Not yet. But given how many people have probably stayed in this room . . ."

"Right. Not helpful. Eyewitnesses?"

"The man at the front desk vaguely recalls seeing Thomas come in. And of course he recalls seeing all the police officers roaming about. They were aware there was some sort of police operation going on in this room."

"And the weapon?"

"Standard handgun. Your guy was lying on top of it."

"He's not my guy."

"Yet. We're tracing the registration number."

"Good. Let me know."

Mike shrugged. "That's the law."

"If anything else comes up . . ."

"Still planning a reelection bid?"

Ben was startled by the abrupt change of subject. "I guess. Why? You think it's a bad idea?"

"I think you and campaigning will fit together about as well as me and high-heel shoes." He grinned. "But you have surprised me before."

"Thanks for the vote of confidence."

"Don't forget you're still honeymooning. These should be tranquil days, filled with love and laughter and promiscuity."

"Was that a poem?"

"No, that was original." He glanced over his shoulder at two nearby hair and fiber analysts. "Ben, can I have a word with you in private?"

"Do I have to?"

Mike took his arm. " 'Let us go then, you and I / When the evening is spread out against the sky . . . ' "

"Would you stop with the poetry already?" Ben sighed. "Why couldn't your father have put you to bed with Peter Rabbit, like everyone else?"

Mike pulled him to the side. "I hope you understand that I am speaking to you now as a friend, not a police officer."

"Am I going to like this?"

Mike put a finger in his chest. "You do not need this case. Seriously. This is a cop killing. People do not like cop killers, particularly in conservative towns like Tulsa. There will be massive publicity. You do not need to be a part of it. Not under any circumstances. But especially not if you're planning to run for another Senate term."

"Got it."

He looked at his friend sternly. "This case will not help you, Ben. The press will not be kind if you represent an accused cop killer."

"The press assume everyone accused is guilty. I don't."

"I don't think you're hearing what I'm saying."

"You're wrong. Message received and understood."

"But taken to heart?"

Ben drew in his breath. "I'm just going to talk to the man. I have no desire to get involved in this. For reasons you can't even begin to comprehend."

"Glad to hear it. Take care." Mike hesitated a moment. "Um, heard anything from your sister?"

"Not much. A few quick phone calls. But that's good, for her."

"And that little boy of hers?"

You mean, that little boy of yours? Ben thought. He still had no idea whether Mike realized what was so patently obvious to him. "Haven't spoken to Joey. I hear he's doing better in school."

"That's good. Not that I care, but if she happens to come to town . . ."

"I'll be sure to let you know."

"Thanks. I better get back to work." He started away, then turned back one last time, holding up a finger. "Now remember—no underdogs. No lost causes. No bad publicity."

"Got it."

"Scout's honor?"

"Scout's honor."

Mike paused a moment, then said: "You never were a Scout, were you?"

Ben smiled. "Couldn't stand the uniform."

CHAPTER

4

BEN HATED how his footsteps echoed as he walked down the metal-floored corridor that led to the county jail holding cells. He had been here before—on one notable occasion wearing orange coveralls, cuffs, and foot shackles—and it never failed to give him the willies. The deliberate austerity, the cold and mechanical environment, and the superior attitudes of those in attendance all made for an indelibly unpleasant experience.

Of course, that was the point.

"Here you are," the man in the tan uniform said, as if those three words left a bitter taste in his mouth. Ben wasn't surprised. The arrestee was accused of killing a police officer. There would be no kindness in these quarters.

"Thanks, Sam." The attending officer unlocked the cell, let Ben in, then closed the door behind him.

Dennis was lying on the cot. The cell had a small table, an open toilet, and a sink, partially obscured by a small wall. It was not the Ritz. It was not even the basement at the Ritz.

Dennis opened his eyes. "Thanks for coming."

"It's a miracle I got here as soon as I did. They were deliberately giving me the runaround."

"I would've thought a senator would have some sway at the jailhouse."

"When it comes to cop killing, no one has sway. And

the police won't make anything easy. The reporters are already gathering outside. I managed to come in through a side door, but I won't get that courtesy again." Ben put down his briefcase and sat on the end of the cot. "So what did you want?"

"I want you to get me off, obviously."

"I'm afraid that's impossible."

"Why?"

"Because I can't suborn perjury."

"I don't even know what that means."

"It means I can't knowingly put someone on the stand and help him lie."

"Who said anything about lying?"

Ben gave him a long look. "You must think I have the memory of a mayfly. I know perfectly well you were planning to kill Detective Sentz. And then you went out and did it."

"I didn't."

"Don't patronize me."

"I didn't."

"Well, good luck convincing the jury."

"I think I should plead not guilty by reason of temporary insanity."

"I thought you didn't do it."

"That's correct. But I think my chances of success will be greater with a temporary insanity plea."

"You'll have to do it with a different attorney. Don't worry—there are lots of lawyers out there. You won't have any trouble finding someone."

"I don't want just anyone. I want you. I hear you're the best in town."

"There are lots of capable attorneys in town. Call my office manager. He can make some recommendations."

Dennis sat up and looked at him with the same pleading eyes that had almost started him crying when they last met. "I need your help."

"That's what you said before. But you didn't listen to me." Ben frowned. "What happened?"

"That's the problem. I don't know. I blacked out."

Ben took a deep breath. "Was that induced by the drugs or the nakedness?"

"I'm serious. I'm not making this up." He took Ben's arm and kept him from rising. "I will admit I hated that man. My wife suffered and died because of him. I will admit I thought about killing him, or making him suffer some semblance of what my wife suffered. But that wasn't why I went to see him. I wanted to confront him. Wanted to find out what was going on."

"I'm amazed he agreed to see you."

"I was, too. When I got to his hotel room, he almost seemed . . ." Dennis stared at the ceiling, searching for the right word. "He almost seemed guilt-ridden. Maybe he regretted what he did, after he saw what happened to Joslyn. I don't know. Something was on his mind. We talked, but at that point my memory gets pretty shaky. I don't know what happened except I remember having the distinct feeling he was going to tell me something, something important . . ."

"And then?"

Dennis clenched his fists. "And that's all I can remember. I know there was more. I just can't bring it back."

"What would cause you to black out?"

"I don't know."

"Did he hit you?"

"No."

"Has this ever happened to you before?"

"No."

"When did you come around?"

"More than two hours later. The police had me in custody. And I remembered nothing since just before I passed out."

"Isn't that convenient?"

Dennis swore under his breath. "Pretty damned inconvenient, if you ask me."

"Well, sorry, but I can't help you. I should be going."

"Please don't." Dennis took Ben's wrist, holding him back. "I don't know what happened to me, but surely this only strengthens our case for temporary insanity."

"Funny how that works out."

"I know there are cases in which blackouts have been used as evidence of mental disorder."

"You know, despite whatever impression you may have gotten from TV shows or the local tabloid news, insanity defenses are rarely successful, and when they are, ninety percent of the time the defendants had been previously diagnosed with mental illnesses."

"I've seen a therapist."

"Was that before or after you came to see me?"

"My capability to function was obviously diminished. I couldn't distinguish right from wrong."

Ben could feel his irritation rising. It was impossible not to be suspicious of a defendant who knew as much about the law as he did. "Diminished capacity is not a defense. It's a mitigating factor. It might get you a reduced sentence, but it won't get you off."

"I know. We have to say I was insane. Didn't comprehend the nature and quality of my actions. Succumbed to an irresistible impulse." He paused. "And we have to say it was temporary. And now it's gone."

Ben looked at him through narrowed eyes. "You're really weirding me out, you know it?"

"Is it a crime to be smart? Well read? Do you only take stupid defendants?"

"Well, no, but—"

"I want you to take my case."

"That's not going to happen."

"There's more to this than you know!"

Ben stopped, one hand already on the cell door. "What does that mean?"

"I don't know exactly. That what I wanted to talk to Sentz about. To find out what was going on. I think . . ." He waved his hands in the air, as though trying to straighten out his muddled thoughts. "I think there's . . . some kind of conspiracy going on."

Ben sighed. As if he didn't get enough conspiracy theories from Loving. "If this is supposed to convince me that you're paranoid and delusional, forget it."

"I mean it! There's something strange about the whole situation."

Ben turned back around. "Okay, I know I shouldn't do this, but I'll give you five more minutes. What are you babbling about?"

"Sentz. His refusal to open a file. Why? I mean, I know they have their rules and regulations, but so what? He could see I was desperate, and he could equally see that my wife wasn't the type to run off without saying anything. There was a moment where I was almost certain Sentz was going to give in and at least issue an APB. And then he looked at someone else in the station house—and that was it. He refused to do anything."

"You're saying someone else forced him to enforce the rules. I don't think we can castigate them much for that."

"You're not listening to me." Dennis stood up, his jaw set. "I'm saying that someone, for some reason, did not want my wife to be found alive."

"What reason could anyone possibly—"

"I don't know! That's what I need you for!"

"You're barking up the wrong tree."

"I'd investigate if I could. But I'm trapped behind bars."

"And unlikely to get bail, on a cop-killing charge."

"Exactly. I need you."

"So you keep saying." He paused, peering at Dennis intently. "Did you think if you got a senator on your side that might get you the publicity you want? Stir up some sympathy and public unrest? Put pressure on the judge, the jury? That's why you keep trying to get me to represent you, isn't it?"

"I'm doing it because I thought you would understand!" Dennis shouted.

His words reverberated through the metal cell long after his mouth had closed, a jarring clamor in Ben's ears.

"I've read about you, Mr. Kincaid."

"Google is a wonderful thing."

"And about your wife."

Ben's chin rose.

"I know she was wrongly accused of murder once. Framed. And probably would've been executed, except that one very determined individual fought for her, fought the system, the courts, the cops, and everyone else who stood in his way." Dennis smiled slightly. "And then he married her."

Ben shuffled his feet. "Well . . . a lot happened in between . . ."

"I want that man to fight for me, Mr. Kincaid. I want him to believe in me enough to stick his neck out and go the extra mile. Or even if he doesn't, I want him to do it for my Joslyn, because she was a good person, an extraordinary person, who did not deserve the gruesome, hideous death she received." He took a small step in Ben's direction. "I—I just want to know that someone still cares about justice. Not winning or losing. Not money. Not reputations. Justice."

He stretched out his hand, his eyes pleading. "Will you be that person, Mr. Kincaid? Will you do it for me? And Joslyn?"

CHAPTER
5

"YOU CANNOT DO this, Ben. Do you hear me? You cannot!"

Ben looked down at the floor and fidgeted with his fingers. "I'm sorry to hear that, Christina. Because I've already done it."

"Without even consulting me? I'm your partner."

"I never consult you before I accept a client. And neither do you."

"This is different."

"How so?"

"There's an unspoken commandment. Thou shalt consult thy partner and helpmeet before representing cop killers."

Ben pressed his fingers against the top of his desk. He could see this was going to be more difficult than he had anticipated. "We have never shied away from taking controversial clients."

"This is way beyond controversial. The whole city is ready to have him drawn and quartered."

"And I've also never shied away from clients everyone believed guilty. Starting with you."

Christina did not back down. "Don't go throwing that in my face. I was framed. That's totally different from some guy who stalked his victim, carried a gun to his hotel room, and blew him away."

"He says he didn't do it."

"I thought he said he blacked out."

Ben hesitated. "Well . . . yes."

"If he blacked out and can't remember anything, how can he know whether he did it or not?"

"I think a murder would probably stick in his mind."

"No, Ben, that's exactly the sort of thing that wouldn't stick in his mind. The human psyche has great built-in defense mechanisms. When a memory becomes too unpleasant, the brain shuts it out. That could be the whole cause for this alleged blackout and memory loss. Selective amnesia."

This was a possibility that had not yet occurred to him. A very disturbing possibility. "You need to meet him, Christina. He's very sincere."

"I don't doubt it. He's probably a wonderful guy, when he's not shooting people."

"Christina . . ."

"But the traumatic death of his wife has caused some sort of personality break. And unfortunately, that's not insanity, temporary or otherwise. That's just a sad case of the right buttons being pushed to turn someone into a murderer."

"In any case, he needs representation."

"Right. And since you couldn't come up with a pardon—"

"Christina . . ."

She flung her arms over her head. "Ben, can you not see how this man is manipulating you? First he wants a pardon. Then he wants to trump up some temporary insanity defense, so he can get away with murder and not even have to do time in the asylum. Then, what do you know, he kills someone and provides a blackout and other circumstances to support a claim of temporary insanity. You're not his lawyer. You're his get-out-of-jail-free card!"

Ben reached forward and took her hand. "Christina, I know you're trying to protect me."

"You're darn tootin'! Someone's got to do it! Do you know I've just come from a two-hour planning session with Harvey? We're supposedly working out your reelection campaign. But if you take this case, you can forget about it. Your candidacy is toast."

"I don't believe that. People understand that everyone is entitled to a defense."

"Excuse me?" She grabbed him by the lapels. "Have you forgotten where you live? This is the land of capital punishment and everyone-should-be-tried-as-an-adult."

"You're being unduly cynical."

"Wait till Channel Six gets wind of this. You'll be the lead story for a week. 'Senator Aids Alleged Cop Slayer!' Do you know what that will do to your approval ratings?"

"I didn't get into this profession for approval ratings."

Christina threw her arms around him and hugged him tight. "I know that, Ben." Ben could feel her pulse, feel her heart throbbing. He knew she was worried about him. "And frankly, I couldn't care less if you run for reelection. I'd probably rather you didn't. But if you're going to take a hit of this magnitude, I want it to be for a good reason. Not because some bitter, scheming murderer is using you."

"Christina." He gave her a little squeeze. "I know you don't think much of my ability to size up people. But I genuinely believe Dennis is sincere. He's not an evil person. I think the loss of his wife has devastated him—as it would me. He's just trying to cope."

"That's not the impression I'm getting."

"I talked to Mike and got some of the paperwork on the case. Dennis did go to the police department every day for a week. Sometimes twice a day. Trying to get them to open a missing persons file. To investigate his wife's disappearance. And this Detective Sentz refused.

Even after she had been gone a week! Doesn't that seem strange to you?"

"I think it's appalling. But I don't think it justifies murder. Neither will the jury."

"Sentz claimed there was no crime, no evidence of foul play, and Mike tells me that technically he's right. They have strong criteria that have to be met before they investigate missing persons because it happens so frequently. Plus, she had disappeared once before, many years before, of her own volition. But still . . . how could any detective resist such a desperate husband? The disappearance of a prominent physician. Someone who worked with cancer patients. Don't you think most people would break a few rules? I know I would."

"You break rules for every sad sack who walks through your doorway, Ben. You can't use yourself as a benchmark. Maybe Detective Sentz was rigid. Maybe even a little heartless. But at the end of the day, it doesn't justify murder."

"I'm not saying it does. I'm just saying I think it's odd. Worth investigating. I want you to ask Loving to look into this. He has a lot of cop buddies. See what he can find out about Sentz. And this whole situation."

"I think you're wasting your time. And Loving's. And mine."

"But you haven't talked to Dennis. Will you at least meet him first? And then if you still don't believe him . . ."

She looked at him expectantly, arms folded. "Yes?"

He smiled. "I will seriously consider listening to you."

Christina grabbed her coat and headed toward the door. "I am not amused, Mr. Kincaid. Or comforted. Not a bit."

CHAPTER
6

BEN WAS ASTONISHED by his first glimpse of Dennis Thomas. As soon as he and Christina rounded the corner and peered into the cell, he realized how much Dennis had changed, or had been changed, by a few days in jail. His skin was white and pasty. Of course, he'd had no sunlight since he was arrested, plus the meals served tended toward starch and white bread. Opportunities for exercise were limited. He appeared to have shaved, but not well. And his brain was probably atrophying; he was used to reading and teaching and other forms of mental stimulation.

But if he looked this poorly after a few days, what would he look like by the time the case came to trial? Ben made a mental note. It was imperative to get this case set as quickly as possible. Before he got any worse.

The guard opened the cell door and Ben and Christina stepped inside.

"Thanks, Sam." The guard closed the door behind him. "Dennis, I want you to meet my partner—and wife, Christina McCall."

Dennis rose from his cot and they shook hands. Ben thought Christina's shake seemed particularly frosty.

"So," Dennis said, almost smiling, "you're here to see if I'm really Jack the Ripper?"

Christina made no apologies. "Something like that. Does that bother you?"

"No. As long as you represent me properly, your private thoughts don't matter, do they?"

"How are you doing?" Ben said, cutting in.

"Oh, as well as can be expected. The guards all hate me, but so far, no one has assaulted me, much as they want to. They've been putting stuff in my food. So I haven't eaten much. And I'm certain that guy in the next cell is a plant. A designated snitch."

Probably so, Ben mused. Smart man. "But how are you feeling?"

"As good as can be expected. I still miss my wife. I talk to her. Sometimes I think I hear her talking back . . ."

Ben and Christina eyed each other. Sounded crazy. Was that the point?

"Do you feel any remorse?" Christina asked.

"Would that be useful?" He didn't blink. "I didn't kill that man, but I could certainly tear up over my wife."

Christina pursed her lips wordlessly.

"Don't stare at me like that just because I'm smart enough to know how to avoid conviction for a crime I didn't commit. Do you think we'll get bail?"

"Unlikely."

"Well, think of an angle. I'm sure two bright people like you can work something out. I have to get bail."

"Why is that?" Christina asked, one arm akimbo.

"Because I don't want the jury to see me looking like I've been in jail for a long period of time. I can see how my appearance has deteriorated. By the time this gets to trial, it will be worse. I also don't want the jury to see me in orange coveralls and a bad haircut."

"I can take care of that, in any case," Ben explained. "We'll have an opportunity to bring you a suit. Get your hair styled."

"That's not enough. I want out. Do you think you could call a press conference?"

Ben felt jolted by the sudden switch of topic. "How would that help anything?"

"They've got television in here, you know. I can see the media frenzy over this case. But no one is presenting my side of the story."

"There's a reason for that," Christina said quietly.

Ben cleared his throat. "We'll have a chance to tell our story at the trial."

"That's not good enough." Dennis looked at him directly. "In the first case, you probably won't call me at trial unless you have to. Even if you do, I'll be cross-examined and the DA will do his best to make me look bad. But at a press conference, I can say anything I want, or you can say it for me, and no one is cross-examined."

"The reporters will want to ask questions."

"You can take questions. From the ones you trust."

"But what good will it do? The press are not the ones who decide the case."

"The jurors do. And there's a very good chance those yet-to-be selected jurors will be watching the coverage of this case. Everyone else seems to be."

Ben had to admit—the man had thought this out carefully. And intelligently. That's what was so scary about him.

"Have you got a psychiatrist lined up yet?"

"Well," Ben said, "I have some possibilities."

"We need a good expert. Someone convincing. My therapist is one of the top in the country. And a very experienced witness."

What a coincidence.

"But you make the call. I've prepared a list of people I've seen in the past, and others I know by reputation."

"Indeed."

"Insanity defenses are more successful when the psychiatric expert knew the defendant before the incident."

"That's true."

"If possible, I think you should go with the name at the top. I think he'll be the most persuasive."

"Do you now."

"We need someone top-notch. Temporary insanity is a tough sell."

"So I've heard . . ." Ben could see Christina was having a difficult time containing herself.

"But I've read that grief coupled with frustration can often lead to an irresistible impulse, which of course is a form of temporary insanity. And the blackout proves something was going on."

"You know," Ben said, "the prosecution will call witnesses of their own."

"Sure, but the state can't afford anyone good, right? And how are they going to explain the blackout?"

"They'll say you were faking."

"No way. They took me to a hospital. The EMTs tried to revive me—unsuccessfully. Took them two hours to bring me around. No way you can fake that."

Ben made a note on his legal pad. "You know, normally at these pretrial meetings, *I* set the agenda."

Dennis snapped his fingers. "That reminds me. I think we should file a civil suit as soon as possible. So it captures the headlines. A suit against the police department for official misconduct leading to death."

"That would be very complicated."

"Can't we bring a claim under 42 USC Section 1983?"

Ben's pencil slowed. "Yessss . . ."

"I think a civil rights suit is the way to go. Otherwise the police have too much immunity. I figure we have excellent claims based upon the Fourth and Fourteenth Amendments to the Constitution. We can claim negligent performance of duty and intentional infliction of emotional distress. I'm sure you can dream up some other causes of action."

Ben tapped the pencil eraser on his pad. "The police have qualified immunity, even against civil rights claims. They're protected from charges based upon anything other than plain incompetence or knowing violations of law. You have to prove they acted in an objectively unreasonable manner to prevail."

Dennis looked at him squarely. "The man directly caused the death of my wife by failing to act in a reasonable manner, Mr. Kincaid. If he had initiated an investigation, she would've been found in three hours. Instead, she suffered for seven days. And died."

"Okay. Civil suit." Ben averted his eyes. "I'll get right on it."

"You seem to have this all worked out," Christina interrupted. "Did you go to law school?"

"No, but I've read a lot of John Grisham novels."

"Oh. Well then, you can't lose."

Dennis folded his arms. "Forgive me for saying so, Mrs. Kincaid—"

"Ms. McCall."

"—but you seem somewhat hostile toward me. Have I done something to offend?"

Ben hoped she'd able to resist giving the obvious answer.

"No," she said instead. "But you do seem . . . preternaturally prepared to contribute to your defense."

"Is it wrong for me to participate in my defense? I thought that was my constitutional right."

"It is, but—"

"Let me save you some time, Ms. McCall. I did not kill that man. But I know there's some stiff evidence against me, so I think temporary insanity is my best shot. I don't plan to go to prison, whether you believe me or not. So if you think the desire to avoid incarceration makes me look guilty, we may have a problem."

"It's not that," Christina replied. "But since we're

being blunt—your cold, level-headed logic is not what I would expect from someone who has just been accused of murder. And is innocent."

Ben suddenly wished this cell were not so pathetically small. There was nowhere to go—not even a way to make the fighters return to their corners.

"And is that what's most important to you, Ms. McCall? Knowing that I'm innocent? Because you would never stoop to representing someone who might be guilty?"

"I wouldn't say that exactly."

"Or perhaps what you're really concerned about is your firm's reputation. Particularly the reputation of your husband, who I understand is currently mounting a reelection campaign. Are you really concerned about my innocence, or that the negative 'presumed guilty' attitude of the self-righteous might tarnish your favorite senator's chances?"

Christina did not answer.

Dennis stepped closer to her, a solemn expression on his face. "Sentz killed my wife, Ms. McCall. He left her to die. Slowly. Painfully. That's what you should keep uppermost in your mind."

He gathered a stack of notes together and passed them to Ben. "Now go set up the press conference. Please. Then get me bail. These coveralls are starting to chafe."

CHAPTER
7

THE COURTHOUSE ELEVATOR doors opened and there they were: the stalwart minions of the fourth estate. Dozens of them, more than could possibly be native to the state of Oklahoma. Which was a bad sign. It meant that this case had already attracted national attention, which was the last thing they needed.

Ben took Dennis—freshly decked out in a new suit, haircut, and shave—and led him down the gauntlet of reporters. He wondered how long the world could go on calling them investigative reporters when so few of them did any investigating. He saw a few old-timers who still worked with pen and paper, but for the most part, they were faces he recognized from television: broadcasters, news readers, people who held microphones in front of cameras and repeated what they had been told, possibly lining up video clips from talking heads to spice up a story that went longer than twenty seconds. They were repeaters, not reporters.

"I think the press conference worked," Dennis muttered under his breath. "They're very interested in me."

"Shhh," Ben whispered. "Say nothing. And never assume they like you."

"They're not all hacks."

"Of course not, but they are all employed by large corporations that like to make money. They're using you to get ratings and they'll turn on you in a heartbeat if that's where the money lies."

Dennis buttoned his lips. The reporters did not. As they made their way to the courtroom, Ben heard a dozen questions tossed out at once.

"Is it true your client shot Detective Sentz seven times—one for each day his wife suffered?"

"How about these rumors that your client drove his wife off the side of the road?"

"Was he angry because his wife made more money?"

"Was she having an affair with his psychiatrist?"

"Is this a vendetta against the police department?"

"Is it true you've accepted a plea from the prosecutor?"

Ben tried not to smile as he opened the courtroom doors. "Is it true" in this case was a cheesy way of suggesting they'd heard something they obviously hadn't, to persuade him to tell them what they wanted to know. It was almost as good as "Some people say," another catchphrase they used to introduce an ugly rumor or innuendo while simultaneously suggesting someone else was to blame.

Ben took his seat at the defendant's table, placing Dennis just beside him. Christina sat on the other side. Ben slowly scanned the room. The courtroom gallery was already packed, mostly by the press. He was not used to seeing this kind of attendance at a mere bail hearing. This case was hot.

Across the aisle, Ben spotted the prosecutors. David Guillerman, the DA himself, was taking the lead. His presence was probably mandated by the enormous press interest. He was being assisted by Greg Patterson, who Ben knew to be hardworking and capable. He would be doing most of the hard stuff, while Guillerman took the limelight. But Ben did not discount Guillerman. He knew Guillerman had started as a trial attorney who somehow managed to make a solo practice not only successful but successful enough to launch a campaign for the district attorney's office. He had graduated from TU law school top of his class and a moot court champion as well. He was single, handsome, and often topped the "Sexiest" and "Most Eligible" lists in local publications like *Oklahoma Magazine*. He would be a formidable opponent and Ben knew it.

Just for the sake of courtesy, Ben crossed the aisle and greeted his opponents. He shook hands with both attorneys. He could tell Patterson was staring at his face.

"Does it show?" Ben asked.

Patterson almost jumped. "Oh—well—I'm sorry. Didn't mean to stare."

"It's all right. A scar is a scar."

"That was a horrible day for Oklahoma," Patterson said. "And the nation. But I admired the way you handled yourself afterward."

"Well . . . thank you." Ben turned his attention to the boss. "David. How have you been? Haven't seen you for ages."

"'Cause you've been hiding out in Washington. Glad you're back home where you belong. Saw your press conference, by the way." He was a handsome man, dark-haired with just enough gray at the temples, telegenic—which was essential when the district attorney was an elected official. "Very dynamic."

"Saw yours, too," Ben replied. "Guess you're hoping for an all-redneck jury?"

"And you're hoping for the liberal bleeding hearts. The result will be somewhere in the middle." He pulled Ben a little closer. "I may have a plea offer for you later today."

"I'm glad," Ben said, "but I doubt my client will accept anything."

"Ten to twenty on a cop killing. It's like a Christmas present."

"Not if you're innocent."

"Don't you mean not if you're insane?" Guillerman smiled, a broad, toothy smile. It was hard not to like him. "And you would have to be to turn this down. Honestly, I'm just trying to save us both a lot of trouble and heartache. You don't know this, Ben, but I've tracked your career for many years. I'm actually a big fan. And I know how surprisingly effective you can be in the courtroom."

Ben maintained a straight face. Surprisingly?

"But this is a loser for you. A dead cop. A family man. And so much evidence of planning and deliberation. Clarence Darrow couldn't win this one."

And you're no Clarence Darrow. The message was so clear Guillerman didn't have to say it. "I'll take any offers to my client. But I don't think it's going to happen."

Guillerman shook his head. "That's a shame. We're both coming up for reelection soon. We really don't need a messy case like this one. No one wins."

"Since you feel so certain you're going to win, why don't you let my bail request go unopposed?"

"Can't do that."

"He's an English teacher, David. What can he do?"

"Look what he's already done." Guillerman smiled. "Can't do it, Ben. The press would crucify me. And I've got a major fund-raiser tonight."

"So long before the election?"

Guillerman shrugged. "It takes a lot of money to mount a campaign these days."

Ben would be appalled at his reducing a criminal trial to politics—if everything he said weren't so true. "I'll wait for your call on that plea."

He returned to his own table. He could see Christina was looking at him eagerly, wondering what they'd talked about. He shook his head. No news.

Judge Leland McPartland was one of the senior members of the Tulsa County judiciary, said to be about three years away from retirement. He was generally considered a competent if uninspired jurist. He was known to be old-school in his approach to the law and conservative in his approach to politics. Ben could just imagine what he thought of this purported cop killer. Or what he would think of the idea of temporary insanity.

The bailiff brought the room to their feet and introduced the judge, who sailed in behind him while he was speaking.

"You may be seated."

The room obliged.

"Is the defendant present?"

Ben rose to his feet. "Benjamin Kincaid for the defense, your honor."

"A pleasure to see our distinguished senator back in the courtroom," McPartland said straight-faced. Ben wasn't sure how to take it. "Are you prepared to proceed?"

"We are. Waive reading. Enter a plea of not guilty."

The judge hesitated for only the tiniest moment. "Not guilty?"

"Yes, your honor. And we will assert the affirmative defense of temporary insanity."

There was an audible reaction from the gallery. The two prosecutors looked at each other with weary eyes.

"Temporary insanity." Judge McPartland made tiny notes on a legal pad, despite the fact that the court reporter was taking down every word anyone said. "Will there be anything else?"

"Yes, your honor. Although it will be tried in another court, you should be aware that there is a parallel civil suit accusing the police department of gross misconduct and seeking damages."

"I am already aware of that, counsel." His voice lowered a notch. "I do read the papers."

"Your honor," Guillerman said, rising, "we all know the police have legal immunity for actions performed in the course of duty."

"That doesn't excuse gross negligence or misconduct," Ben responded. "Or the intentional infliction of emotional distress."

"It's not misconduct to follow the rules. Detective Sentz—"

Judge McPartland held up his hands. "All right, gentlemen. We don't need to have this debate here. Save it for the civil courts. Will there be anything else?"

"Yes, your honor. We request that bail be set."

Guillerman rose again. "Out of the question, your honor. This man killed a police officer. In cold blood."

"I'm sorry," Ben said. "Has a verdict already been rendered? I thought we were just getting started."

"I do not believe it is ever the practice of this court to grant bail in capital cases," Guillerman continued, "and I certainly don't think this is the time to make a change. There can be no leniency when it comes to the execution of duly appointed officers of the law. Our boys in blue. The heroes of 9/11."

Ben was pretty sure Detective Sentz had nothing to do with 9/11, but he let it slide. "I notice, your honor, that the distinguished district attorney has said absolutely nothing relevant to whether my client should be granted bail. The standard is whether he presents a flight risk or any potential harm to society. There is no flight risk. Dennis Thomas has lived in Tulsa all his life except for a few years in college and has no criminal record whatsoever. He has a teaching job at the University of Tulsa and he owns a home in Skiatook. And frankly, his face has been so showcased by the television media that I doubt there's anywhere he could go without being recognized. He has no desire to run. Only to clear his name and see justice done."

"The man is a murderer," Guillerman said. "Case closed."

"Furthermore," Ben continued, "there is no reason to believe he poses any risk to society. Even if you accept the blather the DA has been peddling, my client acted out of grief in retaliation against the man he believed responsible for his wife's death. She's gone now, dead, so there's no chance of those circumstances arising again."

"If a man is dangerous enough to strike once, he can strike again," Guillerman said.

"You could use that argument to preclude anyone ever getting bail," Ben replied.

"Which would be just fine with me. How do we know this man's vendetta is over? Maybe he wants to take out the whole police department."

"That's ridiculous."

"Says who?" Guillerman turned to face Ben. "You yourself said the man was crazy."

"I said we plead the affirmative defense of temporary insanity. Emphasis on the 'temporary.' It's over."

"How convenient." Guillerman turned to face the judge. "You honor, how long are we going to allow this gamesmanship to continue? We all know what happened here. The facts are not in dispute, not to any appreciable degree. This nonsense about temporary insanity is nothing but a cynical attempt to let a man get away with murder."

"Excuse me," Ben said, taking a step toward the bench, "but I thought we were arguing bail, not making closing arguments. There is nothing cynical about this plea. My client poses no flight risk or danger to society. That is a fact. And not even the distinguished DA can bury the facts, no matter how hard he may try."

Ben paused. The reporters were furiously scribbling down his every word.

Well, Guillerman was playing to the media. He would have to play the same game.

Ben turned to face the gallery, though still technically addressing the judge. "Here's a fact they can't deny—this man's wife died because the police did nothing. We can argue about whether they woulda coulda shoulda, but that's the bottom line. They could have saved her and they didn't. How long did it take them to find her once they finally sprang into action? About three hours. But instead of being rescued in three hours, she suffered for seven days. Suffered in the most excruciating way possible, her bones broken, her leg pierced, her very life force slowly ebbing away. In constant pain."

Ben paused, and he was gratified to notice that no one interrupted to fill the gap. He had their attention. "Now imagine being that woman's husband. The man who loves her more than anything else in the world. The man who worships her. The man she doesn't come home to. You search everywhere, with no luck. You ask the police for help, but they can't be budged. You try everything you know—and none of it works. Finally, after seven days, you find her. And it's too late. She dies, right before your eyes. After enduring the most hideous torture imaginable."

Ben paused again, letting the words sink in. "Do you think that might possibly have an effect on a man's mental stability? His rationality? His ability to distinguish right from wrong?" He turned around to face the bench. "This is not a frivolous plea, your honor, and we will prove that at trial. But the point I make now is that, regardless of the outcome of the trial, this man deserves our sympathy. Perhaps even our pity. He does not deserve to be locked away for weeks until this case comes to trial. In the name of humanity, your honor, I beg you to set bail for this defendant!"

Ben sat down. The courtroom remained silent for a long time. Guillerman did not attempt a rebuttal.

"Very well," Judge McPartland said, clearing his throat. "I can see that this is going to be a very interesting case. You are correct, Mr. Guillerman, in your statement that the court does not normally award bail in capital cases. But I think we can all agree that this is far from a typical case. I see no likelihood whatsoever that the defendant will flee, nor do I think it likely that he will cause harm to other persons. And I must say that I think it altogether appropriate that the court give some consideration to the ordeal this man has already suffered. I have been married to the same woman for thirty-seven years now, and . . . well, there but for the grace of God go I. No one should have to endure such an experience, and I will not make it worse."

Guillerman rose but spoke quietly. "The State opposes the setting of any bail in this case."

"Understood," the judge continued. "Objection noted. And I will set bail quite high—a million dollars. But I will make it available. Not intending to set any new precedent, but simply acknowledging that these are most unusual circumstances."

Ben liked the result the judge was rambling toward, but was concerned by McPartland's lack of focus. He seemed to be shuffling about, not really making his point. Ben began to wonder if he was up to a trial of this magnitude.

The judge slammed his gavel. "Bail is set in the amount of one million dollars. When you have your bond together, make the proper arrangements with the officer on the second floor. Now about the trial—"

"As soon as possible," Ben said, rising. "We're ready.

There are few facts in question." And not much evidence that could help them, since they were planning a defense based upon Dennis's mental state, not on the evidence. A long wait till trial would only give the prosecution more time to turn up evidence that might be used against them.

Guillerman looked at Ben, obviously surprised. He shrugged. "If the defense is ready, so are we."

"Very well. I'll plug this into the first available slot. Thank you, gentlemen. This hearing is dismissed."

The tumult rose with such suddenness it was as if a door had suddenly been opened onto an elementary school playground. It was almost deafening. Many people—not all of them reporters—hurled questions at Ben, which he pointedly ignored.

Guillerman pulled Ben to one side. "I'm only saying this because I really am a fan. You'll never win on temporary insanity."

"I guess we'll see."

"I don't blame you for trying. But I know more about the facts of this case than you do, and I'm telling you—you cannot make that stick."

"I appreciate your concern." Sort of. "But I'm not thinking on my feet. I would never advance a theory I didn't believe was viable."

"And if you're contemplating jury nullification, put that out of your head right now. Judge McPartland won't let it happen. No matter how you dress it up. He'll shoot it down."

"Well, you never know. I'm full of surprises."

"I know that. But I think this time you've gone one surprise too far."

"Time will tell, right?"

Guillerman shook his head, then smiled. "Fine. Play it your way. Can't say I didn't warn you."

Ben returned to his own table.

"Nice job," Christina said, but Ben could see she was not altogether pleased.

"Excellent," Dennis said, grabbing his hand and shaking it. "You had me a little worried back in the jail cell. But that was fantastic. You can really pour on the fire when you get worked up, huh?"

"I was doing my job."

"And doing it darn well. The most important thing is that you seemed like you really believed it. That's what sells a jury."

"That, plus evidence. And truth."

"It's important for the jury to believe that the lawyer likes his client. Gives credibility to the claims of innocence."

"We don't have to prove innocence," Ben said. "Only not proven guilty." And he added to himself: Thank goodness.

"Well, anyway, I'm pleased, Ben. I guess everything I heard about you was true. But I don't have a million dollars. I do have a trust fund I could use toward bail, but it's not enough."

Ben nodded. "We'll get a bond. It still won't be cheap, but we'll find a way. You may have to take out a loan. It'll be worth it. You don't need to spend more time in jail."

"You need to spend it in our office," Christina said, packing her materials away. "Now that Ben has so brilliantly put this case on the fast track, we're going to have to work night and day to get ready."

"That's fine," Dennis said. "I'm willing. Whatever you want." He rubbed his hands together. "This is very encouraging."

Ben saw Christina's eyes narrow.

"I've read that people who don't get bail are found guilty nine times out of ten. And the judge's reaction suggests that we've done a decent job of spinning public opinion. I think we need another press conference, Ben. Soon, on the courthouse steps. If the psychiatrist is available, maybe he should come, too. Those potential jurors will be watching."

He moved toward the door, where a dozen reporters eagerly waited to get their hands on him.

Christina gave her husband a fierce look. "Ben . . ."

"I know, Christina. I know."

CHAPTER
8

BEN STOOD shoulder to shoulder with his newly sprung and spruced-up client, staring at the vast array of microphones and minicams assembled on the plaza outside the Tulsa County courthouse. It was important that Dennis be present and that they all see him as he was, a good, intelligent, clean-cut professional who had recently lost his wife. Not a monster, not a violent man.

Just the same, Ben planned to do all the talking.

"We applaud Judge McPartland's actions. It would have been much easier to take the usual path and avoid controversy. But instead of jumping on the media bandwagon, he saw the facts and circumstances clearly and realized that Dennis Thomas is no threat to anyone. He does not deserve to be incarcerated, not now or at any time in the future.

"It is all too easy in this reactionary age to heighten the drama and act as if each and every crime is of equal horror, but that is simply not the case. Not every youth should be tried as an adult. Not every defendant should receive the maximum sentence. We can rise above the visceral need for retribution. We are better than that. Those old attitudes have produced the current mess in the criminal justice system—over 2.2 million people in prison, the highest incarceration rate of any nation, more than four times the world average."

Ben scanned his audience. So far they all seemed

attentive. He suspected he was not swaying the reporter from Fox News, and several others as well, but at least no one was heckling. "The reality, which Judge McPartland recognized, is that Dennis was subjected to circumstances that would tax the mental stability of even the most solid citizen. Who could live knowing that the police department could have saved his wife—and chose not to do so? Who would not be tormented by that knowledge? Temporary insanity is not a gimmick dreamed up by lawyers; it is a very real and debilitating mental state, one that all of us could experience given the right circumstances. It is time that we as a nation recognize that fact and stop acting as if harsh punishment will solve all our problems. Dennis Thomas presents no threat to society. He should not be incarcerated."

Ben never directly said he should be found not guilty, but of course, that was the implicit message. Prospective jurors didn't have to wrestle with whether they genuinely believed in the concept of temporary insanity. That was the tool they would use. The goal was to convince the jury that this man should not go to prison, regardless of whether you think he committed the crime. So, ladies and gentlemen of the jury, make whatever finding you must to make sure he doesn't end up behind bars.

Ben briefly considered avoiding questions altogether, but the crowd had been so respectful during his prepared remarks that he decided, possibly contrary to the lessons of past experience, to give it a go. He pointed toward a woman standing in the front row. She had a ponytail and a fresh, friendly face. The quantum of makeup suggested that she was a television anchorperson, but she looked too nice to be mean.

"What would you say to Detective Sentz's two young daughters, now that you're advocating that their father's murderer should go free without any punishment?"

Ah, well. You can't judge a book . . .

"Forgive me for saying so, ma'am, but you're exploiting those children to drum up controversy and get yourself a lead story. And to avoid the main issue. Dennis Thomas has also been bereaved, if I may remind you. His wife suffered the most extraordinary pain imaginable for seven days running. I would hope that we could extend our sympathies to all the victims of this case. But the question here is whether Dennis Thomas should spend the rest of his life in prison, and I fail to see how that would help those two girls or anyone else."

In the rear of the crowd, he saw Christina tip her curls to him. Slowly but surely, he was getting better at this stuff.

"According to the police report, your client was found at the scene of the crime, lying over the murder weapon—and this is a quote—'apparently unconscious.' Can you explain what happened?"

Ben nodded. "I'm no psychiatrist, but the experts tell me that Dennis's grief reached such magnitude as to temporarily affect his behavior, causing him to potentially engage in activities he would not normally do and will never do again. Apparently at some point the brain, deluged with such potent emotion, reaches overload and shuts down, causing the blackout state." He paused. "I only wish it had kicked in earlier."

That went reasonably well. He tried another reporter.

"Is it true that your client threatened to kill Detective Sentz shortly before he did it?"

Ben hesitated a moment. He hadn't heard this before. He hoped it wasn't true. Unless perhaps the reporter had somehow learned that Dennis had been in Ben's office talking about murder. He hoped that also wasn't true.

"No. Dennis went to the police repeatedly, begging them, literally begging them to take action, to help him find his wife. And they refused. For seven days. While

Joslyn Thomas, a physician who dedicated her life to helping others, suffered the most intense torture imaginable. I don't doubt that Dennis used strong words, trying to move the police into action. I know I would have, had I been in his hideous situation. But there was no death threat."

He pointed toward a reporter he recognized from the *Tulsa World*. "Isn't there a danger that the course you recommend could basically create a crime free-for-all? If your client escapes punishment, what's to prevent anyone with an axe to grind against the police—and I think there are many—to shoot first and claim insanity later?"

"With respect, Jim, I think that question is a typical argument ad absurdum and we both know it. This is not the first insanity plea. They go way back to General Dan Sickles in the first half of the nineteenth century. The previous cases did not trigger a wave of insanity slayings and this one will not, either. Insanity is not contagious. Successful insanity defenses are rare. But this case presents unusual circumstances. We have a model citizen, a man without a blot on his record, driven by the most horrifying events to actions that would normally be far beyond his ken. That doesn't happen every day and it never will, thank heaven. But it is exactly why the temporary insanity plea exists. And we should not be hesitant to use it."

"May I have a few words?"

Ben turned and saw DA Guillerman standing behind him. Where had he come from? This was really in poor taste—crashing another man's press conference.

"Mr. Kincaid speaks very eloquently, but I think he misses the main point. I don't plan to argue my case here, in the media, in the full view of prospective jurors," he added, eyeing Ben sharply, "but I will make one point clear. My job as district attorney, the job to which the good people of Tulsa have elected me, is to ensure justice. And I will do that. No hocus-pocus. No—" He took a deep breath. "—fancy experts and psychobabble. Just justice." He leaned closer to the microphone. "No one will get away with killing a police officer on my watch. That's a promise."

Ben saw countless hands spring in the air, but Guillerman had the sense to ignore them. He'd made his point. He was done.

"Thanks for getting all these folks together," Guillerman said, slapping Ben on the back. "Appreciate the use of the microphone."

"Don't mention it," Ben mumbled back.

All at once, shouting burst out from somewhere in the midst of the assembled crowd. Ben turned and saw a path being carved through the reporters, but he couldn't tell what was happening. The reporters themselves seemed caught unawares. The minicams swung one way, then the other, trying to capture the action.

"Killer! Killlllller!"

In the blink of an eye, Ben saw a wiry, dark-haired man spring out of the melee. He was waving a gun wildly back and forth.

"Murderer!"

Ben tackled Dennis, knocking him to the marble plaza. An instant later, the first shot rang out, followed by two more in rapid succession. Screams broke loose, then chaos. He heard the click of heels, police officers running forward.

Dennis was huddled in a pile beneath him. "Are you okay?" Ben asked.

"I seem to have escaped the bullets, although I think you may have fractured my arm."

"Just as long as you're breathing." Ben scrambled to his feet. Three police officers had the man face-first on the ground. One had captured his gun.

"Christina!" From the back, despite her height, or

lack thereof, he could see her swinging her arms in the air. She was okay, thank God.

"He's a murderer! In cold blood!" The man was still screaming, even as the police hauled him away. "An eye for an eye! An eye for an eye!"

As he watched the crowd disperse, Ben felt Guillerman ease in beside him. "So, Ben, tell me again that part about how insanity isn't contagious."

Ben had no reply.

CHAPTER
9

THE INSTANT Ben passed through the front doors at Kincaid & McCall, he could see Jones was in one of his moods. He tried to ease past as quietly as possible, but Jones still spotted him.

"This phone has been ringing all day!" Jones shouted, his voice dripping with exasperation and perhaps, Ben thought, more than a dollop of self-pity.

"Isn't that usually a good sign? Business on the upswing and all? I would think you'd like that."

"These aren't calls from prospective clients, Boss. It's all about the Dennis Thomas case. Reporters. Radio hosts. Cranks with an axe to grind. It's making me crazy. My arm is tired just from picking up the phone."

"Maybe you should get one of those little phone receivers that clip behind your ear. Then you wouldn't have to pick up the phone."

"What, and sit around looking like Lieutenant Uhura? No chance."

"Right. Might disturb your macho image."

"You even got a call from Nancy Grace!"

Ben took his pink message slips off the spindle. "Should I know who she is?"

Jones slapped his forehead. "No, of course not. Not if you've been living in a cave for the past ten years."

"I like the name. She sounds spiritual."

"Not exactly. She has a show on CNN. Former

prosecutor. Comments on pending cases, usually criminal. She's aggressive and opinionated, and she has a voice that makes you want to slash your wrists. But somehow that works for her."

"And the relevance of all this is . . . ?"

"She wants you to do her show."

Ben stared at the message slip and mulled. "Do you think I should?"

"How can I say this?" He leaned across his desk. "She'll eat you for lunch, Ben."

"Well, then. No Nancy Grace." He saw his burly investigator heading down the opposite corridor. "Loving!"

The barrel-chested man paused and waited for Ben to catch up.

"Have you got anything for me?"

"Not yet, Skipper. None of my friends on the force know anythin' about it. Other'n what everyone knows. And they're not real keen to talk with me, either. They don't take too kindly to us representin' someone who killed a cop." He paused. "Allegedly."

"That's understandable."

"Not real keen on it myself."

"I know you're not. But I need your help. There has to be someone who knows something. Do you have any idea who the guy in the police station was? The one Dennis thinks vetoed any search for Joslyn Thomas?"

"Not yet. But I'm workin' on it. If I get lucky, I might pick somethin' up."

"Then get lucky."

"Do my best. I got a report on that loser who tried to shoot your guy at the press conference."

"Yeah? Who was he? Cop? Cop relative?"

"Not even close." He handed Ben a report. "Name's Lars Engle. Student in the English department. Had some classes with Dennis Thomas. Apparently knew his wife, too, at least a little. In fact, he said he wanted to work with Thomas on his master's thesis. He was like, a fan."

"Those are always the dangerous ones."

"You'd think a fan would be supportive. Not dangerous."

"And if that were true," Ben said, thumbing through his messages, "John Lennon would still be alive." He slapped Loving on the back as he headed on down the hallway to his office. "Get someone to talk, Loving. Pour on some of that homeboy natural charm."

"Well, if you put it that way . . ."

"I do. Get me something I can use."

BEN WAS PLEASED to see Christina and Dennis waiting for him in the main conference room. Dennis looked better every day. Much of the debilitating residue of his stay in jail had washed away. He was a healthy young man and Ben knew he had been exercising regularly, getting fit, getting tan, getting ready to make a good impression in the courtroom.

Dennis spoke first. "Have they found out anything more about that nut at the press conference?"

"Not much." He quickly scanned Loving's report. "I'm surprised you don't remember more about him. He was certainly into you in a big way. Spends most of his spare time reading or on the Internet. Likes to go to the *Tulsa World* website and post anonymous opinions on their bulletin boards. With zero accountability, he was free to say anything. Apparently he posted messages about you more than twenty times with increasing bitterness. Course, no one noticed. Until he pulled out a gun."

"I don't even know why those pages exist," Christina said, throwing down her pencil. "They're just catnip for people who feel powerless and voiceless. 'No one else will listen to me, so I'll post uninformed opinions on this unmonitored bulletin board.'"

"I think the key word is *anonymous*," Ben replied. He remembered a few threatening emails he'd received that had not amused him at all. "Anonymous messages are the last refuge of the cowardly."

"And apparently," Dennis added, "the psychotic." He flipped a page on his legal pad and changed the subject. "Thanks for giving Christina and me a chance to get to know each other better, Ben. I think we've managed to bond."

Ben glanced at Christina, but he wasn't seeing a bonded expression on her face.

"I want Christina to appear at trial with us," Dennis continued. "In fact, I'd like her to sit beside me. Close beside me. I want the jury to see that she likes me. That she isn't scared of me. If she isn't scared of me, why should they be?"

"We can arrange that," Ben said.

"But I'm charging double for the liking part," Christina added.

"From what I read," Dennis continued, "more than half the jurors will likely be women, so having a woman at our table is prudent. Can we get someone black?"

Ben's lips parted, but no words came out.

"To sit at the table with us. A big chunk of the jury will also likely be black. And Hispanic. The Tulsa jury pool tends to draw disproportionately from the north side."

Ben took a deep breath and scribbled on his pad. "I'll see what I can do."

"I mean, it's important that the jury feel commonality with me, right? Makes it easier for them to sympathize?"

"You are very well informed, Dennis. As usual."

"And coldly logical about it, to boot," Christina noted quietly.

"I understand you're going to appear on *Nancy Grace*," Dennis said, changing the subject.

Christina's eyes widened. "This is the first I've heard of it. I think that's a very bad idea."

Ben averted his eyes. "I, um, haven't made a decision yet."

"Ben, she'll tear you apart."

"I don't think that matters," Dennis said. "Everyone expects Nancy Grace to be Nancy Grace. You can still make your case. Few potential jurors are likely to be watching CNN at that particular moment."

"Then what's the point?"

"The point is that the *Tulsa World* will almost certainly run an article about the fact that you will be or were on *Nancy Grace*, right?"

Ben considered. "Probably so."

"And they'll call you for your comment. And they'll run it just as you give it to them. And six-tenths of the people in the potential jury pool will read it." He folded his hands. "That's the point."

Ben wasn't sure whether he should be very impressed or very afraid. Or whether, if Dennis avoided prison, Ben should hire him as a jury consultant.

Dennis continued. "I've been giving a lot of thought to our affirmative defense. Temporary insanity."

"Why am I not surprised?"

"The more I think about it, the more I'm convinced we should argue that I entered a dissociative state."

"Why don't we wait and see what the psychiatrist has to say?"

"Why don't we plan out our defense and tell him what to say?"

"That's not the way it works."

"Oh, please. Offer him a lot of money."

"I won't buy testimony."

"Can't you prepare him to testify? Honestly, we're just talking about giving him an idea what terminology he should use. I don't see why that should bother him." Dennis paused. "Especially if he's getting paid a fortune. Make him earn his fee. Everyone else does."

Christina pushed herself out of her chair. "This is about as much of this as I can take."

Dennis appeared wounded. "What? Just when I thought we were starting to get along."

"I will not be a part of this charade! This man is not grieving. He's scheming! He's got the whole thing worked out to the finest detail. Probably had it all worked out before he came to your office that first time and before he—"

"Christina!" Ben cautioned. "This is our client."

"Well, I'm sorry, but I think it's time we had a serious come-to-Jesus meeting. Long past time, actually. This cold, calculating approach doesn't persuade me."

Dennis raised his chin. He looked at her firmly, steadily, but Ben had a hard time determining what was going on behind his eyes.

"Did it ever occur to you, Ms. McCall," Dennis began, "that it might be easier for me to focus on the details of trial preparation than to think about what happened? Than to think about my wife, trapped in that car, bleeding to death, crying out for me, for some rescue or comfort, but no one coming, not me, not anyone else, for seven days? Did it ever occur to you that I might need a distraction from her voice, the one I hear screaming for me all night long, every moment?"

Christina fell silent. Ben supposed that meant he had made his point. At least for now.

"This does raise something we have to discuss, though, Dennis." Ben laid his pad down on the table. "Listen to me and listen carefully. It doesn't matter what

Christina and I think. Or the media. But if that jury thinks for one moment that you're trying to pull a fast one over them, you're blowfish. History. And nothing I can do will salvage you. That's all she wrote."

"At the end of the day," Christina said, "the most important thing is not that the jury believes you. The most important thing is that they like you. If they like you, they can forgive a lot. If they don't like you, they won't forgive anything."

Dennis nodded thoughtfully. "I appreciate the heads-up. So we have to make sure they don't get the idea that I'm shamming."

Ben leaned forward. "They have to think—no, they have to *know* that you're sincere. Understand me?"

Dennis beamed. "Great. I can do sincere."

Christina threw down her pencil and left the room.

CHAPTER
10

THIS WAS the most difficult jury selection Ben had tackled in his entire career.

Of course every potential venireperson empaneled had heard of the case—how could they not? And of course most said that although they might have formed some opinions about the case they still felt they could weigh the evidence presented in a fair and impartial manner. A few had already made up their minds—guilty as charged—and they were removed. But that still left a big pool that somehow had to be whittled down to eighteen people who might lend a sympathetic ear to Dennis's story. Ben had no idea how to do that. All the traditional questions were useless.

He did learn that none of them had seen him on *Nancy Grace.*

But 60 percent of them had read about it the next day in the *Tulsa World.*

Dennis was right again.

"Let's have a show of hands. How many of you have had some kind of encounter with the police at one time or another?"

Most of them had. A few of them were related to police officers, and one woman was a former police officer herself. They would probably have to be removed by a peremptory challenge. But where to go after that? Upon closer questioning, Ben learned that most of the encounters were simple traffic infractions and no one was particularly angered or frustrated by the police. Yes, the cops were self-righteous jerks, but that was to be expected, they seemed to be saying. No one carried any serious grudges, much less murderous intent.

"How many of you are married?"

Most were.

"How would you feel if your spouse or significant other were in danger—or in pain—and there was someone who could help, but they refused to do so?"

He had hoped this question might stir up some strong feelings, but he was disappointed. Of course they cared about their partners, but it all seemed very abstract. No one would admit they might be moved to extreme action. They'd go through proper channels, they said. Friends and family first. Then police. Perhaps the media. But nothing else. Certainly no recourse to violence.

"I know that for many of you, your faith, or religion, is very important. Do any of you believe that your faith might make it impossible for you to view the case fairly?"

Predictably, the initial response was, No way, dude. All but two of them said that faith was an important part of their lives, but their faith made them stronger and smarter, better able to serve on a jury. Ben continued to press. He knew Guillerman would remove anyone opposed to the death penalty, so he didn't bother asking questions down that line. He did find three who believed that "an eye for an eye" was God's law, and that most likely spelled trouble. Ben used the Good Samaritan story to suggest that the police were lousy Samaritans and didn't help when they could, but it wasn't working. He was pleased to see that many said forgiveness was important. Jesus came to forgive us and wanted us to forgive each other as well, et cetera. But when it came time for them to retire to the jury room, would the Old Testament trump the New Testament? Or the other way around? How could he possibly know?

By the end of the third day of questioning, Ben felt he had targeted the most dangerous ones, the people who absolutely had to be removed. But he had no sense of who the good ones were, which jurors might actually help his case. And he had no idea how to find them.

He was almost prepared to sit down and flip a coin when Christina passed him a scrap of paper.

He glanced down. *Ask if they have a cat.*

Huh? He gave her a puzzled look. And she returned a look that he recognized as meaning: Just do it.

"I was wondering," Ben said, clearing his throat, "how many of you have a pet?"

Almost all did. And even though he knew that, statistically, dog owners outnumbered cat owners, he found that was not true in this jury pool. Almost 70 percent of them had at least one cat at home.

He started with the woman in Chair #1. She was in her midsixties, widowed, retired from school teaching.

"How long have you had your cat, Mrs. Gregory?"

"Almost ten years now. Since my sweet Henry died."

Interesting juxtaposition of facts. "Do you spend a lot of time with . . . ?"

"Percy."

"Yes. Do you spend a lot of time with Percy?"

"Oh, land sakes. As if I have any choice. That little rascal follows me everywhere I go. When I do my crocheting, he drapes himself across my wrists and just lies there. Doesn't seem like a comfortable place to be, what with my constant movement and such. But he never seems to mind."

"I gather you're pretty fond of your kitty."

"I suppose so."

"And I'll bet Percy is fond of you."

"Well, you know cats. I feed him. That gives me an edge." She chuckled a little at her own joke.

"How would you feel if someone tried to take Percy away from you?"

"Mercy's sakes. Why would anyone do that?"

"Just imagine. Maybe something happened to him. Maybe he was hurt. And someone prevented you from helping him."

"Well . . . I wouldn't like that one bit."

"What if someone knew where he was, or knew how to find him, but they wouldn't help you? What if Percy was suffering because someone else could help but refused? Would that make you angry?"

"I should say so. I don't know what I'd do. I—I don't think I could keep my head together."

Exactly. "And if you lost Percy, if he died, because that someone wouldn't help you, what do you think you'd do to them?"

Her chest swelled. "I wouldn't let anyone get away with hurting my Percy. I'd—I'd run them through with my crochet needles if I had to!"

Ben glanced at Christina. She winked back. This was what they needed. People might not be willing to admit to extreme, even uncontrollable emotions with regard to their spouses. But a kitty was a different thing altogether.

BY THE END of the fourth day, the jury was finalized. They had two African Americans, two Hispanics, one Asian, and seven Caucasians. One chiropractor, two teachers, two retirees (including Mrs. Gregory), a software programmer, an oil firm office secretary, and five housewives. Plus six alternates. For better or worse, the jury had been selected. The die was cast. The trial was ready to begin.

After Judge McPartland dismissed them, DA Guillerman pulled Ben to one side.

"I can't believe I'm doing this, because I think we've got a great jury and we're going to bury you at trial, but I've got an offer."

"Go on."

"I mean, I'd love trying this, but it comes at a bad time. I need to focus on getting reelected. Fund-raising. It takes a lot of money to mount a campaign these days."

"You mentioned that before. So what have you got for me, David?"

"Twenty years."

"My client isn't interested."

"In twenty years? Which means he could be out in ten. On a cop killing? That's as good as it's going to get."

"Thanks. Not interested."

"I can get him transferred out of state. Someplace cushier than McAlester. I know he's not a hardened criminal. There's no reason he should be hanging out with them. He can spend his time playing tennis and reading Proust. Maybe crank out some scholarly articles in his spare time."

"His academic career is over if he goes to prison and you know it as well as I do. It's probably already in danger."

He grabbed Ben's arm. "Your boy is not going to like the penitentiary. He seems pretty straight, bookish. Not in great shape. He won't last long. Especially not once word gets out what he did. You may think cop killers are popular in prison. They're not. Not with the guards or the inmates."

"I believe you."

"Frankly, I'm taking a risk here. You know the folks out in the sticks aren't going to think ten years is enough. But I'm willing to take that risk to get this thing out of my hair."

"Because it comes at an inconvenient time."

"Exactly."

And so marches the American justice system. "I'm sorry, but my client already told me to say no."

"Talk some sense into him, Ben. Do you know what a long shot temporary insanity is? Especially given the facts. He'd rather go to trial and almost certainly get death when he could be out by his forty-fifth birthday? That's insane!"

"Well, he's been insane before."

Ben returned to Dennis and Christina and reported.

"All right, my friends, that's it, then. No turning back. He won't make that offer a second time."

"Good," Dennis replied. "I don't want to be tempted."

"And you understand what this means?"

"We're going to trial. Monday morning. On temporary insanity."

"Exactly." Ben took each by the arm and steered them toward the door. He knew there would be a throng of reporters waiting for them outside. "God help us all."

TWO

Insanity Is in the Eyes

CHAPTER
11

BEN SAT UPRIGHT with a start, gasping, covered with sweat.

He was in bed. The sheets were a tangled mess around his feet. He had totally pulled the covers off Christina, probably hours ago. Fortunately, she was an extremely sound sleeper. Nothing bothered her. He could vacuum while she was snoozing and it wouldn't disturb her. Him, not so much.

He was having the weirdest dream, and not the usual one where he appeared before the jury and suddenly realized he was in his underwear. This time, he was driving and something appeared in front of him, causing him to swerve off the road and go over an enormous cliff. He plummeted and there was nothing he could do about it because he was trapped and he couldn't get the seat belt loose, not that plummeting outside a car was necessarily better than plummeting inside a car. He could see the craggy surface rapidly approaching and he screamed in terror, but the impact never seemed to come—he just fell and fell and fell, seemingly forever . . .

Or at least for seven days?

He rolled out of bed, trying to make as little ripple as possible, went to the sink, and splashed water on his face. That felt better. The cool rivulets trickled down the sides, easing the tensions, slowing his breathing.

He hated trials. And the worst part of any trial was the sleepless night before it started.

He checked the clock on the front of the cable box. It was late. He had to get back to sleep. The first day of a trial, a thousand things happened at once and he had to be ready for all of them, including the ones he hadn't anticipated. Although the jurors had seen him during the selection process, it was still important to make a strong impression on the first day of evidence. When the real action began. The prosecution would undoubtedly have a flurry of surprise motions. The reporters would be everywhere. Just his luck that it happened to be a slow news week. They had been covering the pretrial motions as if they were royal weddings. He could just imagine what it would be like once the trial was actually under way. Buzzards circling about looking for any tabloid tidbit to turn into a lead story and boost ratings. Judge McPartland had said he didn't want any comments on the content of the trial made to the press, but Ben knew there was much that could be done in the realm of characterization and innuendo without actually discussing the evidence. Normally Ben ignored the press during a trial, but he knew Dennis wouldn't like that. Dennis thought it was important to court the media, even now, after the jury had been chosen. And, sad to say, he was probably right.

He slid back into bed as quietly as possible, hugging his pillow tightly. He was wide awake. Did it sometimes seem as if the more desperately you needed sleep, the less likely it was to come?

He flipped from side to side for a few minutes, then finally sat up. He thought he felt Christina stir a little.

"Are you awake?" he asked quietly.

"I am now, Insomnia Boy."

"Didn't mean to wake you."

"I know. Got the pretrial jitters?"

"What makes you think that?"

She pounded her pillow, rolled over, and smiled. "Just a crazy whim. Sure, you were nervous before the last fifty trials, but for this capital murder case, you're fine."

"I would hate to see Dennis go to prison. Even if . . . well, you know."

"Yeah. Someday we're going to come up with another way to deal with criminals who aren't evil and aren't mean and aren't going to hurt anyone. But it won't be happening tonight, so why don't you get some sleep?"

"I don't think I can. I keep running every aspect of the trial through my head, wondering if there's something I've forgotten."

"I don't want to raise your blood pressure, Ben, but the truth is, you probably have forgotten something. You know as well as I do how huge and complex trials are. It's simply not possible to think of everything. You'll deal with it when it comes up."

"If that's supposed to be comforting, it isn't working. An attorney has to be prepared."

"And you are. How many trial notebooks have you filled to the brim? About twenty?"

"Twenty-nine."

"Is that a new Ben record?"

"Not quite. But you know, we had relatively little time before trial . . ."

"You're ready. Dennis has nothing to complain about."

"Maybe I should just start reviewing my notes."

"No!" She sat up, and even in the darkness, he could tell she was giving him a stern look. "I absolutely forbid it."

"I didn't know you had that power."

"It's time you did. The honeymoon is over, pal." She sniffed. "Well, technically, the honeymoon never happened."

"Christina . . ."

"I know. Cheap shot."

"What will I do if they ask a question and I don't know the answer?"

"What you always do. Deal."

He ran his hands through his hair and sighed. "I'm a total mess."

She wrapped her arms around him and gently pulled him to her side. "Yes, you are, but I find that endearing. And you know what? I think the juries do, too. We have this post–Perry Mason idea that lawyers have to be perfectly slick bastions of badinage all the time. But sometimes I think that actually turns jurors off. People like human beings. With flaws. Someone they can relate to. And you've got that. Big-time."

"Thank you. I think."

She hugged him tighter. She smelled extremely nice. Christina was one of those special women who seemed immune to morning breath or any other slumber-related unpleasantness. She was always appealing.

"So, Ben. Is there anything I can do to help you sleep?"

"Well . . ."

"Anything that's likely to happen."

He smiled. "I'll be fine."

"Give me a minute." She jumped out of bed, put on her robe, and walked into the kitchen. She returned a few minutes later carrying a steaming mug. "Drink this."

Ben took it cautiously. "This isn't drugged, is it? Because I have to be up at six, ready to rock and roll."

"Relax. It's just chamomile tea."

He looked into the cup and frowned. "You're giving me hot leafy water? Doesn't it have caffeine?"

"No. It's not really even tea. But it will help you sleep."

Ben took a sip. "That's not bad." He drank a little more. "Nice, actually."

She smiled. "I'm glad you're getting some benefit out of the marriage. Now finish it off, then cuddle up close to me and go to sleep."

"Oh . . . I don't want to keep you awake."

"Who are we kidding? You'll fall right back to sleep. Men always do. Me, it will take awhile."

He put down the empty mug and snuggled in. "Thanks for being so nice about it."

She kissed him gently on the forehead. "That's what I'm here for."

CHAPTER
12

LOVING PARKED his pickup a few blocks down Brady so he wouldn't be observed. It probably wouldn't matter, but he didn't want anyone to see him coming. He liked to drink in the environment on his own time.

Sunday night was a surprisingly good time to be checking out a cop bar. Might be more crowded on a Friday night, but a lot of the boys were still working and didn't have the luxury of getting plastered. Sunday night, however, most were off-duty, more than at any other time. There was usually a game on, it was guaranteed to be more exciting on the big screen, and it was a fair bet that no one living off a cop's salary had a ninety-inch screen like the one inside this joint. And it was no small factor that Oklahoma still operated under the barely postprohibition liquor laws that barred the sale of anything other than 3.2 beer anywhere but in liquor stores—which were required to be closed on Sunday. For the heavy drinker who failed to plan ahead, a trip to the local bar was mandated.

Loving heard the singing before he saw the people. Three big burly sorts, arms around one another, standing on the street corner, waiting for a taxi. The guys who regularly pulled people over for DUIs had the sense not to drive themselves home.

"Oh, Danny boy, the pipes, the pipes are playin' . . ."

Loving winced. After a few too many brewskis, the

Irish buried deep inside anyone with Irish ancestry within the last forty-seven generations always seemed to emerge. He knew the lead vocalist. His name was Ginsberg. But there must be some Irish in there somewhere.

His two buddies joined in. "The summer's gone, and all the leaves are fallin' . . ."

Loving doubted they were in any condition to be interrogated. He passed them by, giving them a nod as he did, and entered Scene of the Crime.

This had been the top cop bar for some while. Back in the day, it had been Harry's over on 41st and Peoria, but nowadays this place saw most of the boys-in-blue action. It was low-key enough, and with a reasonably restricted clientele, no one had to worry about what might be reported back the next day. Loving was not much of a drinker, but he could appreciate the need for a swig every now and again, or perhaps even more important, the need for a safe, friendly place to hang. It was easy to forget, given how arrogant some could be and how negative most of their encounters with the populace were, that police officers had a tough job, and at the end of the day, as they approached that car they had just pulled over, they had no way of knowing what they were going to face. Loving would not begrudge them the occasional opportunity to unwind.

As he passed through the front door, his senses were assaulted by so many different sensations they were hard to catalog. The strongest was the smell—pungent beer, mixed with stale breath and pretzels. Smoke thicker than oxygen. The clink and rattle of mugs and ashtrays. Loud music from the juke and the blast of the television even more deafening, especially every time the right team scored. A century of police paraphernalia hanging on the wall, some of it dating back to the Victorian era—billy clubs, truncheons, caps, badges, bullets. A huge television screen, bigger than some movie theaters he'd visited. And way too many people crammed into too little space, lubricated with hops and barley.

Actually, Loving loved it here.

He nodded at the owner, Jake Bradley, a retired cop he had known for probably twenty-five years. Bradley acknowledged him but did not smile. A bad indication, Loving thought. He must realize that Loving hadn't dropped by just for a tall cold one.

Loving decided against the usual surreptitious approach—casual conversation, crazy bar tricks, something to get the tongues wagging. These men weren't stupid. All too many of them spent a good portion of their days trying to get suspects or witnesses to talk. They weren't going to be fooled by anything he tried. He might as well find someone promising and dig in. He'd read Dennis's statement and knew everyone who had been involved or on duty when the week-long drama was playing itself out.

"Jimmy Babbitt! How are ya, you old boozehound?"

Babbitt turned and gave Loving a sharp stare. He was closing in on forty but he didn't look it. He'd gained some weight since Loving had last seen him, but he still didn't have the soft paunch that spoiled the line of too many police uniforms. Loving knew he had been the first responder at the scene of the murder of Detective Sentz.

"Loving." Babbitt looked at him levelly. "Haven't seen you here in a while."

"No. I've been busy." He pointed toward the empty chair at his table. "Mind if I take a seat?"

Babbitt did not respond immediately. "Are you here on business or pleasure?"

"Both." Loving sat down even without the invitation. "No, that's crap. You know I'm here on business."

"Figured as much. You're still working for that lawyer, right?"

"Proud to say I am."

"Representing the man who killed Chris."

"He represents the accused, Jimmy. It's his job."

"Wasn't there a time when he was accused—"

"If you remember that, you must also remember it was a put-up job. A frame."

"That's what I heard." Babbitt poured some beer down his throat. "Still, I don't mind saying a guy as resourceful as you ought to be able to find a better way to make a living."

"I like working for Ben Kincaid. He's a good guy doing good work. And he helped me out when I really needed it. More than once."

"Whatever." Babbitt glanced over at the big screen. "I can't talk about the case."

"I know you can't." Loving fell silent and let several seconds pass. "Heck of a thing, though."

Babbitt's head pivoted slowly. "What are you talking about?"

"Chris gettin' killed. With all those cop buddies swarmin' around the hotel."

"They were working."

"Not hard enough, I guess."

"They were on a stakeout. They didn't expect some nutcase with an axe to grind against Chris."

"Still, you'd think they'd notice somethin'. When that Thomas guy waltzed in the front door."

"For your information, Officer Shaw saw him at the elevator—" He stopped himself, smiled. "Oh, you're good. You're trying to Scooby-Doo me, aren't you?"

"Don't know what you're talkin' about."

"This is how you get me to tell you something you don't already know."

Loving returned the smile. "It was worth a try." He chuckled a little. "Heck of a weird thing, though."

"You're still doing it."

"Sorry, sorry." Loving shifted in his seat. He crossed his legs, then uncrossed them. He folded his arms. "But why didn't they do somethin' about Thomas?"

"They didn't see him coming."

"Didn't see him comin'? Officer Shaw says he talked to him!"

"He was busy with something else."

"Right, right." Loving frowned. "And you didn't see anythin' suspicious when you got there?"

"No, I didn't."

"And there was no sign of a fight, right?"

Babbitt's eyes narrowed. "Are you telling me what you already know, or trying to get me to tell you what I already know?"

"Little of both. No fight, right? No sign of forced entry."

"True enough."

"So Sentz let him in. And they didn't scuffle."

"You have a problem with that?"

"Well, holy moley, Jimmy. Sentz refused to find the man's dying wife. They have a big knock-down grudge match at the scene of her death. Sentz has him arrested. When they meet again, I figure it's not gonna be to play canasta!"

"Yeah, that part is odd, I admit. But I don't think it means anything. You know how Chris was. He probably tried to talk some sense into the guy. Probably felt sorry for him. And paid for it, big-time."

"Why were you the first responder when there were already cops on the premises? You came in from the street."

"Like I told you, they were busy."

"And like you also told me, Shaw stopped the guy on his way to the elevator!"

"Did I hear my name?"

Loving bit down on his lower lip. He didn't have to swivel to know who that was. Served him right for being stupid enough to raise his voice.

"If you've got questions about me, Loving, why don't you ask me?"

Loving turned and saw Peter Shaw standing behind him, bald head, goatee, sour expression. Two of his buddies were standing behind him.

It was never a good sign when they came with muscle.

"I'm just tryin' to find out what happened at that hotel," Loving said, as cool and nonchalant as the circumstances allowed. "Kind of a strange deal."

"What's so strange about it?" Shaw obviously worked out. His arms and pecs were artificially inflated but, Loving reminded himself, size did not necessarily equal strength. He wore a tight T-shirt and, since Loving had seen him last, he had shaved his head. A necessity, Loving wondered, or had he just spent too many nights playing his DVD box set of *The Shield*? "Doesn't seem strange to me."

"What were you stakin' out at the Marriott? No drugs out there. No gangs."

"That's not the only kind of crime in town."

"Then what was it?"

"I'm not at liberty to say."

"How 'bout I run through a long list and you tell me what it wasn't? Gold, silver, rare stamps, old comic books, Krugerrands—"

"Give it up, Loving. I'm not telling you anything." He was inching closer, defensive and irritated and expressing both through his attempts to be intimidating. Which would work fairly well even without his muscle-bound buddies. "Go home."

"And then there's the question of why Sentz was alone in the hotel room. Every stakeout I ever heard about, two men partner up and stay together. It's too dangerous for one to be alone. As I guess this proves."

"Sometimes I was in the room, sometimes one of the other boys. We had a lot of ground to cover. We couldn't afford to stay in one place all the time."

"Sounds like you weren't followin' procedure."

"We weren't expecting a murderer."

"Didn't he threaten Sentz when his wife died?"

"Nobody thought he meant it."

"Or maybe you did."

"What's that supposed to mean?"

Truth to tell, Loving didn't really know. But there was something odd about Shaw's reaction. "I know you were on the premises when it happened, Shaw. Why didn't you stop Thomas before he got upstairs?"

"I was working!"

"In the hotel bar? I can just imagine."

"I was watching the front door."

"With a couple of martinis, I'll bet. Is that why you couldn't stop Thomas? Vision a little blurry?"

Shaw clenched his teeth. "I don't know who you think you are—"

Loving pressed ahead. He wasn't going to make friends with this guy, and he sensed his time was limited, so he might as well play for as much information as possible. "You did stop and talk to him. But then you let him ride on up the elevator. That's weird."

"I couldn't make a big scene! I was undercover!"

"So you let a guy who supposedly threatened your pal a few days before ride up the elevator and plug him."

"I didn't know he was planning to kill Sentz!"

"Your report says you knew he was packin' a gun. Did you think that was for huntin' rabbits?"

"You know as well as I do that carrying a concealed weapon is not illegal in Oklahoma."

"So you let the guy ride up and shoot your friend."

Shaw's fists clenched. "You sorry—" He almost swung, but caught himself at the last moment. "I want you out of here, Loving."

"Gee, you own this place now? Ousted Jake with a hostile takeover?"

"I don't have to own the place to police it. That's what I do."

"I hope you do it better here than you did at the Marriott. Otherwise everyone in the joint is doomed."

This time Shaw's arm swung around, but one of his heavyweight buddies caught it just before it impacted on Loving's face.

Loving did not flinch, did not even blink. Instead, he smiled. "What are you tryin' to hide, Shaw?"

Shaw launched himself again, but his friends still held him back.

Behind them, toward the big screen, Loving heard someone clearing his throat. It was Jake, the owner.

"You know, Loving," he said calmly but firmly, "maybe it would be a good idea if you headed out."

"You sayin' I'm not welcome here anymore?"

"No, no, of course not. But maybe just until this thing blows over?"

"I think Shaw's the one who needs to blow over."

"Just for tonight, Loving. As a personal favor to me."

"Well. If you put it that way." Loving stood and brushed himself off. "What's a little favor for an old friend?" He nodded toward the three huge men eyeing him with venom. "Been a pleasure, boys."

Loving strolled out of the bar, glad once again that he had parked a distance away, this time because if Shaw had known where he parked, he might be walking home.

That hadn't been as productive as he'd hoped. But it hadn't been a total waste of time, either. He'd laid his groundwork. Rustled the bushes. Now he had to wait and see what shook out.

Shaw knew he was being watched. Perhaps he would make a mistake. And everyone in the bar knew Loving wanted information. Eventually someone would produce some. He hoped.

Loving didn't begin to know what was going on here. But the two conversations convinced him that someone was covering something up. Probably several somethings.

Tomorrow night, he'd be back. And the night after that and the night after that. Until he had what Ben needed.

CHAPTER
13

B EN LET C HRISTINA out on Denver, just as close as it was possible to get a vehicle to the front door of the courthouse. He helped her unload the large quantity of materials they would be using at trial. It was their usual pretrial trade-off. She would have to maneuver the loaded dolly through the metal detector, up the elevator, and into the courtroom. He would have to find a parking space. His job was worse.

This time, Ben didn't even attempt to park in the minuscule courthouse parking area maintained by the adjacent Central Library. The parking lot was a great fund-raiser for them, and he liked to support libraries, especially the one where Jones's wife, Paula, worked, but he knew there would be no open spaces. He drove next door to the Civic Center parking lot, and even then he had to hunt a good long while before he found a space. He plugged the meter to the max but he would still have to send someone to plug it two more times during the course of the day.

"Hey, Cassandra." A female officer he knew well was posted at the metal detector just beyond the front door of the county courthouse. He began the usual undressing ritual—off with the watch, the belt, the pocket change. "Christina been through here yet?"

"Of course. She's looking good. You've got a fine woman there, Ben."

"Don't I know it. How's your George?"

"Gets by. Arthritis acts up from time to time."

"Sorry to hear that."

"Rumor around the courthouse is you're running for reelection."

"Election, technically. I was appointed the first time."

"Does that mean it's true?"

Ben stepped through the detector, then began reassembling himself. "Can't think of anything that sounds more unpleasant than campaigning for office."

"You don't seem the type." She looked at him sharply. "But I notice that wasn't an actual denial."

"You're a smart cookie, Cassandra. Have a good day."

She grinned. "Good luck at trial. You're going to need it. The reporters are camped out on the second floor. I'd go in through the judge's chambers."

"Will do."

The Tulsa County Courthouse had been dramatically improved by a series of renovations in recent years. Best of all, there were now several alternatives to what Judge Peterson and others had deemed "the slowest elevators in all creation." Ben decided to take the escalators.

He was surprised to see Loving at the base, apparently waiting for him. He didn't stop walking.

Loving held out his hands to stop him. "I know. You don't have any time because your trial starts today."

Ben banged his forehead. "Is that today? Holy cow!"

Loving frowned. Ben was never quite sure if sarcasm eluded him or just irritated him. "I found out somethin' last night. I think there may be some nastiness going on in the police department."

"Like what?"

"Don't know yet. I may have to step on some toes. Some big, important toes."

"That's never stopped you before."

"Nope. Just thought you should know."

"Appreciate it. But I really—"

"There's one more thing, Ben."

He stopped, obviously impatient.

"I think the cops—and maybe your client—might've been involved in something bad."

That got Ben's attention. "Like what?"

"I don't know. But those cops were at the hotel on a stakeout. Must be some kind of illegal trade. Smuggling."

"You mean drugs? Narcotics?"

"That would be the obvious. But I don't know yet. My sources didn't spill any specifics."

"Illegal golf clubs smuggled into Southern Hills?"

"I dunno. But it occurred to me . . . your guy was on the premises. It might not help your case."

Ben nodded thoughtfully. He wished he had more time to consider the ramifications. But he didn't. "Find out what you can. I'll deal with my client."

"Got it."

Ben rode the escalator up. By this time, he expected Christina would have all their materials assembled in the courtroom and ready for use. Her background as a legal assistant still proved useful.

He poked his head into the conference room beside the judge's office and was not surprised to find both Christina and Dennis waiting for him.

"Is it soup yet?"

"The prosecutor thinks so," Christina said. "He dropped by to repeat the same offer. We turned him down again."

"Sorry I missed that." He gave Dennis a quick once-over. "You look good."

"I did okay?" He was referring to the suit, which was brand-new. Christina had taken him on a shopping expedition to Utica Square and found him a trial wardrobe courtesy of Sak's. It was more than Dennis would normally spend on clothing, but Ben told him to think of it as another legal fee.

He had chosen a blue suit and red tie for the first day, very similar to what Ben was wearing himself. "You did very well."

"Yes," Dennis said, "but do I look sincere?"

Ben's lips thinned. "I hope so."

"I've been practicing sincere expressions in the mirror. Want to see them?"

"No. No expressions in the courtroom."

"Should I cry? I can, you know."

"No expressions whatsoever. Remember the cardinal rule: the jury must never think you're trying to pull the wool over their eyes. They will discount any scornful reactions or protestations. They will not be impressed by emotional outcries. The best course is to maintain an even keel. Be cool. Unfazed. They already know you dispute the prosecutor's evidence. Show them you're not a hotheaded killer. Show them you don't have a violent bone in your body."

"Show them you're not insane." Christina said, adding quietly, "Anymore."

"Insanity is in the eyes of the beholder," Dennis remarked.

"I'll handle the defense," Ben said. "You just keep a straight face. Were you able to get your neighbor to come to trial?"

"Yes, she'll be there. In the front row. Right behind me."

"Good." Normally Ben tried to plant an adoring spouse just behind the defendant, but in this case, obviously, that wasn't possible. Furthermore, Dennis had no living family in the area or, apparently, any close friends. But he did have an attractive neighbor who was the right age to be his mother—even if she wasn't. Ben wanted her right behind him throughout the trial. She could do the facial expressions of scorn and disapproval that Dennis could not. Most important, she could look at Dennis with loving eyes. It was important that the jury see that the people around him, all the people who actually knew him, liked him.

"I just hope that helps," Dennis said softly. "I—I've been reading the press coverage of the case. The press acts as if I've already been convicted. Like the trial is just a formality."

"It isn't," Ben said firmly. "The media know that implications of guilt, like close elections and celebrity tittle-tattle, increase their ratings. You should ignore it. Focus on the trial. I think we've got a good jury."

"We'll see," Dennis said, pushing himself to his feet.

"Yes," Christina said, doing likewise. "We will."

Dennis took Ben's arm. "I want to thank you for doing this. I know how much work a trial is. And I know you had . . . reservations about taking my case. I appreciate it. More than you can possibly know."

Ben nodded. He peered deeply into Dennis's eyes and saw . . . what? Hard to know.

He patted Dennis on the back. "Let's go win this thing."

CHAPTER
14

THIS WAS SIMPLY excruciating, Ben thought, waiting for the trial to begin. It was already ten past nine. What could be taking the judge so long?

He sat at the blond library table that would be his home away from home for the next many days, probably weeks. As usual, Christina had everything so well organized a blind man could find his way through it, which was good, because once the trial began, a blind man is exactly what Ben felt like.

To his right, he saw the prosecutor assembling his team and his materials. For all he had heard about the financial disadvantage the state supposedly had when mounting a trial, it looked to Ben as if they had far more geegaws than he did. Each of the three attorneys sitting at the table—Guillerman, Patterson, and another guy Ben didn't know—all had laptops in front of them, ready to pull up a piece of evidence or testimony with a click. He also knew they had spared no expense assembling witnesses and evidence.

"You think Guillerman will do the opening himself?" he asked Christina quietly.

"I don't think he has any choice, after so much publicity. Besides, it never hurts to get media attention just before an election." She paused. "Well, in this case, it will probably hurt you."

"I'd feel better if he had passed this off to an underling."

"Me too. When the DA himself is on the job, you can be certain of one thing: he doesn't expect to lose. And he will do everything in his power to make sure he's not mistaken."

To their right, Ben saw the all-important jury box, empty for the moment, but soon to be filled with the most important people in the whole drama. Their chairs were rudimentary, and by all accounts uncomfortable, as they were packed shoulder to shoulder in a varnished plywood box. There they would sit in judgment, trying to make sense of conflicting testimony and facts, not to mention complex psychiatric testimony, without even the benefit of being able to take notes. It was a daunting duty, but one, in Ben's experience, that most jurors took very seriously.

Behind them was the gallery, two sections of twelve rows of churchlike pews. They were completely filled, and Ben knew there were many outside who had not been seated but who would be allowed to watch the proceedings on closed-circuit television in the vacant courtroom next door. There were a few people Ben recognized as prosecution witnesses, but not many. Most would come when they were needed. In many cases, they were not allowed to hear the testimony of other witnesses. Most of the people in the gallery were media professionals. They had the know-how to secure a seat, and the people running the court system wanted to keep them happy. Media coverage tended to be pro-prosecution, if only because they heightened the drama by assuming anyone arrested was probably guilty but might not be convicted. They could say the word *allegedly* all they wanted; it was like white noise in the background, a sound barely registered and usually ignored.

The players were all assembled, except the one who would be sitting atop the raised bench, front and center. Ben wondered if he had time to run to the bathroom.

No, better to tough it out. Although intestinal distress
was an unwanted companion to an opening statement,
as he knew from experience.

The door from the deliberation room opened and the
jurors entered the room. Most of them glanced at
Dennis but did not stare. That might be a good sign. Or
it could just mean that, given the enormous media coverage, they had no need to stare at a face they already
knew quite well. Ben would be watching them carefully
once the prosecution started offering its testimony. That
could be supremely telling.

The door from Judge McPartland's chambers opened.
The bailiff came in, which for a trial was the equivalent
of a raised curtain. The show was about to begin.

"All rise." The instant the bailiff said the words,
McPartland entered and headed toward his chair. He
was seated by the time the spiel was over. "The District
Court of Tulsa County is now in session, the Honorable
Judge Leland McPartland presiding. Please turn off all
cell phones and pagers immediately or be held in contempt. This court will now come to order."

"Please be seated," the judge said. He gazed out into
the gallery, then frowned. This was a charade judges
always went through, in Ben's experience, whenever
there was a packed crowd. The judge evinced disapproval, as if somehow the presence of all these people
might disrupt the serious business they had to conduct.
In reality, Ben suspected, like most showmen,
McPartland did not mind having an audience.

The judge nodded at the clerk, who nodded back.
Then he did the same with the court reporter. Everyone
was ready to roll. He read the case name and number,
then read the indictment in short form. He noted that a
jury had been selected, then gave the jurors a few preliminary instructions, mostly about the importance of
arriving on time each day and not talking to the press.

He was not going to sequester them; he expected them to use their own judgment and to stay away from anything pertaining to the case. And with that . . .

Ben gripped Dennis's wrist and squeezed it.

Here we go.

CHAPTER
15

BEN KNEW that District Attorney Guillerman was a man who had earned his job. He hadn't achieved his current lofty position through connections or privileged birth. He'd made his own way through hard work, smarts, and determination.

Guillerman interned at the DA's office when he was still at TU law school. With a successful solo practice, he'd managed to generate the support he needed to run for office successfully. Twice. He had a fine record, was an excellent attorney and, perhaps even more important, could efficiently and effectively manage a large office. Although there had been talk about him running for governor, Ben knew he planned to run for reelection and didn't doubt he would succeed.

"Ladies and gentlemen of the jury," Guillerman began, "first of all, I want to thank you for being here. I know you have already spent many days in this courtroom and mostly likely will spend many more before we are done. Your seats are not comfortable and the food here is keenly mediocre, so for that and many other reasons, I thank you for your service." He smiled a little, something the jurors would not see again for some time.

"Sadly, we are here today on a very serious matter, perhaps the most serious offense in all of the criminal justice system. A blatant case of first-degree murder. The evidence we present in this trial will show that the defendant, Dennis Thomas, did in fact with premeditation shoot with the intent to kill Detective Christopher Sentz, a distinguished officer on the Tulsa police force with an excellent record. He was a husband and the father of two daughters. The evidence will show that the defendant believed Sentz should have acted more quickly to investigate the disappearance of the defendant's wife, who unfortunately perished after a traffic accident. Although the evidence will show that Detective Sentz followed standard procedure at all times, that did not satisfy the defendant. And so on April twelfth of this year, he killed Officer Sentz in cold blood."

Guillerman pressed his hand against his mouth, then blinked rapidly, as if fighting back tears. After a few moments, he stopped, took a glass of water from his table, and sipped slowly. He was doing a good job and Ben knew it. He was showing emotion, showing he was moved by the tragic loss of Detective Sentz, as he should be. At the same time, he was not going too far. Oklahoma juries, for the most part, were a practical, sensible lot. They could sense a phony a mile away. Guillerman was reminding them of the central horror— a good man dead—without engaging in any obvious playacting.

"The evidence will show that on April twelfth, the defendant took a gun—his gun—to shoot Detective Sentz. He learned that Sentz was in a hotel room at the Tulsa Marriott engaged in an ongoing sting operation. The defendant followed him there, entered his room carrying the gun, and shot him at point-blank range. When the police apprehended him, he was lying on the gun and his prints were all over it. Detective Sentz was dead. Witnesses will testify that they saw the defendant enter the hotel looking angry, determined, and cold-blooded, but entirely in possession of his faculties. He knew what he was doing. And he killed a valuable member of our police department—just as he had planned."

Ben couldn't help but admire the flat but effective manner in which the DA had laid out the facts, mentioning everything that helped his case and ignoring everything that did not. He engaged in some speculation, but resisted the temptation to be argumentative, which at this early stage was likely to put the jurors off. He would save that for closing. Ben also noticed that he avoided the potential minefield of the blackout, the hardest aspect of the case for Guillerman to manage. Even if he didn't accept temporary insanity, he could not deny that something had made Dennis unconscious, unable to be revived for nearly two hours. No doubt he would have some answers. But he knew this was not his strength, so he waited to talk about it until he had no choice. For now, he would present his case as if it were perfectly simple and obvious.

"One final matter I would like to touch upon before I yield to my worthy colleague," Guillerman said. "There will undoubtedly be testimony on both sides regarding the defendant's mental state. That is sadly inevitable when a person has been through the undoubtedly traumatic experience of losing a spouse. It is all too easy to get lost in the hugger-mugger of psychiatric jargon. I will not tell you what to think. But I will suggest that you listen to the evidence and decide for yourself. Don't be swayed by long words or impressive credentials. You're Oklahomans. You're as smart as anyone and, more to the point, you're the jurors. Don't be confused by a smoke screen of babble. Use your heads."

He stepped closer to the jurors and looked at them with an expression that Ben noted was, among other things, extremely sincere. "Dennis Thomas bought a gun. He found out where Detective Sentz was. He went there. He pulled the trigger. These systematic, calculated actions were not accidental, and they were not the product of an unbalanced mind. They evidence planning, deliberation, and stone-cold execution. What more is there to say? Don't let yourselves be misled. See the truth for what it is. This was murder in the first degree, deserving the ultimate sanction. And that is exactly what I will be asking for at the conclusion of this case. Thank you."

With that he sat down, never once having used the phrase "temporary insanity," but effectively dismissing it just the same.

And perhaps in that instant Ben realized just how impossible this case really was.

As ALWAYS, Ben had the option of delivering his opening statement immediately, or waiting until the prosecution's case had closed and giving it at the start of the defense's case. And as always, he chose to do it now. He never liked to let the jury go too long without hearing from him, especially after such an effective opening. He knew he had to get their side of the story in the jury's heads immediately, to let them know what the points of contention were, so they could be thinking about them while the prosecutor presented his case. They could say anything they wanted; the smart jurors would always remember what points were in doubt. And for the defense, doubt was what it was all about.

"The prosecutor has done an admirable job of summing up some of the facts of the case," Ben began, doing his best to seem agreeable and not argumentative. "There are, however, a few things he got wrong and, more important, many things he left out. And that, ladies and gentlemen, is where the entire case lies.

"Mr. Guillerman would have you believe he has an airtight case, but that is far from the truth. Consider, if you will, everything he told you the prosecution would be presenting at trial. Dennis Thomas believed Detective Sentz was responsible for the horrible death of his wife. That much is true. As the evidence will show, she suffered the most unimaginable agony, unbelievable pain, for seven days. *Seven days.* The police had the ability to locate her in a few hours. Imagine how that would make any loving husband feel. After you hear what happened, you may well think the police are ultimately responsible for her death, too.

"It is also true that Dennis sought Detective Sentz out. Wanted to confront him, to talk to him, to get some explanations. Who would not want to confront the man you thought killed your wife? I don't doubt that there are many people who saw Dennis at the hotel. He made no attempt to hide it—and that in itself is telling.

"But that's where the prosecution case falls apart. Because once Dennis was inside that hotel room, they have no idea what happened. Do they have any eyewitnesses to this alleged crime? No. Do they have any proof Dennis fired the gun? No. They seem to think that if they can just put Dennis in the room, that will be enough. But it isn't. They have to prove his guilt beyond a reasonable doubt. And that means, at the very least, two things: the prosecution has to prove that he pulled the trigger, and you have to believe he was not insane at the time."

Out the corner of his eye, Ben saw Guillerman twitch. He was undoubtedly tempted to object, but he didn't, probably because he knew jurors didn't like objections during opening and closing and he didn't want to irritate them this early in the game. Ben had chosen his words carefully. He hadn't actually said that the prosecution had to prove Dennis was sane when he shot Sentz, because temporary insanity was their affirmative defense and the burden of proving it was on them. At the same time, Ben had put a critical idea into their heads: they didn't have to find Dennis guilty even if they thought he pulled the trigger.

Ben strolled back to his table as he began the next section of his opening. Dennis looked good, respectable, honorable. Ben wanted the jury looking at him while he talked about him. "There is one important detail the evidence will reveal that you have not yet been told. The district attorney does not dispute it, but still, oddly enough, he failed to mention it. When the police found Dennis in that hotel room, he was unconscious. In fact, he did not regain consciousness for over two hours. Why? The prosecution has no explanation. Did someone hit him over the head before shooting Detective Sentz? It's possible. Did Dennis experience some kind of mental breakdown? Possible. The evidence will show that Dennis experienced extreme trauma after losing his wife in such a horrific way, trauma that would have driven the best of us to unimaginable extremes. Trauma that prevented him from understanding what he was doing, that literally unraveled his fundamental understanding of what is right and what is wrong."

Ben casually moved from one end of the jury box to the other, never for a moment relinquishing his hold on the eyes of the jurors.

"I know that some of you may be dubious, perhaps even cynical about the science of psychiatry, or the idea of temporary insanity. It's understandable. We're Oklahomans. Good, honest, commonsense people. All I ask is that you listen to the testimony presented and view it with an open mind. Try to imagine for a moment what this man was going through, what his wife had gone through, and how that would have affected him. What that must have done to his powers of reason. To his sanity. The defense will show that, regardless of what took place that day, the circumstances rendered Dennis temporarily insane, and under the law, a man who is temporarily insane cannot be held accountable for his actions. And then ask yourself—what if it had been you? What if it had been your spouse? Wouldn't you have reacted the same? Wouldn't anyone?

"And most important . . ." Ben leaned against the rail, getting as close to them as possible. "Most important, I ask that you remember the oath you took when you were sworn into your current position. You swore to uphold the law. The law says that you must presume that Dennis Thomas is innocent. You must presume his innocence and continue presuming it unless and until the prosecution proves otherwise—beyond a reasonable doubt. That's what matters most. That is the single most important part of your duty."

He took a few steps back, making sure they could see District Attorney Guillerman. "No amount of political ambition is a substitute for the truth. No desire to win a highly publicized trial is a substitute for the evidence. If the prosecution does not prove their case, regardless of what you think, you must find Dennis not guilty. That is the oath you swore. And I'm counting on you to abide by it."

Ben slowly walked back to his seat. Just under the table, he could see Christina giving him a subtle thumbs-up. That was a good sign. But he didn't fool himself. This was a tough case. And he had no way of knowing whether he was getting across to them until they rendered their verdict. When it would be too late for him to do anything about it.

"Thank you, counsel," Judge McPartland said, without the slightest trace of inflection or comment. "Mr. Guillerman, you may call your first witness."

CHAPTER
16

THE FIRST WITNESS was Bob Barkley, the county medical examiner. Barkley had been the lead witness in every case of murder or serious injury Ben had tried in Tulsa county for many years, ever since the supremely distinguished—and impossible to work with—Dr. Koregai had passed away. Barkley apparently had the Dick Clark gene: he didn't seem to age at all. He had a full shock of blond hair and a trim figure. One could almost see the abs rippling through his bright blue shirt. Ben still had a hard time convincing himself there hadn't been confusion back at headquarters and someone switched a surfer dude for a coroner.

Barkley had nothing controversial to say. His job was simply to establish that a murder had occurred. This was not in dispute; nonetheless, if the prosecution didn't establish it, the whole case could be dismissed on the technicality that no crime had been proven. This was the sort of potential technical gaffe that kept lawyers awake at nights.

Patterson, Guillerman's assistant, competently established his credentials and that he had examined the remains after Sentz's body was brought to the coroner's office. He conducted the autopsy and filed his report. Death was caused by a gunshot wound to the frontal lobe. There was not much more to say about it. Ben normally didn't even bother cross-examining this sort of witness, but today he thought he saw an opportunity to score a few points, or at least to plant a few seeds of doubt in the minds of the jurors.

After Patterson rested, Christina began her cross-examination. To some it would probably appear that, since Guillerman used his assistant on this witness, Ben would do the same, rather than let it appear that he was concerned about a witness Guillerman thought so unimportant that he passed him off to an underling. But Ben had a much better secret motive. He knew Barkley had a crush on Christina, and he doubted her recent marriage had changed that. He would be easy for her to lead around.

"Dr. Barkley, I've heard you testify about the cause of death," Christina began. "You said death was caused by a gunshot wound, correct?"

"That's correct."

"But I noticed you didn't say anything about how the wound occurred, did you?"

"Well, the fingerprints—"

"Dr. Barkley, are you a fingerprint specialist?"

"No."

"So why don't we leave that to them and let you testify about what you learned from the autopsy, okay?"

Barkley was just too affable to be stung, especially when that cute redhead was asking the questions. "Sure. Whatever you want."

"Your examination didn't yield any information regarding who might have inflicted the wound, did it?"

"There was only one person in the room—"

"Were you there?"

"Well, no, but—"

"So let's stick to what you personally know. Because in point of fact, there were two people in the room, weren't there? At least. Counting the victim?"

"Well, yes, but—"

"Doctor, is it possible this wound could have been self-inflicted?"

Behind him, Ben sensed the stirring in the gallery. This was a line they were not expecting. But he didn't fool himself into thinking he'd surprised Guillerman. The DA was smart enough to know that Ben's job was to create doubt whenever and wherever possible. Technically, since their primary defense was temporary insanity, the testimony of these fact witnesses wasn't relevant—all that mattered was whether Dennis understood the nature and quality of his actions. But of course, that wouldn't stop Guillerman from calling fact witnesses any more than it would stop Ben from refuting them. They both knew that doubt worked to Dennis's advantage, that the jury was much more likely to accept the temporary insanity plea if they found him sympathetic and if they had doubts about his actual guilt.

"The bullet struck him square in the center of the forehead. It would be extremely awkward to do that to yourself."

"In your opinion. But is it possible?"

"I doubt it."

"I can do it." Christina reached a hand around and pointed a finger at her forehead. "You look pretty limber, Doctor. Can't you do it?"

"The question is whether Detective Sentz could do it. He suffered a gunshot wound to the right shoulder several years ago that restricted his mobility."

"Could he have used his left hand?"

"I suppose he might have. But why would he? He had no reason—"

"You're not answering the question, Doctor. Is it possible he could have done it?"

Barkley sighed. "Yes, I suppose it is possible. But why—"

"Thank you. Were you close to Detective Sentz, Doctor?"

"No."

"Do you have any knowledge regarding his mental state?"

"I have no reason to believe—"

"Please answer the question, sir."

Barkley still wasn't showing the slightest irritation, but Ben sensed he might at least be getting marginally closer. "No, I was not familiar with his mental state. But why would he want to kill himself?"

"Maybe because he was responsible for the death of Dennis Thomas's wife?"

Guillerman sprang to his feet. "Objection!"

Christina turned toward the bench. "The witness did raise the issue of whether Detective Sentz had any motivation for suicide. And this is cross-examination."

Judge McPartland nodded. "The objection is overruled. But counsel—don't waste my time with a lot of nonsense that serves no purpose other than confusing the jury."

"Of course not, your honor." Why on earth would they want to confuse the jury?

Christina returned to the witness. "All we know for certain is that there was at least one person in that hotel room who believed Sentz killed Joslyn Thomas. What if there were two? What if Sentz was racked with guilt, guilt that only became even more profound when he met the bereaved husband face-to-face?"

"Your honor," Guillerman said, "I object again. This is not closing argument."

"This time I agree with him," McPartland said. "Sustained."

Which was fine, because Christina had already made her point, and any further remarks from the witness would only mess it up.

"Thank you, your honor." Ben smiled. Christina had learned to always thank the judge, whether she won an objection or not, because jurors often didn't understand the meaning of the judge's rulings. If she said thank you, they thought she'd won. Even when she hadn't. "Dr. Barkley, can you tell this jury that you can absolutely rule out the possibility of suicide in this case? To a medical certainty?"

"Well, gosh, Christina, if you put it that way, I guess not."

"Thank you. No more questions."

THE NEXT WITNESS was Detective Sentz's dentist, who presented the victim's dental records and showed that they matched the impressions produced by Dr. Barkley from the autopsy. In other words, the victim was definitely Christopher Sentz, a point never in dispute, but another fact the prosecution had to prove to make their case. Ben didn't cross this witness. He knew he could play with these quickie tech witnesses once and get away with it, but twice would be pressing his luck with both the judge and the jurors. He had no reason to interrogate the man, and Ben had learned some time ago about the danger of going on a fishing expedition during cross-examination. You might not like what you catch.

"WELL, THAT WENT well enough," Dennis said during the lunch break. "I don't think they've laid a glove on us yet."

"They haven't tried," Christina said bluntly. "But they will."

"I thought your cross was excellent."

She shrugged as she scarfed down a french fry. "I

don't believe for a minute that Sentz killed himself. But doubt is doubt. And you never know what evidence might turn up later to support it."

Dennis stared down at his meal. He hadn't taken a bite. "I was so worried last night I couldn't sleep."

Ben and Christina looked at each other. "Imagine that."

"I was so angry before, but . . . now all that seems to have gone away. I think Joslyn took it away. That was her last wish for me. Took it awhile to sink in, but it's starting to become clear. And now that I'm getting my head on straight, I'm afraid . . . I'm afraid it won't matter because—"

Christina patted his hand. "It's much too early for this kind of talk. Eat your lunch. You need to keep up your strength." She inhaled another fry. "You ain't seen nothin' yet."

CHAPTER
17

THE FIRST WITNESS after lunch was much more important: an eyewitness who placed Dennis at the scene of the crime. Officer Peter Shaw was an eight-year member of the force and had been working with Sentz at the time of the murder. He claimed he was at the hotel in the downstairs lobby and saw Dennis approach the elevator. He couldn't quite put Dennis in the hotel room, but he could put him practically on the front doorstep. More important, he testified that Dennis appeared angry if not enraged, determined, and potentially violent. He also said he thought Dennis was packing a gun.

Ben had previously determined that Christina should take this cross. Loving had given him the lowdown on Shaw, a bully but still a young man who apparently hadn't had a date in a long time and tended to put his foot in his mouth around women. Hence Ben thought a smart, comely redhead might do a better job on the man than he could. Worked on the coroner. Not that he wanted Christina to think he valued only her feminine charms. But he certainly didn't have any.

"I have a few things I'd like to clear up," Christina said, with a casualness that was not likely to disarm anyone. "Why were you at the hotel on April twelfth?"

"Detective Sentz was captaining a stakeout we hoped would evolve into a sting operation. We believed there was a smuggling ring planning a major operation at the hotel. Sentz had taken a room near theirs and planted surveillance equipment so he could monitor what went on next door. I was planted in the dining area near the front door so I could see who went in and out. We maintained contact via cell phones."

"How long had you been at your post?"

"Over three hours when I first spotted the defendant."

"Did you get breaks?"

"Not unless one of the other men on the case came by. We had to keep the door monitored at all times."

"I see." Ben suppressed a smile. He loved watching Christina cross. She seemed so sweet, so fresh-faced and innocent. There was no reason at all to think she might be up to something—until she sprang the trap and you felt the cold metal teeth breaking your neck. "And when did you see Dennis Thomas?"

"Eleven fourteen at night. I made a note."

"What did you do?"

"At first he seemed content to just sit in the lobby. So I left him alone. Eventually, though, he made a move for the elevators. I followed him."

"Did you believe he was part of this smuggling ring?"

"No. But I recognized him."

"Why did you recognize him?"

"I'd seen him in the police station. When he was— you know. Coming by."

"When he was trying to get the police to open a missing persons investigation on his wife but they refused while she bled to death in her car?"

Shaw averted his eyes. "Uh, yeah."

"So you followed him. Why?"

"Well, I was afraid he might interfere with the operation."

"Why would you think that?"

"It was hard to imagine he was there by coincidence."

"Why? It's a popular hotel, isn't it?"

"Yeah. But he obviously wasn't there to spend a relaxing weekend. He seemed angry."

"How angry?"

"Very."

"Enraged?"

"I'd say so."

"Irrational?"

Shaw's eyes darted to the prosecution table.

"Don't look to the DA for your answers," Christina said. "Answer for yourself!"

"I wasn't—" He took a deep breath. "I didn't think he looked crazy, if that's what you mean."

"Why? Because the DA told you not to say he looked crazy?"

"I just . . . didn't think he was that bad."

"But he was bad enough for you to leave your station, which you previously wouldn't even leave to go to the bathroom, to try to intercept him."

"Well . . . yeah."

"Sounds like you must've thought he looked dangerous."

Shaw thought a long time before answering. "I thought he might be dangerous to our operation."

"Why did you think he was angry?"

"He had an intense expression on his face."

"You're telling me you left your post and went after him because he was making a frowny face?" As Shaw's eyes darted, she added, "And this time, answer without help from the peanut gallery!"

"I just . . . thought he was mad."

"Why?"

"He was muttering to himself. Under his breath."

"He was talking to himself?"

"Constantly. Over and over again."

"Did that concern you?"

"Yes."

"But it didn't seem crazy."

"Objection!" Guillerman was on his feet before Christina had finished speaking the magic word. "She's putting ideas into his mouth."

"I can lead on cross," Christina said. "He's a big boy. Can't he take care of himself without help from his master?"

"That's enough," Judge McPartland said crossly. "I'll allow the question. The witness will answer."

"I didn't think he seemed crazy," Shaw said. "Just very angry."

"What's the difference?"

Shaw hesitated a long time before answering. "I . . . I don't know."

Ben knew that was as good as it was going to get, but it was pretty good. Christina let that sink into the jurors' brains before she moved on.

"You also testified he was carrying a gun, right?"

"Yes."

"Did you see the gun?"

"I saw a bulge under his leather jacket."

"Ah. So when you told the jury he was carrying a gun, you actually meant that he was carrying a bulge."

"We found his gun in the hotel room."

"Move to strike," Christina said, not missing a beat. "The jury wants to know what you saw, Officer Shaw. And all you saw was a bulge."

He blew air through his teeth. "That's correct."

"And that could've been his iPod for all you know."

"Whatever."

"Did you stop him?"

"I tried."

"So what was the problem? Did the English professor overpower you?"

Ben could see Shaw was getting angry, which of course was Christina's primary objective. Angry people sometimes said things they shouldn't.

"No, but I was undercover. I couldn't flash a badge and I didn't want to create a scene. I did try to pull him to one side so we could talk, but he pushed me away and got in the elevator."

"Did you do anything further?"

"I watched the numbers light over the elevator and saw that it went to the seventh floor. Where our surveillance room was. I called Chris. Detective Sentz. Told him he might be getting a surprise visitor."

"I see. Did you have any further contact with Detective Sentz or Dennis Thomas?"

"No."

"Did you see him go into Detective Sentz's room?"

"No."

"Did you ever see him holding a gun?"

"No."

"Did you see who pulled the trigger?"

"No."

"Thank you for your honesty." She turned and started toward the defendant's table, then stopped. "Oh, one more thing."

Ben's eyebrows rose. Shades of Columbo. What was this about?

"You said Dennis Thomas was muttering. Could you hear what he was saying?"

"Um, yeah. Some of it."

"And what was he saying?"

"The same thing, over and over again. I didn't understand it at the time. Now I do."

"What was it, Officer?"

"A name. Joslyn." He paused, swallowed. "He just said her name, with that same weird fixed look on his face. 'Joslyn. Joslyn. Joslyn.' That was all."

"Thank you," Christina said, a solemn expression on her face. "No more questions for this witness, your honor."

CHAPTER
18

ON THE SECOND day of the trial, there was no evidence that public interest had subsided at all. The morning news shows had been full of coverage, reporting and predicting and commenting. Ben still had to pass through a gauntlet just to get into the courtroom. And the gallery was still full.

DA Guillerman seemed considerably less cheery than he had been the day before. This warmed Ben's heart. Perhaps he and Christina had done more damage to his case than they realized.

Ben had an easy morning. Guillerman started with a few softball witnesses. Apparently the DA subscribed to the common belief that jurors mostly saw jury duty as a sort of holiday, free time off work, so they tended to sleep in and get to the courthouse as late as possible. Consequently, there was no point in putting important witnesses on early, because most of the jurors weren't really awake yet.

He started with forensics witnesses. The first confirmed that the handgun found in the hotel room had in fact fired the bullet that killed Christopher Sentz. He also mentioned that the police had run a search and found that it had been sold and registered to one Dennis Thomas several years before.

The next two witnesses were considerably more problematic. The fingerprint analysts established that there were more than sufficient correspondences between the prints on the gun and the prints Dennis gave when he was arrested to show that he had fired the gun. On cross, Ben made the point that the prints at best showed that Dennis had held the gun—hardly unusual, since he owned it. It was a thin point—especially since no one else's prints had been found—but Ben made the most of it. The truth was, in the post-DNA universe, fingerprint analysis was not nearly as important as it once had been. But juries were comfortable with it and they expected it, and the DA wanted to keep them happy.

Guillerman's next forensic witness testified that they'd found GSR (gunshot residue) on Dennis's clothing. Ben argued on cross that since Dennis was found lying on the gun, that was hardly surprising. He also established that they did not find residue on Dennis's hands, but the expert asserted that since the test had not been taken until after Dennis had been in the hospital for several hours, he might well have washed his hands, several times over, with hospital-strength cleansers. Basically, the testimony was a wash. It didn't help Dennis, but Ben didn't think it hurt him much, either.

The final forensic witness was the DNA expert. Traces of dead skin on the gun demonstrated that Dennis had held it. Some of those flecks were found on the trigger. It didn't take a science degree to understand what that implied. But it still was far short of conclusive proof.

THE PRIMARY WITNESS for the afternoon was Lieutenant Jimmy Babbitt. Ben knew he'd been the first responder, the first man at the crime scene, not counting the undercover agents who were already on the premises. He'd been responding to two calls, one from another resident at the hotel who'd heard the gunshot, and one from one of the undercover agents who'd become concerned when Sentz didn't call in at the appointed time. Babbitt found the hotel room door locked. He broke in and found two figures lying on the floor. Detective Sentz was dead. He had a bullet hole in his forehead. Dennis was not wounded, but he was lying on the floor only two feet away, on top of what had been established as the murder weapon. His gun.

Ben took the cross-examination. "Let's make a few things clear. You didn't see who pulled the trigger, right?"

"True." He paused. "But there were only two people in the room. And the door was locked."

"From the inside. It locks automatically, does it not? So anyone could've exited the room and left the door locked behind them."

Babbitt was a natty dresser, especially for a police witness. He was actually wearing a suit, rather than the usual sports coat and slacks. He wore a bright tie that appeared to be silk and even sported French cuffs. "I suppose. But the other officers didn't see anyone."

"The other officers themselves could've gotten in and out of the room, right?"

"Yes."

"Thank you. So the truth is, we have many potential suspects. In fact, we have no reason to exclude anyone, since the door was not monitored and anyone could've left without being observed, right?"

"If you say so."

"Did you see any signs of a struggle?"

"Not really. One chair was overturned."

"Would you expect more mess from a murderous man on a rampage?"

"Or a crazy man."

Touché. This witness was stylish *and* smart. Ben would have to be more careful.

"Have you ever participated in an undercover operation?"

"Yes."

"Is it typical to allow civilians into the stakeout room?"

"Well . . . no."

"So how did Dennis get in?"

"I don't know. I wasn't there."

"Do you think Dennis overcame Detective Sentz with brute strength?"

"He didn't have to. He had a gun."

"Detective Sentz also had a gun, did he not?"

"True enough."

"Why would Detective Sentz let him in? This man had allegedly assaulted him only a few days before."

"I don't know. It's possible he let himself in."

"There doesn't seem to be very tight security on this stakeout."

"Objection, your honor," Guillerman said wearily. "Is this relevant to anything? It sure doesn't seem so. We're trying a murder, not questioning departmental stakeout procedures."

Judge McPartland nodded. "I would appreciate it if you could move things along, Mr. Kincaid. This trial will likely be long enough just sticking to the issues that actually matter."

Ben took the hint. "I don't believe you mentioned the state you found Dennis in when you entered the room, Officer."

"I said he was lying on the ground."

"Was he conscious?"

"I'm not a doctor."

"Did he appear to be conscious?"

"His eyes were closed and he did not respond when I spoke to him. But that doesn't mean anything."

"Did he show any signs of consciousness?"

"Well . . ."

"Did he blink?"

"His eyes were closed."

"Did he move?"

"No."

"Did he do anything that would suggest to you that he was conscious?"

Babbitt shrugged. "I've seen fakers before."

"I didn't ask you about your past experience, Officer. I asked you about Dennis Thomas. Did he do anything that suggested to you that he was conscious?"

"I guess not."

"In your experience, do murderers normally remain at the scene of the crime?"

"No."

That was as far as Ben could take it. If he asked if there was any reason for Dennis to remain, Babbitt would suggest he was faking to set up an insanity defense. He'd established the fact of unconsciousness. He'd let the psychiatric witness connect the dots.

"Did you remain with Dennis when he was taken to the hospital?"

"Yes."

"Were the medical experts able to get a reaction out of him?"

"Not for about two hours. Then he came around."

"Did you question him?"

"Yes."

"What did he say?"

"Not much. He claimed he couldn't remember what happened after he got to the hotel."

"Thank you, Officer. No more questions."

AFTER COURT recessed for the day, Ben huddled with Christina.

"How did you think that went?" he asked.

"About as well as possible."

"What does that mean?"

"It means you've got an impossible case. You can't expect to be winning, especially not while the prosecution is still putting on their evidence."

"You think we're losing?"

She dodged the question. "I'm hoping your expert is really good."

"He's written a book."

"Well, that makes him an expert. I wonder if that's why Dennis chose to see him in the first place."

"Christina . . ."

"Dennis is going to have to be good, too."

Ben glanced back at his client. He had been well behaved during these first two days of trial. No overt reactions. No overt scheming. No meddling in the case. But he was still a cause for concern. "You think we should put Dennis on the stand?"

"Only if you have to. But . . ."

"You think we'll have to."

She gave his shoulder a squeeze. "We'll make that decision when the time comes. After this next witness."

"You think this witness will be important."

She nodded. "I think if this goes badly for us, we'll need a lot more than Dennis Thomas on the stand to make it right again."

CHAPTER
19

As soon as Dennis entered the courtroom the next day, Ben could tell he was worried.

"Do you think we're winning?"

"I have no idea. And unless you're a psychic, neither do you."

"I don't like that woman at the end of the front row of the jury box. The young one. She keeps staring at me like I remind her of her old boyfriend. The one who had an affair with her best friend and then dumped her."

Ben smiled a little. "Maybe you do. But she won't convict you for that."

"You're sure of that?"

"Yes." He was sure she would have much better reasons to convict him if she was so inclined. "Just keep doing what you're doing. The jurors are watching. They'll see that you're a good person. That will go a long way."

Dennis looked down at the table. "Ben . . . I know we kind of got off to a rocky start, but I appreciate what you've done for me."

"I know. You've said that."

"And I hope you also know that even if I come off a little . . . cold, or . . . calculating, it's just my way. I can't show what I'm really feeling inside. If I did, it would destroy me. I'd fall apart. Totally."

"Please don't. We need you here. One hundred percent."

"Did I ever tell you Joslyn could sing? Like an angel. She studied opera in school. Thought about doing it professionally, then decided to go into medicine. But sometimes, late at night, just for me, she'd sing." His voice caught. "Sweetest thing you ever heard."

Ben saw that his client's eyes were watering.

"I loved my wife so much."

Ben laid his hand gently on his back. "I know you did. Do."

BEN EXPECTED Guillerman to rest his case soon, but before they could get to that blessed moment, he knew they would have to endure the man Guillerman considered his smoking gun—the "death threat" witness. Ben had interviewed him before trial and wasn't all that impressed, but it was impossible to know how something would play at trial until you observed the expressions on the jurors' faces when they heard it. Ben had no doubt the man had been woodshedded for days, rehearsed over and over again until he was just where Guillerman needed him to be.

Officer Oliver Conway was dressed in a sports coat and a bolo tie—Oklahoma chic. He worked at the downtown police station. He was what they called a triage officer; after the front desk clerk took the preliminary information, Conway helped decide whom, if anyone, the complainant would see. Consequently, he was on duty and watching most of the times Dennis had come to the station, pleading for help.

"Unfortunately, we couldn't assist him. It wasn't just Detective Sentz. We all knew the rules. We get too many of these complaints that turn out to be some kid who went over to a friend's house or a wife who got mad and moved in with her mother. We all felt sorry for him—me, Detective Sentz, Shaw, Officer Torres at the front desk. But there was nothing we could do."

Something he said triggered a lightbulb over Ben's head. He rustled through some papers to confirm what he already knew. There was no Officer Torres on the prosecution witness list.

Why not? If this man had seen it all, including everything Conway was about to describe, why wasn't he on the list?

Ben didn't have any problem with most of Conway's testimony. In fact, he thought it helped his case, letting the jury hear once again the story of this desperate man begging the police to act while they refused. Even the hardest heart would have difficulty not sympathizing after hearing that woeful tale.

Unfortunately, Officer Conway was also part of the team that was finally dispatched on the seventh day to find Joslyn Thomas.

"She must have been traveling at an extreme speed on those winding country roads," Conway explained, "because she didn't just go off the side. She plummeted down a steep ravine and then careened through some thick blackberry bushes. As a result, her car was entirely invisible from the road."

Guillerman nodded. "But you still managed to find her?"

"Yes. One of the officers suggested that we try to trace her cell phone. We got lucky. Her phone was on— it's a miracle the battery hadn't gone dead—and her position was only a few miles from the nearest signal tower. We were able to narrow her location down to a relatively confined area. We deployed several cars and a helicopter to get an aerial view. As a result, we were able to locate her in just over three hours."

Like all police officers, Conway had been trained to make his testimony precise and unadorned. Tell the facts and be quiet—don't leave the defense attorney any ammunition to use against you. Still, it was impossible not to notice that he was trying to portray the police department as making a heroic effort to find Joslyn Thomas—perhaps to compensate for the fact that they did nothing for so long.

"Unfortunately, she was almost dead when we found her. We had medics with us, but there was not much they could do. They eased her pain, primarily. And we allowed her to see her husband one last time. I'm glad for that."

"How did Mr. Thomas react?"

"He was angry. Very angry."

"Irrational? Crazed?"

"No, he was as rational as anyone. Just mad. Furious. He blamed Detective Sentz. I couldn't figure out why. Sentz didn't write the regulations. All he did was enforce them."

"Objection," Ben said quietly.

"Sustained," Judge McPartland replied. "The witness will avoid editorializing. Just testify about what you saw and heard."

"Sure," Conway said, with apparent aw-shucks good nature. "Anyway, Mr. Thomas was angry. He threw himself at Detective Sentz, shouting mean, threatening words. Sentz didn't know what to do. He tried not to hurt the man, but Thomas just kept coming. Finally, Sentz was forced to physically push him away. That's when his face was scraped up."

Guillerman showed the jury a photo of Dennis with the right side of his face bloodied and scabbed. Of course, the photo he chose was the mug shot taken after Dennis was arrested. Because no one looks good in a mug shot.

"Two officers took him away on a charge of assaulting a police officer. We didn't want to press charges, and we dropped them after he'd had a weekend to cool off. Of course we felt sorry for him. But we couldn't let him go nuclear on a police detective."

"Of course not," Guillerman said, nodding. "Tell me, Officer. Did the defendant say anything as the police were taking him away?"

Conway took a deep breath. "I'm afraid so," he said, as if it really pained him to bring up such unpleasantness. And who knows? Ben thought. Maybe it did.

"He kept shouting, 'There will be a reckoning. You haven't seen the last of me. There will be a reckoning.'"

"A reckoning. Hmmm." Guillerman picked up a forensic photo of Detective Sentz in the coroner's lab. His suggestion was obvious. "Anything else?"

"Yes. He said, You'll pay for this. You'll pay! And he was looking right at Detective Sentz when he said it."

Guillerman nodded, a grave expression on his face. He laid the autopsy photo on his table, in full view of the jurors. "No more questions."

"YOU WERE PRESENT, were you not, when Dennis Thomas came to the police station asking for help?" Ben decided not to mess around with this witness. The impression he had left was too damaging. Ben had to get right to the heart of the matter.

"I was."

"And you saw Detective Sentz refuse, time after time."

"He had no choice."

"Answer the question," Ben said sternly. Wimps ask the judge to direct the witness to answer. Macho lawyers like Ben could handle it for themselves. Or at least that's what he told himself.

"Yes, I was there."

"And in fact, Detective Sentz did have a choice, didn't he?"

"The regulations strictly state that, absent special circumstances, such as the involvement of a minor or evidence of foul—"

"I'm not asking you to recite the regulations to me," Ben said forcefully. "Both Dennis and I have heard enough about the regulations. I'm asking you whether Detective Sentz had a choice."

"In my opinion, no."

"You're saying he had no discretion at all."

"Well . . ."

"Of course he has discretion. He's a detective. I know detectives, and I know that for the most part they call their own shots, right?"

"I don't know."

"True or false, Officer. If Detective Sentz wanted to open a missing persons investigation, did he have the power to do it?"

Conway shrugged. "If you put it that way . . . yes."

"But he chose not to."

"Yes."

"Did he take his cues from anyone else?"

"Not to my knowledge."

"Did anyone else participate in Sentz's decision not to help?"

"Chris could make his own decisions."

"You're sure? He didn't look to anyone else for permission?"

"Chris Sentz was a full detective. The only person he answered to was the chief, and Chief Blackwell doesn't get involved in issues like this."

Ben let it go, though he still had a feeling he hadn't gotten all there was to get. "So finally, on the seventh day, Sentz saw the light and decided to authorize an investigation."

Conway's head tilted to one side. "Well . . . no."

"What do you mean?"

"As I understand it, Sentz was out and Officer Torres took the complaint to another detective. That's why there was an investigation."

Torres. Again. Who was this mysterious man who'd finally showed the heart that the others had not?

"But Detective Sentz was at the scene. When Joslyn Thomas was found."

"Eventually, yes. He heard that he had been effectively overruled in his absence, and he—" Conway stopped short.

"Yes? Finish your sentence."

"No, that was all I had to say."

"It was not. What were you about to say regarding Detective Sentz?" Ben leaned closer. "That he was not pleased that someone else ordered an investigation?"

"You know how it is. No one likes it when people go around them. Or over their heads."

"So Sentz was angry when he arrived at the scene?"

"I wouldn't say angry. A bit perturbed, perhaps. He just wanted to know what was going on."

Ben continued to press. "He was angry, and Dennis was angry, and they began to fight. Isn't that what happened?"

"Not at all."

"You told the jury that they fought."

"I told the jury that the defendant attacked Detective Sentz."

"With no provocation at all?"

"Right. Just seeing Sentz was enough to set him off."

"Does that strike you as a rational reaction?"

"Objection," Guillerman said. "Officer Conway is not a psychiatric witness. Although," he added in a lowered voice, "I'm sure there will be one."

"Sustained."

Ben didn't miss a beat. "How would you describe Dennis Thomas's demeanor at this time?"

"As I said, he was very angry."

"The man had just seen his wife die in his arms."

"Yes."

"He had just been told by the medics that she had been in extreme pain for days."

"I know, it's horrible."

Ben's voice rose. "And then he saw the man he believed was responsible for that pain, for his wife's death. Don't you think you might go a little crazy?"

"Objection!" Guillerman shouted, rising to his feet. "Not a psychiatric witness."

"I'm sorry," Ben said, not bringing his tone down at all, "but this man testified that Dennis made statements that we all know the prosecutor will try to turn into a threat. I want to show where those statements came from. They were not the statements of someone cold-bloodedly planning a murder. They were the words of a man driven to the brink of insanity by the relentless refusal to investigate by the Tulsa police department!"

Judge McPartland pounded his gavel. He looked angry. "Approach the bench, counsel." They did.

He leaned close to Ben's face. "I will not have this grandstanding in my courtroom, Mr. Kincaid. Do you understand me?"

"Your honor—"

"I don't care who you are. If I see another outburst like that, your co-counsel will be finishing this trial."

"Yes, your honor."

"I will allow this witness to answer questions about what he saw and heard. And that is it. Do you both get that?"

They answered in the affirmative.

"Then get out there and finish. I'm ready for the weekend."

Ben returned to his place before the witness box. "Officer Conway, you had the rare opportunity to witness Mr. Thomas over a long period. A week. Did he seem to change during that time?"

"I'm not sure what you mean."

"Was he more agitated the second time he came to the station than he had been the first?"

"Yes, definitely. He became more and more upset as the week passed. And tired, haggard. Wrung out."

"I would imagine so. When you saw him at the scene of his wife's accident and death—"

"He was a totally different person." Ben saw his eyes dart to the prosecution table. "I mean, I'm not saying he'd, you know, lost it or anything. But he was definitely more upset."

"Upset enough to do things he would not normally do?"

"Yeah."

"Or to say things he would not normally say?"

"Probably so, but that doesn't mean he was crazy."

"Are you a psychiatrist now?"

"No, but I looked into the man's eyes. Right there, at the scene, and that's something not even your expert can claim to have done. I looked into his eyes and I didn't see a crazy man. I saw a murderer."

"Objection!" Ben shouted.

But the witness continued. "I looked into those eyes and I saw someone who wanted Detective Sentz dead. At any cost."

"Objection!" Ben repeated. "The witness—"

"He's a murderer!" Conway continued. "He tried to kill Sentz right there in the ravine. And he finished the job a few days later! It was all planned." He thrust his finger toward Ben. "And that lawyer was part of it! They planned the whole thing!"

"*Objection!*"

"It's true! He saw his lawyer just before he went to the hotel! It was all planned! All of it!"

By now the judge was pounding his gavel thunderously, ordering the witness to be silent, but Ben knew the damage had been done.

The gallery was in turmoil. Ben saw reporters rushing toward the back door. There was just enough time to get this latest bit on the five o'clock news broadcasts, reporting everything Officer Conway had said as if it were fact.

The worst part was, Ben knew he had let it happen. He had opened the door and Conway had jumped right in.

Ben glanced at Dennis. He looked worried, and no amount of coldness or cleverness was sufficient to mask it.

Then he glanced at Guillerman. The DA was smiling. Not gloating, nothing that overt. But pleased.

And he should be. He had created the fine distinction the prosecution needed to win this case.

Dennis had been angry when he went up to that hotel room, yes, but not crazy. Just determined. Murderous and determined. A critical difference.

The difference between a man who gets off on a charge of temporary insanity and a man who gets the death penalty.

THREE

Our Adversaries Are Insane

CHAPTER
20

BEN HUNCHED OVER the living room table. His back hurt and his eyes were red and watery. He'd spent the entire weekend working from sunup to sundown—and not sleeping much or well in between. But he couldn't altogether blame the condition of his eyes on that. In truth, he was mildly allergic to cats, including the one that was currently sitting in his lap. He and Giselle had spent many years together, ever since Christina first gave her to him. And she had been a great comfort to him. But not to his eyes. They still reddened every time she came near. And if he petted her and then made the mistake of rubbing his eyes . . . Visine alert!

He leaned back and stretched, careful not to dislodge Giselle from his lap. He had not covered nearly as much material as he had hoped to get through before the trial resumed tomorrow. This case was moving too fast, much faster than he had anticipated. The speed of light, compared to the glacial pace of the usual pretrial and trial process. The prosecution had already rested its case, and now the burden was on him to come up with something to salvage the mess.

Whether he cared to admit it or not, the last day of the trial had been a disaster. The prosecution had set him up and he'd fallen for it. They'd dealt with the defendant and his alleged defense perfectly. Ben would have a very difficult time trying to undo all the damage that had been done. And Dennis's life hung in the balance. Whatever might or might not have happened, he shouldn't be executed. Unfortunately, the burden of making sure that didn't happen rested squarely on Ben's shoulders.

And Christina wondered why he didn't sleep well . . .

No one had actually seen Dennis pull the trigger, but he knew he couldn't rely on that, not when the prosecution could put him in Sentz's room and his prints and DNA were all over the weapon. All their hopes were riding on the plea of temporary insanity. And what did they have to support that? Some medical testimony. Dennis had passed out, but Ben knew that could be spun in a number of different directions, including some that were not helpful. Their psychiatric witness was strong, but juries were wary of paid experts who purported to tell them what had really happened. In the final analysis, it was going to depend upon whether they liked Dennis, whether they felt sorry for him. If they did, they had a mechanism for allowing him to escape punishment. And if not . . .

Ben checked his watch. Christina had suggested a movie earlier, but he had insisted on working. He knew the film would be wasted; he would never stop thinking about the case long enough to enjoy himself. For that matter, he would've liked to call Mike, see if he wanted to go get a bite, catch up on the latest with his nonromance with Lieutenant Baxter. But it wouldn't be fair to Mike. He would end up talking about the case, which would put Mike in an uncomfortable position since he was a member of the police force. No, better to stay home. If he was going to be obsessed, he might as well be obsessed in a semiproductive way.

He heard Christina shout from the kitchen. "Haven't you worked enough? Take a break."

"I've still got tons to do."

"You work too much!"

"We're in the middle of a trial, remember? This is how we support ourselves. We work long hours in the courtroom so we can goof off . . . well . . ."

"Yes? The woman who still hasn't had a honeymoon is waiting for you to complete the sentence."

"You know what I mean."

The swinging doors separating the living room from the kitchen swung open. "All right, F. Lee Bailey. It's dinnertime."

He pushed away from the table. "Perfect timing." He glanced at the plate she slid under his nose. "And the perfect meal, too." An egg sandwich, just the way he liked it. None of that fancy-schmancy egg salad stuff. Just scrambled eggs on mayonnaise between two slices of toasted bread. Heaven!

Ben took a huge bite out of the corner. "Mmm. So good."

"I thought you were probably ready for some quality nourishment," Christina replied, with only a hint of sarcasm. "I initially thought grilled cheese, that other great favorite of yours and others with a ten-year-old's taste buds. But that would sit too heavy."

"I owe you one," he managed as he chugged down another bite. In normal practice, Ben and Christina shared the cooking duties. But when a trial was on, that changed, even when Christina was second-chairing. He knew her contributions to the trial were absolutely as important as his, maybe more so. But her obsession level was considerably less, and that was a positive thing. They made a good team. He could obsess, and she could scramble the eggs.

"Maybe some coffee to go with it?" he mumbled, his mouth full.

"You know what coffee does to you."

"I need the caffeine. I have to stay up late. There's much more I want to do."

"Yes, and then you won't be able to sleep because you've had so much coffee, and then you'll be whining because you can't sleep, and then your stomach will hurt because you're allergic to coffee, et cetera, et cetera."

He wiped his face with a napkin, grinning. "You think you know me pretty well, don't you?"

"As a matter of fact, yes. Much better than you know yourself. How about a Sprite?"

"I guess that will have to do. And if it's not too much trouble . . ."

She rolled her eyes. "Chocolate milk?"

"If you don't mind."

"I suppose I can't deny a man his comfort food in the middle of a murder trial." She pulled a face. "Eggs and chocolate milk. Pardon me while I vomit!" She started toward the kitchen, then stopped at the television. "The evening news is about to start. Mind if I turn it on?"

"Is there any point? It's just going to be more of the same."

"More of the same I can deal with. I'm concerned about that last cheap shot Conway took on the witness stand."

"Oh, police officers hate defense attorneys. They'll take any shot they can get."

"True. But Guillerman doesn't do anything without a reason. I think he had that witness prepared to deliver his fatal harpoon. I don't believe anything there happened spontaneously. And how did he know you saw Dennis before he went to see Sentz?" She clicked on the console television.

". . . the News on Seven. This is Annie Rhodes." The young woman holding the microphone was attractive, but she downplayed it with a stern expression. "Startling new developments in the murder of one of Tulsa County's most trusted and honored police officers . . ."

Ben frowned. "How do they know it was murder?"

"Shhh!"

". . . took an unexpected turn Friday when one of the prosecution's chief witnesses testified that Dennis Thomas planned the murder of Detective Christopher Sentz in advance and, furthermore, that he did so in conspiracy with his defense attorney and current U.S. senator, Benjamin Kincaid."

Ben frowned. "Didn't she forget to say *allegedly*?"

Christina waved him down. "Shhh!"

". . . but Channel Seven has learned that Dennis Thomas actually spoke to Senator Kincaid in his office on the day of the shooting, before the murder was committed. Evidence of conspiracy? Some Tulsans believe so."

Ben watched as the image cut to a video of someone Ben didn't recognize. Her name appeared at the bottom of the screen.

"I just happened to be at Two Warren Place that day when I was approached by a twenty-four-year-old man who said that he worked in Kincaid's office . . ."

"Huh?" Ben screeched. "Who?"

Christina scowled. "No one that age works for us. I mean, I may still look twenty-four, but I'm not." She pondered. "Maybe that kid who delivers sandwiches saw him."

". . . and said that he wanted to consult with a leading defense attorney about how he might get away with murder. Apparently he and Kincaid talked for some time. That's probably when the topic of temporary insanity was raised first."

"That's not true!" Ben yelled at the glass box. "I mean, it is, but—but not the way they're making it sound!"

The television image reverted to the female reporter. "There you have it, John. An alleged eyewitness to the premeditated murder that robbed Tulsa of a fine officer and a family of its father."

"Eyewitness? It was hearsay!" Ben said, outraged.

"Speculation. All she did was repeat what someone else supposedly told her. Can you get away with saying anything on the news if you get someone else to say it for you?"

"This evidence—and I use the term lightly—wouldn't be admissible in the most informal court hearing," Christina noted. "But apparently hearsay is good enough for the evening news."

The reporter continued. "We consulted the district attorney for his reaction to this startling development in the case that has already shocked and horrified Tulsans."

This time the on-screen image shifted to David Guillerman, apparently sitting at his desk. He spoke hesitantly, as if he hated to comment at all, which would probably be useful when he had to explain to the judge why he'd violated the gag order.

"Of course I'm shocked and appalled by the new information Channel Seven has brought to light in this case. I had no idea."

"Is it my imagination, or is his nose getting longer?" Ben asked.

"Shhh!"

Guillerman continued. "I prefer to try cases in the courtroom, not the media, but this is unacceptable behavior, made all the worse because the attorney is also our elected—well, our appointed representative in the U.S. Senate. The peddling of influence has already turned many people off government and caused enormous cynicism in this country. To have someone actually collaborating with criminals, just to make legal fees, is truly shocking. I hope the state bar association is paying attention. I understand that Kincaid's colleague in the Senate, Senator Hardwick, is preparing a formal motion to censure him as soon as Congress reconvenes."

"Hardwick's a Republican! He hates me!"

"Which pretty much guarantees his participation in

this lynching." Christina shut the television off. "This changes the trial landscape."

"No joke. This is horrible! Those TV people totally trashed me."

"What do you expect from tabloid news channels? You're famous. You're a target. That's how they pay their bills."

"They said I conspired with Dennis!"

"Honestly, how long did you think you could stay in politics before someone flung some mud your way? This is probably overdue."

"But he said I helped plan a murder!"

"Which was probably a mistake. Guillerman took it too far. If he had simply said you had some idea of Dennis's mind-set, he could've done almost as much damage, with a lot more credibility." She cleared her throat. "Since that's more or less true. But helped plan a murder? You? With your record? I don't think there are many people gullible enough to buy that. Even if it does come from an attractive news reader."

"But I have no opportunity to defend myself."

"You will. As soon as the judge clears it, you can make a statement. Explain that at no time did Dennis say he planned or even wanted to kill anyone. This will blow over. In the end, all anyone's going to remember from this mess is who won the trial."

"I hope you're right." He clenched his fists together. "It just makes me so mad! They intentionally misled their viewers. They melodramatized the facts. And everyone in the city was watching."

"Exactly." Christina looked straight into his eyes. "Do you not see? That's what you can use to your advantage. It may look grim now, but this could actually turn out to be the biggest break you've had in this entire impossible trial."

CHAPTER
21

LOVING WAS NOT excited about the prospect of a return visit to Scene of the Crime. He'd come to this bar almost every night this week. Wasn't all he had done, of course. He'd been surreptitiously following some of the officers who were at the hotel the night Sentz died. He'd run deep background checks on Sentz, Conway, and Shaw, as well as Dennis Thomas and his late wife. He'd bugged the police locker room, which was probably illegal and almost certainly would be fatal if they found out. He'd talked to everyone present when Joslyn Thomas was found and everyone at the hotel on the fateful day.

But all of that had produced nothing. So here he was, back at Scene of the Crime, hoping to hit a home run when no one was even pitching. He knew Ben had been cross-examining the police witnesses, and he would have loved to have brought Ben something useful, but so far it hadn't happened. He had to come up with something before this trial was over and done.

His first visit here had been mildly productive, in a macho confrontational sort of way. But the follow-ups had not fulfilled the promise of the original. Officer Shaw had obviously put the word out. No one was to talk to Loving, or anyone else associated with Ben Kincaid. And so far the other cops had toed the line. Loving had sat in silence for several nights running. Not stirring up any trouble, but not stirring up anything else, either.

A more sensible person would probably give up, but sensible had never been Loving's strong suit. Ben needed help. That was good enough for him. Loving frankly couldn't care less about this Thomas guy. He didn't hold much with killers, crazy or not. But Ben he cared about. Ben had reached out to him when he really needed help, when the rest of the world was heaping scorn and abuse. He would do anything for the Skipper. And if that meant one more miserable night at Scene of the Crime, so be it.

"Psst!"

Loving looked both ways. He didn't see anything. But he supposed if the person hissing at him wanted to be seen, he wouldn't be hissing at him.

"Psst!"

Loving followed the general sound to a grove of trees a little ways off the road, still a good distance from the bar. He could hear the hooting and the music and the blare of the big-screen television, but there was no chance that anyone hanging out there could have heard the hisser.

"Am I hot or cold?" Loving said as he entered the grove.

"Over here."

Loving walked slowly into the darkness. The scant moonlight eventually cast its glow on a man around thirty years of age. He was a police officer. Loving had seen him before, although he wasn't sure they'd ever been formally introduced. What was his name? Something Hispanic, but Loving couldn't quite place it . . .

"I'm Joe Torres."

"Good to meet you." Loving extended his hand, but the other man did not shake it. "You wantin' me?"

"Yes. Are you still investigating the Sentz case?"

"You know somethin'?"

"Maybe. I was the front desk clerk most of the times Dennis Thomas came in asking for help."

Loving eased in closer. "What happened?"

"It's all pretty much as they all say. Thomas was desperate. He begged, pleaded, argued. Sentz wouldn't relent. Nothing seemed to matter. He said there were no grounds for opening a missing persons investigation, so he didn't."

"Was anyone else involved in this decision?"

"I never saw anyone out of the ordinary in the station. But it did seem weird. And I heard Thomas say he thought someone else was pulling Sentz's strings."

"Dennis said he saw another man in the police station once when you were there. He didn't see the guy's face, but Dennis thought he was tellin' Sentz to lay off. Did you see anyone there?"

"No."

"Do you know who that might've been?"

"No. But I wouldn't be—I mean—" Torres stopped, started again. "I know Sentz said he was going by the book. And it's true. Technically there were no grounds for action. But we all know that those rules are written mostly to give officers the ability to allocate manpower as necessary and to get rid of crackpots. Cases that aren't really cases. Thomas wasn't a crackpot. He was intelligent, resourceful, and obviously very worried about his wife."

"Still, if the rules are on the books . . ."

"Sentz had discretion. I've seen him use it before. If he wanted to start an investigation, he'd start an investigation. He'd find a way to make it good."

"But he never did that for Dennis Thomas."

"Exactly. Not even after seven days, when it was pretty obvious something had happened to her. That part was . . . unusual."

"Why did you think he was stonewallin' Thomas?"

"I don't know. But I can't help but think there was a reason. That's why I finally got something going myself."

"*You* did?"

Torres nodded. "I got one of the other detectives to sign off on it. Someone who didn't know the whole story. Sentz was furious when he found out. But we did find Joslyn Thomas."

"Not in time."

"Yeah." Torres's head lowered. "Not in time."

"And Dennis Thomas attacked Sentz."

Torres frowned. "He wasn't the only one who wanted to."

"What do you mean?"

"Sentz came in angry, furious. He was out for my blood. He was hurling abuse and outrage. But the fact is, Joslyn Thomas was in danger and we found her. It would've been a good time for him to be contrite and admit his mistake. Instead he came in like he didn't care about the woman who had just died. All he cared about was that someone went over his head. It was just twisted. Didn't make any sense."

Loving pondered that a long moment. "And Thomas attacked him?"

"Yeah. But Sentz went after him beforehand. Threw him down, scraped up his face. He was the first one to get physical."

"What about all those ugly things Thomas supposedly said? The threats."

"He said them. But put it in context. The man's stalling caused his wife enormous pain. He acted angry that we found her. He physically manhandled him. He had him arrested!" Torres shook his head. "I think I would've said a lot more than that if it had been me."

"Why do you think Sentz was so determined not to investigate? And so angry when you did?"

"I don't know. It was weird. No one will say anything now, because they don't want to get crosswise with Guillerman. But it was really bizarre."

"What about that deal at the hotel? The stakeout. There had to be somethin' goin' on there."

"I don't know much about that. It was very secret. Certainly nothing they'd share with a desk clerk."

"How did they pick the men who would be involved?"

Torres moved in closer, dropping his voice another notch, as if what he was about to say was particularly sensitive. "It was all the Benedict's Bunch. Sentz. Shaw. Conway. A couple of others."

"The what?" Loving had been investigating this case a long time, but this was a new bit of terminology. "What did you call them?"

"It's a reference to St. Benedict's. The hospital."

The hospital where Joslyn Thomas worked. "What did those cops have to do with the hospital?"

"They were moonlighting there."

"As what?"

"The word was, they were security."

Off-duty cops working as hospital security? He supposed it was possible.

"But I think there was more to it than that."

"Why?"

"I don't know exactly. I could just tell they were up to something. The whispers. Furtive looks. Sudden disappearances. Covering for one another."

"Cops always stick up for one another."

"This went way beyond that." Torres wrung his hands together. "Look, it's true I'm new on the force and I don't know all there is to know."

"Sounds like you know a heck of a lot."

"I worked hard to become a cop. I'm proud of where I am. I'm the first guy in my whole family to go to college. First to wear a uniform, you know? It means something to me. And I don't like it when—when some-one else tarnishes what I worked so hard to get."

"So what are you tellin' me about these men, Joe?"

"I don't have any proof."

"But . . . ?"

Torres inhaled deeply. "I thought they were dirty. I think they were involved in something dirty. Maybe that's why they were at the hotel. I wouldn't be sur-prised if it explains this whole mess."

"How long had this been going on?"

"I don't know. Long enough."

"And you think it has something to do with Joslyn Thomas?"

"I wouldn't be surprised. Especially after Sentz repeat-edly refused to look for her. That was not something any normal red-blooded person would do. Unless he were covering something up."

"Are you sayin' what I think you're sayin'?" Loving moved in tighter. Despite the darkness, he managed to look the man straight in the eye. "First Joslyn Thomas disappears. Now the husband is on track to disappear. And every time, the same guys are involved."

"That's how I see it."

No wonder he hadn't come up with anything. He was totally barking up the wrong tree. And so was Ben.

"Who did they report to at the hospital?"

"Sorry. I don't know."

"What department?"

"I still don't know."

"Any hints? Clues? Anything that might tell me where to look?"

"I'm sorry." He glanced nervously over his shoulder. "I think I should go now."

"Wait." Loving pulled a card out of his back pocket. "Before you leave. Take this. I want you to see Ben Kincaid."

"I can't do that."

"He'll take care of you."

Torres began backing away. "I told you, I can't do that."

"It's important. He needs to hear this."

"I can't testify."

"Then he'll have you swear out an affidavit."

"No!"

"We can protect you."

"You can't. Not enough."

"At least talk to him. Or talk to Thomas."

"No!" Torres moved backward, fast.

"It's important, Joe. A man's life is on the line."

"I won't testify."

"He can subpoena you."

"No!" Torres turned and began to run.

"What are you afraid of? Losing your job?"

"I'm afraid of losing my life!" Torres shouted back. And then he disappeared into the night.

Loving didn't bother chasing him. What would be the point? Even if he caught him, he couldn't make him talk. And the truth was, Torres was right to be concerned for his life. Smart, even. Cops did not like being ratted on, especially by one of their own. Other people came after cops, they circled the wagons. But when it was one of their own mounting the challenge . . .

Well, he had a right to be concerned.

Loving checked his watch. Hell with the bar. He wasn't likely to get more than he already had. He'd drive crosstown to St. Benedict's. He had no idea what he was looking for. But he needed to find something. Something Ben could use in court.

Time was running out fast. If he didn't come up with something useful soon, it would be too late.

CHAPTER
22

"A MISTRIAL?" Dennis looked back at Ben, perplexed. "Why would I want that? We've been in trial more than a week!"

"There are a million possible reasons. You're the defendant. And you're not currently in jail. Time is on your side."

"Do you think we're losing? Is that why you want to start over?"

"No. I have no idea what the jury is thinking. But we have taken some hits. This could be our chance to start from scratch."

Ben had asked Dennis to come to the courthouse conference room early so they could discuss this all-important issue before he saw the judge. Mistrial was a delicate subject. A corporate defendant will always go for it; given the time value of money, the longer they can delay paying a judgment, the better. But with human beings, there were many more emotional issues. Humans wanted closure, resolution. Even if the trial process was nerve-wracking, even if they were uncertain about the result, there was always a strong desire to get it over with.

"Guillerman made a critical error when he spoke to the reporters. Judge McPartland issued a no-exceptions gag order. No comments to the press. Ironically, it was Guillerman who first raised the issue, because he was tired of our press conferences. Of course, Guillerman will claim he wasn't commenting on the case as such—only on the breaking news story. But McPartland isn't an idiot. He won't be happy."

"And the judge will give us a mistrial over that?"

"He might. We'll have to impanel the jury, ask questions. If any of them watched the news report, they're off the jury. If more than six of them saw the news report, then we don't have enough alternates. We have to start over. And if one of the jurors mentioned it to the others, the entire jury pool is tainted. Automatic mistrial."

"How long before a new trial would begin?"

"Depends on the judge's schedule. I'm thinking it would be a good long while. Assuming the case remains with Judge McPartland."

"It could go to another judge?"

"It could go to another county. Or another state." Ben leaned across the conference table. "We could ask for a change of venue, arguing that the media coverage has irredeemably tainted the local jury pool."

"Does that happen often?"

"No. But it does happen, usually in high-profile cases. This is why Timothy McVeigh was tried in Colorado, not Oklahoma."

"Do we have any idea what kind of judge we might get somewhere else?"

"No. Potluck."

"Would it be an improvement?"

"Depends on how you think McPartland is leaning. And I have no idea. He's kept his cards pretty close to his vest so far."

"So basically, asking for a mistrial is a big crapshoot."

"Basically, yes."

Dennis rubbed his fingers against his forehead. For once, the trial strategist who held all the answers seemed uncertain. "What do you think we should do?"

Ben took a deep breath. "I think I have to ask for a mistrial. I think it would be malpractice not to ask for a mistrial."

"I'm not going to sue you for malpractice."

"Thanks. But what if we have to appeal, you know? If we . . . we . . ."

"Lose?"

"Yeah. That. If the appellate court finds my representation incompetent, it would destroy me as a lawyer. And it could interfere with our appeal."

Dennis ran his hands through his precisely coiffed hair. "I don't know, Ben. I really just want to get this over with."

"I know you do. But we have to be smart about this."

"I suppose."

This was where the conversation was going to get sticky. If Ben had his way, he wouldn't go here at all. But he had no choice.

"Dennis . . . there's one more possibility I have to raise. If I ask for a mistrial, it's possible we could get even more than a delay of the game. We could conceivably win the whole shooting match."

"What? How?"

"A tainted jury pool is one thing. Definitely grounds for a mistrial. But if the judge finds deliberate misconduct on the part of the prosecution . . ."

"Is that possible?"

Ben shrugged. "Guillerman obviously knew something. He planted the seed with Officer Conway. He didn't have to appear on that news broadcast—but he did."

"Okay, so he's guilty of misconduct. What does that get us?"

"A mistrial, for sure. But in this scenario, there might be a little more. Here, the mistrial is the result of deliberate acts by the state. That being the case, the court could find that double jeopardy has attached."

"And if double jeopardy has attached . . . ?"

"You can't be tried again for the same offense. Not even in a capital murder case. In other words, you go free."

Dennis's lips parted. "No."

"It's a long shot. A remote chance. Judge McPartland obviously will not be eager to dismiss a high-profile case involving the death of a police officer. But it is possible."

"And I would be acquitted."

"In effect."

Dennis's eyes seemed to draw inward. "But without a finding of innocence. Without ever really being tried."

"True."

Dennis sat up, squared his shoulders. "I don't know if I like that idea."

"I understand. But you can't expect to be exonerated by a court. Even if you were found not guilty, some people will never believe it. Especially not if you get off on a charge of temporary insanity."

Dennis remained strangely quiet. "Ben," he said at last, "I don't know if I've even said this to you before, but . . . I didn't kill Detective Sentz."

"I thought you didn't remember what happened."

"I don't. But I still . . . I can't believe I would do that. Even under the circumstances."

"I understand," Ben said. Though, he thought silently, *your subsequent belief proves nothing about what happened.*

"You know . . . this trial has been very hard."

"I'm sure."

"Are you? Sometimes I think you believe—and I know Christina does—that my willingness to plan and scheme and orchestrate the trial means I'm a cold, rotten person who wants to kill and get away with it."

"Oh, no—"

"You don't have to bother denying it. I know the score."

"Maybe you were a little more . . . present than most defendants."

"But I needed that. You know?" He looked at Ben with pleading eyes, and it occurred to Ben that this might have been the most vulnerable he had seen this man since the whole drama began. "That gave me an edge. When I lost Joslyn, my world was shattered. Into pieces, tiny little shards of glass where a life had once been. I didn't know what to do. I had to distract myself. First with talk of revenge. Then with plans to escape punishment."

He looked away. Ben could see his eyes were watering. "I'm starting to lose it, Ben. I really am. I can feel the heat, the fire, the . . . the anger, ebbing away. And if I lose that, I don't know what I'll have left. I can't get through another trial. And I can't live in a world filled with people who think I'm a murderer. I—I—" He shook his head. "I don't know if I can live at all."

"Hey now." Ben placed his hand on the man's shoulder and squeezed. "Let's not talk like that."

"I'm just telling you how I feel."

"Let me make the motion, Dennis. Then we'll take it from there. Okay?"

"I guess. I—" He looked up at Ben with sorrowful eyes. "I trust you."

Ben nodded, took his briefcase, and headed for the judge's chambers.

Why had Dennis said that? Ben would have rather heard "I hate you."

What Dennis had said instead was the worst curse a client could possibly lay on his lawyer's shoulders. Especially in a capital murder case.

CHAPTER
23

BEN HAD NOT been inside Judge McPartland's chambers before, so he was surprised at what he found. Judges were free to decorate in any way they wanted, but most kept it on the conservative side. Members of the judiciary must be distinguished, it seemed, even away from prying eyes. Decorating tended toward Western art, macho Remingtons and such, with the occasional cowboy or OU football paraphernalia.

McPartland liked dogs. Ben hadn't known it before, but the evidence was all around him. He had at least four, judging from the photographs, and apparently took them to shows on a regular basis. There was Judge McPartland, motioning to his Pomeranian to sit up on cue. There was the mighty Doberman strutting down the walkway. Even a fluffy white poodle, and if Ben wasn't mistaken, it had painted toenails. They all appeared groomed and brushed, and in one case even clothed. Their pedigrees hung on the walls, as did their graduation certificates from obedience school.

Ben found himself liking the judge a lot more than he had before, even though, technically, Ben was a cat person. Still, it was good to see the judge had outside interests. After a week of criminal trials, a dog show must seem very relaxing.

They only had to wait a few minutes before the judge arrived. McPartland did not appear surprised to see Ben and District Attorney Guillerman waiting in his chambers. Not surprised, but not pleased, either.

"Let me guess," he said, leaning back expansively in his padded recliner. "Senator Kincaid has a motion."

"Darn tootin'," Ben said curtly.

"And the state opposes?"

The DA shrugged. "I don't know what we're talking about yet."

"Mr. Guillerman, I've been a judge a long time. Don't play games with me."

"Honest, Judge, I don't—"

"Well then, let me inform you." The judge leaned forward, his brow sharply creased. Ben got the impression that Guillerman might have made a major tactical blunder. "Do you recall a while back when we were selecting a jury?"

"Certainly."

"And do you recall the conclusion, when I mentioned to you both that I didn't want any more discussion of the case with the press?"

Guillerman pointed at Ben. "He was the one who kept calling the press conferences."

"Yes, and you intruded whenever you could, but it doesn't matter. The point is, I issued a gag order. And you have violated it."

Guillerman pressed his hands against his starched white shirt. "I didn't call a press conference. All I did was answer a few questions."

"From the press."

"And they didn't even pertain to the murder trial. They were about the defense attorney."

McPartland was not impressed. "And you thought that would have no relevance to the trial?"

"Not really."

"Amazing that a man with your naïveté could survive so long in the world of politics."

"I just do my job." Guillerman shook his head with dismay. "I'll admit, I had no idea the media would sensationalize my remarks on the evening news. Very tabloid. Might as well be *Entertainment Tonight*."

"I guess you've never watched the evening news before."

"Well . . . I stay pretty busy at work."

McPartland drew in his chin. This was the most overt display of irritation Ben had seen since the trial began. "You know, I'm enjoying this inane repartee, but it's essentially irrelevant. I issued a gag order and you violated it."

"I don't recall you ever using the words *gag order*. You just said not to talk to reporters about the case."

"That's what a gag order is, counsel. You're making me wonder if you went to law school. Except I'm pretty sure that's a requirement for becoming district attorney, and last I heard, you were teaching night classes."

"Your honor, I mean no disrespect. But I maintain that I did not violate your order because I did not discuss the substance of the case."

"You told a city full of couch potatoes that the defendant conspired with his attorney to get away with murder, which is basically your whole prosecution theory. That's commenting on the case. And it's exactly the same line your man was dishing from the witness stand last week."

Guillerman chose to remain silent. Ben was glad he was not in his shoes. The judge was displeased, and that never worked in a lawyer's favor, as he knew all too well.

Judge McPartland ran his hand back and forth over his chin. "You know what this means? I'm going to have to sequester the jury now. I've got no choice. The press won't let go of this anytime soon. I heard about it on the radio driving to work this morning, and I was listening to a hip-hop station. The jurors will not be happy. And I don't blame them. City hall won't be too pleased, either. Sequestration costs a fortune." He leaned back in his chair. "The jurors will go into a major tailspin."

"Are the accommodations provided that bad?"

"No, they'll stay at the Ambassador Hotel down the road. But these people have already given up days of their lives and expect to lose more before it's over. Imagine their reaction when they find out they don't get to go home anymore."

"Who knows?" Guillerman said optimistically. "Some may be happy about it."

"No, Mr. District Attorney, no one will be happy about it, not even the housewife with six kids who hasn't had a vacation in eight years. And let me tell you why. Two words: no television."

Ben gulped. "No TVs at the hotel?"

"We have them removed. Can't take the risk, especially not when coverage is all over the airwaves. So now imagine the scenario: away from home, away from family—no glass teat. Horrifying, huh?"

"Dreadful."

"It gets worse. We take out the minibars, too."

"No!"

"Have to. State can't buy liquor for anyone. Against the law."

"Do they at least get pay-per-view?"

"No. I'm telling you, Uncle Sam can be a cruel master. But I'll do this to those poor public-minded citizens to cure this mess you've created."

Ben raised a hand. "Shouldn't we consider my motion first?"

"Good point. Because you're hoping there won't be any need for the jury." He thumbed through a stack of papers on his desk. "I assume you're moving for a mistrial."

"Yes, your honor." Ben cleared his throat. "Um, sort of."

McPartland peered at him over his bifocals. "Sort of?"

"I am moving for a mistrial, your honor, but specifically I'm asking for a finding of prosecutorial misconduct and a ruling that double jeopardy has attached."

Judge McPartland gaped. "You want me to set your man free?"

"In effect."

"Do you know what those reporters you two are so fond of would do to me if I complied?"

Ben shrugged. "It's not your fault, your honor. If there's been deliberate prosecutorial misconduct, you have no choice."

"The rank-and-file Joe Beer Can NASCAR pork-rind-eating voter won't see it that way."

"I understand. But of course the court has to rule on the law, not the potential professional ramifications."

"Of course."

"And I know we can count on your honor to do just that."

McPartland pointed a finger Ben's way. "My momma told me never to count on anything till I see it in writing. That was good advice." He swiveled his chair around and stared out the expansive window at downtown Tulsa. "What if I declare a mistrial but simply order a new trial?"

"We're not asking for that relief, sir."

"You're telling me you wouldn't accept a new trial?"

"No, your honor."

He looked incredulous. Guillerman appeared more than a bit surprised himself. "May I ask why?"

"Because my client doesn't want that. He's willing to accept a double jeopardy ruling—though he isn't happy about it. He wants a jury to declare his innocence."

"Every defendant does, counsel. Few get it."

"But he does not want a new trial at some point in the distant future. This trial has been hard on him, especially coming so close on the heels of the loss of his wife. He wants it over, one way or the other."

McPartland's eyes narrowed. "Counsel, is this some kind of twisted trial tactic?"

"No, sir. And I don't think I'm violating any confidences to say that this is not what I recommended. But it is what he wants."

"All or nothing, huh?"

"Exactly."

Judge McPartland swiveled back around to his desk. "You boys are not making my job easier, you know that?"

Guillerman smiled his million-watt smile. Seemed he could be charming even when he was under fire. "Do we ever, Judge?"

"No." He took a deep breath. "Well, the first thing you should know is, I brought the jury in early this morning and quizzed them with a court reporter present. Only two say they saw any of the news coverage of this case over the weekend."

"They're lying," Ben said succinctly.

"Very likely. I know I'd be watching if I were them. How could they not? They are human beings, after all. But what I did not get, as I questioned them, was a sense that anyone had changed their mind because of what they saw, or that anyone's mind was made up, or that the jury pool was tainted. Even the two who admitted seeing the coverage said it didn't affect them, and I believe them. One of them turned it off before it was over."

"Your honor—"

"Let me finish. I'm going to remove the two jurors who admit to seeing the televised story. I will sequester the rest. I will give them strict instructions not to consider anything they didn't get in the courtroom. And I'm also going to instruct them to disregard that last little salvo from your witness, Mr. Guillerman." He gave the prosecutor a harsh look. "I'm hoping that will get the message across. Whether they know what the witness was implying or not, they will decide this case on the relevant evidence presented at trial."

"That works for me," Guillerman said. And no doubt it did, Ben thought. He was getting away with prosecutorial misconduct with virtually no substantive penalty.

"Your honor," Ben said, "I respectfully object. This is not enough. We're talking about deliberate misconduct."

"But for what purpose?"

The question took Ben aback. "What do you mean?"

"Well, see, Senator, I've read the law on this subject. Reviewed it just this morning, in fact. And prosecutorial misconduct doesn't necessarily mandate a mistrial. That extreme sanction only kicks in if the misconduct was engaged in purposefully."

Ben frowned. "I hardly think he gave that interview by accident."

"Agreed. But it has to have been done for the purpose of causing a mistrial. Then it would offend public policy to give him what he wanted. A dismissal is the appropriate penalty. But I don't think the district attorney gave that interview because he wanted a mistrial. Do you?"

"Well . . ."

"Why would he? His case went well and you haven't even started yours yet. No, he wasn't after a mistrial. He did it to win. He did it to bury you before you've even started. Didn't you, Mr. Guillerman?"

"Um, well . . ."

McPartland chuckled. "Yeah. Tough question. Assumes facts not in evidence. At least that's your story."

"But your honor," Ben said, scooting forward in his chair, "this was a serious and deliberate offense."

"Oh, I don't think it did your case that much harm, Mr. Kincaid. And that's the main thing. Because as those of us who went to law school know, not all error leads to a mistrial—not even violations of gag orders. The effect has to be prejudicial to a significant degree. There has to be a showing that the prejudice was great enough to affect the outcome of the trial. And I don't think that's the case here. The prosecution alleged something they can't prove. So what? That's what they do. You'll probably do some of that yourself, huh, Mr. Kincaid?"

"I would never—"

"Unless you're planning to put on evidence to support a possible finding of suicide. Which I very much doubt."

Ben fell silent.

"Good. So we all know where we stand. The jury will be sequestered, and the motion is denied."

Both lawyers rose to their feet and started toward the door.

"I'm not finished yet." The judge looked Guillerman straight in the eye. "This will not happen again. Do you understand me? There is a gag order in place. A total and absolute gag order. Any further violation *will* result in a mistrial with double jeopardy attached. This defendant will go free and it will be your fault. Plus I will personally recommend disbarment, in writing." He lowered his voice. "And I would imagine your shot at reelection would not be enhanced. Understand, Mr. District Attorney?"

"Yes, sir. I do."

"Good. Anything else?"

Ben leaned forward. "I want to call an Officer Torres to the stand. My investigator tells me he may have relevant information, and he's been mentioned—"

McPartland cut him off. "Is he on your witness list?"

"No, I just found out—"

"Then forget it."

"But the prosecution witnesses have mentioned him and—"

"You're the one who wants to be a stickler for the

rules, Mr. Kincaid. He's not on your list. So you're not going to call him. Anything else?"

Ben smoldered silently.

"Fine." McPartland waved his hands at them. "Now get out of my chambers. Go forth and sin no more."

BEN STOPPED Guillerman in the hallway before they got to the courtroom and the reporters. "Tough guy" wasn't really his best mode, but he knew this situation called for a little grit. Or at the very least a furrowed brow.

"I don't appreciate you spreading that crap about me to the press," Ben said, blocking his path.

Guillerman smiled with such amiability as to be truly annoying. "Don't take it personally, Ben. It's just trial tactics."

"Don't take it personally? You told people that I conspired to commit murder!"

"No, all I did was say I was shocked by the news reporter's story. That doesn't make it true."

"You're mincing words."

"But you've got to understand something, too." The smile faded. "You're representing a cop killer. Most people take that pretty seriously. Including me."

"So you're saying you were justified in violating a judicial order?"

"All I'm saying is, if you want to remain in office, you'd better snap on your political weather vane. Because the wind is blowing against you on this one and the elections are not far away. You'll never be able to raise funds if you cling to this case. And it takes a lot of money—"

"To run for reelection these days. Yes, I remember." Ben wasn't finished. "Thanks to you, I've got a call from the bar association."

"What did you expect? Sometimes I think they spend more time going after lawyers than they do promoting them these days, apparently never noticing how much damage they do to the profession in the process." He took a breath. "Of course, that was off the record. Don't want them to find an excuse to come after me."

"I want you to make a public apology."

"Ben, I can't do that. For starters, it might violate the judge's gag order. Furthermore—"

"At least admit that you yourself have no evidence of any premeditation or conspiracy."

"With a capital trial pending? I'm sorry, Ben, but you're dreaming. I can't do it. And honestly, it wouldn't do you a bit of good if I did. Those evening news shows love it when you're being accused. But me calling a press conference to say something good about you?" He made a dismissive snort. "They probably wouldn't even show up."

"It's a matter of principle."

"No, Ben, it's not. It's about winning and losing. Why do prosecutors brag about their win/loss records? Why do athletes take steroids? Why do politicians claim we won wars when we won nothing? Americans love winners." He paused. "Until they get too successful. Then we love to watch them fall. It's the American way."

Ben stepped out of his path. "You're a cynical so-and-so, you know it?"

Guillerman passed on down the hallway. "Maybe. But I got elected to my office, unlike you, and I plan to retain mine, probably also unlike you. And I'm going to win this case." He stopped and gave Ben a parting look. "If you thought what's happened so far was bad, stay tuned."

CHAPTER
24

BEN SAT at the defendant's table waiting for the judge to enter the courtroom. No one was talking. Dennis was absorbed in his own thoughts. Ben wasn't sure if he was pleased or displeased that the judge turned down the mistrial motion. Probably a little of both. But it left him exactly where he had been before—hanging on to this case with only the most tenuous of tethers.

Christina was keeping herself busy, as usual. With the defense case about to begin, there were a million things to manage. Making sure the witnesses were on tap and prepared. Making sure all the exhibits were copied and ready to be admitted. Making sure the legal research was available when Guillerman made his inevitable objections. Making sure the extra-large bottle of Maalox was close at hand.

"Where do you think the jurors' heads are right now?" he whispered to Christina.

She didn't stop organizing whatever it was she was organizing. "They're confused. They're wondering if Dennis really is the type to make a death threat, much less to act on it. They're wondering what Conway was getting at when he dragged you into his testimony. Except for the ones who watched the news report on television and lied about it. They know what the accusation was about and are wondering if it's true. In any case, they will be watching very closely. Both Dennis and you."

"How do we convince them we're not a scum-sucking murder squad?"

She smiled a little. "Just stick to the plan. Put on your case. Be the straight arrow you usually are." She winked. "At least in public."

"And you think that will be enough?"

She plopped his first witness outline on the table in front of him. "I never said that."

THE FIRST defense witness was a professor, Gordon Taylor, who worked at TU in the English department with Dennis. He had known Dennis—and Joslyn—for many years. His testimony had two important aspects. First, he established that Dennis and Joslyn had been a loving couple, deeply devoted to each other. Despite the busyness of their schedules and the disparity in their incomes, he testified, the two were deeply in love and appeared to have a healthy relationship.

Taylor was also able to testify about the change that had come over Dennis after his wife disappeared. Although Dennis had stopped coming to work, Taylor saw him twice and on one occasion accompanied him when he searched for his wife. He described Dennis as worried, obsessed, and deeply distressed. He said that physically, Dennis had been tired, haggard. He'd begun to stutter when he talked and often drifted off in the middle of his sentences, never completing his thoughts. Since he wasn't a medical expert, Ben couldn't quite have him say that Dennis's mental stability was affected, but the implication was obvious.

Taylor was a useful witness, but Ben didn't kid himself that he was a case winner. Guillerman didn't even bother to cross-examine.

The next witness was another personal friend, a woman who lived next door to Dennis and Joslyn. Not

the woman sitting behind him masquerading as his
mother, but another woman named Joanne Sultan. She
was also able to confirm that Dennis and Joslyn had
been a loving couple. She had heard some arguing from
time to time while she was out working in her garden,
especially when Joslyn came home in the wee hours of
the morning, but she never thought anything of it. She
had been watching people all her life and she could tell
Dennis was still as in love with her as he had been on the
day they married. She also personally admired Dennis—
his sunny personality, his eager willingness to help a
neighbor.

The portrait she painted of her neighbor after his wife
died could not have been more dramatically different
had she said he'd been imbibing Dr. Jekyll's potion. He'd
stopped going to work. He'd stopped shaving in the
morning or changing his clothes. He'd muttered to himself, mostly unintelligibly. Sultan had gone over to his
house on several occasions during this period; she'd been
worried about him and felt he probably should not be
alone. But he'd refused all assistance and virtually barri-
caded himself in his home. Sultan admitted that on one
occasion, after Joslyn was dead, she had peered through
the kitchen window, just to check on Dennis. She'd seen
him poring over a photo album with tears in his eyes.

Their wedding photos.

The last time she'd seen him, she'd been encouraged.
She'd thought he might be getting over it, because she
could see that he had dressed and groomed himself. In
fact, he'd been wearing a suit and looked quite attractive. This was the day of the murder.

Ben realized that she must have seen him on his way
to Ben's office.

"Did you ever observe him doing anything violent?"

"No," she assured Ben readily. "Never. Not before or
after he lost his dear wife. Never."

"Did you ever hear him talk about doing anything violent?"

"No. Of course not."

"Ever see anything that suggested he might be planning something violent?"

"No."

"How would you describe his demeanor on the last occasion you spoke to him?"

She thought several moments before answering. "I would say he was a changed man. Dramatically altered. I'm sure there was a glimmer of the old Dennis in there somewhere, but I couldn't spot it. He was not himself."

"Thank you. I have no more questions."

Guillerman, however, had several.

"You've testified that you never saw any indications that the defendant was planning anything violent."

"That's so."

"But you have said he muttered a lot. What did he mutter?"

"Mostly his wife's name. Joslyn."

"Anything else?"

She smiled sadly. "Fizz. It was a nickname he had for her."

"Anything else?"

"I'm sure I can't recall everything . . ."

"Did he ever mention Detective Christopher Sentz?"

The elderly woman's lips turned down in a small frown. "On occasion."

"And did he mention the detective favorably?"

"No."

"What did he say?"

She took a deep breath. It was obvious she did not want to continue but felt honor bound to answer the question truthfully. "He called him a murderer."

"I see. Did you detect any anger when he said this?"

"What do you expect?"

"He was very angry at Detective Sentz, wasn't he?"

"Can you blame him?"

"You're not answering the question."

"Yes. He was very angry at Detective Sentz. But that doesn't mean—"

"Just answer the questions, ma'am. Would you say he thought about Detective Sentz a lot?"

"Probably."

"That would be my guess as well. Now, one final matter, and let me thank you already for your cooperation today. You described in some detail how changed you found the defendant after he lost his wife, right?"

"Yes. Dramatically so."

"As I'm sure is to be expected when someone loses a spouse, something which, sadly, is not all that uncommon. Thousands of people lose spouses every year, but they don't all go out and commit murder as a result."

"Objection!" Ben said.

"Sustained."

"I'm sorry, your honor. I was distracted. What I meant to ask was, Ms. Sultan, you've said you thought the defendant was different. But would you describe that difference as insane?"

"Objection!" Ben said again. "The witness is not qualified to render a psychiatric opinion."

The judge shrugged. "She can give her personal opinion, based on her observations, and the jury can give it whatever credence they deem appropriate."

"Thank you, your honor." Guillerman repeated the question. "Did he ever strike you as insane?"

There was a long pause before the witness answered. The silence hung between them, weighted and immoveable.

It seemed an eternity before she answered. "No," she said quietly. "He did not."

"Thank you," Guillerman said, walking away. Ben sensed it was taking everything he had not to gloat. "No more questions."

CHAPTER
25

BEN'S LEAD WITNESS after the lunch break was the first of two medical experts he would be calling. Dr. Stanley Hayes was an emergency medicine specialist operating out of a hospital in Oklahoma City. He was in his mid-fifties, bald on top and salt-and-pepper on the sides, slightly pudgy but certainly no more than might be expected from a successful man of his age and height. He was active in several state and national medical organizations and had been the keynote speaker for the National Council of Emergency Room Personnel. Ben established his credentials and then revealed that he had reviewed all the records pertaining to Joslyn Thomas and was familiar with the case.

"Your honor," Guillerman said, "let me renew my objection to this witness and his entire anticipated testimony. It has no probative value."

Judge McPartland looked annoyed. Perhaps he was still angry about the gag order violation. "Mr. Prosecutor, I have already ruled on your objection and you have made a record. Please sit down."

Ben continued his direct. "Could you explain what caused the death of Joslyn Thomas?"

Hayes spoke directly to the jury box. "Dr. Thomas suffered numerous injuries from the crash, which, after not being treated for many days, led to her death. Upon impact, she was impaled by a jutting piece of metal that pierced her leg, right about here." He pointed to a spot on his upper thigh. "This rendered her immobile, although given the condition of the automobile, I doubt she could have gotten out in any case. She also suffered a severe concussion, though it did not render her permanently unconscious. She had numerous lacerations, all over her body. One wound to her forehead bled profusely. She also suffered a broken arm, a broken clavicle, and two broken ribs, injuries she presumably received upon impact."

"Of all these injuries, which were the most profound?"

"The most dangerous would be the impalement of her leg, though they were all serious. Broken limbs can be especially nasty when they go too long untreated. With the leg wound, though, there was profuse bleeding, not to mention the deadly danger of gangrene. Blood poisoning from the metal is also a danger. Worst of all, her kidneys had been damaged, causing a buildup of toxins in her system. That, coupled with the dehydration and malnutrition, is probably what caused her death."

"I noticed you used the word *probably,* Doctor. Is there some uncertainty about it?"

He spread his hands wide. "In a case such as this, when there are so many factors at play that could have caused death, it is virtually impossible to know which one delivered the final killing stroke." He paused, then his voice dropped a notch. "And I don't really see that it matters much."

"Indeed." Ben flipped a page in his outline. This was where the examination got tricky. "Dr. Hayes, this is a delicate matter I'm about to raise, and I apologize in advance, but it's something the jury needs to know. During this time that Joslyn Thomas was trapped in her car . . . would she have felt any pain?"

"Objection!" Guillerman said. "I must raise the same

argument again, your honor. This is entirely inappropriate. This testimony is not relevant to any matter at issue in this trial."

"I'm going to allow it," Judge McPartland said, "just as I told you all the previous times you made this same argument. And if you make it again, your associate will have to take over the prosecution, because you will no longer be at liberty."

Guillerman sat down, not pleased.

"You may answer the question," Ben said, urging the witness onward.

"Oh my, yes," he said. He seemed genuinely distressed. "Almost nothing on earth hurts as badly as a broken rib. She had two. Plus a broken arm. Plus a sharp piece of metal jabbed into her leg. The pain would have been . . . well, unimaginable. Indescribable."

"I don't doubt it," Ben said, "but just so the jury can understand, I'm going to ask you to try."

"In the medical profession, we have what is known as the pain scale. There are many different factors involved in measuring and evaluating pain, but for the purposes of this trial, all you need to know is that basically it's a one-to-ten scale. One is relatively minor pain, and ten is the maximum it is possible for human beings to endure."

"And where on the scale would you place the pain that Joslyn Thomas experienced, Doctor?"

"Ten," he said, his face set and grim. "And if there were any higher numbers, I would say that."

"I see. And she would have felt this pain throughout the period she was trapped in the car?"

"Of course. Her concussion did not induce unconsciousness. There was nothing to alleviate the pain. She was still conscious, albeit only barely, when her rescuers arrived." He squirmed uncomfortably in his seat. "She would have felt the pain."

"For seven days."

"Yes," the doctor said. "Day and night."

Ben remained silent for a few moments, appearing to search through his outline for his next question. He wanted to let that horror linger in the juror minds before he dropped the next bomb.

"Doctor," Ben continued, "you've described Joslyn Thomas's injuries as being ultimately fatal. Could she have been saved had help come sooner?"

Guillerman was halfway to his feet before he stopped himself. Ben could see he desperately wanted to object, but apparently not desperately enough to get himself locked up on a contempt-of-court charge. The image of the DA sitting behind bars was not one likely to win votes.

"Almost certainly so," Dr. Hayes answered. "Although she had many injuries, no one of them was so catastrophic as to guarantee death. What ultimately killed her was time."

"Can you explain what you mean, Doctor?"

"I mean injuries of this sort will only get worse if they are not treated. She bled more. The poison spread. The toxins multiplied. And perhaps most critically, she remained dehydrated and without nourishment. The more time passed, the worse she got. Until finally it was too late and she could not be saved, not even by the best team of medics imaginable."

"Can you give us an estimate of when she would have reached the point of no return?"

He leaned forward, nodding his head. "Of course it's impossible for me to set out a precise timetable, because no one was there collecting data. But based upon my analysis of the records, I see no reason why she couldn't have been saved, had she been found, after several days. In fact, I would go so far as to say she could have been saved had she been found a day earlier. Possibly even a few hours earlier."

"So if the police had launched their investigation sooner, as Dennis Thomas had been urging them to do for days, she might have lived?"

Out the corner of his eye, Ben could see Guillerman gnashing his teeth. But he kept his mouth closed.

"Almost certainly," Dr. Hayes said. "I'd stake my reputation on it. They could have saved that young doctor's life. If they had just moved sooner."

"Thank you," Ben said. "Pass the witness."

"Permission to approach the bench," Guillerman said. He appeared near the smoldering point. The judge nodded and waved his fingers. Ben followed Guillerman up to the front.

"Your honor, I renew my objection, and I further formally protest the scurrilous tactics being used in this trial."

"One thing at a time, counsel." McPartland appeared underwhelmed. "What's the basis for the objection?"

"This testimony is irrelevant. What difference does it make if the poor woman suffered pain? What difference does it make if she could have been saved? None of that is relevant to whether Christopher Sentz was murdered."

"The testimony goes to our affirmative defense," Ben said quietly.

"That was my understanding," the judge added. "It goes to the state of mind of the defendant at the time the killing occurred."

"What is he saying?" Guillerman asked. He was visibly angered, and Ben didn't doubt it was genuine. "That this guy's wife died in pain, so it was okay for him to take out a cop?"

"I doubt if that's how he'll put it in closing argument," the judge said dryly.

"Probably not," Guillerman barked, "because that would be too honest!"

The judge put his hand over the microphone. "Counsel . . ."

"This is the most offensive defense I've encountered in my entire career!" Guillerman continued. "Who are we kidding? This defendant killed a police officer. A senior detective. He planned it, then he consulted with his attorney on how to construct a good defense, and then he put the plan in action. He killed Detective Sentz in cold blood and faked a blackout so that he would look—" He pointed a finger to his temple and drew circles in the air. "—craaaaaazy!"

"None of this alleged premeditation has been proven," Ben felt obliged to point out. "I'm simply presenting a textbook, by-the-numbers case of temporary insanity."

Judge McPartland gave him a long look. "Well now, let's not push it too far, Mr. Kincaid."

"That's not what he's arguing at all," Guillerman said, "and you know it as well as I do, Judge. What he's asking for is jury nullification."

"That's not true!" Ben insisted.

Guillerman continued. "No one believes his client was insane, even temporarily, and he's not really asking them to. What he's saying is, his wife died a horrible death and it was all the police department's fault, so forget about the law and let my man walk."

"That is not correct. But what's wrong with asking for justice? When the application of the law would produce an unjust result, don't jurors have the right to use their own judgment?"

"That's jury nullification, and it's unethical and grounds for disbarment."

Judge McPartland did not respond nearly as quickly as Ben would have liked. "I will admit that this aspect of the defense case troubles me."

"Your honor," Ben said firmly, "all I'm trying to do is

show the jury what could cause a perfectly ordinary and harmless man to contemplate the most extreme actions. He didn't just lose his wife—he lost her in the most horrible way imaginable. It wasn't an unavoidable accident. The police had the power to find her a few hours after she disappeared. They chose not to. I am not in any way saying that made it okay to kill Detective Sentz. But I am saying that such dramatic and catastrophic events can render the most healthy brain temporarily unhinged. And this theory will be reinforced by my psychiatric witness."

"For the price of six hundred dollars an hour," Guillerman muttered. "That's a lot of money for an opinion of insanity."

"I'm reminded of something Oscar Wilde said," Ben remarked. " 'In all matters of opinion, our adversaries are insane.' "

"For that much money, our adversaries could be declared insane."

"That's enough, counsel." McPartland leaned back in his chair, obviously taking a few minutes to collect his thoughts. "I'm not happy about this aspect of this case, as I said. What else is new? This case has been a thorn in my side from the start. But I will see it out."

He took another deep breath, then glared at the two attorneys. "I will allow Mr. Kincaid to call his psychiatric expert and to tie his testimony in with the other testimony we have heard. For the purpose of establishing a case of temporary insanity. And nothing else. Do you hear me, Mr. Kincaid?"

"I do, your honor."

"Mr. Guillerman?"

"Loud and clear."

"Good. There will be no arguments for jury nullification or any other inappropriate claims. Got it?"

"Yes," they both answered.

"Good." He banged his gavel on the bench. "We're taking fifteen before the next witness, gentlemen. I need my blood pressure medicine."

The judge left the courtroom, and most of the people in attendance headed toward the back doors. Guillerman stopped Ben before he could go anywhere.

"I'm filing a complaint with the bar association, Kincaid."

"What, another one?"

"You know what that means?"

"You think I'm winning?"

He jabbed a finger into Ben's chest. "I've got a lot of friends on the Grievance Committee. You could lose your license over this."

"That would free up a lot of time."

"Even if you don't, we can tie you up in so many investigations and proceedings your candidacy will be impossible. I've got friends on the Democratic Party committee, too. No one will support you."

"Are you threatening me?"

"You heard what I said."

"What I think I heard was the district attorney making a personal threat for the purpose of gaining an advantage in a criminal trial. And that really *is* grounds for disbarment."

"You're in over your head, Kincaid," Guillerman growled, bearing down on him, "and you're going to lose. I will see to that personally. You're going down in flames." He turned on his heel and stomped away. "Both you and your client."

CHAPTER
26

PERSEVERANCE, AL. The key to uncovering the unknown.

That's what his father used to tell him, Loving mused, daydreaming a little as he stared at the hospital for the third day running. Before he shoved off, Loving's dad used to take him on camping trips down near Tahlequah. Sometimes they'd float the Illinois; other times they'd go on long hikes through the woods. They would pretend to be pioneer scouts, Kit Carson and his men, tracking bad guys through the dense brush. They would look for clues, broken twigs, telltale footprints in the mud. What kind of animal has a foot like that? his dad would ask.

And of course, his father had been strangely fascinated with the analysis of what he called "scat." You can tell what animal had been there by analyzing the scat. At the time, Loving had doubted his father's credibility on this subject. Turns out it was true, although it took him many years to learn that. A friend at the Nature Conservancy had even given him a pictorial scarf illustrating the various types of scat indigenous to the Oklahoma prairie.

His father had been a good man before he disappeared. Loving still didn't know why he left. He knew his mother was high-strung and not the easiest to look after. He should know—he'd been doing it on his own for almost thirty years now. But why his father had made such a sudden break, as if he just couldn't stand it another day, that he didn't understand.

Just as Loving could not comprehend why his father had never wanted to come back since he left. Not even just to stop in and say hello.

Loving rubbed his eyes and slapped the sides of his face. Funny how your mind wanders when you've been staring at the same urban structure for three days. The point of the reverie was that his father had taught him patience, perseverance, the ability to wait for what you want. That was a lesson that served him well in his current life as a private detective.

Ever since that strange meeting with Officer Torres in the grove of trees outside Scene of the Crime, Loving had staked out St. Benedict's Hospital. He wasn't sure what he was looking for, but this was the only lead he had, so he was not letting it go. If there was something happening here, surely he would eventually see a hint of it. He'd been watching all around the clock. He moved his van to a new position every now and again, to avoid attention. But he always made sure he had a view of the front doors and the loading dock on the side. If something unusual was going down, that would most likely be where he would get a glimpse.

St. Benedict's filled a midtown niche, closing gaps between St. John's modern urban complex and St. Francis's sprawling pink cinder block. Despite the fact that he was a detective, Loving still didn't know what had motivated the St. Francis powers-that-be to paint a hospital pink. He had heard so many contradictory stories, they had taken on the sheen of urban legends. Pink paint surplus. Comforting to the ill. St. Francis of Assisi's favorite color. As if you would pick your color scheme based upon the preferences of a guy who talked to birds. It was even more strange now that they added the Children's Hospital, which was bright blue with green windows. It looked like a giant Lego construction with a mismatched piece at the end.

By contrast, St. Benedict's was smaller and lower-key. The entire building was a single story, like a hospital designed by Frank Lloyd Wright. It was not as large as either of the other two major hospitals but was renowned for its research and its willingness to tackle difficult cases. Almost too successful: they had a reputation for dealing with those in the worst, most terminal condition. Telling someone that a mutual friend had "gone to Benedict's" was guaranteed to produce a sorrowful expression; it was tantamount to saying the funeral service would be held next Monday. Loving had only been inside a few times, and none of the visits were experiences he liked to recall or hoped to repeat ever again in his life.

Well, what could he do next to keep himself awake? He'd played the alphabet game solo, particularly difficult when there were so few signs around, impossible now that it was dark outside. He'd decoded every personalized license plate within view. He'd heard every song on his iPod several times over. It was possible that it was time to chuck it in, try something else. He wasn't a quitter, but he knew Ben needed help, and if this wasn't going to pan out, perhaps it was time to try something different. He hated to go against his dad's advice, but he was in his forties now, after all, and there came a time when a man had—

Loving sat up straight in his seat. Wait just a minute. Was that who he thought it was?

He smiled. Daddy had been right. Again.

It was possible the man was just going to visit a sick friend. But Loving didn't think so.

Loving slowly eased out of his van, careful not to attract any attention. He crept between the cars, staying well behind Officer Peter Shaw. One of the Benedict's

Bunch. The darkness helped, even though the parking lot was illuminated with several high fluorescent lamps.

He stepped through the sliding front doors and waited, staying out of sight. Shaw would recognize him, and the last time he and Loving had met, he'd threatened to punch his lights out. A big scene in the hospital lobby would not likely generate the information Loving needed.

Shaw nodded at the front desk receptionist but did not stop or sign in. That in itself was interesting. Told Loving at least two things: he'd been here before, and he didn't want to leave a record of his presence.

Once Shaw had disappeared down the corridor, Loving started forward. He knew he would not get past the front desk so readily. He would have to be clever.

Loving started talking before he even reached the desk. "Did Peter Shaw come through here?"

The woman sitting behind the desk did not immediately answer.

"You know Pete. Shaved head. Goatee. Cop. He left his pager. He'll get in big trouble if I don't give it to him."

"You can leave it with me and I'll see—"

"No, sorry, I can't. Appreciate your offer, but it's police property. I put it into anyone's hands other than his, I'll get drilled by my boss, and I've got enough of that already."

"Well, he didn't sign in, so I don't know . . ."

"I can find him. Do you have any idea which way he went?"

The woman seemed a bit confused, which was understandable, given the circumstances. Loving's primary goal here was to keep her talking before she had time for thinking.

"I believe he usually goes to Oncology."

Oncology. The same department where Joslyn Thomas worked. This case just got a whole lot more interesting.

"Thanks! You're a lifesaver!"

Loving brushed past her. She held up her hand, but he was too quick. Her hand fell and he passed without question. He had a suspicion that she was not entirely satisfied with their interaction. But he also suspected that Shaw and his buddies had been visiting the hospital for some time, and she probably wasn't satisfied with that interaction, either. Bottom line, she knew that something out of the ordinary was going on but had decided it didn't behoove her to be curious.

Loving read the sign dangling over the corridor. The arrow indicated that Oncology was to the left. He veered down the corridor and almost immediately saw Shaw at the other end of the hall.

Loving opened a door and dove inside. It was a spacious closet, filled with supplies. It would do for now, but he needed to get out of here before he was accused of trying to steal something. He wasn't exactly wearing a clever disguise for undercover work. His white T-shirt and torn jeans would not allow him to blend in with the doctors or the staff. He needed something better . . .

Hospital greens would do. They were a common sight here, plus he could just pull them over his clothes. He could pass as an OR intern or some similar no-education-required employee. But where would he find the greens?

He opened the door just a crack and checked the hallway. Coast was clear. He slipped out and read the signs on the doors as furiously as possible. There had to be a lounge or sitting room where staff waited for their calls . . .

He found the locker room quickly, before Shaw reappeared in the corridor. Just inside, a big linen laundry basket on wheels held lots of dirties. Where were the clean clothes?

He supposed that given his circumstances, he couldn't

afford to be choosy. He rooted around in the basket, searching for something that would fit his large frame, preferably not too soaked with blood or flesh or any other surgical remnants. After that, he found a stack of masks on a shelf. Obscuring his face would be a good idea, too.

A minute later he was back out in the hallway. He didn't kid himself that this getup would prevent Shaw from recognizing him if he got a good look. But it might shield him from a distant casual glance.

Slowly he made his way down the corridor to where he had last seen Shaw. He had no trouble locating him. He was visible in the window of a closed office door. He was talking to someone else, a man in a white coat. A doctor, unless Loving was mistaken. The conversation seemed uncomfortable. Shaw appeared agitated. His volume was increasing.

Loving retrieved a mop from the closet where he had hidden a few minutes before. He stood just outside the office door, pretending to wipe up a nonexistent mess, straining his ears to hear what was being said inside.

Once he was close, the conversation came through with surprising clarity.

"I'm telling you, the deal is off," Shaw said. "It's too risky."

"Just one more time. That's all I'm asking," the doctor replied.

"No way."

"Chris would've done it."

"Yeah, and look how he ended up."

"That's not fair and we both know it. He . . ." Loving couldn't hear the last part of the sentence. He scooted in closer. People were passing by him in the corridor, but so far no one was taking notice. Still, he knew that condition would not last forever.

"I'm in charge now, and I say no way."

"You're being unreasonable," the doctor replied.

"I'm being smart. You weren't the one up on that witness stand."

"What are you complaining about? It went fine."

"Did you hear that chump lawyer quizzing me? He got close, Gary. Dangerous close."

"He got nothing. And now it's over."

"It ain't over, not yet. And I think we should lay low till it is."

"That's not possible. It's all been arranged. I'll have a truck ready at the back loading dock. It will only take a few minutes. I'll take care of everything inside. You take care of everything outside."

"You're not listening to me. I don't want any part of this."

"You're already a part of it. And if something happens to me, you're going down, too. So maybe you better show up just to make sure nothing goes wrong."

"Are you threatening me?"

"You call it what you will. I want you here."

"I'm not coming."

"Who should I get, then? Your assistant? Maybe I should call Torres. He usually fills in when you guys screw up, right?"

"Don't go anywhere near Torres!"

"Fine. Do this one more job for me, Shaw. Just one. Then you'll be fixed to do anything you want. Give me your cell phone number. I'll text you the details as soon as I know when and where."

Shaw recited his number. "The money won't help me if I'm not alive."

"You will be. And then you can quit this crappy police work. Take care of your sister. Take early retirement. Take it in the Cayman Islands. The world will be at your doorstep."

"It's too risky!"

"Nothing good comes easy, my friend. So just ask yourself. Do you want to spend the rest of your life barely scraping by, handing out traffic tickets and chasing drug dealers? Or would you rather be sitting on the beach drinking booze out of a pineapple? Your choice."

"Excuse me. Can I help you?"

Loving looked up abruptly. Someone was talking to him.

"I don't recognize you." It was the floor nurse, who according to her name tag was Ernestine Tubbs. "Are you assigned to this wing?"

"Uh, no. Not normally." It seemed like the smart answer. "I'm supposed to see the doctor." He pointed through the door. "He's, um, busy."

"I'll go in and get him."

"No, no. Don't do that." Loving held her back. "He's, um, havin' a conversation. It's pretty intense."

Tubbs glanced through the window, saw Shaw, frowned. "I'm not surprised."

"I'll just wait," Loving said, grinning. "I don't mind. Beats scrubbin' down the operatin' theater."

"We can't have you just standing around. Who sent you?"

Loving licked his lips. "Um, who sent me?"

"Yes. Who sent you to see the doctor?"

"Um . . . he did."

Tubbs blinked. "The doctor sent you to see the doctor?"

"Uh . . . yeah. He called for me. I came right down, but as you can see, he's tied up. Doctors. Always think the world revolves around them."

"Well, I'm not afraid of him. I'll go in—"

Loving grabbed her. The mop clattered to the floor. "Please don't."

"I insist."

"I really don't want you—"

"What on earth is going on out here?"

Loving slowly pivoted. The doctor stood in the door-way behind him. The first thing Loving noticed was that he looked extremely irritated.

The second thing he noticed was the name tag on his white coat identifying him as Dr. Sentz.

CHAPTER
27

DENNIS'S THERAPIST, Daniel Estevez, M.D., Ph.D., was not a man Ben would normally choose for his most important expert. He was too young, for one thing. Medical testimony usually went down better when it descended from a lot of gray hair. He also had a disturbing tendency to avoid medical and psychiatric jargon. Usually, Ben had to coach people the other way. He had to get them to simplify what they were saying so a jury could readily understand it. Estevez was largely babble-free. This made him more readily comprehensible, but Ben worried that it might also rob him of that sense of intellectual superiority that made so many medical witnesses almost unassailable.

Ben could have sought a different witness, but in the end he thought he was better off with a witness who actually knew the defendant than with one who had been hired to get to know him after the fact.

After Ben established the man's credentials, he began the main testimony.

"When did you begin seeing Dennis?"

"Almost two years ago."

"Why were you seeing him?"

"Dennis was suffering some anxiety. Mostly work-related. There were a few other stressors. Nothing uncommon."

"How was the therapy going?"

"Well. He was sleeping better, being more productive at work."

"Was he on any medications?"

"Eventually. I prefer not to start prescribing drugs until I can reliably diagnose if there's a serious and immediate need. Initially I felt we could deal with Dennis's problems without medication, and that of course is more desirable. Later, I prescribed a mild antianxiety drug."

"Did his mental state change during the period of time you were treating him?"

"Yes."

"And when would that be?"

"After the loss of his wife. Wait—let me change that. After his wife disappeared. I didn't see him during the time she was trapped in that car, but I did talk to him twice on the phone, and I could tell I was speaking to a very different Dennis."

"How so?"

"His stress levels were off the charts. He was having trouble speaking and thinking clearly."

"What would cause such a change?"

"He was desperately searching for his wife, and he felt he was the only one doing so. He had an intuition that she was in trouble and was frustrated that he could do nothing about it. Plus I suspect he was not eating properly or getting enough rest. If any."

"How would you describe his mental state at this time?"

"I would say he was suffering from panic attacks and an extreme anxiety disorder. Which is hardly unusual, given the circumstances."

Ben crossed the courtroom and positioned himself closer to the jury. He knew this would encourage Dr. Estevez to look at them occasionally. It would also block their view of Guillerman and his overt expressions of disbelief.

"Did you see him prior to the time they found his wife?"

"No. I asked him to come in, but he said he couldn't. He was spending every night and day looking for her."

"When did you see him next?"

"I saw him in my office two days after she died. And I have seen him since he was arrested, of course."

"Would you describe for the jury your observations about Dennis on these occasions?"

"After Joslyn died, he was in a bad way. He had suffered a total nervous breakdown. Was barely functioning. He looked terrible physically. Red eyes, pale complexion. Was totally consumed with grief for his wife. Grief, and perhaps guilt."

"Why guilt? He had nothing to do with his wife's death."

"You and I know that. But he wasn't thinking clearly. He was suffering from a form of survivor's guilt, even though he had not been in the car with her and had nothing to do with the accident. Nonetheless, he knew she had suffered for seven days. He tried to find her, tried everything he knew. But he failed. So he blamed himself for her suffering."

"In your opinion, was this a normal way for a bereaved spouse to respond?"

"Obviously not. The horror of what happened, coupled with his natural predisposition to experience stress, triggered something inside him. He became irrational."

"Thank you, Doctor. When you saw him on these occasions, did he mention the police at all?"

"Oh, yes. Many times."

"Did he blame them for his wife's death?"

"Not exactly. He said they could have rescued her sooner. Which is obviously true. But I don't know that he blamed them, exactly. It was more as if . . ." He thought for a moment. ". . . as if he blamed himself for not being able to motivate them into action."

"Did he mention Detective Sentz?"

"Yes. He seemed to think Sentz had some reason for not opening an investigation, something personal or . . . well, I don't know what. He was not really making sense."

"Were you concerned about Dennis at this point?"

"Yes. An unbalanced mental state is always a cause for concern."

"What action did you take?"

"I gave him a prescription. For Risperdal. It's a stronger medication I thought would help calm him down. And I told him I wanted to see him the next day."

"Why?"

"I felt that part of his problem stemmed from his feeling of helplessness, that there was nothing he could do about the situation. We have techniques for helping someone out of that mental state. Helping them turn their grief into something positive."

"Did he show up for the next appointment?"

"He did not. And that night, on the news, I heard what happened."

"Have you seen Dennis since his arrest?"

"Yes. Many times."

"Have you drawn any conclusions about what happened?"

"Yes."

"Would you share them with the jury, please?"

Estevez straightened up. "I believe that his mental capacity was severely diminished at the time of Detective Sentz's death."

"Is that all?"

"No. I also believe that he was motivated by an irresistible impulse to want to harm Detective Sentz."

"When you say he had diminished capacity, what exactly do you mean?"

"That his ability to control himself was greatly reduced. That his ability to comprehend the nature and quality of his acts was all but eradicated. That he could no longer discern the difference between right and wrong."

"How long did this condition last?"

Estevez thought a moment before answering. "I can't say with certainty, but after the shooting occurred, Dennis suffered a blackout. I believe this was the brain shutting down, protecting itself from the overload caused by too much stress, too much guilt. With Detective Sentz's death, the target of all that negative energy had been eliminated."

"Are you saying this is the result of Dennis's actions against Detective Sentz?"

"No, and perhaps I should make that more clear. I have no idea what happened in that hotel room. Neither does Dennis. From a psychological point of view, it makes no difference who did what. What matters is that Detective Sentz did in fact die, and when that occurred, the subject of Dennis's abnormal fixation was gone. With nothing to fixate on, the obsession began to lose its hold. The blackout signals a sort of mental changing of the guard, if you will. The brain shut down so it could begin healing itself."

"And did it?"

"Yes. He's been getting better ever since the incident, and now I believe he has returned to the same mental state he was in before his wife disappeared. He's still dealing with a great deal of stress, obviously, as a result of the charges and this trial. But he's much better than he was before."

"Does he present a danger to others at this time?"

"Objection," Guillerman said, undoubtedly grateful

to finally have an opportunity to break up the flow. "Not relevant."

Technically, he was correct. The defendant's current mental state didn't matter; what mattered was his mental state at the time he allegedly pulled the trigger. But Ben wanted the jury to hear it, just the same.

"I'll allow this," the judge ruled.

"No. He is not a danger to anyone. The extreme circumstances that produced this anomalous situation will not and cannot recur."

"Thank you," Ben said, returning to his seat. "I'll pass the witness." And pray to God for deliverance from the barrage he knew was soon to follow.

CHAPTER
28

GUILLERMAN STRODE UP to the witness box without missing a beat. He was coming on strong, and clearly he wanted everyone to know it. He couldn't afford to let this witness step down without putting a few dents in his highly educated armor.

"Just so the jury knows where everyone stands, Doctor, are you being paid for your testimony today?"

"No. I'm being paid for my time."

"So you are being compensated for being in the courtroom today."

"Yes. Just as you are, counsel."

Guillerman smiled. "I'll bet you're getting more. What's your hourly rate?"

"I get two hundred dollars an hour normally, but I charge three hundred for court time. Obviously, there are more problems when I have to come to court."

"Gosh, I'd hate to think of you being inconvenienced. What are the additional problems?"

"Having to drive downtown, find a parking place. And put up with cross-examination, of course."

Even though his delivery was totally flat and dry, Estevez was managing to get in a few zingers. Ben had no idea how that would play with the jury, but he was enjoying it.

"Does that three hundred dollars an hour include time spent in preparation for appearing in the courtroom?"

"Yes."

"How much of that time have you logged?"

"About twenty hours."

Guillerman whistled. "This little murder trial is turning into a real cash cow for you, isn't it?"

Estevez's reaction was cold. "I wouldn't put it that way."

"During this preparation, did you meet with the defendant?"

"Of course."

"And you met with his attorney?"

"I talked with Mr. Kincaid and his partner, Ms. McCall."

"And they told you what they wanted you to say?"

"Don't be offensive. I told them what conclusions I had reached regarding the incident. They didn't tell me anything."

"And you pocketed about ten thousand dollars for your trouble."

"Something like that."

"I would imagine you could get most people to say just about anything for ten thousand dollars."

"Objection," Ben said. He kept it quiet. The objection had to be made, but he didn't want to start a fuss. Expert witnesses got paid and the jury could do with that what they would.

"That's all right," Guillerman said. "I think I've made my point."

Several times over, Ben thought.

"Dr. Estevez, you mentioned that at some point prior to the murder you prescribed medication for Dennis."

"Yes."

"You described it as a mild antianxiety drug."

"Yes."

"It sounded as if his anxiety levels were rather high, at least at the time."

"Yes."

"Why didn't you prescribe something stronger?"

"This was the first time he had taken anxiety medicine. You don't start anyone on the strongest medication. You start with something mild, then see if more is required."

"But you could have prescribed something stronger, right?"

"I have the ability, if that's what you mean."

"And you chose not to. Tell me, sir—is it correct to say that if you had prescribed something stronger before all this happened, we might not be here today?"

"Objection," Ben said. "Speculation."

"I'll allow it," the judge ruled. "He is an expert."

The witness answered, "I seriously doubt it. I mean, I suppose if I had given him something so strong that it knocked him out he couldn't have done anything. But short of that, I don't think it would've made any difference."

"And that was because his anger was so intense, he was going to kill that cop no matter what."

"Objection," Ben said. Again, he played it weary, rather than angry. Better to give the impression the objection was obligatory, even though he knew no juror could be foolish enough to be swayed by it, rather than to act as if it were of great importance.

"Sustained."

"Well, let me come at this a different way." Guillerman rested his hands on the witness box and stared directly at Dr. Estevez. "That stuff you prescribed later—Risperdal. It's actually used for a variety of reasons, isn't it?"

"Yes."

"And one of those reasons is that it's supposed to improve impulse control. Or to put it another way, to suppress strong feelings. Violent impulses."

"It is used sometimes for that purpose, but—"

"So what you actually prescribed was something to help the defendant control his violent and angry temper."

"I had no reason to believe—"

"Tell me, Doctor. Is having a bad temper the same as being insane?"

"Of course not."

"But the defendant does have a history of violent temper, right?"

"I would not agree with that statement."

"He was in fact having troubles with his wife, the one whose loss supposedly drove him over the brink, right?"

Estevez took a deep breath. "Every marriage has its problems. Even the good ones."

"And he had in fact been violent with his wife."

"There was one incident that—"

"Dr. Estevez, isn't it true that the defendant was angry, even before his wife disappeared, because he believed his wife was having an affair?"

"Objection!" Ben rose to his feet. This one would require more strength. Where had this come from? He glanced at Christina. She was just as puzzled as he. "This is not relevant."

Judge McPartland tilted his head to one side. "I suspect it may be. Overruled."

"Please answer the question," Guillerman directed the witness.

"Dennis did believe that at one time."

"And he was particularly angry," Guillerman said, "because he believed she was having an affair with a cop, right? Isn't that the truth?"

The courtroom buzzed with whispering and murmuring. Spectators moved back and forth as if a fire had been lit beneath them. Several reporters made for the rear doors.

Ben glanced at Dennis. He was doing an admirable job of not reacting to this latest bombshell. But Ben himself would like to know if this was true. Because if it was, it changed everything. The jury would never be satisfied until they knew the truth.

And the only one who could tell them about that was Dennis.

Even Estevez seemed surprised by this revelation. "He never mentioned that."

"Did he mention an affair?"

"He had some suspicions, but—"

"And if his wife was cheating on him with a police officer, that would certainly give him additional motivation to kill a police officer, wouldn't it?"

"I suppose, but—"

"So in fact, the defendant's vendetta against police officers began even before his wife disappeared!"

"Objection!" Ben insisted.

Judge McPartland nodded. "This time I have to agree. The witness already said he hadn't heard this before. Rein it in, counsel."

"Of course, your honor." Guillerman tucked in his chin. "I just want the jury to understand the source of the defendant's anger." He looked at the witness again. "Because it's possible for someone to be so angry that he is driven to extreme action without being insane, isn't it?"

"It's also possible to have anger, frustration, guilt, and worry consume the normal personality and produce an aberrant psychological reaction."

Ben was glad to see their witness earning his money.

Guillerman did not relent. "But it doesn't always happen that way, does it? In fact, that would be the exception, not the rule."

"True."

"And isn't it also true that insanity should not be

assumed in cases of extreme or atypical action simply to grant mercy to sympathetic cases?"

Ben eased forward in his chair. He didn't like where this was headed. He wanted to object, but he knew the judge would slap him down, since he had been implicitly asking the jury for mercy all along.

"I wouldn't put it quite that way," Estevez answered weakly.

"Oh, but Doctor, you did put it exactly that way." Guillerman returned to his table and pulled out a thick book. "Dr. Estevez, are you the author of a book called *The Psychotherapy of Extreme Violence*?"

Estevez did not evidence the usual pride Ben associated with authorship. "It's been some years."

"But I'm sure you genuinely believed what you wrote when you wrote it."

"Well, yes."

"Have you subsequently determined that what you wrote was wrong?"

"No, but—"

"In fact, you won some awards for this book, did you not?"

"The American Psychiatric Association was quite kind about it."

"You have published excerpts from it in professional journals."

"That's correct."

"You have several copies in the waiting room of your office."

He smiled slightly. "That's true."

"And it helped you obtain a part-time position at the University of Tulsa, correct?"

"It didn't hurt any."

"So I think we can assume that not only did you believe what you wrote, but you still do and others do as well. Right?"

Estevez seemed resigned. Ben desperately wanted to know what was in that book.

"That's correct."

"Good. Let me read what you wrote specifically on the subject of the use of the insanity defense in criminal trials. You said, and I quote: 'Too often, the definition of true insanity is muddied for the purpose of justifying mercy in criminal actions.'"

"Objection," Ben said. "This book is not on the prosecution exhibit list." It was a weak objection and he knew it, but he had to distract the jury and break up Guillerman's flow.

Judge McPartland was unimpressed. "I don't believe the prosecutor is planning to admit it as an exhibit. Are you?"

"No," Guillerman answered. Because then he would have had to list it and Ben would've been alerted to this tactic. "Just using it to impeach the witness."

"Very well. The objection is overruled."

Guillerman continued reading. "You go on to say: 'It is normal for persons in civilized societies to believe that certain individuals do not merit the harsh penalties dispensed for criminal actions. Consequently, the concept of temporary insanity was defined into existence in order to allow courts to absolve those who undoubtedly committed the crimes but whose circumstances are sympathetic and whose behaviors are unlikely to be repeated.'" Guillerman closed the book with a slam. "Is that true, Dr. Estevez? Was this whole idea of temporary insanity . . . what were your words . . . 'defined into existence'?"

Estevez appeared supremely uncomfortable. "Every psychological diagnosis is an intellectual construction. We define terms so that we may treat real illnesses."

"But according to you, Doctor, this one was 'defined into existence' in order to get criminals off the hook."

"That's not what I said."

"That's what it sounded like to me."

Estevez leaned forward, straining. He was starting to look as if he was struggling to maintain his credibility, never a good sign. "You have to make a distinction between the psychiatric concept of temporary insanity and the legal concept of temporary insanity."

"Why? Because one is real and the other is invented to get guilty people off?"

"Mercy is the best attribute of humanity. There is nothing wrong with it."

"No, but there is something wrong with trying to pull a fast one on the jury. Let me ask you one final question, Doctor. Do you believe Dennis Thomas killed Christopher Sentz?"

Estevez was already flustered, and now it became worse. He pursed his lips and swallowed. "I wasn't there."

"I know you're not an eyewitness. You're a psychiatric expert. And based upon your examination of the defendant, your awareness of his mental state, not to mention his temper, do you believe he pulled the trigger and killed Detective Sentz?"

"Dennis was functioning under an extreme psychological—"

"You're not answering the question, Doctor. Do you believe that Dennis Thomas killed Christopher Sentz?"

"I—I don't know."

Guillerman leaned forward, his frustration apparent. "What do you *think*? You're an expert witness. Give us your expert opinion."

Estevez looked across at Dennis, then returned his gaze to the district attorney. "I assume that he did."

"Thank you. Finally. No more questions."

And he sat down, with Ben still gritting his teeth. Guillerman had handled that brilliantly. If he had gone

one question further, Ben would've been on his feet. But Guillerman hadn't let it go that far. He'd made his point and sat down. He would return to the theme later, no doubt, in closing argument. When it really mattered.

Ben considered redirecting. He hated to leave it as it was, particularly as the last bit of testimony of the day, what the jurors were most likely to remember. But he couldn't think of anything he could do to fix this. Better just to let it go and not make a bigger deal of it than it already was.

Judge McPartland recessed the trial for the day and the jury was dismissed to their sequestration hotel. Christina began packing up. She did not look happy.

Guillerman did. Their eyes met briefly and he winked at Ben. The message was all too clear. You tried for jury nullification, and I just killed it. Your move.

Dennis had a worried expression on his face. "That didn't go as well as we had hoped, did it?"

"We'll talk about it when we get back to the office."

"I saw the looks on the jurors' faces, and—"

"We'll talk about it when we get back to the office." Among other reasons, Ben needed more time to process what had happened. At this point, he wasn't sure which was worse. Was it the suggestion of the affair, which gave Dennis an additional motivation to murder a cop and also suggested that he had a violent temper? Or the testimony indicating that the temporary insanity defense was a kindhearted crock? Or the fact that, ironically enough, their own expert was the first witness who could actually portray Dennis pulling the trigger? None of them was good.

"We'll get some dinner, then we'll try to sort this all out."

"Is—Is it too late to ask for a mistrial?"

"I'm afraid so. That ship has sailed."

As they left the courtroom, Dennis said precious little. But the hollow expression in his eyes said it all.

FOUR

The Most Delicate Balance

CHAPTER
29

THEY ALL needed sleep. And yet Ben could not make himself call it a day. Or a night, he supposed, since it was well after dark. The normal human diurnal cycles had little meaning during a trial. All the usual daily habits and procedures became meaningless. There was only the trial, omnipresent and all-absorbing. And a client who desperately needed him to succeed.

He stared out the window of their seventh-floor conference room at the slumbering city. Tulsa was lovely at night. He liked it during the day, too, but the day gave you not only the rolling hills and long lines of trees but also refineries and dirt and far too much pavement. At night all that faded away. The lights winked at you. The traffic moved slowly, oozing down Yale like neon gas in a very long tube.

A dramatic contrast to the turmoil roiling in his brain. No amount of visual tranquility was going to calm that, much as he might wish it would.

"We have to make a decision," Christina said, trying once again to drag them back on topic. "Preferably before we all pass out from exhaustion."

"We may have to spend the night at the office," Ben remarked.

"I am not wearing this skirt to court again tomorrow."

"I doubt anyone would notice."

"I would notice." She paused. "And you should notice." She flipped a pencil into the air. "I hate trials."

Dennis looked back at her with the same sad eyes he'd had all day. "Then why do you do it?"

"Because we're making a difference," Ben answered.

"Because we're making a living," Christina answered.

Dennis almost smiled. "And you two live together?"

Christina nodded. "We thrive on conflict."

"That explains a great deal."

Ben returned to the conference table. He looked at Dennis squarely. "Here's the main problem with putting you on the witness stand. It's not that I don't think you can handle yourself. I'm sure you can, probably better than most. But Guillerman is very good. He will score points at your expense. And there will be nothing I can do to stop him."

"I get that," Dennis said earnestly. "But surely the potential benefits outweigh the harms."

"Honestly, that's something we can never gauge until it's all over. But this is something I know for certain. He'll ask you what happened in that hotel room. So far as we know, you're the only person alive who can tell him."

"I don't remember."

"And that answer is not one that will please the jury."

"But it's true!"

"I know, Dennis. But the jury really wants to know who pulled that trigger. Do you blame them? I can't answer that question for them. I can't even put anyone else in the room other than Sentz himself. And I don't have anything to support that suicide theory."

"It's grounds for doubt," Dennis said.

"Yes, but is it reasonable doubt? I don't know. I can't show that he was suicidal, because no one I've talked to thinks he was. And I can't produce a motive for anyone else to kill him, even if they were in the room."

"What about Loving's investigation?"

"I haven't heard from him lately. Last I heard he had a lead at the hospital where your wife worked."

"What has that got to do with anything?"

"I don't know. Mike is all tied up, too. Neither of them is going to help us, at least not before tomorrow morning. I have to either call a witness or rest my case. And I don't like either possibility."

Christina slid in beside Dennis. "Don't you remember anything about what happened at the hotel?"

He thought for a moment. "I remember driving to the Marriott. I remember going inside, riding up the elevator. I even vaguely remember him letting me in. I think we talked about . . . something. And then—it's all a blank."

Ben gave Christina a searching look. This just wasn't good enough. The chances were too great that the jury would think he was hiding something.

"But what happens if I don't testify?" Dennis asked. "That DA told everyone that I have this raging temper, like the Incredible Hulk of English professors."

"The jury will make their decision based on their own observations."

"But if I don't take the stand, they don't have much to observe."

Ben sighed. Dennis was right, of course.

"I want to set the record straight. Yes, of course Joslyn and I had problems occasionally. Who doesn't? But I loved her dearly. And I wasn't on any anti-cop rampage, either."

"I don't think anybody bought that shot in the dark," Christina said, "and I was watching the jury closely."

"Thank goodness."

"But they might think it predisposed you to anger, given what happened later."

"That's not good."

"No. It isn't."

Dennis drew himself up. "Ben. Christina. Put me on the stand. Let them see me. They'll realize I'm not violent, not an anger management case."

"I don't even know if that would be a good thing!" Ben said, exasperated. "Our whole case depends on them thinking you were temporarily insane. If you come across too normal, we lose."

"But it was just the extreme circumstances of the moment, right? It passed."

"Yeah, that's the argument. But the jury is going to be leery of that now that our witness has explained that temporary insanity is just a device to allow jurors to show mercy to sympathetic defendants. They don't want to be accused of doing anything inappropriate. Guillerman will hammer them in his closing, reminding them of their oaths and insisting that they apply the law."

"Let him do his worst," Dennis said defiantly. "He still can't prove I pulled the trigger. And I don't believe the jury will convict me if they like me and sympathize with me. I don't care what Guillerman says."

"I wish I shared your certainty," Ben said. "But I don't."

"What do you think, Christina?"

She contemplated a long time before responding. "I think the jurors do sympathize with you, Dennis. And they always will. But most also think you killed a police officer, and they will be concerned that showing any kind of leniency, regardless of your circumstances, sends the wrong message."

"So you think they'll convict me?"

She laid her head on the table. "I think that ultimately juries are unfathomable, and none of us will know what the jurors are thinking until the foreman tells us."

Dennis fell back in his chair. "So this is why you guys get the big bucks?"

Christina rolled her eyes. "Show me the big bucks. I've been waiting a long time. Instead, Ben keeps bringing home stray cats."

"What?"

She averted her eyes. "Never mind."

"Look," Dennis said, "I researched this whole trial six ways to Sunday. But even I can't pretend I know the answer to this question. I know this: I do not want to spend the rest of my life in prison. And I don't want to be executed."

Ben shrugged. "I know that, but—"

Dennis held up a hand to cut him off. "I just don't see any way I get out of this unless the jury likes me. I mean really genuinely sympathizes with me. And I don't think that can happen unless I take the stand."

Ben pressed his palms against his brow. "I hate to say it—because this is so fraught with risk—but I think you're right."

"So you're putting me on the stand?"

He closed his eyes. "Yes."

"Do you want me to cry?"

"No!" Ben shouted, too loudly. "I want no showmanship. No histrionics."

"I can do it."

"I know you can. But juries are smarter than you think. And as I said before, if they detect any falseness in you—"

"I'm history."

"Exactly. So I will put you on the stand, and you will tell them what happened. How hard you tried to find your wife. How hard you tried to get the police to help. And you can tell them as much as you remember about what happened the day Sentz died. But that's it. No irrelevant digressions. No big emotional plays. No Helen Hayes moments."

"Okay. Got it."

"Christina, I want you to watch the jury every second. If you think they're hearing something they don't like, you signal me immediately."

"Got it."

"Send me a note. Tell the judge there's an emergency. Whatever. Better that we stop and regroup than go on with something the jury doesn't like or believe."

"You got it, tiger."

"This is a very dodgy business we're undertaking. We have to be careful."

"Understood. We're skiing the black diamonds."

"But I still have one question," Dennis said. "What do I do during cross? That man will try to rip me to shreds."

"Answer every question directly and succinctly. Don't say any more than you have to say to be responsive. At the same time, don't let him walk all over you. He will try to suggest that this was a premeditated murder and that you concocted the insanity plea to get yourself off. Don't let him get away with it."

"I—I'll do my best."

"Good." Ben felt so weary he wasn't sure he could make it to the parking lot. "Let's all go home and get a little rest. Because tomorrow is the day when we determine how this thing ends."

Tomorrow is the day, Ben thought but did not say, when we determine how Dennis lives the rest of his life. Or whether he lives at all.

CHAPTER
30

SENTZ? Loving took a long look at the doctor's face, his age. The resemblance was unmistakable.

This doctor had to be the brother of Christopher Sentz, the police detective who was shot.

Curiouser and curiouser . . .

"Who are you?" Sentz asked, giving Loving a fast look up and down.

"You don't know?" Nurse Tubbs said. She turned to Loving. "I thought you said he called for you."

Oh, this was just peachy. Loving's brain raced. He had to defuse this situation and fast. He couldn't afford to get hauled in by the hospital security. In fact, he couldn't afford to stand here long at all, because it was only a matter of time before Shaw wandered out of that office to see what was happening. And he was sure to recognize Loving when he did. Not only would it blow his cover, but it would almost certainly mean he and the doctor would cancel whatever it was they had planned.

"He didn't call for me by name. He just called for one of the scrub boys."

Tubbs placed her fists squarely on her hips. "Well, why didn't you say so? If that's all it is—"

"Wait a minute," Sentz said. "I'm confused. I haven't called for anyone."

"Are you sure?" Loving replied. "That's what the

boss told me." He glanced down at Sentz's name tag. "Oh my gosh. I thought you were Dr. Thomas."

Tubbs and Sentz exchanged a look. "You thought I was Dr. Thomas?"

"Yeah. Did I get that wrong?"

"You could say that," Tubbs replied. "Because Dr. Thomas was a woman. And she's been dead since April."

"Oh, gee, maybe I misheard."

"And who gave you these instructions?"

"Who?" Loving took a deep breath. "My boss."

"Yes, but who?"

"That would be, um . . . Bob."

"Bob Finlay?"

"Yeah. That's the one."

"When did they put him in charge of Intern Dispatch?"

"Just this morning. I think it's a temporary thing."

"Thank goodness. He's already off to a flying start."

The doctor cut in. "What did you say your name was?"

Loving coughed. "I don't think I said."

"Well, say it now, Einstein."

"My name is . . . um . . ."

"Is this too hard for you?"

"No, it's . . . Kit. Kit Car . . . lisle."

Sentz frowned. "I don't think I've heard that name before."

"I'm new."

"That explains a great deal. Are you sure they said Thomas? Perhaps it was Tomlinson."

Loving snapped his fingers. "You know, I think it was."

Sentz pointed to the opposite end of the corridor. "You need to be down there."

"Oh, wow. I didn't know. Hope I'm not too late. Thanks."

Loving skittered away, dragging his mop with him. Had he covered okay? He hoped so. He sensed more irritation than suspicion. In his experience, doctors were usually very smart, but that intelligence often came with a decided lack of patience. He hoped Sentz would go back to his work without any alarm bells ringing in his head, or anything else that might inspire him to alter his plans.

He decided to wear the greens out of the hospital. He didn't want to spend any more time here than necessary. If Shaw spotted him he would be in serious trouble. And he would lose his only lead.

Loving left the same way he came in, careful not to attract the attention of the woman seated at the front desk, then made his way to his van. He climbed into the back, opened his tool box, and retrieved a small GPS homing device. He slid open the magnetic base and then, making sure no one was watching, attached it to the inside of the metal cover over the rear driver's-side wheel of Shaw's car.

Just in case their plans changed, Loving would be able to follow the man or find him anywhere within a twenty-five-mile range.

He returned to his van and called Ben. He didn't answer. Probably in court or prepping. He left a message telling him to reply. Not that Loving really had anything to tell him yet. But he at least had some prospects.

He drove to a nearby Starbucks. Personally, he thought the coffee was ridiculously overpriced, and he wasn't sure you could call it coffee after they slathered whipped cream and chocolate sprinkles on it, but he wasn't really interested in the menu. He wanted the Internet access. He didn't have time to drive home.

He logged on to some of the PI websites and did a detailed search on Dr. Sentz. Dr. Gary Sentz, as it turned

out, was indeed the brother of the deceased detective.
One brother into med school, the other into the police
department. That had to make for some interesting family reunions.

He kept searching. Dr. Sentz had graduated from OU
medical school about ten years ago and had been
working in Tulsa for most of the time since. He had
only come to St. Benedict's in the last year. He was a
specialist in nuclear medicine, whatever that was.
Loving assumed it meant he had the unhappy job of
administering chemotherapy and similar treatments. He
had noticed signs inside the hospital bearing radiation
warnings.

What Loving couldn't find, no matter how hard he
looked, were any criminal connections, any signs of
Sentz being involved in nefarious activities. He had a
perfectly clean record, other than a few traffic offenses.
He didn't appear to have any friends or family involved
with gangs or smuggling. He lived in a nice neighborhood. He had no discernible access to contraband.
There was no evidence of a drug habit or dependency
problem.

Loving closed the lid of his laptop and pondered.
What the heck was this man orchestrating? Why did he
need Shaw and his accomplices?

He didn't know. And he suspected he wasn't going to
find out from a laptop.

He brought out his cell phone, which was no ordinary
cell phone. He remembered a time when his investigative work had primarily involved tracking people down
and bashing their heads together. Unfortunately, those
days were long gone. Like it or not, he had been forced
out of his Luddite state into the brave new technologi-
cal world. If the bad guys were going to be playing with
these tools, he had to as well.

Some months ago he had downloaded a piece of

critical (and illegal) firmware off the Internet. It basically turned his phone into a radio capable of picking up other messages broadcast on the same channel, rather than the usual phone, which was limited to picking up messages addressed to you. It was similar to phone cloning, but for that you needed temporary access to your target's SIM card. Loving didn't see how he was going to swipe Shaw's phone, even for a little while, and he doubted Shaw would give it to him. He would have to content himself with intercepting messages.

He entered Shaw's phone number, which he had overheard at the hospital. He also needed to know Shaw's service network. He didn't, but there were only so many choices—Verizon, Cingular, T-Mobile, and the rest. Trial and error would get him there in time. He had to stay within range of the same base station, but that shouldn't be too hard. He knew where Shaw lived and worked and he had a GPS transmitter on the man's car.

When the good Dr. Sentz got around to texting the details to Shaw, Loving would get the same message. And he would respond, too, in his own way.

He just hoped it was in time. He felt bad about not having been any more useful to Ben in this trial. He didn't like to let the Skipper down. If he could figure out what was going on between Shaw and Dr. Sentz—and quite possibly the late Chris Sentz as well—there was a good chance it might be useful to Ben. Shaw had said something about Ben getting close during his cross-examination. Close to what?

He checked the transponder screen to make sure the GPS signal was working. It was. Shaw had left the hospital and returned to police headquarters.

Loving would be watching this signal very carefully over the next few days. When they made their move, he would be ready.

CHAPTER
31

"Yes, Joslyn and I had our spats, just like I would imagine every couple does. But we still loved each other deeply. We'd been married seven years, and we were together two years before that, and those were the happiest days of my life. I never before had a relationship anything like it. She was my entire life. She was everything to me."

Ben watched Dennis carefully as he testified. He had been concerned that, having been so calculating throughout the pretrial period, Dennis would try to put on a show. But he seemed to have taken Ben's cautions to heart. If anything, he was leaning in the opposite direction. He was coming off a little cold, a little robotic. Even as he talked about how much he loved his wife, Ben was not sure his vocal inflection and body language carried the force of his words.

And he knew the jurors were watching very closely.

"Yes, we'd had a fight recently, but it wasn't about an affair. No one was having an affair. I don't know where the DA got that. I notice he didn't put on any evidence about it. Joslyn had lunch one day with an old boyfriend, someone she knew in high school. I overreacted. It was stupid, I know, but I do have a jealous streak. At one point, she shoved me a little, and I lost my head. I swung my hand in the air, not really meaning anything. But I slapped her. I felt horrible about it. It ended the fight right then and there. I took her in my arms and apologized and we both had a long cry about it."

"And you told your therapist about this later?" Ben asked.

"Of course I did. I felt terrible. I am not a violent man, not at all. I won't even step on cockroaches. I capture them and throw them outside. And even though hitting Joslyn was largely accidental, it still tore me up inside. So I brought it up at my next session."

"Did it ever happen again?"

"No."

"Did you ever believe your wife was having an affair?"

"No. There was one time when she stayed out late and I had concerns. Not even concerns, really. The thought just flashed into my head. She came home and I got over it."

"Were you ever concerned that she was having some kind of relationship with a police officer?"

"No."

"Prior to your wife's disappearance, have you ever had any hostility or ill will toward police officers?"

"No."

So far so good. Ben could tell the instant he walked into the courtroom that everything was different. Part of it was the surprise turn the trial had taken the day before. Part of it was the knowledge that the testimonial part of the trial could well end today. And Ben had to acknowledge that part of the reason for the increased tension arose from the possibility that Dennis Thomas might take the stand.

Throughout the pretrial period, Ben knew the local pundits had debated whether Dennis would testify. Most felt certain he would not, and for most of that time, Ben had agreed with them. But now, after the dangerous testimony that had gone before, expertly planned by Guillerman to have the maximum and most disastrous impact, that had changed. Even Guillerman recognized that. When Ben entered the courtroom, he didn't ask who Ben's next witness would be. He asked which exhibits Dennis would be using.

"Had anything changed in your relationship with your wife prior to the evening of April twelfth?"

"Nothing dramatic. It had been a rough week. She was very stressed about her job."

"How so?"

"Joslyn worked with cancer patients. Mostly women. As you might imagine, it's difficult, emotionally numbing work. No one is ever happy to see her. Treatment is difficult, often painful. She has to subject people to chemotherapy and radiation treatments. Successes are uncommon and usually temporary."

"I can see where that might be difficult."

"You can't imagine. Not unless you've done it. Many nights she would come home in tears. She was such a loving person. She would become attached to her patients, even though she knew their dire circumstances. And the likely outcome. It's one thing to deal bravely with bad news when you receive it. But Joslyn was thoroughly healthy. She chose this work. She chose to put herself out like that. A lot of people talk about helping others, but there aren't many who are willing to do it like she did." Dennis fell quiet. "She was a very special woman. Strength like you can't imagine."

"What happened on April twelfth?"

"It was mostly a normal morning. She left a little earlier than usual. Said she had to talk to someone. I was the usual breakfast chef at our house. She was actually a much better cook, but I had more time before I had to get to work. I made her favorite—a western omelet. She barely tasted it. And that was unusual for her."

"When did you talk to her next?"

Dennis pressed his lips together. Ben knew they were beginning to approach the material that would really be delicate and difficult.

"I called her during her lunch hour. I usually did, when I wasn't in class. Just to chat. She seemed fine. Didn't refer to anything outside of the usual work stuff."

"Did you get any idea what was troubling her?"

"Not really. She told me she'd taken a stroll through the children's ward. That usually brightened her spirits, even though the children were very ill. Apparently on this occasion it had not done the trick, though."

"Anything else?"

"I know she had an elderly patient she really liked who was dying. She'd been treating the woman a long time." Dennis smiled a bit. "She called her 'flinty.' Joslyn liked flinty." He paused. "That may have been getting to her."

"Was there anything else?"

"Not that I know of." His voice dropped a notch. His eyes fell. "That was the last time I spoke to her. Until . . . you know." He cleared his throat, coughed a bit. "Until she was almost dead."

Ben stepped away from the podium. The jury appeared riveted by the testimony. That did not surprise him. But what were they thinking about Dennis?

"What happened next?"

"For me, it was a day much like any other. Two classes, a few student advising sessions. Until Joslyn didn't come home. I wasn't concerned at first. It wasn't that unusual for her to be late. She worked very hard. But when it was nine and she hadn't even called, I knew something had happened. I couldn't get her on her cell phone. That's when I began to worry."

"What did you do?"

"I called her office. Someone at the front desk of the hospital had seen her leave. She'd signed out. Her car was no longer in the parking lot. So that left two possibilities. Either she had gone somewhere on her way home and not mentioned it to me, or she'd run into some trouble. I didn't believe the former. She would've called, even assuming she went somewhere, which was unlikely. She would've answered when I called her cell phone. I knew she was in trouble."

"What did you do?"

"I got in my car and drove. It was dark by then, but I searched everywhere, using my brights and a flashlight. We live out in Skiatook. Well outside the city limits. You take Lombard Lane and keep going on curvy country roads for about fifteen minutes. These roads aren't on maps—not even a GPS can help you. We journeyed quite a distance out of town so we could buy a significant piece of property. It was worth it—or so I thought. That night, I wished we lived closer to the city."

"Did you have any success?"

"None. I worked all night—didn't sleep a wink. I called her friends—no one knew anything. I looked for signs of car trouble, signs that she'd had an accident. I called hospitals. Nothing. And no one had any information for me. No one could help."

"So what did you do next?"

"That morning, as soon as the sun came up, I went to the Tulsa Police Department, Uniform East Division, since Tulsa was the last place she was seen. I'll admit it—I had been up all night and I looked a mess. Hadn't shaved or showered or changed clothes."

Ben nodded and gently steered him back to his story. The most challenging part of direct examinations was that you could not ask leading questions—meaning your question could not suggest an answer. In cross, of course, virtually every question was leading. But in direct, the attorney was primarily limited to drawing out the relevant story and asking what happened next.

"What occurred at the police station?"

"At first, they were helpful, encouraging. An officer took my report. He couldn't have been more kind. But as it turned out, he was the exception, not the rule. My report was filed. Nothing happened. I was told later that it had been referred to a detective downtown who would decide what to do. Still nothing happened. So I went downtown to see the detective. I talked with an Officer Torres at the front desk. He, too, was encouraging and helpful. But he told me that I would have to see the detective. He was the one who would decide what course of action should be taken."

Ben recalled what Loving had told him about his private conversation with Torres. He wondered how much more that man knew than he had told. "So then what happened?"

"Officer Torres took me to Detective Christopher Sentz. He said that Sentz would take care of me. Boy, did he ever."

Ben could immediately see a change come over Dennis—and he knew the jury would see it, too. He seemed to harden. His neck stiffened. His eyes became cold. Every time he said Sentz's name he looked as if he had a bad taste in his mouth.

"Detective Sentz was uncooperative, almost from the start. He told me that she had not been gone long enough to be a cause for concern. So I asked him how long she had to be missing. He said there was no set number of hours, it just depended on the circumstances. I asked him to tell me what circumstances were required. He said that since Joslyn was not elderly or a minor or off her medications and had no history of mental illness, he would need some evidence of foul play."

"What was your reaction?"

"I was stunned. The evidence of foul play was everywhere! The most responsible, reliable woman on earth had failed to come home, failed to call. Obviously something had happened to her. Either she'd had an accident or someone had gotten to her."

"What was Sentz's response?"

Dennis shook his head. "I wanted to scream. He said that even if she had an accident, that didn't constitute foul play. So I guess if she was hurt and bleeding on the side of the road—which she was—that wasn't a police concern. What do we pay these people for? And then he oh so nonchalantly said that they got these kinds of complaints all the time and that they almost always turned out to be nothing. He implied that she had run off with another man. He thought it was a big joke. A joke! My wife—gone without a trace!"

Ben cut in. "I'm sure that must have been very difficult for you, Dennis. That would have been unbearable for any loving husband." Dennis was becoming agitated, and although Ben wanted the jury to feel his emotion, he did not want them to see a temper. That was the problem with temporary insanity; the tightrope was just too slender. He had to show that the events could have driven Dennis insane, without giving them the impression that he actually was insane. "Did the detective offer you any other assistance or advice?"

"Sentz ran a check on her credit card, but that turned out to do more harm than good. He found a charge for gasoline the night she disappeared. So he explained that it proved she was not in any danger. But it didn't. I was the one who made that charge. I used the same credit card account."

"I guess he made a mistake."

"I think he knew." Ben heard a sharp intake of air from the jury box. "I'm sorry, but I do. He had access to the receipt—unlike me, at the time—and it was clearly my name on the receipt. If I hadn't been so tired and muddled, I would've recalled sooner. But I didn't."

"Anything else?"

"Sentz also noted that Joslyn had been reported missing once before. Said she had a history of this sort of behavior. He was using that as an excuse to do nothing. Here's what really happened. More than ten years ago, when she was in college, she was taking a few days off after breaking up with a boyfriend. But her mother wasn't able to reach her and got worried, so she called the police. As if that was remotely the same!"

"Did you make any further requests?"

"I asked if he could at least issue an APB. Get the other cops looking for her car. He explained that he wasn't permitted to do that for the same reasons. I pressed him. I insisted that he could do it if he wanted and he did not disagree. For a brief beautiful moment, I actually thought he was going to do it. I could see it in his eyes."

"And then?" Ben urged.

"It never happened. I saw him look across the room at some guy. I never knew who he was. I haven't found out since." Which was true. Both Ben and Loving had been looking, without success.

"And you don't know who it was?"

"No. I never got a good look at him. No one else seems to know what I'm talking about. Everyone at the police station says this person doesn't exist, that I must be—" He caught himself, though not so quickly that the jury didn't know what he was about to say. "Anyway, I've never located him."

Ben didn't know how much he should encourage this line. It was certainly interesting, but none of the police witnesses had indicated that the decision was made by anyone other than Sentz, and Ben didn't know that suggesting otherwise got them anywhere.

"And Detective Sentz did not issue the APB?"

"No."

"Did you ever see him again?"

"Oh, yes. Many times. I continued to search. I did not go to work once that entire week. I continued to call hospitals. I called everyone Joslyn knew, never once turning up anything helpful. And I went to the police station over and over again, every day. Nothing changed. Sentz was just as stubborn as ever. I tried coming at other times and going to other stations, but my report was in the system, so they always referred the matter back to Sentz. But he never changed his mind. And he became increasingly offensive."

"How so?"

Dennis's neck straightened. He sat up in his chair. He was visibly suppressing anger. "As the week progressed, it was clear to most people that something had happened to Joslyn. Something bad. So you would think Sentz would consent to open an investigation. But he didn't. Even after seven days missing, he wouldn't agree that there was any indication that something was horribly wrong. Instead, he kept suggesting that Joslyn had run off with another man."

"Really?"

"Yes! To my face he said that. I was tired and desperate, and this man was suggesting that my wife probably disappeared with someone. He made some slimy comment about how a doctor could do better than an English teacher. He looked at her picture and said she could have any man she wanted, then looked at me as if to say, Who wouldn't leave a schmuck like you?"

Dennis was becoming more agitated by the second, but Ben thought that was okay. These were extreme circumstances. Who wouldn't be angry, given what happened?

"When did Detective Sentz finally change his mind?"

"Never. Never once did that—" Dennis caught himself in time. Ben wasn't sure exactly what descriptive term had come next, but he knew it wouldn't have been pretty. "It was Officer Torres who finally authorized the investigation. And he took all kinds of grief for it afterward, too."

"Why?"

"Sentz said it was because he acted outside his authority. But I know better. He did not want Joslyn's disappearance investigated. And Torres did it anyway. They put the poor man on suspension, till the media got wind of the story. Since his action did lead to Joslyn being found, they reinstated him. Although I understand he still has some bad marks on his record."

"What happened when Torres initiated the investigation?"

"At my suggestion, they traced her cell phone. I knew she'd have it with her. I was afraid it would be dead, but by some miracle, it wasn't. Maybe she didn't leave it on all the time, to conserve battery power. I don't know. But they traced the signal. Turned out she went off the road not far from a signal tower, out in the backwoods of Skiatook. They were able to narrow her location down to about a five-mile radius. Given how few roads there were out there, that didn't leave many possibilities. They found her in about three hours." Dennis sat up straight, his back arched, his teeth clenched. "Can you believe that? She had been out there suffering . . . bleeding . . . for seven days. And they had the power to find her in three hours."

"I'm so sorry," Ben said. It was an almost impossible situation, trying to calm his witness down without seeming as if he was calming his witness down, because why would this nice temper-free man need to be calmed down? "That must have been horrifying. Were you there at the crash site?"

"Oh, yes. I stayed with them every step of the way. It was a dirt road, so there were no skid marks, but one of the other officers finally detected an unnatural depression, just at the lip of a sharp declivity leading to a ravine. Two officers went down. Her car had plowed through some thick brush. Blackberry bushes, I think. That's why her car wasn't visible from the road."

"And your wife was down there?"

"Yes."

"And she was still alive?"

"Barely. She was trapped in the car, bleeding and gashed—"

"Objection," Guillerman said, but Ben noticed he was very quiet about it. "We've already heard expert medical testimony about Dr. Thomas's injuries."

"Overruled. The witness may proceed."

"The police officers and the medics did everything they could for her. They had to rip the roof off the car to get to her. That took some time. Once she was out, the medics injected her with something—epinephrine, I think. They stopped the bleeding and treated all the major lacerations. But in only a few minutes, they came to me shaking their heads."

"What did they say?"

Dennis's head bowed. He trembled a bit the first time he tried to speak. When he lifted his head again, there was a tear in his eye. "They—they said she would never make it back to a hospital alive. And they asked if I wanted to see her."

Ben's voice grew quiet. "What did you say?"

"Of course I wanted to see her. I ran to her. I put my arms around her, as much as was possible. I told her that I had been looking for her and I apologized for not finding her sooner. I—I cried."

Ben found it difficult to hold back tears himself. "Was there anything else?"

"She told me not to worry. She—she could see how this was affecting me. She told me to be strong and not to mourn for her. That was so like Joslyn, always thinking about others, even as she was dying. And—and just before she died—"

His voice broke. He turned his head away.

Ben cleared his throat. "We could take a break . . ."

"No. I can continue." Dennis sat up straight and wiped his face dry. "She told me to outwit the stars. It was a phrase she knew from a famous teacher, a yogi. Part of her ongoing search for meaning, for peace of mind. I'm no expert, but I think it means, Don't let yourself be controlled by outside forces. Or other people. Chart your own course. Your own destiny." Dennis pressed his fingers against his forehead. "She wanted the best life possible for me. Even . . . even without her." He covered his face. His shoulders heaved.

"Your honor . . ."

Ben didn't have to finish his sentence. "Let's take a fifteen-minute break, shall we?" McPartland rapped the gavel. "We'll pick this up right where we left off."

CHAPTER
32

BEN TOOK Dennis into a nearby deliberation room and left him there so he could collect himself in private. While he did, Ben and Christina conferred.

"How do you think it's going?" Ben asked, knotting his fingers together.

"I think it's going well. Hard to be sure."

"That's supposed to be your specialty."

"This is a tough case. Too many nuances. I think they are genuinely moved by his loss. And that's good. But I'm not sure they blame the police, certainly not enough to justify a murder. I think they like Dennis and believe him so far, but we really haven't gotten into the tricky stuff yet."

Ben ducked his head, hoping that the reporters in the corridor would leave him alone. "Bottom-line this for me, Christina. I don't have much time."

"They like and believe him, but that doesn't mean they believe he was temporarily insane. And we need that. Without it, all we have is jury nullification. Dennis's situation was horrible, but to impel the jury to let him go unpunished, we would have to also show that the police were unreasonable. If we could show that Detective Sentz had some deliberate reason for not investigating, some ulterior motive, that would be good."

"But we don't have that," Ben replied. "And the mystery man in the police station isn't going to be enough."

"No," Christina said sadly. "I don't think it is."

"So that leaves us with making the jury like him so much they want to let him off, or making the jury think he was temporarily crazy, which are rather contradictory goals."

"Don't I know it. And that contradiction is playing out big-time right now, inside the heads of each and every member of that jury."

BEN STEPPED INTO the deliberation room. Dennis seemed to have recovered himself with surprising speed. Or perhaps he shouldn't be surprised.

"I just talked to my investigator," Ben said. "Did you know that the late Officer Sentz had a brother who worked at St. Benedict's? With your wife?"

Dennis blinked rapidly several times, as if he was having a hard time processing the information. "No, I had no idea."

"Surely she mentioned the name."

"Not that I recall. But the name didn't mean anything to me—until after she disappeared. And she was always careful to observe patient confidentiality."

"It's a heck of a coincidence," Ben said, frowning. "Does he know anything about the case? About what his brother was doing?"

"I don't know. Yet. My investigator is looking into it. Unfortunately, I have to take you back into the courtroom and finish the direct. I'm beginning to wish we hadn't moved to trial so quickly."

"Could you get the judge to delay the trial?"

"A reasonable judge, maybe. This judge, no. But I'll try."

THE HEARING in the judge's chamber took fewer than five minutes. Ben had said he was ready for trial and now he was going to have to stand by his word. Justice would not be delayed because "some investigator had a hunch of no apparent significance." And so the direct examination of Dennis would proceed.

"Dennis, if you're ready to continue, I have a few more questions," Ben said.

"Of course." He seemed a little steadier. His voice was almost back to normal, though his face was flushed.

"What did you do after they found Joslyn?"

"I kind of lost control at the scene of the accident. Detective Sentz finally showed up and he was angry and bellowing because Torres had initiated the search. The search that found her, if too late. That was just the last straw. I'm embarrassed to say I got in his face and he grabbed me and threw me to the ground. That's when my face was scraped up. He later made it sound as if he had to take precautions to protect himself. That was a crock. He was covering his rear, once he saw how much attention the case got."

"You had been through a horrifying experience," Ben said. "Were there any further incidents?"

"Yes. After Joslyn died. I attacked him and I managed to get one good punch in before his buddies pulled me away. He had me arrested. I spent the weekend in jail. By the time I was released, Joslyn had been cremated. I never got to see her again. Never really got to say goodbye."

"That must have been heartbreaking." Ben was having to fight back tears, as were many in the gallery. "What about later? After you got home?"

"For days, I did nothing. I pretty much fell apart. Let myself go. I felt so bad. So . . . guilty. As if there were something I should have done. Something more. Beating myself up night and day."

"I can understand that."

"And I was angry at Detective Sentz. I will admit that. Thought about him all the time. But please realize—this man had the power to save my wife's life. I didn't! I couldn't save her. But he could. He could and he chose not to. That was . . . that was a very hard truth to deal with."

"You saw your therapist?"

"Yes, and he tried to help, but there was only so much he could do. I was totally consumed with these thoughts about Detective Sentz."

"Did your therapist give you medication?"

"Yes."

"Did you take it?"

"Of course. Couldn't tell that it made any difference, though. I was too far gone."

Not the words Ben would've chosen. Keep it moving . . .

"When did you obtain the gun?"

"I had it already. We lived out in the country, remember? Everyone has a gun. It isn't unusual. It made Joslyn feel safer. But I never used it. Never once. Couldn't even remember where it was at first."

"But you did remember eventually."

"Yes." His features seemed to slow as if he was trying to recall, trying to revisit someplace he didn't really want to go. "I found it. Loaded it. I had become increasingly obsessed with Detective Sentz. I couldn't think, read, watch television. I saw him everywhere I went. I just—" He looked skyward. His eyes were watering. "I wanted him to acknowledge that he did a bad thing. That's all. Just wanted him to take responsibility."

"So what did you do?"

"I went to the police station. Turned out he wasn't there, he was on some kind of stakeout. So I made a stakeout of my own. I watched the police station until he turned up. When he did, I followed him, all the way to the Marriott. I went in and waited. If you sit in the central lounge, you can see the outside of every door on every floor. I watched and waited. Eventually, I saw him go into a room. I took the elevator up."

"Did you meet anyone along the way?"

"Yes. That police officer. The one who testified. Shaw. He tried to stop me. But he didn't try hard. I think he was sloshed. You know." He made a drinking gesture with his hand. "I'd seen him sitting in the hotel bar swishing martinis for several hours. So I pushed past him and went on up to the hotel room. I wasn't planning to hurt Sentz. I just wanted to force him to acknowledge what he had done. I wanted him to take responsibility for the death of my wife."

"And what happened next?"

Dennis took a long deep breath. He seemed almost lost in thought, his eyes turned inward. "I don't know. That's all I can remember."

"Nothing more?"

"I know I got in the elevator. I got off. I have a vague memory of seeing Sentz, of him letting me in the room. We talked. I don't remember what was said. And that's it." He shook his head, obviously frustrated. "I woke up several hours later in the hospital. Apparently I blacked out."

"Objection," Guillerman said quietly.

"Sustained," Judge McPartland replied. "The witness will limit himself to what he saw and heard."

"Do you remember anything more?" Ben asked. "More than what you've told us?"

"No. Nothing. But I want to say this—I did not go to the hotel to kill that man. Yes, I took a gun. Maybe I even wanted to scare him a little. And definitely I wanted him to admit that he had been wrong, that his actions had killed my Joslyn. If there was something going on with him and that man at the station, I wanted to know about it. But I did not plan to kill him. Never in a million years. Joslyn would not have wanted that. And neither did I."

"Thank you," Ben said. "I'll pass the witness."

As Guillerman approached, Ben realized that his chore now was almost as difficult as Ben's had been. This was cross-examination. The DA had to be aggressive. At the same time, if he came on too strong with a man who had just lost his wife in a horrible manner, it could well put off the jurors. He had to find a middle ground, at least until he uncovered some lie or inconsistency. Then, and only then, could he pounce.

"Mr. Thomas, you talked a great deal about your life after you lost your wife and what you did then. But aren't you leaving something out?"

Dennis's head tilted to one side. He obviously didn't know what to say. Questions like that were insidious. The correct answer, of course, was no. But even the most confident witness had to wonder what the DA was about to spring on him. And nothing eroded confidence like uncertainty.

"I'm not sure what you mean."

"You talked about seeing your shrink, going to the funeral . . . but for some reason you're leaving something out. Aren't you?"

"I'm still not aware of what you mean."

"You saw Mr. Kincaid. Didn't you?"

Ben sat up straight, ready to respond. Guillerman was entering dangerous territory. He could establish the fact of a meeting, but any questions regarding the nature or content of the discussion were strictly forbidden. And given that Guillerman had already narrowly escaped a mistrial motion for a closely related leak, he expected the DA to toe the line carefully.

"I—I saw my lawyer, yes."

"And when did you see him?"

"Well . . ."

"It was the very day you shot—excuse me—when you were arrested on the charge of shooting Detective Sentz. Right?"

"Yes, it was."

"How long did you and your lawyer chat?"

"Perhaps fifteen minutes."

"That was all it took. Wow." Guillerman shook his head from side to side, commenting without commenting. "Did you do anything else that day?"

"Only what I've already described. From there I went to the police station."

"So after you had your little chat with the good senator, you went directly to the station, where you waited for Detective Sentz to arrive and then stalked him with a gun."

"Objection!" Ben said.

Guillerman held up his hands. "I'm only repeating the man's testimony."

McPartland was unimpressed. "I think there might have been a little rephrasing mixed in with the repeating. Sustained."

Guillerman continued. "You left Mr. Kincaid's office, you went to the police station, you followed the detective to the hotel, you discovered his room, and you went up. With a gun. Is that correct?"

Dennis exhaled heavily. "That's correct."

"But you want this jury to believe that you did not go there with the intent to kill him."

"That's correct."

"The thought never entered your mind."

"I can't say that. At that time, I had a lot of thoughts going through my mind, some of them pretty bad. But I didn't act on them."

"You did carry the gun for a reason, I'm assuming."

"I thought I might need it to get in to see him. And I

thought I might want to scare him. Intimidate him a little. Get him to tell the truth about what he had done."

Guillerman whistled. "That's very logical thinking."

"I doubt it."

"I must say, Mr. Thomas . . . you don't strike me as crazy at all."

"Thank you. I guess."

"You strike me much more as a planner."

"Objection," Ben said.

"I would prefer it," Judge McPartland said, "if your questions were actually questions, Mr. Prosecutor."

"Sorry," Guillerman replied, not looking very sorry.

"We're not that far away from closing arguments. Can't you wait?"

"I will do my best." He turned back to the witness. "You were apparently level-headed enough to see an attorney before anything happened that might cause you to need one, right?"

"I've already said that."

"And you were level-headed enough to track down Detective Sentz."

"I did."

"And you managed to find out which room he was in."

"It didn't require Jessica Fletcher."

"And yet now we learn that all this time you were temporarily insane, under the control of an irresistible impulse. That was one doggone smart, cold, and logical irresistible impulse."

"Your honor," Ben said, rising, "I'm sorry, but I must object again. This is nothing but closing argument thinly disguised as questioning."

"I have to agree with Mr. Kincaid," McPartland said. "If you have no more real questions, Mr. Guillerman, sit down."

"I'm sorry, your honor. I'll move along. I think I've made my point."

Unfortunately, Ben knew that was the truth. He had made his point, and he would make it even more strongly later. "Now let's talk about this mythical other man you claim you saw at the police station, the one who conspired to force Detective Sentz to . . . well, to abide by the rules of the Tulsa Police Department. You don't know his name, right?"

"Right."

"You can't describe him."

"True."

"No one else saw him."

"No one else will admit to seeing him."

"What about Officer Torres? He stuck up for you at other times."

Dennis lowered his head and frowned. It was obvious this question bothered him. "He said he didn't know who or what I was talking about."

Guillerman spread his hands wide. "Doesn't it seem like someone else should have seen this mystery man?"

"Yes," Dennis said firmly, "it does. And I think it's very suspicious that he could be there and no one recalls it."

"So I guess he was also out to get you? Good thing you didn't know who he was when you were toting that gun around."

"Your honor!" Ben protested. The judge reprimanded Guillerman again, but Ben knew all the legal wrangling would have little impact on the jury. Guillerman was scoring his points, slowly, one by one, chipping away at Dennis's credibility.

"You do understand, do you not, Mr. Thomas, that Detective Sentz was abiding by the written rules of departmental procedure?"

"I know that is technically correct. I also know that he had the discretion to open an investigation if he saw fit. And I believe that most human beings would have done so given the circumstances. The fact that he repeatedly refused to do so is suspiciously—"

"Right, right. I know. The great conspiracy to get you. Or your wife. Do you know of any reason why anyone would want to hurt you and your wife?"

"No. Apparently there was one."

"But you don't know what it could possibly be."

"That's what I was trying to find out!" Dennis leaned forward in his chair. Veins throbbed on the sides of his head. "That's why I wanted to talk to Detective Sentz."

"You mean, that's why you wanted to shoot him."

"No! I just wanted to know what happened. I wanted to know why my wife had to die! Is that so much to ask?"

He was shouting now and it didn't sound good. Ben wished there were something he could do to slow this down, break it up. But there was nothing. A frivolous objection would not help Dennis.

"Let me ask you another question, Mr. Thomas. That whole week she was missing, did you really even want to find your wife?"

Ben closed his eyes. Now Guillerman was being intentionally provocative, taking advantage of Dennis's agitated state.

Dennis was floored, literally sputtering. "I—I can't believe you would even ask that. Of course I did. I—I tried everything—"

"Isn't it true that her car was found less than two miles from your house?"

"As the crow flies. But I didn't know where she was."

"You had a week. In seven days you couldn't find someone who was two miles away?"

"I didn't know where she was!" Dennis was practically shouting now.

"Are there many roads out there, sir? Out to your place?"

"Only one."

"So you couldn't effectively search one road two miles from your home?" Guillerman shrugged. "Of course. Who would think to look there?"

"She wasn't visible!" Dennis was on the defensive now and he acted like it. He was straining, trying to convince the unconvinceable, which never made for effective testimony. "You couldn't even tell a car had gone off the road!"

"What if you got out of your car and looked around?" Guillerman asked. "Like the police ultimately did. Didn't take them long to find her."

"They knew where to go."

"Why did you need a cell phone signal to tell you the obvious? That she was probably not far from home?"

"It wasn't obvious! I didn't know!"

"I'll tell you what I think, Mr. Thomas. I think you didn't want to find your wife. That's why you didn't think to look in the obvious place."

"Noooo!"

"Maybe the real reason you were so angry that day is because the police found her!"

"It's not true, you—"

"You were mad at her. You wanted to be free of her. That's why you hit her!"

"Nooo!" Dennis rose to his feet. "I loved my wife! *I loved my wife!*"

Ben slumped in his seat. It was horrifying. Dennis was melting down right before their eyes.

"Your honor," Ben said, "could we take a short break?"

"No!" Guillerman barked. "I'm not done. Don't let this man have another powwow with his attorney. Who knows what they might cook up next!"

"I'm going to allow the cross to continue," Judge McPartland said.

Guillerman pressed ahead. "You planned this murder,

didn't you, Mr. Thomas? Planned the whole thing from start to finish."

"I did not! I never—"

"You did your research, found out what you needed, got your gun, tracked Sentz down, and shot him in cold blood."

"No!"

"You hated him!"

"I never wanted to hurt him!"

"Then why did you hit him?"

Dennis fell silent.

Guillerman continued. "First your wife, then the cop. You have a nasty little temper, don't you?"

"I never meant to hurt him. I just—I lost control."

"I believe it. More than once."

"It wasn't like that!"

"Didn't you hit Detective Sentz at the scene of your wife's accident?"

"Yes, but—"

"Objection!" Ben shouted.

"Overruled," the judge said in a firm tone that permitted no rebuttal.

"Funny thing to do to someone you didn't want to hurt," Guillerman continued. "Logical thing to do to someone you wanted to kill."

"I just swung—"

"So hard he was scheduled for root canal surgery. Except you killed him before he could get there."

"I did not want to hurt him!"

"He could've pressed charges against you, but he didn't. He withdrew them. An act of charity that cost him his life."

"He scraped up the entire right side of my face!"

"You probably wanted to kill him right then and there, but others stopped you, so you waited until he was alone and did it then!"

"That isn't true!"

Guillerman leaned in for the kill. "And after you hit him, you threatened him."

"No!"

"Didn't you scream, 'There will be a reckoning!' over and over again?"

"I didn't mean—"

"Don't bother lying about it. I have lots of witnesses."

"I said it, but—"

"And that was a death threat, right? By a 'reckoning,' you meant a murder!"

"That is not true!"

"There will be a reckoning, you said repeatedly. And a few days later, there was! You shot Detective Sentz in cold blood!"

"*No!*" He looked at Ben, as if pleading for help. "*No!*"

"One last question, Mr. Thomas. Just one and then we're done. And be honest, because if you are not, this jury will see through you, just as I do. My question is this. You claim you weren't out to get Detective Sentz. You claim you blacked out and you don't know what happened. Very well. When you finally came to, when you awoke and someone told you that Detective Sentz was dead, murdered—what was your reaction?"

Dennis's eyes darted to the defendant's table.

"Don't look to your lawyer for an answer! I think he's done quite enough for you already. I want the truth this time. I want to know—when you found out that Christopher Sentz was dead—how did that make you feel?"

Dennis hesitated. His lips parted, but no words came out.

"We're all waiting for an answer, sir. Tell us the truth! What was your reaction?"

"I—I—"

"Don't pretend you were filled with remorse. Don't give this jury any more trash. Tell us the truth. What was your reaction?"

After all the shouting, Dennis's voice seemed so tiny he was barely audible. "I was glad Sentz was dead."

Ben's eyelids closed.

"What was that, sir? I'm not sure the jury could hear you!"

"I was glad," Dennis said, much louder. "I was glad, okay?"

"You were glad!" Guillerman turned to the jury. "Did you hear that? He was glad!"

"The man killed my wife!" Dennis said, matching his volume. "He deserved to die!"

"Thank you for your honesty." Guillerman threw up his hands. "Nothing more. I've had as much of this calculating killer as I can take."

"Counsel!" the judge said, eyes flared.

"No more questions. I will pass the witness."

"You will pay a five-hundred-dollar fine for contempt of court, that's what you will do. I will not tolerate this kind of behavior in my courtroom. You are an experienced . . ."

The judge's chastisement went on for some while, but Ben knew it wouldn't matter. Guillerman's tirade was well worth the five hundred dollars his office would pay, and then some. The judge would instruct the jury to ignore his remarks, which was rather like asking a mouse to ignore the elephant about to step on its head. Impossible.

Dennis had been seriously damaged during this examination. He wasn't sure Guillerman had actually brought out anything new. What he had attacked was not so much Dennis's veracity as his character. If the jury didn't trust him, they wouldn't cut him a break.

They wouldn't believe he was temporarily insane and they wouldn't be motivated toward jury nullification.

If they bought what Guillerman was peddling, the only thing they would be motivated to do would be to find Dennis guilty of murder in the first degree.

CHAPTER
33

It was ten past two in the morning when the blip on the transponder screen told Loving that Officer Shaw had finally arrived at the hospital.

He slumped down in the front seat of his van, making sure he wasn't spotted. He had waited too long for this to screw it up now. The floating beam of the headlights told him that Shaw's PT Cruiser had passed him by. Then he slowly inched upward in his seat and waited for something to happen.

As far as he could tell, the operation was going down exactly as Dr. Sentz had planned. Loving had successfully intercepted the text message: LOADING DK THU 2. He had picked up a few other text messages, too, which told him more than he ever wanted to know about Shaw's personal life and those massage parlors on Cherry Street.

They were at the hospital's rear loading dock. A truck had been parked here more than an hour. It was not a large truck, however. More like the size of your average armored car. So what exactly was going to be transported? Money? Gold bullion? And why were they picking it up at the hospital? There had to be a reason. No one would choose this location if they could avoid it. Unlike most buildings, a hospital remained active all through the night. It was a dangerous place to be doing anything you didn't want other people to know about.

Why did the oncologist need to be involved? And why was it happening here? He remembered that Sentz indicated to Shaw that someone else was the primary boss orchestrating the operation. Who was it? Loving had no answers—yet. But he was determined to get them.

Shaw left his car. Loving wanted to be in a position to keep an eye on him. He had intentionally parked his van far enough away to avoid attracting attention. But he was too far removed from the loading dock. He needed to be closer. He could try to follow the truck, but he might lose it, and even then there was no guarantee that following the truck to its destination would give him the information he wanted. He would feel much better if he could see and hear what happened. Better yet if he could get a GPS tracking device on that truck.

He was a little worried about exiting without attracting notice. But he had rigged his van a long time ago so that no noise was made and no lights went on when he opened his door. Carefully he eased the door just enough and slid his wide frame through the opening, then began creeping forward. Didn't appear to have attracted any attention.

There was no moon tonight, and that was cutting two ways. It decreased the chances that anyone would spot him. But it also decreased the chances of him being able to spy on them. He wondered if they hadn't chosen this particular spot because there were no lamps or any other prominent illumination. Fortunately, he had retrieved his night-vision goggles from the kit in the rear of his van. He put them on. He didn't much care for the way they made everything look neon green. But it was better than stumbling around in the dark. Especially when you were stumbling around people who seriously did not want to be detected—and might have resorted to extreme means in the past to avoid it.

There were two men standing close to the hospital, in

front of the truck. Shaw joined them. Loving crept a little closer, still not getting anywhere near close enough to be spotted. There was a retaining wall on the edge of the driveway that gave him some cover. He wanted to be close enough to hear what they were saying.

He slid a small plug into his left ear. It was a direction amplifier. Sort of like those eavesdropping dish guns you saw in toy stores, except more powerful and much smaller. He hated the James Bond gimmickry. But they lived in a Google-driven world. The technophobes were not going to rule the earth, much less catch very smart doctors engaged in nefarious activities.

Careful not to make any telltale sound, Loving crept to the rear of the truck and slid a GPS transponder under the bumper. Now he had a backup plan. Time to figure out what was going on.

He hid behind the retaining wall. A few more steps and he was able to pick up some of the conversation, even though they were talking in whispers.

"Everything ready?" Loving did not know who was speaking.

"It will be." That was Sentz. "I didn't want to break in until I knew you were ready to take it away."

"I didn't think you had to break in. Don't you have access?"

"Do you want it to be obvious?" Sentz spoke to him as if he were a child, which Loving was beginning to believe was his usual way of speaking to everyone. "There are only a handful of people who have access."

"And did you make sure everyone else was out of the way this time?" The speaker gave the last two words a particular emphasis.

"Absolutely. Only one other oncologist on duty, and he is very busy."

"Good. We can't afford screw-ups."

"Agreed. Eventually someone is going to notice what's missing—probably soon."

"I got a question." This time it was Shaw speaking. "Shouldn't I be wearing some kinda suit?"

"You're good as long as you don't open the pig. And you wouldn't do that, would you?" The doctor's question seemed particularly pointed.

"Of course not. I just want to be sure. I saw that guy."

"It won't happen again."

"Make sure it doesn't. I'm doing this so I can have a life. It would spoil the whole plan if I ended up dead."

"Granted." Sentz glanced at his watch. "I'll go to the vault now. I'll be back in a few minutes."

"Good. Hurry."

The pig? What are they smuggling, farm animals?

The doctor disappeared. Shaw lit a cigarette. The other man rubbed his hands together, glancing occasionally at the sky.

Loving wondered how long this would take. Every moment he was out here, he was potentially in danger. He didn't have any doubts about what these guys would do if he were spotted. Shaw was surely carrying his service revolver. Loving didn't care to test his aim.

He wasn't sure whether it would be best to rush them as soon as Sentz emerged with the contraband or to wait and try to follow the truck to its destination. The surest way to find out what was being smuggled would be to rush them as soon as Sentz presented the goods. But there were three of them, and it was dark, and at least one of them was armed, probably all of them. It would be safer to wait, though riskier, because even with the tracer, they might escape. On the other hand, the police would be able to charge them with more if the goods were actually transported, and they would need big charges to threaten these people enough to get them to talk, maybe offer some immunity deals to find out what was going on and how it related to the Dennis Thomas case. Decisions, decisions . . .

There were too many questions, and it was too hard to know—

A hand gripped Loving around the mouth.

His eyes went wide. Loving tried to shake the hand free, but he couldn't. Whoever was behind him had locked his other arm around his chest. He was strong. Loving's cover was probably already blown, but he still wasn't anxious to attract the attention of the men on the loading dock. Maybe he could still get out of this alive . . .

Loving kicked back against the retaining wall, knocking his assailant on his butt. His grip on Loving remained strong, even on his back. Loving tried to break away, unsuccessfully. This guy had some serious muscle. Loving pushed again and they went rolling down the grassy hill, locked together like lovers, Jack and Jill, tumbling out of control.

They hit the bottom with a thud. Finally the attacker's grip loosened just enough for Loving to wrest himself free. He swung around, then pushed himself up on his knees and took a swing.

The other man ducked, then lunged under Loving's arms and wrapped his arms around him, tackling him. They both crashed once more to the ground. It knocked the breath out of Loving. He shook himself, trying to get his bearings. The darkness made it almost impossible. He felt a fist clock him on the right side of his jaw.

Enough. He wasn't going to be anyone's punching bag. He jumped up and lunged.

The other man pulled a gun. Loving froze in his tracks.

"Police," the man said breathlessly.

Blast. Probably one of Shaw's buddies. Now Loving would never find out what he needed to know.

He heard the hammer of the gun cock. "You've got ten seconds to tell me what you're doing here."

"I'm not sayin' anythin'."

After a brief pause, the man said, "Loving?"

The dirty cop recognized him. He was a goner now.

"Is Ben here?"

Loving wasn't sure how to answer. He decided to go with the truth. "No."

"Thank heaven for that. For once, he actually showed some sense. Now get down before those jerks on the dock see you."

"You mean," Loving whispered, "you're not with them?"

"With them? I told you, I'm with the police."

"So is Shaw."

"Good point." He took a small pocket flashlight out of his coat and shone it on his face. "Now are we both on the same page?"

It was a face Loving had seen in the office a dozen or more times. Ben's best friend. Homicide detective Mike Morelli.

CHAPTER
34

"LADIES AND GENTLEMAN of the jury, this is not a complex case. The defense has tried to complicate what even they admit is a simple matter, but I think you're smart enough to see through that. You may remember what I asked of you all those days ago when we began this trial. Nothing has changed. All I ask is that you honor the oath you swore when you took on the most important civic duty, that of being a juror. All I ask is that you weigh the evidence fairly and intelligently and that you apply the law."

Guillerman was starting low-key, Ben observed, but he suspected the man would work himself up to a fiery frenzy before he sat down. He would begin with appeals to logic and common sense, but before he was done there would be dramaturgy worthy of a Baptist preacher, filled with tears and invocations of "the thin blue line."

"The crime with which Dennis Thomas has been charged is murder in the first degree. What are the facts that led to this charge? I will tell you. And please remember: these facts are not in dispute."

He raised his hand and began ticking them off, one after another. "He has admitted that he blamed Detective Sentz for the death of his wife. He has admitted that he attacked the man, causing serious injury, and stopped only because other officers were present. He has admitted that he met with a high-profile defense attorney on the day of the murder. He has admitted that he took deliberate steps to discover Detective Sentz's location. He has admitted that he purposefully and intentionally went to the hotel room where he learned Sentz was." Guillerman lowered his chin, looking at them levelly. "And he has admitted that he went there with a gun."

Guillerman moved into the center of the courtroom, taking their attention with him. "This is the honest truth—I've gotten murder convictions on a lot less than that. There's not much doubt about what happened in that hotel room, and I notice that the defense hasn't tried very hard to convince anyone differently. Did we believe for one second that Detective Sentz would harm himself? No. Is there any indication of a third party? No. So why isn't this trial over already?

"There is only one reason. Because they have asserted the defense of temporary insanity. This is called an affirmative defense, meaning that the burden of proof is shifted. They must prove the truth of their defense. As the judge will later instruct you, if they do not, the defense must fail, and you must find the defendant just as responsible for his own actions as you would anyone else."

He took a few more steps backward, bringing himself up beside the defendant's table. "So what actual evidence of temporary insanity do we have?" He gestured toward Dennis. "What proof did you receive that this man was insane? We know he was angry, yes. Obsessed, certainly. We know he had a serious temper and was given to bouts of violence, not only with his wife but with others. He was given medication that might help suppress his violent impulses. But insanity? Where was the proof of that? The entire process of getting the gun, tracking down his intended victim, stalking him at the hotel—none of that sounds like the irrational act of a crazy man. It sounds like the cold, calculating, deliberate act of a man determined to take a life."

Guillerman glanced at Dennis, forcing the jury to do the same, then he moved on. "Excluding the psychiatric evidence, which I will talk about in a moment, the only real proof you have of anything remotely resembling mental illness is his blackout. He says he blacked out and now, conveniently, he doesn't remember what happened. Please remember that he never once, in the entire time he was on the witness stand, denied that he killed Detective Sentz. He just says he doesn't remember. What does that tell you?

"Did he really black out? Or was he faking? What you should be asking yourself is this: Is this one act, this one fainting spell, quite possibly feigned, enough to demonstrate that he was mentally ill? Or was it perhaps induced by the revulsion and horror a rational mind experienced after he completed the murderous act? Was the blackout the result of a brain desperately trying to erase the memory of what it had done?"

Guillerman returned to the jury box. "That leaves us with only one final element that bears on the defendant's excuse. The paid psychiatric witness. The man who himself called temporary insanity a merciful device invented to absolve the guilty. The man who only saw Dennis Thomas once between his wife's death and the murder but still wants to be considered an expert. The man who didn't see sufficient danger signs to take any action, but now wants to tell us that the defendant was temporarily insane. How seriously can you take this man?

"He says Dennis Thomas was under a lot of stress. Well, who isn't? All I can say to that is, with something like six million Americans taking Prozac every day, I seriously hope you do not turn stress into a license to kill. He says that the defendant was disturbed by the loss of his wife and I do not doubt it. Even though it is apparent that the marriage had problems, problems that the defendant has tried to withhold from the jury, I do not doubt that it was hard to lose a spouse, particularly in that way. But there is no good way. Death is a part of life, and each and every day many loving people lose their partners. I hope that you will not allow this to stand as a justification for anyone to vent their rage by taking the life of another human being."

Guillerman moved closer, leaning against the rail. "Here is what we know for certain about this witness. He has received a fortune for his role in this case, somewhere in the range of ten thousand dollars. How many psychiatrists would sell their souls for ten thousand dollars? Sadly, I suspect there are more than a few. He told us that Dennis Thomas had a violent temper, that he had actually struck his wife on at least one occasion. That they were having marital troubles and Dennis was upset about it. That he blamed Detective Sentz and was obsessed with him. That after his wife's death his temper grew to such proportion that the doctor prescribed a temper-reducing medication."

He held up a finger. "But here is the most important thing we learned from Dr. Estevez. We learned that he doesn't believe temporary insanity actually exists. In his own words, taken straight from his book, which he did not disavow on the stand, he said that temporary insanity was 'defined into existence.' That means it doesn't really exist. That means no one had even used the term until lawyers invented it to get their clients off the hook. To prevent them from taking responsibility for their actions. Or to put it charitably, to give juries an excuse to ignore the law."

Guillerman leaned even closer, burning into their eyes, not allowing them to escape his gaze. "These are the two questions you must ask yourself." His voice began to rise. "Do you believe that the defendant was temporarily insane? Seriously? And even if you do, is this a case where it is appropriate to set aside the law and give mercy to a murderer?

"The defendant's lawyer is basically asking you to ignore your head and listen to your heart. But is your heart really saying to let the murderer off? Mine isn't. I have a heart a big as anyone's, but my heart goes out to Christopher Sentz, who gave the best years of his life to this community and got thanked with a bullet to the forehead. Our police officers are the thin blue line!"

Ben drew in his breath. Here we go . . .

"They are all that stands between us and chaos. Crime rampant in the streets. Is this how we want to reward our protectors? By allowing them to be murdered without consequence?" His voice continued to climb. He was in full dramatic dudgeon now, and the jury seemed rapt with attention. "God help us, I hope not. My heart does not go out to the slayers of men who put their lives on the line for us every day. My heart goes out to his wife, now a widow, and his two lovely daughters, now fatherless. My heart does not go out to a man who, for whatever reason, deliberately decided to take another man's life. And it never will!"

Guillerman drew himself up, folded his hands, and added calmly, "You swore an oath when you took a seat on this jury. You swore to apply the law. Nothing else. To apply the law. Please honor that oath."

And with those words, DA Guillerman concluded.

BEN KNEW he could never match Guillerman in terms of oratory. He just wasn't that slick, not even after spending time in the U.S. Senate. Guillerman was probably better than Ben would ever be. And he lacked the weapons in his arsenal to counter his content. In terms of dramatic potency, he simply had nothing to compete with the slaying of a public servant, husband, and father. Bottom line, Guillerman had the better case. If Ben was going to salvage this, he was going to have to take a different approach. Disarm the jury. Find another way to win.

"Ladies and gentlemen of the jury, Mr. Guillerman is right. He's absolutely right. You probably didn't expect to hear me say that. But it's true. He's right."

Out the corner of his eye, Ben saw his cohorts back at the table looking concerned. Dennis was no doubt wondering if Ben was throwing in the towel. Christina knew this wasn't the closing she'd heard him practicing earlier in the day. Well, that was a fundamental part of criminal law—sometimes you had to make adjustments along the way.

"In the main, Mr. Guillerman has not misrepresented the facts. Shaded them in a dramatic manner, perhaps, but he has not misrepresented them. Dennis did in fact follow Detective Sentz. He did in fact go to that hotel room. And he did have a gun. He told you all this. He admitted it. So there's absolutely no reason whatsoever why you should not find him guilty as charged."

Ben turned and started back to the table. Several of the jurors appeared confused, concerned. There was a definite stir in the gallery.

Just as he reached the table, Ben stopped. "Unless, of course, you are concerned about justice." He turned slowly to once again face the jury. "Because surely, even in this day and age, there must be some room for justice in what we almost mockingly call the criminal justice system." He took a step closer. "As I listened to the words of the district attorney, I heard no consideration of justice whatsoever. In fact, I heard him explicitly ask you to disregard justice. And I think that is very sad."

Ben continued to approach, gazing at the jury levelly. "Mr. Guillerman wants to suggest that a blackout could be faked, but I think you know better. The doctors testified that he was out for more than two hours and they were unable to wake him. No one is that good a faker. Dennis Thomas blacked out. So that leads to another question: Why? Dr. Estevez explained it. He said that with Detective Sentz's death, Dennis's dissociative state burst like a popped balloon. The brain literally shut itself down to heal. What contrary evidence have you heard? None. What other evidence have you had to explain the blackout? None. The only explanation that has any evidence in support is that Dennis was gripped by temporary insanity. We have presented our evidence and the prosecution has not refuted it. We have also shown the numerous flaws in their supposedly airtight case. Does this give you sufficient cause for doubt?" Ben paused, letting the jury be reminded of the importance of that word. "Absolutely. An alternate explanation for what happened, never refuted by the prosecution, is always grounds for reasonable doubt. And a man acting while temporarily insane must be acquitted. Like it or not. That's the law."

Ben moved forward, casting a quick glance back at his table. He could see that Christina was still confused. But she wasn't frowning.

He could definitely see concern in Dennis's eyes, though. Worry. He hoped the jury couldn't see it, too.

"The district attorney wants you to believe that this case is a referendum on Detective Sentz. To the extent that he is interested in justice at all, he wants justice for Sentz, his representative of the thin blue line. But Detective Sentz is not the one on trial today. Neither is the police department. Dennis Thomas is on trial. This is a referendum on him. You will decide his future."

Ben moved to the side, inviting the jury to give the defendant another look. "Mr. Guillerman has repeatedly attempted to demonize this man. It's not good enough for him to simply say his trauma after the loss of his wife led him to take an extreme action. He wants you to believe he's evil. He wants you to believe he has an explosive temper, based on the scantiest of evidence. He wants you to believe he's dangerous. He wants you to believe he's a wife beater, based on one minor incident, one Dennis readily admitted. He wants to transform a man suffering from the worst sort of grief imaginable into Hannibal Lecter, a cold-hearted, scheming, calculating killer."

Ben gestured back toward his client. "This man is a literature professor. He specializes in the classics. *The Iliad. The Odyssey.* His students like him, because he goes the extra mile to help them with their problems. He was a loving husband and his wife returned his love. Yes, he has problems, as do we all. But he is a good person, and that did not change in the least until he was hurled into a maelstrom of the most nightmarish events. Days on end of frustration and fear, unable to find his wife, unable to obtain the slightest cooperation from the 'thin blue line.' I don't know whether you think the police are to blame for what they did—or did not do—but this is a fact: their failure to act when they could have acted resulted in the death of Joslyn Thomas. How would you feel about that if it were your spouse in the car? Or your mother? Or you?"

Enough of this. Ben moved to the side, blocking off their view of the defendant, closing in to make his final points. "Yes, Dennis reacted to his wife's death in an extreme fashion. Regardless of what you think happened in that hotel room, it is clear that he did things he should not have done. But that in and of itself proves that his brain was not functioning in a normal manner. He was behaving extraordinarily—like he had never acted before. That is not a strike against him, as my opponent would suggest. That is perhaps your greatest evidence that Dennis was acting under the influence of an altered mental state. That most delicate of balances had been utterly skewered."

Ben paused, giving the jury a chance to register all he had said. "I also have sympathy for Detective Sentz. I'm sure we all do. But that is simply not the subject of this trial. That is a side matter the DA has introduced to distract you from your task at hand. This case is about Dennis Thomas. It is possible to have sympathy for both men—indeed, I don't see how we cannot. But Dennis Thomas is the one on trial. One man has died already. Do we need another? Haven't we had enough death result from this tragic, almost Shakespearean series of events? Isn't this exactly when we as a society should have the courage to resist the temptation to pursue revenge and retribution? The Bible says, 'Blessed are the merciful, for they shall receive mercy.' Mr. Guillerman thinks the fact that temporary insanity allows a jury to grant mercy is a bad thing. I think it's perhaps the one final element that allows us to retain some semblance of justice in the criminal justice system."

Ben folded his hands, signaling the jury that he was coming to a close. "Like Mr. Guillerman, I urge you to fulfill your oath. You agreed that you would listen to the judge's instructions and would apply them to this case. The judge will read those instructions to you in a few minutes and you will be able to take a copy back with you to the deliberation room. All of them are important, but two are paramount. One that says that in order to convict, you must find the defendant guilty beyond a reasonable doubt. If you find the degree of proof is anything less than that, you must acquit Dennis. It is not a choice. If you believe the case against him has not been proved, if doubts still linger in your mind, you must set this good man free and let him get on with his life. And if you believe that he was temporarily insane, you also must acquit him."

Ben moved in closer. "Let's be honest here. Dennis is not a criminal. These circumstances will never be repeated. He is no danger to society. Hasn't there been enough death already?"

Ben held up his hands like trays on opposite ends of a scale. "Justice? Mercy? Or retribution. The choice is yours."

Ben gazed at them one final time, making eye contact with each. Then he took his seat at the table.

The judge read his instructions to the jury, then cautioned them about what they could and could not do in the course of deliberation. Less than half an hour later, they were dismissed. The bailiff led them back to the main deliberation room, where they would remain for the foreseeable future.

After the court session was adjourned and the spectators were leaving, Christina tapped Ben on the sleeve. "Just so you know, I thought your closing was brilliant."

He smiled a little. "Persuasive?"

She did not answer immediately. "Brilliant."

Dennis swiveled around in his chair. His eyes seemed dark, tired. The strain of the trial was definitely showing on him. Probably on all of them.

"But was it enough?" Dennis asked, keeping his voice low so no one would hear. "Will they believe it?"

Ben did not immediately answer.

"I was watching their eyes, but I couldn't tell what they were thinking."

"We'll talk about it when we get out of here."

Dennis appeared surprised. "We're leaving? Going back to the office?"

Ben began packing up his trial materials. "I think we should all go home. I have a feeling the jury is going to be out for a good long time."

CHAPTER
35

LOVING DID a double take. "Mike?"

"Yeah. You're sure Ben isn't lurking around some-where?"

"He's busy with the trial. What are you doing here?"

"Keep your voice down." Mike glanced up the hill. It was a steep slope they had just rolled down, but there were still men in the driveway waiting for Dr. Sentz to return with the mysterious goods. "We don't want to tip off those smugglers upstairs."

"Do you know what's goin' on? What they're doin'?"

"Don't you?"

"Well . . ."

"Then why are you here?"

"I'm tryin' to find out who killed Christopher Sentz."

"I thought that was obvious."

"Ben doesn't think so."

"What else is new? Ben thinks all his clients are pure as driven snow. Even the cop killers."

"Yeah, but I'm beginnin' to think he may be right this time. Something weird was goin' on at that hotel."

Mike cocked his head slightly. "And you think that has something to do with the smuggling ring?"

"I know Peter Shaw is one of the goons up in that driveway. And he was also at the hotel that day."

"Then the foxes were guarding the henhouse." Mike

paused a moment. "You know, that would explain a few questions I've had."

"Why are you tracking smugglers, anyway? Isn't homicide your beat?"

"There was a homicide. A man who died in the most grotesque manner."

"Some kinda mutilation?"

"Worse. Intense radiation poisoning. What the docs call ARS—acute radiation syndrome. Burns all over the body, even more serious internal damage. Organs baked from the inside out. Immune system shutdown. GI tract disintegrated. Stomach lining aspirated. Stress on the body triggers a cardiac arrest in the most painful—"

"I get the idea."

"That's what started my investigation."

Loving remembered the radiation warnings he had seen on the hospital doors in the oncology wing. "There's something inside the hospital? Something dangerous?"

"Very dangerous. And valuable. If you're a terrorist."

Loving glanced up the side of the hill, making sure they weren't doing anything to attract the attention of the men waiting for Dr. Sentz to come out with the contraband. "Can you clue me in?"

"Ever heard of cesium?"

"Can't say that I have."

"It's one of several radioactive materials used by hospitals today for radiation therapy. That's one of many purposes. It's also used in the oil industry to create a more effective drilling fluid. Scientists use it in atomic clocks. Photoelectric cells. But cancer treatment hospitals are the primary users in the United States."

"For what, chemo?"

"It's primarily used to treat gynecological cancers."

Loving thought for a moment. "That was Joslyn Thomas's specialty."

"Cervical and uterine cancers?"

Loving nodded.

"Apparently they place the cesium inside a woman's uterus to irradiate the cancerous growth." Mike swore under his breath. "That's the real irony here. The same stuff docs use to cure cancer patients can also be used by murderers and terrorists to make dirty bombs."

"Dirty bombs? Is that for real? I thought that was a myth. Like Red Mercury."

"Just because we haven't seen one explode in the United States doesn't make it any less real. *Dirty bomb* is basically a catchphrase for any radiological dispersal device. A weapon that combines conventional explosives with radioactive material."

"Does that make it more effective?"

"In a way. You can actually kill more people immediately with conventional bombs. The primary purpose of the dirty bomb is to spread radioactive material over a large area. High-intensity exposure to radiation can kill a person in a few hours. If released in a limited and controlled environment, it could make the place uninhabitable for centuries. In any scenario, thousands could be irradiated. Even if it's not fatal, you know what that means."

"Panic."

Mike nodded grimly. "Terror. Which is the primary objective of terrorists."

"How hard are these bombs to make?"

"Unfortunately, not very. Contact with water is enough to set cesium off. Ice, even. Like all alkali metals, it's highly reactive."

Loving's lips tightened. "Criminy. I thought this case was about vengeance. Not weapons of mass destruction."

"More like weapons of mass disruption. It's all about the psychological effect. Which can actually be a great deal more devastating than killing a lot of people in an explosion."

"You think those guys up there are terrorists?"

"I think they're supplying materials to terrorists. Through the black market."

"There's a black market for this stuff?"

"Big-time. Has been steadily growing since the mid-nineties. The main problem is transportation. This junk can be deadly. You've got to have a protective carrier. Most people wear protective clothing, especially if they're handling it. Even your major-league zealots don't want to be around it. Who would?" He sighed. "But the black market still seems to flourish. Greed and zealotry can be a lethal combination."

"In Oklahoma?"

"You might be surprised. It's everywhere. Haven't you read about the Chechen bombs? The spy assassinated with radioactive materials in London? Surely you remember that Jose Padilla, the al-Qaeda terrorist, was planning to detonate a dirty bomb in the United States. The first robbery from a radiotherapy clinic occurred in Brazil; the thieves got a capsule filled with cesium-137. It usually takes the form of a powder, or sometimes a piece of silvery metal about the size of a postage stamp. They keep it in stainless-steel tubes, but that doesn't stop the radiation—only lead can do that. Those Brazilian thieves planned to sell it but got sick before they could. In the meantime, they managed to contaminate two hundred and fifty people and kill five."

"Geez Louise."

"Not too long ago there was another robbery on the East Coast. These little creeps made off with twenty-seven tubes. We know the stuff ended up on the black market. The authorities couldn't stop it, but they shut down the facility. Terrorists started looking elsewhere. That brought them to Oklahoma."

"When did you find out?"

"When we found the irradiated body in the woods just north of the Arkansas River."

Loving winced. "Who was it?"

"That's the thing—we don't know. The body was too ravaged to be recognizable. Print and DNA checks didn't produce results. After Dr. Barkley determined that it was radiation poisoning, I started investigating the hot lab at St. Benedict's—the only source of radioactive materials in town. After talking to the head administrator, we began an inventory and I eventually learned that some of their cesium was missing."

"How much?"

"A scary amount. Almost twenty tubes."

Loving whistled.

"The security in there is a lot less than what you might find at a government stockpile or a nuclear power plant. Which is why those jerks upstairs have been able to get away with this."

"There must be some precautions."

"Only a few of the docs have access. You need a magnetic key card to get in and you're supposed to sign out for anything you take. Not hard regulations to get around. Especially if you have an oncology doctor working for you."

A light went off in Loving's head. "Joslyn Thomas worked in oncology. Would she have had access to this stuff?"

"Probably."

"You think she was in on this operation?"

"Either that or she found out about it." Mike paused. "Maybe her accident wasn't all that accidental."

"Why did you come here tonight?"

"My investigation led me to the remaining oncologist, Dr. Gary Sentz."

"The brother of Christopher Sentz."

"Another disturbing bit of synchronicity," Mike murmured. "I found out about his little rendezvous tonight because I, uh, managed to find a way to intercept his text messages."

Loving grinned. "That was one busy signal tower."

"What do you mean? You haven't been doing anything illegal, have you?"

"Perish the thought." He jabbed Mike in the side and pointed. "Look! Sentz!"

Loving pushed his night goggles back into place and started up the hill, careful to cling as closely to the ground as possible.

Dr. Sentz emerged from the back door. He was wearing some kind of outfit. A big baggy uniform with a helmet.

Loving looked more closely. It was a hazmat suit. Guess he couldn't blame Sentz for being careful, given what Mike had told him.

"What's that thing he's pulling?" Loving whispered. It looked like a lawn fertilizer, but Loving suspected that wasn't it.

"That's the pig," Mike whispered back. "It's a transport vehicle. Basically a covered bucket on wheels. Made of lead, of course. Hospitals keep them around to transport cesium from one facility to another."

"Or from a facility to a terrorist."

"That, too."

They both crept closer. Loving could pick up some of what Sentz was saying.

". . . map will get you to the exchange point in the desert. Everything has been arranged. They take charge of the stuff. All you have to do is be there."

"Why aren't you coming with us?" Shaw asked.

"Because I'll be the first suspect when they notice radioactive materials are missing. I have to be inside making sure everyone remembers that I was here all night."

"Shouldn't we be wearing one of those suits?"

"Are you planning to open the canister?"

"No chance."

"Then you'll be okay. I had to handle it. You don't."

"How do I know these guys we take the hot stuff to won't kill us?"

"You've been watching too much 24. They don't want to kill off their source. Who knows when they might want more? Now stop talking and open the back of the truck."

Loving steeled himself. If they were going to do something, this was the time.

"What's the plan?" he asked Mike. "Do we move in or follow the truck?"

"I don't want to rely on following the truck in the dark."

"I put a GPS tracker on the back bumper."

Mike arched an eyebrow. "I can see now why Ben pays you so well."

"I wish."

"But I still think it's too risky. I want to bring these thugs in now. Especially if they have something to do with two murders."

"I'm ready when you are."

"Uh-uh. There's more of them than us. And I think there's at least one more accomplice somewhere on the premises."

"Don't you carry a gun?"

"Yeah, and so do both of those men up in the driveway. I don't want to start a shoot-out with radioactive cesium in the cross fire."

"Good point."

"I'm going to crawl back to my car and radio for reinforcements."

"Better hurry."

"I will. It won't take long." He grabbed Loving's arm.

"I know your rep, Loving. Do not go in there on your own. Understand? No matter what. Wait for me."

"Whatever you say. You're the professional. I'm just the talented amateur."

Mike grimaced. "Back before you know it."

Mike skittered down the hill and into the parking lot. Loving decided to move in for a closer look. He had no intention of doing anything stupid. But the more he saw and heard, the more useful he would be later when they were trying to drag out a confession. Or to extract information about the murders.

Lying flat on the ground, he crept forward, pulling himself along by his elbows. In less than a minute, he had made it back to the retaining wall. He was barely fifteen feet away from them.

Shaw and his accomplices finished loading the pig into the back of the truck. Loving saw now why only a small but secure truck was required. Their cargo didn't occupy that much space. But it was far more valuable than most cargo that did.

"Careful going over any bumps," Sentz said.

Shaw gave him a harsh look.

"That was a joke."

Shaw wasn't laughing. "This stuff is secure, right? No chance it's gonna go off and blow us sky-high?"

"Of course not." He smiled. "It wouldn't blow you anywhere. It would burn you up from the inside out."

"Like what happened to Parsons?"

"I had nothing to do with that. That was my boss. But still . . . I wouldn't take any sharp turns."

"You want to drive this rig yourself, jerkface?"

"No, I do not. Safe journey, gentlemen. Text me when you've achieved your goal. We'll meet later to distribute the proceeds."

Sentz started back inside the hospital.

Where was Mike? Loving turned around—

The fist careened out of the darkness and knocked him in the face so hard his head slammed back against the retaining wall. He barely had a chance to react before the second blow came, even harder than the first. A thunderous hammering sound split his skull even more than the blows.

He spread his wobbling arms, trying to push himself to his feet. A well-placed kick to the pit of his stomach stopped that short. He fell back onto the ground with a painful thud.

"Hey, Shaw!" an unfamiliar voice cried. "Look what I found!"

Loving heard footsteps running toward him. He tried to get his bearings, but the pain and the darkness made it impossible.

Someone grabbed him by the hair and jerked him upward. "Know this guy?"

Even though his vision was blurred, Loving could make out Shaw's ugly mug right in front of his face. "I sure do."

"He made us. You know what we have to do with him."

Shaw took a deep breath. "We can't do it here."

"We can't be late, either," the accomplice said.

Shaw slammed the flat of his hand against Loving's face, hard. "We didn't need this complication, Loving."

Several replies came to Loving's mind, but he knew none of them would help his situation.

"We'll take care of him somewhere else, after we drop off the goods."

"That'll be days."

"You in a hurry?"

"No, but—it seems kind of dangerous. He could get loose or something."

Shaw shook his head. "Give him some of that stuff. You know. Like you gave Thomas at the hotel."

Loving's ears pricked up. Did he hear that right? It was hard to hear anything over the ringing in his head.

Loving heard something liquid pouring from a bottle, followed by a strong acrid scent permeating the night air. He didn't like this at all.

Shaw was back in his face. "You just couldn't leave well enough alone, could you, Loving? Had to butt into stuff that didn't concern you. Turn against the cops and cuddle up to the cop killer."

Loving knew any explanation would be futile. What he needed to do was make a break for it before it was too late. If he could just get free, he could run fast, all the way down the hill. Sure, they had guns, but it was dark. There was a chance he might make it. Better than his chances if he didn't.

Before he could try anything, someone pressed a cloth over Loving's nose and mouth. He knew he would soon be unconscious.

"Now put him in the back of the truck," Shaw growled.

"You mean with the—the—"

"Yeah. What does it matter?" Even as consciousness faded, Loving felt himself being dragged over the pavement. "He's gonna die anyway."

CHAPTER
36

BEN SAT UPRIGHT, gasping for air.

What was that about? He was lying in bed, dripping with sweat, heaving like he was in the throes of a major heart attack.

He glanced at the clock on the cable box. Not quite four in the morning. This would be another mostly sleepless night.

This time, the dream had been different. There was no falling, drowning, or burning. This time, instead of being the victim, he was the victimizer.

He was somewhere in medieval England, deep within the Tower of London. An execution was in progress. Hordes of commoners surrounded the scaffold, hurling insults and rotten vegetables. Armed guards slowly marched the prisoner out of his cell and up the steps to the top. The condemned man took his position, then the executioner shoved him down onto his knees, forcing his head over the chopping block. Just before he swung the axe, the executioner pulled the white hood off the condemned man's head.

Not Ben. Dennis.

Ben was the executioner.

Didn't take Sigmund Freud to figure that one out.

Trials always wreaked havoc on a lawyer's normal sleeping patterns, but this one had been worse than most. Part of it was the uncertainty, the feeling that every day brought a new surprise. Part of it was the gnawing suspense, especially now as they waited for the jury to reach a verdict. But part of it was also undoubtedly that Ben couldn't shake the feeling that he was losing. It had consumed him the moment he first walked into the courtroom, and nothing had occurred since to change his mind.

Christina had told him this was an impossible case. He just hoped and prayed that this time she wasn't right.

There was little chance he would fall back to sleep, and it might not be a good thing if he did, given that he had to be wide awake and getting ready at six. This part of the trial—waiting for the jury—was in many respects the worst. You still had to appear, even though the jury might not emerge from deliberations. There was nothing you could do to change what had gone before, nothing you could do to affect their decision. A lawyer could only toss about, worrying that he should have done something different, could have done it better, while biding time and waiting for the axe to fall. The insecure man's nightmare.

He was all too aware that this time the axe could fall—on Dennis's neck.

Since he wasn't going back to sleep, he decided to get up. He stretched, cricked his back, and carefully eased off the bed. For once, he was not going to wake Christina. She had been working just as hard as he. She needed rest.

He passed silently out of the bedroom and into the kitchen. Ben had moved into this boardinghouse not long after he got out of law school and moved to Tulsa. Many years later, he inherited the place from the landlady, Mrs. Marmelstein. After they married, Christina had moved in with him, and now they lived here together when they weren't in Washington. It was a little cramped, since Ben still had tenants downstairs, but she didn't complain. They both agreed it would be foolish to buy or rent something else, especially when they were still maintaining an apartment in D.C. Ben had many happy memories of this place, where so much had happened. Moments of sweet glory. Moments of great loneliness.

He had spent six months here trying to raise his nephew on his own. He still missed Joey. Hadn't seen him for years. Julia kept saying she was going to come for a visit, but it never seemed to happen.

Since coffee was off-limits, Ben fixed himself a piping hot cup of Earl Grey tea. It had plenty of caffeine, but what he really liked was the sensation of hot water cascading down his throat, restoring his strength. Helping him imagine he could function for another day despite extreme sleep deprivation.

He passed the row of plants on a table next to a large window where they could get sun. The flora were all Christina's work. Ben had tried to liven up the room on many occasions with greenery, but they'd never lasted long. Christina referred to the spot as Ben's memorial garden—a memorial to all the plants that had died as soon as he brought them home.

He leaned forward and breathed deeply. She had a thriving lavender, a little bonsai. All full of life.

He loved her so much.

Playing the piano was not an option at this time of the morning, so he tiptoed back into the bedroom, opened the closet, and slowly ascended the ladder, carrying his tea with him. A rooftop portal opened up on a ledge between two gables on the roof. Ben and Christina had discovered it years ago. They both loved to come out here to relax, breathe in the night air, enjoy the cityscape. And on one occasion, this little nook had saved Christina's life.

The sun was just beginning to rise in the east, toward

the TU campus and beyond. There was a low-lying mist hugging the ground and the rays of the rising sun were just beginning to cast an orange corona over the horizon. Spectacular. The city was waking. Cars trickled onto the main arteries of traffic. A few lights were lit in the tall downtown skyscrapers. Shifting shadows played in the niches and corners of the rooftops, changing by the second in the rising light. A few muffled sounds of the city in springtime reached his ears, but it was still mostly quiet. Peaceful. Despite all the life he knew was teeming around him. All the good-hearted people. All the families, the lovers, the children, all involved in their own lives and all a part of one another's, fitted together like glittering tiles in a huge beautiful mosaic. This was when he loved Tulsa best.

"Boo."

It had barely been more than a whisper, but he still jumped almost a foot into the air.

He turned to see Christina in her pink nightie, smiling at him, wriggling her fingers.

Ben took a deep breath. "Are you trying to kill me?"

"I don't know. Have you paid the life insurance premiums?"

"I could have fallen off the edge of the roof!"

"I would've caught you."

And she probably would have, too.

"Having trouble sleeping?" she asked.

"Good work, Miss Marple. You shouldn't be up. You need your sleep."

"Like you don't? I'm pretty sure even Daniel Webster occasionally got a good night's snooze."

"Not during a trial."

"He did. Regularly. Never missed a wink. Snored through the night. And he went up against the devil."

"I know the feeling."

"So come back to bed."

"It's pointless. I won't sleep."

She scooted closer and put her arm around him. "You're worried, aren't you?"

"I think I have good reason."

"It won't help anything. The trial is over. There's nothing more you can do. It's in the jury's hands."

"That's a terrifying thought."

"Only because you start to panic anytime you have to rely on someone else."

He gave her a dismissive frown, even though he knew she was mostly right. "You yourself have many times said that juries are unpredictable."

"All the more reason not to beat yourself up worrying about it."

"You think Dennis feels the same way?"

Christina sighed heavily. "I think that just because one person is undoubtedly in misery doesn't mean we all have to be."

"He's suffered enough."

"I agree, Ben. But there's still nothing we can do. You should learn to meditate. It would be good for you."

"Ugh."

"It's not healthy, the way you take these impossible cases and obsess over them. I know you're trying to help other people but . . . honestly, sometimes I wonder if it's a good thing. For you." She sighed. "Come with me to my class tomorrow night."

"I don't need to meditate."

"No. Clearly you already have achieved nirvana."

"It won't help."

"You'll learn how to breathe."

"Been doing it for years."

"You'll learn how to clear your mind. See things in perspective. Improve your life."

"Sitting cross-legged on a mat is not going to improve my life."

"You can't know that until you've given it a try."

"I can." Ben watched as the municipal garbage trucks pulled away from their central station and dispersed into the city. He saw joggers huffing and puffing down the street, the air still so cold they could see their breath. He spotted teachers pulling into the neighborhood school parking lot, embarking on another day of molding young minds. There were so many good people in this town, so many who genuinely cared about one another, who would go the extra mile to help someone in need.

That was why he had gone to law school. Why he'd chosen the life he now led. He had made enemies and seen many negative headlines, but he had also made many friends and seen so much kindness. He had a wonderful life and he knew it. He should be able to focus on that. That should be enough.

But no matter how much he tried to convince himself, his mind always moved in another direction.

"Have you ever thought about it?" he asked.

"Thought about what?"

"You know. What you would do in a similar situation. If something happened to me."

"You mean if you were left trapped and suffering in a car for seven days because the police wouldn't get up off their butts?"

"Yeah."

"I don't have to think. I know. I'd do the exact same thing, except I'd do it the first day and I'd use a bazooka."

Ben smiled. "And then claim temporary insanity?"

"And then claim justifiable homicide."

"You'd go to prison."

"It would be worth it." She grinned a little. "What about you, you hopeless romantic, you? What would you do?"

"I—certainly wouldn't be happy."

"Oh, not so much emotion, Ben. I'm going to swoon."

"But murder? I don't think I could ever do that. Under any circumstances."

She wrapped herself around his arm and pulled him close. "I know that, sweetie. I wouldn't want you to."

"I know that, too."

They both fell silent. They stared out for a long while, watching the city arise.

"We have a good life," she said.

"It's because of you."

"It's because of us, you silly." She kicked open the portal door. "Come back to bed."

"I can't sleep."

"Who said anything about sleep?"

His head tilted to one side. "Scrabble?"

She gave him a long look. "Yes, that's it. Scrabble. You goat." She rolled her eyes and descended the ladder. "The things a woman has to put up with . . ."

CHAPTER
37

"YOU'RE SURE you haven't heard anything from Loving?"

"I'm sure, boss."

"Not even a hint? A disconnected call?"

"No." Jones handed Ben his mail. "Not a coded letter. Not a message in a bottle. Not a cuneiform tablet etched in ancient Sanskrit. Nothing." He pushed away from his station, juggling phones and files and messages all at the same time. "What were you expecting? The trial is over."

"I know. I just . . . hoped. That he'd call in with something."

"Ride in with the cavalry at the last minute and save the day?"

"I never said the day needed saving."

"You didn't have to."

The front door opened and Christina sailed into the room—then tripped. Her briefcase fell to the floor and skidded across the tile floor.

"Whoa there." Ben ran to her side and helped her back to her feet. "You okay? You seem a little unsteady."

"I didn't get much sleep last night."

"I'm sorry."

"I wasn't complaining." She glanced over at Jones. "Any word?"

"No."

"Have you talked to Dennis?"

"He's standing by. Wringing his hands. Worried sick. Do you blame him?"

"No. I don't. Talk about torture."

The phone rang. The three of them stared at it. No one moved.

Ben made a small cough. "Jones, I believe this is your job."

Jones picked up the phone. "Hello?" He listened for a good long while, then put down the receiver.

"And?"

"The jury has reached a verdict."

DESPITE THE FACT that every single seat in the court-room gallery was filled, there was a strange silence as they waited for judge and jury to return. Even with all the reporters in the rear, each of them eager to hear the outcome and relay it to their masters, there was a pro-nounced funereal atmosphere.

Ben couldn't help but flash back to his nightmare, his mental horror movie. With himself essaying the role of the executioner.

"They were out a long time," Dennis said, wringing his hands. "What does it mean when they're out a long time?"

"It means they're out a long time."

"So there must have been some disagreement, right? Like at least one person believed what we said."

"It's possible."

"And it only takes one, right?"

Ben's throat was dry. "It's not a hung jury. They've reached a verdict. One way or the other."

Dennis's eyebrows knitted close together. Ben could see he was in turmoil, but there was simply nothing he could do for the man at this time.

Guillerman entered the courtroom but did not stop to chat with Ben. No taunts, no bragging, no speculation. The trial was done. He apparently had no more use for collegiality. Ben was relieved.

A few minutes later, Judge McPartland entered the courtroom. His opening remarks were brief and to the point. He did caution the reporters that he wanted no inappropriate outbursts or disruptions when the verdict was read, although Ben had a hard time seeing what he might do about it, unless he had wired the seats to produce electric shocks. They would all be gone before he had a chance to issue sanctions.

When the preliminaries were complete, the judge signaled his bailiff. A few moments later, the man reappeared with the jury trailing behind him.

Ben saw that Mrs. Gregory, the elderly woman with the cat, had been chosen jury foreperson. He hadn't seen that coming. But then, he had tried many cases and he had never correctly predicted the foreperson yet.

Over the years, Ben had heard so much contradictory speculation about the meaning of whether the jury looked at the defendant as they reentered the room that at this point he preferred not to even watch. He stared straight ahead as they took their seats. Why speculate? They would all know soon enough.

"Would the foreperson rise?" the judge said. Mrs. Gregory complied.

"Have you reached a verdict?"

"We have, your honor."

The judge signaled the bailiff again. He took the piece of paper from Mrs. Gregory and brought it to the judge. The judge glanced at it with a perfect poker face. Then he passed it back to the bailiff, who returned it to the foreperson.

"You may read the verdict."

Mrs. Gregory cleared her throat and began. "In case

number C-09-8563, the State of Oklahoma versus Dennis Fitzgerald Thomas, on the charge of murder in the first degree, we the jury find the defendant . . ."

Why did they always have to pause there? *Why?*

". . . guilty as charged."

Ben felt the bottom drop out of his stomach. A gnawing hollowness replaced it. He reached for the edge of the table and missed it.

Dennis stared at him wordlessly.

"Pursuant to the guidelines set forth in the judge's instructions," the foreperson continued, "we recommend that the defendant, having been found guilty of the crime of murder in the first degree, should be sentenced to execution by the most expedient legal means."

The judge polled the jury, but Ben was barely aware of it. "Is this your verdict?" It was, in all twelve cases. "The court will accept the jury's recommendation."

Ben felt as if he had been dropped into a vacuum chamber. It was almost as if it were happening somewhere else, somewhere far away from him. The clamor of the reporters, the applause from the prosecution table, the banging of the gavel, all in some faraway land.

"I want to thank the jury for their service. I know this has been a long and burdensome trial, particularly after you were sequestered, and I want to thank you for your cooperation."

The judge turned to face Dennis. "The defendant will be immediately rendered into the custody of the county authorities. Bailiffs."

Two officers swooped in from the sides, one on either side of Dennis. Ben spotted two marshals in the rear of the courtroom. They were ready.

"Isn't there anything you can do?" Dennis asked, tears springing from his eyes.

"I'll visit you as soon as they allow it," Ben replied. "We will begin immediate work on your appeal."

"Do we have grounds?"

Ben didn't answer. The truth was, he couldn't think of any procedural errors. But he and Christina would put their heads together and come up with something.

One of the bailiffs pulled Dennis's arms back and slipped on a pair of handcuffs.

"Stop this, Ben," Dennis said, weeping profusely. His voice broke. "Please stop this."

Ben felt a dry catch in his throat. "There's nothing I can do."

Dennis fell to his knees. "Please stop this. Please!"

Ben felt his mouth working, but no sounds came out. Tears sprang to his eyes as well. "I—I'm so sorry . . ."

The bailiffs hauled Dennis to his feet and dragged him toward the doors. "I'm sorry, Joslyn!" he screamed. "I'm sorry! *Ben, help me!*"

Ben felt Christina squeeze his arm. "I am so sorry."

They were both sorry, and they were both totally helpless as they watched the authorities drag Dennis away. Within a few days, he would be transported to the penitentiary in McAlester, where he would be placed on death row. To await execution.

"*Help me!*" Dennis screamed one last time before they pulled him out of the courtroom. Ben watched in despair as they hauled him away, the man who had bet it all on Ben Kincaid and, as a result, had lost everything.

CHAPTER
38

LOVING WOKE SCARED.

Too many sensations rushed together at once, all of them confused, none of them good. His head hurt. He was parched. Worst of all, his skin itched. He felt hot, as if he were . . . burning.

His eyes flew open.

Slowly, he assimilated what few facts he could be sure about. He was outside. It was daylight. He was lying on the ground, restrained in some manner. He didn't know where he was, but it didn't look like Oklahoma. More of a desert. New Mexico, maybe. Arizona. He was tied down to something—not that he was likely to go anywhere soon, given how he felt.

He glanced down at his right arm, exposed beyond his short-sleeved T-shirt.

Oh dear God . . .

"Loving! You're awake! About time."

That was Officer Peter Shaw. He recognized the voice. Hard to forget a man like that, after he had . . .

Had what? He tried to remember what had happened when he saw Shaw last. He had a strong sense that something important had occurred, but he couldn't remember the details, nothing after he was spotted by Shaw's accomplice. It was as if he had gotten drunk and had a blackout—but he was pretty sure nothing nearly so entertaining had been involved.

"Don't bother trying to get free. You can't. Don't bother trying to escape. You're going to die."

"Then why haven't you done it already?" Loving managed to say. His voice was slow and creaky.

"Haven't had time, sadly enough. Been racing across the country to make an appointment. And then I get this text message. Turns out our contacts are running late. I'm irritated beyond belief. I hate people who aren't punctual, especially when I'm carrying stuff that can get me arrested. Or kill me dead."

"Sorry you're inconvenienced," Loving grunted.

"You're the one who's inconvenienced," Shaw said. "This leaves me time to deal with you."

Loving bit down on his lower lip. "You're a real piece of work, you know that, Shaw? You make all cops look bad."

"Is that what you think?" He leaned down into Loving's face. "Well, let me tell you something, Mr. High-and-Mighty Private Investigator. You don't know squat!"

Shaw pulled back up, pacing around Loving's prone body.

"Why don't you educate me?" Couldn't hurt to keep him talking. Better than the alternative.

"You think I'm going to start monologing and tell you my whole sad story?" He laughed bitterly. "Why not? You're dead already."

What did that mean? His skin felt so hot . . . "I've known you for a long time, Shaw. You used to be a straight arrow. What happened?"

Silence hung between them, heavy as a hippo. Loving still could feel the sun beating down upon him. At least, that's what he hoped he was feeling.

"My sister. That's what happened. Did you ever meet Nikki?"

"Don't know that I did," Loving answered quietly.

"She's a sweetheart. An angel. Best sister a guy could have. Always there for me. Job troubles. Divorce. Always there. Never had the sense to link up with any guy halfway worth her salt, but she's a princess. Never had a boss halfway worth her salt, either, but she's a queen."

"I'm not seein' the connection."

"Haven't you guessed, Loving? She got cancer. Cervical cancer. Had no medical insurance. Turns out her boss didn't cover her. I took her to St. Benedict's. They're supposed to be the experts, right? But without insurance, she couldn't afford treatment. Think I could afford it? In one month they billed more than I make in a year. It was hopeless. My sweet sister was fading away, turning skeletal right before my eyes. And there was nothing I could do about it."

"So you went dirty. To get money."

"I went dirty to get treatment," Shaw said, kicking his feet in the sand. "What else could I do? When did medicine stop being about healing and start being about money?" He stomped angrily around Loving. "Dr. Sentz approached me privately. He knew who I was. Said his brother had recommended me. Said I might be just right for a very special job."

"Smuggling cesium."

"Chris was already helping his brother set it up. They were taking their lead from some major muckety-muck."

"The guy in the police station. The one who nixed lookin' for Joslyn Thomas?"

"All I know is that I went from catching crooks to being one. They had already made one smuggling attempt that went sour. Pig leaked and their accomplice got killed. Some poor clown named Parsons. Radiation poisoning."

Loving remembered the victim Mike had told him about.

"They said it would be easy. It wasn't. It went bad, right from the start. First time Dr. Sentz tried to sneak cesium out of the hot lab, Joslyn Thomas caught him. He tried to make some excuses, but she wasn't an idiot. She ran out of the hospital. Probably had no idea what to do. But Sentz did. He called his brother. Told him to meet Joslyn on the way home."

Loving's lips parted. "That's why she went off the road."

"Chris drove her into the ravine. She wasn't dead, but he knew she would be in time, and it was better that way. Looking like an accident. If he had shot her or strangled her, everyone would know it was murder. He made sure she wouldn't be found anytime soon. Hid her car behind the blackberry bushes. Smoothed out the dirt, any sign that her car had gone off the road. And that was it." Shaw took a deep breath, then released it. "So you can imagine his reaction when this guy comes into the station wanting someone to look for his wife."

"Small wonder he didn't want to open an investigation."

"Into the accident he caused. Right. He wanted to make sure she was good and dead before anyone found her. And he did." Shaw crouched down beside him. "What he didn't reckon on, of course, was the husband."

"Dennis blamed Sentz."

"He was righter than he could ever imagine. Sentz knew that. Guilt was eating him alive."

"So what happened at the hotel?"

"I saw Thomas as soon as he entered. Called Dr. Sentz, asked him what to do. Sentz brought over a drug to slip into the coffee Thomas sipped while he watched for Chris. I did it while he was in the restroom. Didn't work immediately. He still managed to ride up the elevator, just like I said. I wanted that. See, I was worried about Chris. His guilt was getting the best of him. He was making noise about going to the chief, telling him what happened, trying to make some sort of immunity deal in exchange for a lead on the terrorists. I thought that was a very bad idea. I couldn't let that happen." He paused. "Chris had to die."

Loving clenched his teeth. "Did you let Dennis go up to the room so he would do the killin' for you? Or so he would get blamed for what you did?"

"What difference does it make? Chris is dead. Dennis Thomas took the rap. And here we are."

"Yeah," Loving said bitterly. "What are you gonna do with me?"

"Well, there's really only one choice, right?" He walked away for a moment, then returned with something in his hands. "And it has to be done in a way that cannot be traced back to me. No clues. Not even a bullet."

Loving stared with horror at the small stainless steel tube in Shaw's gloved hands. "Don't do it, Shaw. You don't want this on your conscience. Do not do this."

"Did you know they still haven't identified Parsons? That's how bad this stuff is. Tears you up like nothing else. Add that to the effect of the sun and critters, plus the fact that you won't be found for weeks, probably years, out here in the vast desert." He pulled out the plug in the tube. "It isn't pretty. But it is necessary."

"Don't do this, Shaw."

"Don't have any choice."

"Do you think this is what your sister would want? Do you? You said she was an angel. Would an angel want to live at the cost of so many others?"

"She will never know."

"How can you be sure of that? Three people have died already."

Shaw began to tremble. "Do you think I don't already know that?"

Slowly, he tilted the brim of the tube. A silver-gray powder drifted downward onto Loving's chest.

Loving's eyes ballooned. He twisted from side to side, but he had been tied so tightly he could barely move. "Get that off me!"

"If it's any comfort," Shaw said, "you'll be dead in about six hours. On the down side . . . it won't be a very pleasant six hours."

"Shaw!"

"Goodbye, Loving. You'll understand, I hope, if I don't stick around. Got an appointment to keep. And now that that stuff's loose, I want to be as far away as possible."

"This is wrong, Shaw! Wrong!"

Shaw turned away, covering his eyes. "I can't stop it now, Loving. Don't you see that? It's gone too far. Too far. There's nothing I can do."

"There's always something, Shaw. It's never too late. You can do anything you want. You can be whoever you want to be. Get this stuff off me!"

Shaw shook his head. "No." And then he disappeared.

"Shaw!" Loving bellowed as loudly as he could, but there was no response.

He heard the sound of a vehicle driving away. He was alone. In the desert. Under the hot sun.

The powdered cesium was burning him. Burning a hole straight through to his heart.

YOU CAN'T SAVE everyone.

Ben stared out at the darkened city streets. He had climbed onto his rooftop perch, but tonight he found no solace there. The air was brisk, but it did not invigorate him. The electric blue moonlight cast a shimmering, ethereal glow around the midtown neighborhood, but the sense of forgiving and forgetting that he usually obtained here, at least in a small and temporary fashion, was not forthcoming.

The streets were always busy on a Friday night. Everyone was going out to dinner, it seemed, and each of Tulsa's restaurants would be packed to the brim. He and Christina usually stayed in, but it was fun to watch everyone else hopping about. Movie theaters would be packed with those anxious to get out of the house to see the latest Hollywood extravaganza in the eyeblink before it showed up on DVD. He could see a group of teenagers walking along, singing, shouting, raising a ruckus. A local gang? They didn't look dangerous. Bored, mostly. Looking for something to do. Something to define their existence on a warm spring Friday night.

And what would Dennis Thomas be doing right now? Ben closed his eyes tightly shut. He didn't want to think about it, but the imagery came unbidden. By now the booking would be complete. He'd be in coveralls to-night. Guards acting out power fantasies, or hiding their insecurities with bitterness. Either way, the effect would be equally unpleasant for Dennis. He would not be allowed to bring books. He would not be allowed a window. He would be put in a cold cell block in a small room with someone he didn't know and had nothing in common with until it was time to haul him away to the penitentiary where he would in all likelihood spend the rest of his life. However brief that might be.

Ben ran his fingers through his hair. Christina had tried to comfort him, of course, but it hadn't worked. He not only didn't respond to it, he resented it, if he were to be honest with himself. He didn't want to hear a lot of claptrap about how he had done his best. What good was that? He hadn't been asked to do his best. He had been asked to win. It was no consolation to hear that you can't win them all. At this moment in time, there was only one case, and he had lost it. That was why Dennis was spending the night on a metal cot staring at the ceiling, wondering if he would ever sleep well again.

This was not like most cases. Ben had been reluctant to get into this mess at all, but that didn't matter. He had taken the case, and he had bumbled and lost it. Dennis had placed enough trust in him to put his life in Ben's hands. His faith had been misplaced. His gamble, lost.

To Ben it was never just a case, never could be just a case. He was there to help his client, to do the right thing, to try to extract a little justice from a system that had all too often forgotten that justice was its goal. He'd failed.

Why did he do it? Why was he driven to take these impossible cases? To defend the lost, the hopeless, and, as Jones would point out, the invariably unprofitable. Was he still desperately trying to prove to his long-dead father that he had not made a fatal mistake, not chosen a profession of no value? Or was he trying to prove something to himself? Was he trying to calm the demons roiling inside by showing that he had something to contribute, that he could make the world a little better, one case at a time? Was he trying to find his worth in his work, or was his work trying to tell him who he really was? And how long would Dennis have to suffer because Ben had tripped and fallen on his journey to find his life purpose?

Ben leaned back against the roof, wishing there was some way he could neutralize the thoughts racing through his head. Nothing worked—not food, not television, none of the usual diversions. He had tried playing the piano, the most natural mood elevator he knew. But he couldn't get his heart into it. Not even a good Eliza Gilkyson tune could cure this angst. There would be no release, not even in sleep, when it finally came, because the sleep would be filled with dreams, and his dreams tonight would be nightmares, dark and nasty and remorseless.

Christina had reminded him that this had been an impossible case and that he'd still given the jury a lot to think about despite the absence of any facts or evidence to help him. Ben bought none of it. He had been trying cases for a good while now. He knew the score. The fact was, Guillerman had beaten him because he'd put on the better case. He had outmaneuvered and outfoxed Ben from the beginning. Seen him coming. Outflanked him. The courtroom was a battlefield, and Ben had been pummeled by enemy artillery. Decimated.

That stung.

You can't save everyone, Christina had tried to tell him. And the logical part of his brain knew that she was right. But what he was feeling at this moment had nothing to do with logic.

He knew he wasn't being fair to himself. He didn't care. He didn't want to be fair. He didn't deserve it. On this warm spring Tulsa night, he had no memory of all those he had helped in the past. All he could remember was the man lying on the metal cot staring at the ceiling for what would be the first of so many sleepless nights, alone, apart, separated from everything he ever knew or loved. Until it was time for him to be put down. Because Ben hadn't been able to save him.

CHAPTER
40

LOVING SAW the first sores appear on his arms, then his legs. Big pustulous sores. Ugly ones. Scars that would never heal.

Next, he felt extreme nausea. He was heaving, puking uncontrollably. He couldn't stop himself. It felt as if he were vomiting up his stomach, lining and all, spewing out his insides.

The sores continued to bubble, boil. They hurt. They spread across his entire body.

Inside, he could feel the poison eating away at him, his insides turning to fleshy mush. His GI tract giving up. His internal organs boiling and bursting, spilling even more poison into his system.

Worst of all, he knew his immune system had shut down, so there was no hope that anything happening to him would ever get better. His body was falling apart, melting. Liquefying.

He was on fire! The pain was so intense, like nothing he had ever felt before, and he had felt a lot of pain in his time. He was being cooked on a high-power rotisserie, inside and out. Burning him alive.

"Ahhhhhh!"

Loving squirmed from side to side, desperately trying to get loose. He knew he was hallucinating. He knew it wasn't really happening, not like he imagined. But it felt just as intense. He was ashamed of himself for giving in to fear and panic, but what could he do? There was a mushroom cloud on his chest! It was killing him!

How long had it been? Seemed like hours, although some small remaining remotely rational part of his brain said it had not been nearly so long.

Shaw had said it would take six hours to kill him, but Loving knew it would hurt a long time before that. He had felt as if he were roasting since he awoke. He was in the desert, under the sun, perhaps that was natural. How could he know? Was it the cesium or the heat? Or his imagination? Which one would kill him first?

He took deep breaths, trying to calm himself. There was no point in panicking, he muttered. Then again, was there any point in remaining calm? Was there any point in anything? He would be dead in six hours. His body was melting!

He wished he'd had a chance to say goodbye to his father. He did regret that. Maybe his ex. She had hurt him badly, but he had loved her once and in some part of his heart that would never change. He would have at least liked to have dropped by and said something to her, tried to patch things up. Before he melted!

Why did people play with this stuff? Did they not understand how dangerous it could be? How could we possibly justify keeping any kind of radioactive materials around for any reason at all? Anyone who thought that was a good idea should have to sit with a tube full of cesium on their chest for a while and see if they changed their minds.

He wondered what had happened with Ben and the trial. That was the worst part of this, knowing he had let Ben down.

Who was he kidding? Melting alive was the worst part of this. But he did worry about Ben. The Skipper had done so much for him over the years. What had happened? He had no sense of time, but he knew the trial was winding down even when he was last conscious, back in Tulsa. What would happen to Ben if he lost? There should be some way to convey the information he had obtained, before . . .

Before he boiled.

He closed his eyes and prayed, prayed like he hadn't since he was a child. He knew better than to ask for deliverance. That kind of miracle did not occur anymore. He asked for assistance for Ben or, failing that, for comfort. He asked for happiness for his friends, his family. His ex. Everyone back at the office. And then he prayed that the radiation would kill him quickly, before he had thoroughly experienced the excruciating pain he knew was soon to follow . . .

The sun was still beating down on his face when he first heard the sound of a car engine. More hallucinations. Only explanation. Could he not, please, get the one about the bright white light? Because he was ready to be out of this . . .

The footsteps came so loud and so fast he thought they were going to trample over him.

"My God, is that what I think it is?"

"Yes. Get the freaking pig!"

More footsteps. Loving felt something hard brush against his chest. He hated to open his eyes. He knew it would only lead to more delusions. But it was hard to resist . . .

"Mike?"

"I'm here, buddy. Sorry it took so long."

"Mike?"

"Don't try to talk. You've been out in the sun too long. You're severely sunburned."

"Is . . . that what it is?"

"Yes. We caught Shaw and his friend just down the desert a few miles. Thank God you put that tracker on the truck. After you were nabbed, I got the transponder screen out of your van, but I didn't know the frequency.

Figured it out eventually, but by that time they were out of range. Knew they were going to New Mexico, though, from their text messages. Called the local authorities and got a helicopter to track down the signal. That's how we found you."

"You're . . . talking too fast."

"Sorry. Doesn't matter."

Loving felt the tension in his arms and legs relax. They had cut him loose.

"Don't try to stand. We're wearing hazmat suits. We'll carry you back to the truck, then copter you out of here. You've been exposed less than an hour, so you should be okay, but we're still going to fly you into Los Alamos for a very special chemical shower."

"That sounds . . . nice."

"It will do the trick."

"Need to call . . . Ben."

"Doubt if he's in a very good mood. He lost that trial."

"What?"

"Yeah. And you know how he is."

"But—Dennis is innocent."

"I know you think so, but—"

Loving grabbed Mike's arm. "I know he's innocent. Shaw told me so."

"What? When?"

"Let me get to Shaw. We'll make him a deal. Get him to testify."

"First we have to get you that shower. I can't guarantee the DA will make any deals. Or that Shaw will cooperate."

"He will. Now that it's over." Loving was so tired. Maybe it would be okay, just for now, to rest. For a little while. "He'll do it."

"Maybe if we can make it in his own best interest."

Loving shook his head slowly. His body was beginning to relax, and he wasn't even out of the sun yet. "He'll do it for his sister."

FIVE

Those Who Danced

CHAPTER
41

"Mr. Kincaid, I know why you're here. Again. Do you recall the last time?"

"I do," Ben said contritely.

Judge McPartland pointed his gavel. "Then you may recall my telling you that if you brought another motion before this court, without new grounds, I would cite you for contempt and throw you in jail."

"I recall that distinctly, your honor."

"It is one thing to be a zealous advocate. One cannot help but admire that. Up to a point. But when the trial is over, it is over. Your remedy, if any, is to appeal to a higher court, not to keep badgering the trial court."

"Yes, sir. But an appeal takes a year or more. A motion to set aside—"

"I don't need a lecture on trial procedure, Mr. Kincaid."

"No, sir."

"Especially not during your third attempt at the same motion. You are very lucky that I have not already—"

"He's innocent!" Ben exclaimed.

A hush fell over the packed courtroom. Despite the fact that most of those in attendance were reporters, there was not so much as a cough. Perhaps they were stunned that he had raised his voice. Or perhaps, like Christina, they thought it was long overdue. If dangerous. Especially with an old-school judge. Good thing he'd brought a toothbrush . . .

"I am aware of your position, Mr. Kincaid. And I do not doubt that you genuinely believe it. But we have rules and procedures in this justice system of ours. Surely you must realize—"

"I've been down this road before," Ben said firmly. "Trying to get someone out of the clutches of the criminal justice system when I knew he was not guilty. Seeing a good man rot away in prison because the wheels of justice turn so slowly."

"I admit the system is flawed—"

"But no one ever wants to do anything about it. That's why so many trials go bad. That's why more than a hundred people have been released from death row because DNA evidence proved the criminal justice system totally screwed up. That's why—"

Behind him, Ben felt Christina tugging at the back of his coat. He coughed into his hand. "But I digress . . ."

Since Dennis Thomas's conviction, Ben had alternated between halfheartedly planning an appeal and mostly wallowing in his own guilt. He should've done this, he should've done that. Nothing made him feel better. Despite Christina's best efforts to bring him out of his funk, all he could think about was the fact that there was a man in prison—a man on death row, no less—because he'd let himself be outmaneuvered by a sharp district attorney positioning himself for reelection.

Then he got the call from Loving. Mike, actually, on behalf of Loving. Slowly he was able to put the pieces together. Within twenty-four hours, he was back in front of this court with a motion to set aside judgment based upon newly discovered evidence. Ben presented an affidavit from Loving in which he described in detail everything that Shaw had told him. The intentional killing of Joslyn Thomas. The deliberate refusal to investigate. The drugging of Dennis Thomas. The cesium black market operation that lay behind the whole complex drama.

His motion was denied. The judge took it all into consideration, but he noted that the standard for setting aside a jury verdict was very high, and rightly so. Otherwise there would never be any finality in any case. He noted that the affidavit had been sworn out by someone who worked for the defense attorney, which of course went to its credibility. He also noted that it was all hearsay, a form of evidence disfavored by the courts, and that Loving had recently been drugged and was suffering bouts of memory loss as a result.

A week later, Ben was back with another motion. This time he had an affidavit from Mike detailing the entire police investigation, not only of the death of Christopher Sentz but also of Joslyn Thomas. A subsequent, more intensive investigation at the crime scene revealed evidence that Joslyn's accident had been engineered, then covered up, by a third party—Christopher Sentz. He also detailed the investigation into the cesium robberies and how they related to the Thomas case, and noted that Peter Shaw had perjured himself at trial and others might have done so as well.

The judge admitted that he was impressed. He admitted that it appeared the whole truth had not come out at trial. But he saw no clear indication of anything that likely would have altered the jury's verdict. Mike was unable to explain what had happened in that hotel room. Motion denied.

Dennis had sat beside Ben for both hearings. Ben had warned him that this was a difficult business and that he should not get his hopes elevated. But how could he not? He was a human being. How could he help but hope that this would be the time he finally found justice? But it never happened. Ben let him down again, just as he had done at the trial.

And every time, Dennis looked a little older, a little more tired, a little more beaten. It had only been three months, but his hair was already grayer. His eyes sagged. His skin was pale, almost translucent. This was not a man who needed to be in prison. Or who, Ben suspected, would survive long there.

"The point of this third appearance, your honor, is that we have even more newly discovered evidence. And this time it's being provided by the district attorney's office."

Judge McPartland raised an eyebrow. He looked over at the prosecution table. "Is this true?"

Guillerman nodded. He didn't look happy about it. Truth was, Mike had orchestrated the whole thing, and it had taken a long time. He had to get the cooperation of a host of law enforcement officials, both state and federal. Eventually he brokered a deal. Shaw received a reduced sentence—and his sister was guaranteed medical treatment. In exchange, he agreed to testify at this hearing. Once Mike had the whole matter arranged, Guillerman had little choice but to go along with it.

"Very well then. Mr. Kincaid, please call your witness."

"I SEE NOW that my head was all messed up. I couldn't think straight. I wasn't sleeping well. Drinking too much. Taking pills to help me stay calm. You got to understand—I've never been married. I have no children. My sister is my whole world. The one who was always there for me. The one who stood beside me when the rest of the world couldn't care less. I could not watch her die because we couldn't afford the health care she needed!"

Shaw, like Dennis, had also changed much in the three months since the trial. He'd lost a good deal of weight. He'd shaved his goatee. His skull was stubbly. Ben knew he had spent most of that time incarcerated at the Tulsa

County Jail. Perhaps he did not have access to the usual grooming tools.

But Ben also sensed a certain calm about him. A rectitude, perhaps. As if, now that all the secrets were out, he didn't have to hide anymore, and he was relieved about it. Better to bask in a harsh sun than to cower in shadows.

"I was horrified when I heard what Chris had done. Driving that poor woman off the road like that. Covering it up. She never did anything to anyone. She spent her days trying to help the sick and dying. And this was her reward? Just because Dr. Sentz was sloppy? It wasn't right."

Ben felt Dennis flinch each time Shaw talked about the horrors that had been visited upon his wife, but somehow he managed to keep it together. Ben didn't know how. Perhaps Dennis had also acquired some strength during the intervening months.

"I knew Chris was stonewalling the investigation. I thought it was a mistake. Better to seem to cooperate than to create suspicion. But he didn't see it that way. He was afraid she might still be alive—which was correct, as it turned out—and he didn't want her found anytime soon. That's why he was so upset when he found out what Officer Torres had done. He was afraid he would be found out. Didn't happen. He overreacted. And his overreaction set the whole drama into motion.

"After the body of Parsons was discovered, dead from radiation poisoning, the Tulsa police began an investigation into the murder, and then later into the cesium smuggling operation. Unfortunately, since Sentz was in charge of that one, too, it never got anywhere. He figured the safest way to make sure the cops never got close to him was to run the investigation himself. The stakeout at the Marriott was a big smoke screen based upon faked nonevidence. The irony was, we were the smugglers we were supposedly hunting."

Behind him, Ben saw reporters scribbling furiously. The clickety-clack of laptops had been deemed too distracting, so they were forced to resort to pen and paper, which for many of them, Ben suspected, was a new and strange experience.

"I totally used Dennis Thomas. Dr. Sentz knew his stupid guilt-ridden brother had to be eliminated, but he was too weak to do it himself. He just made little hints, you know? Basically hoping someone else would do it, so he wouldn't have to come face-to-face with what he was—the kind of monster who could contemplate killing his own brother. So I drugged Dennis Thomas. He was our patsy. He took the fall, and covered up our whole operation in the process."

Beside him, Ben felt Dennis's arms shaking. Seething with anger? Furious about the great injustice that had been done to him? Or trembling with anticipation? Perhaps he was beginning to feel, as Ben did, that this time the result might be different. This time the evidence went into the hotel room.

"Mr. Guillerman, would you like to cross-examine?"

"No," he answered succinctly. "I have no reason to doubt anything the witness has said."

Ben's eyes widened a bit. He was not only not challenging but implicitly endorsing the witness. A brave move from the district attorney who had fought to put Dennis away. He was signaling the judge that even if his office did not allow him to support this motion, he certainly did not oppose it.

After Shaw finished testifying, he was taken by two marshals and escorted back to the jail. Eventually he would be moved to prison, where he would serve several years. Given all that he had done, the deal let him off easy. But it would be worth it if it got Dennis out of the coveralls.

"Is there anything else?"

Both attorneys shook their heads.

"Very well, then. I want to check a few precedents and gather my thoughts. Please do not leave the premises. I will render a judgment before the close of business today."

Christina and Ben looked at each other. They weren't even going to say what was in their heads, as if voicing any hopes might jinx them.

Dennis did not have the same control. "He's thinking about it, right? We know he's at least thinking about it?"

"We do know that."

"But what if he denies your motion again?"

"Then we take it to the Court of Criminal Appeals. Justice Johnson and that lot. At least now we've got some real issues."

"But no sure thing."

"That doesn't exist in the legal world."

"And that will take a year to be heard?"

"At least."

Dennis fell silent. Ben took his hand and squeezed it tightly.

That wasn't much. But at the moment, it was all the attorney had to offer his client.

LIKE ALL BREAKS, this one gave Ben a chance to contemplate everything that could possibly go wrong. It was still possible that the judge could dismiss the testimony as lacking credibility, since Shaw was a known perjurer and he had basically sold his testimony to get a lighter sentence. It was possible he could find any of a thousand other flaws as well. And Ben contemplated each and every one.

He was greatly relieved when the judge finally returned to the courtroom.

"It may well be that we will never know everything that happened in this case. I for one would like to know who masterminded this sale of radioactive materials, and the identities of the intended buyers. I would sleep better tonight if I had that information. But my job here is to analyze the new evidence that has been presented in terms of the case tried. Specifically, my job is to determine whether the new evidence justifies setting aside the jury's verdict."

He took a deep breath before answering. It seemed it was not only jurors who instinctively drew out the big moment of revelation.

"Most motions for new trial can be dismissed out of hand. Most newly discovered evidence is neither new nor evidence of much. But this is different. Here we have a confession from a key player in a criminal operation. To use his own words, Dennis Thomas was their patsy. And I for one am ashamed that both law enforcement and the justice system played a part in this ongoing misuse of a grieving husband."

McPartland drew himself up to his full height. "It is with this in mind that I announce that the defendant's motion is hereby granted. The court will entertain any writ for relief the defense may care to subsequently submit and my ruling will be forwarded to the court of the pending civil action. The judgment against Dennis Thomas is hereby set aside and double jeopardy has attached. Therefore, Mr. Thomas, as of this moment, you are a free man. Marshals, remove those shackles."

Dennis jumped up into the air. Most of the reporters in the gallery did the same. He heard a cry from the back row, then another. A few moments later, a spontaneous round of applause broke out.

The judge hammered down his gavel. "This court is still in session!" he barked. "Therefore, there will be order in this court!" His stony glare melted into a smile. "However, what you do afterward is your own business." He brought down the gavel again. "This court is in recess."

The crowd once again burst into applause. The back doors slammed repeatedly as people raced in and out.

Before Ben even knew what was happening, he felt Dennis's arms wrap around him. "Thank you," he said quietly. Ben could tell he was weeping. "Thank you so very much. From both of us."

Ben didn't have to ask what that meant.

Over his shoulder, Ben saw Guillerman approaching.

"I know you might not want to hear from me," Guillerman said, speaking to Dennis, "but I am genuinely sorry about what happened."

Dennis reached out his hand. "I don't blame you."

"Thank you. But I won't stop blaming myself." He looked past to Ben. "Congratulations, counselor."

"Thank you for not opposing the use of the Shaw evidence."

Guillerman shook his head. "I'm not a total jerk, you know. Honest." He reached out his hand to Ben. "Thank you for your damned tenacity. You are a testament to this profession. What it should be."

Ben didn't know what to say. So he simply took the man's hand and shook it.

"Hey, do I get in on this celebration?" Christina was standing on her tiptoes, trying to break into the circle.

"If you insist." Ben turned around and gave her a big hug.

"I always have to beg for it." She hugged him back. "Way to go, slugger. I'm proud of you."

"Thank you, my dear."

"But if you think this means I'm going easy on you tonight on the Scrabble board . . ."

"Don't be ridiculous." He wrapped an arm around both his wife and his client. "Dennis, how long has it been since you had a really good New York–style pizza?"

"Ben, I've been in prison."

"Right. Well, as it happens, Mario's is still open . . ."

CHAPTER
42

BEN PROBABLY should have stayed home. It always took at least a day to recover from a major trial. Or even a minor one. To transition from having one event totally subsume your life to reintegrating everything that used to be important was not something that could happen in a day. He knew many attorneys who got on a plane and disappeared for at least a week after a trial. Granted, the actual trial had ended some months ago, but Ben had been just as obsessed in the following months as he had been when he was going to the courtroom every day.

Christina was ready to get out of town. He knew that. She was still reminding him that they had never actually gone on that honeymoon he'd promised.

Maybe later. For now, he needed to catch up. Hadn't had lunch at Goldie's for a while. Or played the piano. Worked the Sunday *Times* crossword. And if he just spent more time studying those *Q*-without-*U* words, he was sure he could finally beat Christina . . .

There was a knock on his office door.

"Loving!"

Ben jumped up and ran to greet him. He had only seen him a few times since Mike and the rest of the police officers rescued him from Shaw and his thugs. Loving had asked for a leave of absence and taken some time off.

"How are you?"

"I'm . . . tryin' to get myself together."

"Still feeling a little shaky?"

Loving paused a moment, as if struggling to come up with the right words. Ben knew he was not typically a garrulous sort, especially when it came to anything as squishy as his personal feelings. "Yeah. It's hard."

"I don't doubt it."

"I totally cracked up out there," he said. "I cracked like a . . . a . . . cracker."

"Oh, you did not."

"You weren't there, Skipper. I did."

"Mike told me he was very impressed by your fortitude."

"He was bein' nice. I lost it. Hallucinated."

"The sun was hot—"

"Thought I was at death's door. And I hadn't even been out that long. It was all in my mind."

"You'd been knocked on the head. Given a drug. They had you for three days."

"I don't even remember that. But I sure remember what happened when I woke up. I was a basket case. Loserville." Loving shook his head. It was an amazing thing, seeing this gruff barrel-chested man talk in such an introspective, emotional manner. "I've been through a lot in the last few years—most of it thanks to you. Embarrassment. Beatings. Even torture. None of that was fun. But when that guy poured the cesium on my chest, I went to pieces."

"Anyone would, Loving."

"No, not like that. I—I think I've been hidin' somethin'. For too long. Somethin' knocks me down and I get right back up, like I'm one of those inflatable toys you hit but they swing right back up at you. I'm not an inflatable toy!"

"I know that, Loving."

"And this time, I'm not bouncin' back up again. I need some time."

"Take all the time you need. Please."

He took a deep breath. "I'm goin' to Colorado. To the Shambhala Meditation Center. Where Joslyn Thomas went." He looked at Ben squarely. "I'm gonna learn to meditate."

Ben resisted asking if this was Christina's idea. He already knew the answer. "You?"

"I wanna find some peace of mind."

"Well . . . we all do."

"I'm on a journey. And this breakdown has shown me there's some stuff inside me that I haven't gotten in touch with. I wanna know the real me. I wanna understand my life purpose."

"I thought it was, you know. Working with me."

Loving gave him a long look. "I've been driven by fear. How else do you explain what happened to me? How else do you explain all those crazy conspiracy theories I've been chasin' all these years? I've been readin' this book." He pulled it out of his back pocket. "*How Not to Be Afraid of Your Life*. Written by this gal who practices Buddhist meditation. She's really smart. Look at her picture on the cover. See how happy she is? She's runnin' the retreat."

"Sounds splendid."

"So that's why I'm here. I have something I want to ask you."

"Like I said, take all the time you need."

"Would you come with me?"

Ben's lips parted. "Me? At that . . . retreat thingie?"

Loving gripped him firmly by the shoulders. "I think it would be good for you, Skipper."

"Well . . . no doubt . . ."

"Seriously. You think I don't know you've got issues?"

"Excuse me?"

"Skipper, I'm only sayin' this 'cause I love you."

"You do?"

"You're one big ball of neurosis and insecurity. You always have been. You worry all the time. You're lonely even though you've got great friends, a great wife. You're dissatisfied even though you're doin' great work, got a great job, helpin' other people. You've got the whole world in the palm of your hands, but you don't know it."

"Do tell . . ."

"Sure, Christina keeps you from going totally off the deep end—"

"Does she now?"

"—but even she can't do it forever all by herself. Skipper, your friends love you. We don't wanna see you have a total meltdown. End up in the nuthouse or dead in a ditch."

"We have that in common."

"So whaddaya say?" He squeezed Ben's arms even tighter. "Come with me. Let's make the journey to inner peace together."

"Loving . . ."

"Are you gonna claim you already found peace of mind? 'Cause you're about the least peace-of-mind person I know."

Ben gave him a piercing look. "I appreciate your concern. But it's not for me. I hope it works well for you."

Loving looked as if Ben had just run over his cat. "Are you sure, Skipper?"

"I'm sure."

"Nothin' I can do to change your mind?"

"Absolutely nothing." He opened the door and let Loving out. "Best to the Buddha." And closed the door behind him.

NOT TEN minutes later, Ben was interrupted by another knock at his office door.

"Loving, I don't need no more dharma."

"Ben?"

He looked up. Dennis Thomas was poking his head through the door. "Have you got a moment?"

"Of course I do." Ben showed him to the chair opposite his desk. "How's life on the outside?"

Dennis grinned. "A lot better than life on the inside. That's for darn sure. I'm very excited about my future."

"Well, that's two of you."

"Huh?"

Ben smiled. "Loving is going on a meditation retreat. He wanted me to go. But obviously, I declined."

"I'm not surprised."

"I'm glad to hear that you don't think I've got issues."

"I didn't say that. I just said I'm not surprised you're not going."

Oh. "What can I do for you, Dennis?"

"I wanted to give you a gift."

Ben held out his hands. "That's not necessary."

"Please. As little as you charged me, it's the least I can do." He reached into his side bag and handed Ben a big blue book. "I hope you'll like it."

Ben stared at the cover. *Autobiography of a Yogi,* by Paramhansa Yogananda. *It's like an epidemic around here . . .*

"I gather this has something to do with meditation?"

"The Yogananda was one of the great spiritual guides of the twentieth century," Dennis answered. "Joslyn loved him. Read everything he wrote."

"Well, I'm sure it's a fine book, but you know, I'm an Episcopalian . . ."

"Buddhism is a philosophy, not a religion. And the Yogananda wasn't Buddhist. He was spiritual, not religious."

"What's the difference?"

"I just wanted to give you a message. From Joslyn."

Ben blinked. "From Joslyn?"

"The last thing she said to me. Outwit the stars. At first, I thought it was some sort of mantra or something. But after I read that book, I realized she was trying to tell me something very specific. The Yogananda knew that many people believed in astrology. That our fates are steered by the stars. But he was a great believer in the strength of the spirit and the eternal nature of the soul. He believed that we could change what the stars dealt us. He believed we could become whoever we longed to be."

Ben fell silent.

"Everyone has issues with which they must deal. Baggage from parents, lovers, spouses, ex-spouses, children. From traumatic events. They deal with their problems in different ways. Or find ways to avoid them. Some of those ways actually benefit other people, but that doesn't change the fact that they are not dealing with their issues. More like self-medicating with good deeds. And how long can anyone keep that up? Not forever. It's impossible to know exactly what another person's triggers might be . . ."

He seemed to be peering at Ben very closely. It was making him uncomfortable.

". . . but I know what Joslyn was seeing. She knew she was dying. And she knew how I would react. Because I do have a temper. That's one of the attributes the stars dealt me. She knew that could potentially get me into a lot of trouble."

Dennis averted his eyes toward the floor. "After she died in my arms, I was filled with rage. When I saw Christopher Sentz, I wanted to do more than just punch him in the face. I wanted to kill him. For days thereafter, I wanted to kill him." He shook his head. "I didn't really get my head clear until I read this book, after I got out of prison. Then I understood what Joslyn was telling me. And I did it. I let go of my anger. Not just toward Sentz. Toward everyone.

"Have I told you about the foundation?" Dennis asked eagerly. "Whatever we get from the state, I'm putting into the Joslyn Thomas Foundation. To help those with medical difficulties who can't get proper care. It's not right that people have to endanger their health because they can't afford to pay for it. It's not right that children go uninsured through no fault of their own. Let's face it—if Officer Shaw's sister had been able to afford treatment, this whole mess might never have happened. So I'm going to try to make sure it never happens again."

He leaned back in his chair. "I'm a better person now, Ben. Much better than I was before. It took a tragedy to get my life in order. But sometimes I think that's why tragedies happen. We need something dramatic to shake us by the shoulders." He smiled. "So we can outwit the stars."

He leaned forward, gripping Ben's wrist tightly. "We all can."

He stood up and clapped his hands together. "Well, I suspect you've had about enough of me for one lifetime. I'm going to get out of here. So you can move on and obsess over something else."

His eyes twinkled a bit. He walked toward the door, and just before he left, added, "Thank you, Ben. For giving me my life back. And making it better."

He left the office. But even halfway down the hallway, Ben was able to hear him shout, "Now read the book!"

Ben blew air through his teeth. Honestly. He supposed it was sweet, in a way. So many people wanting to help him. As if he needed it. The only thing he needed right now was a little time off. Although he saw from the message on his desk that Jones had a potential new client for him. She had no money and the evidence was totally stacked against her, but she seemed sincere and her trial was scheduled to start in less than a week—

He looked up. What was it Dennis had said?

Slowly, almost grudgingly, he flipped open the pages of the big blue book.

". . . the soul is ever-free; it is deathless because birthless; it cannot be regimented by stars . . ."

CHAPTER
43

THE MAN standing in the shadows checked his watch for the third time in a minute. He hated this. He did not like doing it. At least, he did not like doing it himself. That was why he used others, a carefully chosen chain of well-paid associates who could get the job done with virtually no trail leading back to him. Nothing that could flow back. Except the money.

That was the way he liked it. But now that everyone with whom he associated had been either killed or arrested, he was hard-pressed to get the job done. Dr. Sentz had made one last withdrawal after he sent Officer Shaw on his merry way. And now that Sentz and Shaw had been arrested and the leaks from the hot lab at St. Benedict's had been discovered, there were likely to be no more. He needed to get rid of this stuff as profitably as possible.

Who would've imagined he would end up doing this? He had barely paid attention to high school chemistry. When he was first approached by those in the black market, he had no idea substances of such value existed anywhere in Tulsa, much less at a medical facility. It had been time for his real education, the kind you don't get at Will Rogers High School. Learned cesium was first discovered in 1860 in mineral water in Germany, the first element detected by spectrum analysis based upon the distinctive bright blue lines. An alkali metal, found naturally occurring all over the world, most especially at Bernic Lake in Manitoba. And he learned how useful it could be as a hydrology measure, an ion engine propellant, a hydrogenation catalyst, in magnetometers, in organic chemistry, as an oxidizer to burn silicon in infrared flares.

And oh yes. You could make bombs with it. Dirty bombs. Bombs capable of causing great destruction and also spreading radiation over a wide area. The former attorney general John Ashcroft had raised the alarm. This could be the means of the next terrorist attack on the United States, he had said. I mean, we all know it's coming, right? We just don't know when and how.

If he had been better educated, he might not have been so surprised when the dark men first came to his office.

A relationship was forged from mutual interest and need. He needed cash. They had lots. They needed cesium. He knew everyone.

How much did they have now? He couldn't be certain, but it was no small amount. He knew they were using a great deal for testing. But how long could it be until they were ready to use it in a more productive manner?

The Chechen separatists had been the first to make the attempt. Two times they tried to plant dirty bombs. The first ever attempt at radiological terror was in 1995 with a canister of cesium-137 wrapped with explosives in Izmaylovsky Park in Moscow. The second came two years later. The bomb was found near a railway line not far from the Chechen capital, Grozny. KGB agent Alexander Litvinenko was killed by exposure to polonium-210.

People had been stealing radioactive materials ever since that first time in Brazil, then elsewhere all across the globe. So long as these materials were processed, for medicine, for nuclear power, for weapons, for anything at all, there would be terrorists trying to steal them. And inevitably some would be successful. So he really had done nothing, he told himself, nothing that would not have happened anyway. The only question was who would profit. Why not him? He would use it a good deal more purposefully than most of the people in the black market arena.

He saw headlights flicker down the long desert trail. Saints be praised. He had been out here ruminating long enough. Let's get this thing done.

They pulled up in a blue van, a Town and Country, if he was not mistaken. Tinted windows, dark. So clichéd.

The man who stepped out was not smiling. He was rough and angry and obviously in a hurry. Presumably that was his way of dealing with nervousness—to mask it under a veneer of arrogance and presumed macho toughness. It reminded him of nothing so much as the police officers he dealt with so often. Ironic, given what this man was doing.

"Do you have it?" the man asked brusquely. He spoke with a thick accent. Talk about another cliché. Was it wrong for him to wish there was no Middle Eastern origin? Why couldn't he get a nice white backwoods bully determined to bring down the federal government by blowing up innocent citizens?

"I have it. Do you have my money?"

The man opened a steel-shell briefcase. It was all there, all in cash, all in small unmarked bills. More than enough to take care of his immediate needs.

"I'll get the pig."

He walked to the back of his truck and wheeled out the small covered bucket. He would not be sorry to get rid of that. He had been keeping it far too long. The cesium was supposedly safe so long as it stayed in the bucket—safe from contamination and safe from being detected by law enforcement officials with spectrometers. But it still creeped him out. Made him wonder if he should be sleeping in a hazmat suit.

"Still active?" the other man asked.

"I'm no scientist. But I'm sure it is."

"And no one knows? We have heard what happened in Tulsa."

"Dr. Sentz may have been an idiot, but at least he had the sense to realize that he couldn't keep making little withdrawals forever without eventually being noticed. He took everything he could get the last time, then only sent as much as you asked for with Shaw. This is what's left."

"We are concerned that the police will find us."

"No chance. Shaw knew nothing about you."

"But if they investigate—"

"They will find nothing. Trust me. I've been watching the investigation very carefully."

"And if they find you?"

"They won't. The only one who knew I was involved was Christopher Sentz, and he's dead. The rest reported to him. I communicated with his brother through anonymous text messages. They knew there was a higher boss, but they didn't know who he was. Who I am."

The man smiled with admiration. "We do things much the same in our own cells."

"I know you do. That's where I got the idea."

"I hope we can do business again sometime."

"I appreciate that, but I have to keep my nose clean for a while. I'm going to be under a lot of scrutiny. Besides, my source has run dry. But who knows?" He shrugged. "In four years, I'll probably need money again. And that should give me about enough time to find another source of cesium."

They made the exchange with minimum fuss. He took the briefcase full of cash and returned to his truck. He waited for them to leave, then started his engine.

It was a long drive back to Tulsa.

He plugged in his iPod and spun up the John Prine playlist. Nothing better than Johnny for a long drive. Down-home, smooth, easy to listen to, and very smart. Country music for those who can't stand country music.

He thought about what the man had said. Would the police ever trace the cesium back to its buyers? He knew the current investigation would never get them there. He would like to think something would, someday. Before the big boom. Not that he wanted to see his most reliable source of funding dry up. But he did feel an itching at the base of his conscience that was hard to ignore. Like he should be a member of the French Resistance, but instead he was collaborating with the enemy. Still, he knew it was going to happen, and he knew someone was going to profit . . . and there was no point in beating himself up about it. Right?

He chuckled a little when he thought about the whole Dennis Thomas inquiry. Who was the mystery man who'd signaled Christopher Sentz to refuse to open an investigation into Joslyn's disappearance? Kincaid was all around it, but he couldn't see the answer, even when it was right before his eyes. Dennis had never gotten a good look at him, barely a glimpse, back at the police station. And no one else had noticed he was there. Ironically, those dunderheads assumed that if such a person existed, it must not be anyone they knew because they didn't remember him. The truth was, they didn't remember him being there because he was in there all the time.

David Guillerman adjusted his rearview mirror and peered into his own eyes. Still blue, still crystal clear. Nothing had changed. He was the same person he had always been. Right?

It takes a lot of money to mount a campaign these days.

CHAPTER
44

BEN OPENED the door of his Senate office in the Rayburn building, R-222, and inhaled. And started coughing. This place had been closed too long.

"Glad to be back?" Christina asked.

He shrugged. "I'd rather be back on our roof at home, staring at the stars."

Christina immediately walked toward her desk and started sorting through the huge pile of mail that had accumulated while the Senate was in recess. As his Chief of Staff, she generally got more mail than he did. She had tried to keep up with some of the work at home, by email, but there was no substitute for being here, in the locus of governmental power.

"You seemed pretty absorbed during the flight. Spent most of the time gazing out the window. What were you thinking about?" Christina asked.

"Oh . . . I don't know."

"Fine, I'll guess. You were gazing at the constellations and thinking, One of those beauties should be named for my Christina."

"Got it in one."

She walked over to him and laid her hand on his shoulder. "But seriously."

"I tell you, that was it."

"You were wondering if the stars are really big gaseous nuclear reactors spitting helium into the universe."

"Uh, no."

"You were wondering if there's extraterrestrial life."

"Not at the moment."

"You were trying to remember if Ursa Major is the same as the Big Dipper."

"No."

"You were trying to count the stars."

"Still no." He sighed. "I was trying to . . . outwit them."

She pulled a face. "What are you talking about?"

"Nothing. Anything beats thinking about the case. Over and over again."

"Still beating yourself up, huh? Pretending you could have done a better job?"

"Sometimes."

"It worked out in the end."

"No thanks to me."

She took his hand. "Look, Ben. I want to apologize."

"For what?"

"For being such a pain. From the start. I'll admit it—I just didn't like Dennis. I didn't trust him. I know how easily you're bruised, and I didn't want to see you hurt."

"Who says I'm easily bruised?"

"Are you kidding? You're like the most hypersensitive person since Spider-Man. Except his Spidey-sense is useful. Yours, not so much."

"A lawyer should be able to empathize with others."

"Is that what you're doing? Because I think it would be hard to go around feeling the way you do."

Ben made no reply.

"My point is just that I didn't mean to make this affair more difficult than it already was."

"You didn't," Ben replied. "It's always good having someone thinking over your shoulder. Catching what you miss." He squeezed her delicate freckled hand. "I need you."

She blushed a little. "Well, yes. You do. But it's nice to hear you say it." She fluttered her eyelashes. "So if that's not what's troubling you, what is?"

"Our temporary insanity defense failed."

"Well, insanity is such a subjective concept. You remember that quotation I showed you from Angela Monet? 'Those who danced were thought to be quite insane by those who could not hear the music.'"

"Clever. But it doesn't change the fact that my defense flopped."

"I know. I was there."

"We did eventually get him off."

"There for that one, too."

Ben paused for a moment. "But . . . we never proved he didn't pull the trigger."

Christina stared back at him. "Shaw testified that they drugged him."

"Which explains why Dennis doesn't remember what happened. No matter how intense and memorable it might have been. They gave Loving the same drug, and as a result, he lost his memory of everything that happened after he was captured. Anything could've occurred after Dennis went to that hotel room. Dennis would've forgotten it."

"But Shaw said that he and his boss wanted to eliminate Christopher Sentz. That he was getting a bad case of the guilts. He was dangerous. Had to be eliminated."

"True. So several people had motives to kill Sentz." He looked at her pointedly. "That still doesn't tell us who pulled the trigger. Shaw never said he did it, not specifically. And if he didn't, then . . ."

She took Ben's hand, led him to the window of the reception area, and silently gazed out at the panoramic view of the Washington skyline.

Finally, after five minutes that felt like fifty, Christina spoke. "I think Dennis is innocent."

"You do?"

"Of course. He's such a nice man. So spiritual."

"He told me that after his wife died he was consumed with fury."

"But he wasn't a criminal. Shaw was a criminal."

"But not a murderer. As far as we know. And it was really his boss who wanted Sentz dead, not him."

Another silence fell upon them. This one lasted even longer.

"I still don't think it was Dennis."

"Really?"

"Yeah." She inhaled deeply. "In fact, I'm certain of it."

"You are?"

"Yeah. Certain."

Ben nodded. "Good. So am I."

"My instincts are good."

"They are."

"So there. That settles that."

"That settles it."

"We did the right thing, Ben. We did."

"Agreed."

"I mean it."

"Sure."

"Really."

"Absolutely."

And they stood in silence for the longest time, arms entwined, staring at the stars.

Acknowledgments

As usual, I am indebted to many people for their assistance. First, I want to thank the home team at Ballantine: Gina Centrello, who proves that successful publishers can also be nice people; my editor, Junessa Viloria, who made numerous helpful comments about the manuscript; Cindy Murray and David Moench, who master the murky waters of publicity; Kim Hovey, my longtime friend and an extraordinary talent; and all those in promotions and sales, without whom you would not now be reading this book.

I want to thank Dave Johnson for his help and advice regarding police procedure, specifically with regard to missing persons cases. The Joslyn Thomas horror is based on several true cases, the worst of which differs from this fictional case only in that even more time elapsed before the police finally decided to take action. I want to thank my father, Dr. William Bernhardt, for his help with medical and hospital issues. I want to thank Debbie Newton and James Vance for reading and commenting on an early draft of the manuscript. And I want to thank my children, Harry, Alice, and Ralph, for making my life so rich and interesting, and my dear wife, Marcia, for making every day a joy beyond measure.

Sadly, all the facts and statistics cited herein are accurate as of the time of this writing. The United States does have a higher incarceration rate than any civilized nation and we have more women behind bars than any other nation on earth. We treat all crimes the same: victimless crimes, white-collar crimes, crimes arising from dependency problems (believed by some to be as high as 70 percent of the total), and crimes motivated by need or hunger are in most cases all punished in the same manner, essentially the same way crimes were punished five hundred years ago. The cost to the taxpayer of maintaining this huge, antiquated system is enormous. Meanwhile, DNA evidence proves over and over again how often our criminal justice system gets it wrong. Instead of another "law-and-order" candidate suggesting that stiffer sentences will solve everything, perhaps what we need is someone who will seriously consider alternative approaches to redressing society's mistakes.

Readers are always welcome to email me at wb@williambernhardt.com or to visit my website: www .williambernhardt.com.

—William Bernhardt

Read on for a preview of William Bernhardt's
next exciting novel

CAPITOL BETRAYAL

Available in hardcover from Ballantine Books
in March 2010

April 14
7:17 a.m.
(Two hours before)

BEN KINCAID STOOD rigid and still as his wife,
Christina McCall, adjusted his tie, smoothed the lie of
his shirt, and ran a lint brush over the shoulders of his
navy blue suit coat.

"There," she said, taking a step back to survey the
view. "Now you look like someone who's ready to
advise the leader of the free world."

"That's a relief."

"Remember to smile and say something nice about
his wife. And don't remind him about—" She stopped
in midsentence. "Wait just a minute." She hiked up the
leg of his blue slacks. "Are you seriously wearing red
socks?"

Ben's eyes moved downward. "They're my lucky
socks."

"No."

"But I need all the luck—"

"No." She pointed toward the clothes closet.
"Change."

Ben obeyed without further protest. Of course, he

always made a great show of being put out when
Christina made these sartorial demands, but in truth, he
didn't mind a bit. Given that he had no sense of fashion
and was partially color-blind, he needed all the help he
could get and was capable of accepting it without feeling his manhood was threatened. For years his mother
had picked out and paired up all his clothes. Now she
had passed the torch to his wife. All this meant, he
reminded himself as he changed into a pair of blue
socks, was that he was a very fortunate man.

The irony was that, once upon a time, Christina had
been known for her dubious fashion sense, for dressing
more like a member of the Sex Pistols than a practicing
attorney. All that had changed last year when Ben made
his run for a Senate seat. In addition to the five thousand
other consultants they'd consulted, they'd hired a fashion
consultant to tell them how to dress for formal functions,
casual events, and television appearances. For Christina, it
was a road-to-Damascus experience. Now she had the
reputation of being one of the sharpest dressers in
Washington; Ben had been asked more than once if she
had acquired a fashion degree at some point in her past.
With her gorgeous red hair styled in a fetching shoulder-
length coif, Ben found her absolutely stunning. Not that
he was prejudiced or anything.

"That's more like it," she said when he reemerged.
"And just for the record, you're not wearing those
Superman boxer shorts, are you?"

"I'm not planning to strip at the White House."

"Yes, and nothing unplanned ever happens to you,
does it?"

"Good point. No, I'm clean."

"Thank you." She smiled, and the smile made his
spirits soar. Such a beautiful woman. Her face seemed
to absolutely glow. Was it all his imagination? She even
seemed taller these days. Although he supposed that

could have something to do with the heels. "Anything else you need, *mon cher amour*?"

"No. I'd better go. Traffic is terrible this time of day. And it still takes half an hour to get cleared to enter the White House."

"Still?"

"Yup." Ben had been working for almost two months now as a member of the president's legal team. Robert Griswold was the official special counsel to the president, but he had a staff of four lawyers, and after his Senate defeat Ben had been appointed to fill a temporary vacancy on that staff. Despite the loss—not exactly unusual for a Democrat in Oklahoma—Ben's rankings in popularity polls remained high nationwide as a result of his work during his brief time in the Senate, particularly his work on the controversial Emergency Council bill, which garnered nationwide daily coverage. His oration on the floor of the Senate was widely credited with being the cause of the bill's ultimate defeat, which endeared him to many, especially in the Democratic party. Still, he'd been flabbergasted when the newly elected president, Roland Kyler, invited him into the White House. "I want the president to have a chance to read my brief. So I'm out of here."

"Did you have Jones proofread it?"

"I'm an adult, Christina."

"And you're the worst speller on earth. Spell-check is not enough for you. Email it to Jones now. He'll have it proofed by the time you get to the White House."

He raised his chin a bit. "If you insist. Parting is such sweet sorrow, but—"

"Wait." She took both of Ben's hands and snuggled close to him. "Can you believe that sometime today you're going to see the POTUS?" Christina had always loved hip slang and catchphrases. She'd picked up on the Beltway acronyms in no time at all. "You work hard and try to help him. He's a good man."

"You just say that because he did you a favor."

"No, I say it because it's true."

"You're talking about his inspirational politics?"

"I'm talking about him, the human being. He's good to his wife. That's the surest sign of a good man."

Ben arched an eyebrow. "Is it indeed?"

"Yes. I read that he's given up smoking after twenty years because his wife didn't want smoke to ruin the White House—or him. That can't be easy, but he's doing it for her. So you help him out, Ben. He doesn't need any extra trouble."

"I'll probably get ten minutes with him. If I'm lucky."

"Look at you!" She grinned and pulled him closer. "You're talking about meeting with President Kyler all calm, cool, and collected. I remember when you couldn't think about talking to a judge without your knees shaking so badly you could barely walk."

Ben shrugged. "Times change. People grow up."

"They do indeed." She wrapped her arms around him. "And may I just say, Mr. Kincaid, that I like the way you've grown up, very much." She pressed herself against him and squeezed.

"Oh, I almost forgot." Ben grinned. "I have a surprise for you."

"What a coincidence. I have a surprise for you also."

"Well, you'll never top mine."

"Never say never."

"No, that's what you always do. You always top my story. But not this time."

"Okay," she said, arching an eyebrow, "you go first."

Ben beamed. "Robert says there's a good chance that after this temporary appointment expires, I might be appointed to the president's energy commission."

"That's terrific! Who better than a good Oklahoma boy to advise the president on energy concerns?"

"Well, he knows we have to shift over to natural gas, the sooner the better. Our dependency on foreign oil is killing this country on numerous fronts. And we simultaneously need to develop alternative energy sources—"

Christina held up her hands. "Hold on, tiger. I've already heard the speech. Save it for the president."

"Right. Sorry. But isn't that great news?"

"Terrific."

"So what's your news, huh? Go ahead and try to top a presidential commission appointment."

She batted her long eyelashes. "I've signed LexiCo as a firm client."

Ben's lips parted. "No."

"Yup. We're their counsel for all litigation matters, civil and criminal."

"No!" Ben knew LexiCo was a huge East Coast technology firm that Christina had been courting for months. Having them on the firm roster would not only generate much revenue but start a precedent. Where LexiCo went others would surely follow. Ben had been concerned about the firm and its nascent D.C. satellite office, especially after he went "Of Counsel" so he could take the White House appointment. Now it appeared that Christina had landed a client who could keep the firm busy well into the future. "That's fantastic!"

"Yup. I'm hiring a new associate. Just in case I want to take some time off."

"Good thinking."

"And?"

He sighed. "And your news is bigger than mine."

"Like I said, never say never." She pulled him close once more.

"Can we make a date to watch *Jeopardy!* together tonight?"

She made a small moue. "Because you've read, like, every history book ever written? I don't think I can stand to hear you ace all the history questions again."

"Hey, at least you don't have to listen to someone talking about how sexy Alex Trebek is."

"I only did that once!" She squeezed him all the tighter. "It's just 'cause he reminds me of you, you smarty. So tell me the truth—do you like me a lot, or do you really truly love me, Mr. Kincaid?"

He hugged her with all his heart and soul. "Yes."